MURDER BY THE BOOKS

Ron Atkinson

No part of this publication may be reproduced
in whole or in part, or stored in a retrieval system,
or transmitted in any form or by any means,
electronic, mechanical, photocopying, recording,
or otherwise, without written permission of the author,
except for the inclusion of brief quotations in a review.
For information regarding permission, please write to:
info@barringerpublishing.com

Text and Illustrations copyright ©2010 by Ron Atkinson
All rights reserved.

Barringer Publishing, Naples, Florida
www.barringerpublishing.com
Cover, graphics, layout design by Lisa Camp
Editing by Elizabeth Heath
Back Cover Photography by Angela DeStafano

ISBN: 978-0-9825109-5-7

Library of Congress Cataloging-in-Publication Data
Murder By The Books/Ron Atkinson

Printed in U.S.A.

This book is a work of fiction. Names, characters, places and incidents are products of the author's imagination or are used fictitiously. Any resemblance to actual events or locales or persons living or dead is entirely coincidental.

*To my grandson Jake,
already growing up way too fast.*

In memory of my mother who, when I was seven, introduced me to the first novel I ever read, the Reader's Digest Condensed Books version of "The Year the Yankees Lost the Pennant" (1955, Volume 21). I've loved good baseball and great storytelling ever since. Thanks, Mom.

10:30 A.M., Wednesday, December 24, 1986
Fort Myers, Florida

The sixty-seven year old founder of the generic pharmaceutical company that bore his name acknowledged her arrival with his usual sinister grin. The one that reminded her of Lee Van Cleef in *The Good, the Bad, and the Ugly*.

"You've heard?" Leonard Manetti asked.

She nodded and smiled, as if to say *No hard feelings,* her anger tempered by the fact that in roughly fifteen minutes her nemesis would be dead of an apparent heart attack. He just didn't know it yet.

The office stunk of stale cigarette smoke and sickly-sweet aftershave, causing her to pinch her nose as she locked the soundproofed door that guarded Leonard's treasured privacy. After removing a bronze notary stamp from her briefcase, she took a seat at the glass-topped conference table where Leonard sat tapping his pen against the cover of a brown vinyl binder.

The temperature was seasonally mild for southwest Florida in late

December, in the mid-70s, but the AC had been set on frigid. Her fingers felt like shards of Arctic ice, which wouldn't do for the task ahead, and she placed them under her thighs for warmth.

"Don't sit like that," Leonard snapped, reaching inside his shirt pocket for his bifocals. "You look like a schoolgirl." She ignored him as he opened the binder to a page marked with a yellow sticky note.

"As you know, I've had a change of heart," he said, "which requires modifying the Revocable Living Trust. I want you to witness the change and affix the stamp, just to make it official."

He removed a page from the binder and pushed it across the table for her inspection. She returned it without comment, hoping he wouldn't notice her cheeks burning despite the room's deep freeze.

She wasn't at all surprised by his actions. A lifetime of emotional cuts and bruises had prepared her to expect almost anything rude, insensitive and hurtful from this man. Still, what a monster he was to pick Christmas Eve to rob of her birthright like this, designating as his successor—and messenger—the one person he knew would upset her the most. And for what?

But she knew the answer. Leonard wanted to drive home his point one more goddamn time: I blame *you*!

No, she wasn't surprised. But thanks to the inadvertent heads-up Leonard's enmity had provided—a full seventeen hours advance notice—she was prepared to end the years of persecution.

"I'm thirsty," she said.

Leonard spoke to her over his shoulder as she edged around the table to a water cooler stationed behind him. "I plan to hang around awhile," he said, his pen poised above the paragraph in question. "Things could change."

Indeed they could.

She made a point of filling a paper cup with water and took a sip, then tossed the cup into a small wastebasket adjacent to the cooler. Next she removed a 5cc syringe from a plastic bag tucked into a pocket of her suit jacket. Though the drug was virtually undetectable once injected, a pathologist searching for the cause of an unexpected death would spot the entry point of a 22-gauge needle, which would spark uncomfortable questions. But she knew no autopsy would be ordered. Not for an aging, sallow-skinned, recalcitrant smoker afflicted with severe coronary heart disease. She wouldn't be surprised if the cardiologist wanted his insufferable patient dead and buried as much as she did.

"*Happy holidays,*" she whispered.

Leonard's pen never touched paper as she slammed his head into the side of the conference table, not hard enough to kill him but sufficient to propel him to the floor, face down, disoriented and at her mercy. The size of the gash on his forehead was an unexpected bonus.

Before he could react, she pressed a knee into Leonard's shoulders, then cleared a patch of hair at the nape of his neck. Seconds later, her task accomplished with clinical efficiency, she returned the spent syringe, plastic bag and embosser to her briefcase as her victim moaned, rolled over, and pushed himself up on an elbow.

Running a sleeve across eyes fogged by blood, pain and confusion, he stared at his attacker, uncomprehending. Only after the back of his neck began to burn and he saw the syringe in her hand did he understand.

And then he screamed.

Though she knew no one else could hear it, she instinctively rushed to cover his mouth. "*Watch it!*" she yelped, yanking her hand back a second before Leonard's dentures chomped at her fingers. He followed with a wild right that grazed her left ear, but the effort cost him his fragile balance, and he tumbled onto his back.

Instantly she straddled his chest and squatted, the forward weight of her knees constricting Leonard's upper arms, her own easily blocking the few feeble punches he could manage. How long they sparred that way she wasn't sure—five minutes, maybe more—but long enough for the paralytic agent to cause Leonard's vision to blur and his extremities to twitch and cramp uncontrollably.

She observed his final minutes from his desk chair, taking a moment to smooth the wrinkles in her suit. His arms and legs were in limp paralysis now, chest and diaphragm soon to follow. From there he would proceed to respiratory paralysis and hypoxia. Through it all, he would be awake and aware—how fitting!—until unconsciousness and death.

When at last Leonard stopped breathing, she knelt beside him and checked for a pulse. Finding none, she used a handful of tissues to place the binder into his top desk drawer. Her final act, a quick rehearsal of her lines.

Oh, God, it was awful! He grabbed his chest...fell right onto the table...it happened so fast, there was nothing I could do!

Satisfied, she gave the office that would soon be hers one last glance, then jerked open the door and screamed for help with all the panicked emotion a loving daughter could muster.

1.

Twenty-two years later,
8:45 A.M., Thursday, August 7, 2008
Naples, Florida

I settled into a lounge chair on my elevated back deck, head still aching from a bout of over-imbibing last night. That's when I spotted the owner of "Gator Done" Alligator Removal Service standing a foot from the pond behind my house.

From an earlier encounter I knew that his name was Dale Beecher and suspected he wanted to take a look at "Sneaky Pete," the fat old alligator I'd named after a popular dance hall five miles up the road. As Dale peered intently at the pond's untroubled water, his jeans hovering an inch above a pair of scuffed work boots, I guessed my gator-in-residence wasn't long for the tranquility of Palms Away.

Among other responsibilities to the residents of this gated community of millionaires, Dale's job was to keep an eye on the larger of the several hundred alligators that swam in our sixty private ponds and lakes and hid in our fifteen hundred acre preserve. When one grew too big or aggressive or strayed too near to a path reserved for golf carts, as lately ol' Pete had been wont to do, Dale had to remove it.

"North end," I shouted.

He turned and waved—"Thanks, Mr. McDermott"—and disappeared around a bend. My good deed for the day thus dispensed, I leaned back and wet my lips with a glass of orange juice, trying to relax a nervous stomach spinning like a washing machine with an unbalanced load. I should, in fact, have been dressed for my golf game by now, but I was still in tee shirt and boxers, all motivation on hold until I got the call I'd been dreading from Señor Diego Sanchez.

We met by accident in the early '90s at the lobby elevators of downtown Chicago's Sears Tower where we both worked at the time. I was a CPA on the verge of jumping headlong into the world of the financial fraud investigator; he was a few years into building a lucrative career in financial management. Talking sports, business, women and the vagaries of the stock market, we became good friends. Not longer after, I put him in charge of the once healthy stock portfolio now straining to finance my forced early retirement.

I'd been ignoring Diego's depressing quarterly investment summaries for weeks now, certain the stock market would reverse course in the next month, or maybe two or three, and I'd escape a humiliating exit from the comfortably insular southwest Florida paradise I was certain held the key to my redemption. Unfortunately, the power of positive thinking had done little to prevent my portfolio from plunging into severely negative territory, along with everybody else's.

Diego had left a curt message yesterday. He said if I wanted to continue living the privileged life of an unemployed rich guy, I'd better answer his next call. Which I did when the phone rang at exactly 9:00 A.M.

He inquired about the weather.

"Humid as hell," I said.

Diego replied, "Then I suggest you shut off the air-conditioning you can no longer afford and turn on your ceiling fans as I try to keep you in the style to which you had better not become accustomed."

At which point he gave me the numbers. It felt as if a pair of wet tennis shoes were banging against my esophagus.

"Shouldn't we have learned something the last time we went through this?" I asked, referring to the collapse of the dot.com bubble eight years earlier. It was one thing to miss the first one, but a second in the same decade? *C'mon.*

I was ignoring, of course, the fact that if not for Diego's financial savvy, I would have been in trouble far earlier. And that the plan we'd put together before I left Chicago hadn't included moving into one of the area's ritzier communities and then putting off gainful employment for—what was it now?—*four years.* But he held his tongue, graciously declining to engage in a pissing contest in which his friend was destined to be the sore loser.

Finishing my juice, I asked how much longer I had to live.

"Six months," Diego said without equivocation. "Much beyond that I fear your options will prove severely limited and decidedly inelegant, no matter what the stock market does from here on. If you ask my opinion, which I know you will not, I would tell you to put the house up for sale this afternoon."

Bad idea. With the real estate market on life support down here, it would take a miracle to sell my home in a year, much less six months, and I'd likely suffer a financial beating even then. Discounting his advice, I told him I'd cancelled my landline phone service and had decided to keep my three year old BMW sedan rather than opting for a new model. It was a pathetic response to the black hole of financial doom I'd created, and Diego knew it.

"Cutting expenses is mandatory," he said, "but generating income—*and lots of it*—must be your first priority."

I heard an exasperated sigh. "When you left Chicago," he said, "you told me it was to get yourself together before starting your own firm. But I fear you are ducking the rigors of financial fraud investigation to avoid certain... temptations. I must tell you, looking at the amounts you've been withdrawing from your account, and then not hearing from you, I've wondered if...?"

I thought about using the phone's camera to email Diego a picture of my raised middle finger but thought better of it. "Do me a favor, okay? Drop that line of questioning. I'm as clean as an *Irish Spring* shower, and I'm going to stay that way."

All due credit to a rehab clinic renowned for its rigorous discipline—with fees to match—I'd kicked the habit that had destroyed my career and nearly wrecked a marriage that was still in deep doo-doo. While I suffered the occasional craving, I wasn't about to go that route again, even if I ended up on some I-75 off-ramp dressed in tattered clothes with a ratty old cardboard sign around my neck that read, "Rainey McDermott, CPA. Will do taxes for food."

The truth: I'd snapped at Diego partly because the memory of my screw-up still stung and partly because I knew he was right. I *had* been procrastinating, though I had my justifications. My goal wasn't just to get "a job" but to land a high six-figure position equivalent to what I'd been earning in Chicago, a salary that would keep me ensconced in my Palms Away home, hopefully far from the prying eyes of those who might be investigating how I landed here in the first place. At the same time I could continue to surround myself with the kind of money, power and prestige I figured necessary to start my own consulting firm.

But first things first.

I needed something that would pay the bills and shore up my depleted savings while I sniffed around for prospects. Never mind that the number of high-paying positions in my field had shrunk dramatically, right along with the value of my home, the available credit on my home equity line and credit cards, and the funds in my stock portfolio. It had become easier just to play golf, fool around with the bongos Diego had introduced me to as a stress-reliever years ago, and wait for a miracle. Sadly, as had just been made clear, the time for waiting was over.

Just as I was about to hang up, he asked about Colleen.

"Not a good subject right now," I said of the wife who'd left me two months ago.

An awkward silence followed, he told me to give her his love and then asked about my mother who was living out the rest of her emphysema-shortened life in a Cape Coral care facility about an hour north of me. I'd helped to move her there from Chicago around the end of 2002, just after my caseload exploded and just before I got hooked. The weather was somehow supposed to help her feel better, but that didn't turn out to be the case. All I knew then was, she'd be somebody else's responsibility.

I told Diego she didn't have long, but that she was doing as well as could be expected. Translation: not the way any of us would want to spend our last days.

Before I could cut him off, he asked about Frank. Another sore subject.

Last I heard, my long-estranged father was cohabiting somewhere in Fort Myers with a babe who was about a decade north of wounded cougar country. I didn't care to go into it and tossed off a curt no comment.

The skies had darkened over the past five minutes and a gust of cool air signaled an imminent cloudburst approaching from the east. A minute later, with thunder rumbling in the distance and rain beginning to descend in torrents, I ended my call, promising Diego I'd spend the weekend getting more familiar with the Help Wanted ads.

As I scampered inside, I glanced at the pond, past a row of dwarf Fakahatchee grass lining the bank along the back of my property. And there they were, two alligator eyes staring at me from the middle of the pond, as if Sneaky Pete were telling me that although his days here might be numbered, he wasn't going down without a fight. Neither was I.

Flimsy as the odds might be, maybe even bordering on wishful thinking, I decided to pursue a possible solution to my problems that had arrived yesterday in the form of an unexpected invitation.

Perfumed, at that.

2.

I left Sneaky Pete to fend for himself and in deference to Diego fired up a selection from *Santana*. If I finished dressing for golf fast enough, I might have time to hit the bongos for a song or two before heading for the course, revved up and ready to kick some ass.

Assuming I cared about my Irish roots, which I could take or leave, I should be playing a traditional *bodhran*. Or maybe the spoon and bones. But the bongos? Yet Diego had been right: beating the natural rawhide skins until my fingers ached had somehow soothed an anxious soul desperate for relief. It just hadn't been enough. Maybe if he'd thrown in a set of congas back then, things might have turned out better.

As "Evil Ways" boomed from the speakers, the front door opened and in staggered my friend Billy Ray Hammonds, now five years retired from the FBI. He shook the rain from the bill of his cap. "Must of got hold of some bad Scotch, partner," he said, obviously suffering from the same varicose veins of the eyeballs with which I'd been afflicted. "What are the odds, huh?"

I'd asked Billy Ray to join me last night at the Palms Away Golf & Country

Club where, stimulated by an over-abundance of adult beverages, we discussed McCain versus Obama, the unsolvable mess in the Middle East, and the surprisingly competitive Tampa Bay Rays baseball team. We talked about everything but Colleen and our plans for the future—or lack thereof.

Before the night was over, he'd talked me into partnering with him in a grudge match today against two former FBI pals who'd been making a habit of stealing his pocket change. Billy Ray hefted two hundred and twenty pounds on a five-foot, ten-inch frame. Even at sixty-two, with a couple of blocked arteries nearing the danger zone, the man cut an imposing figure.

Rotating his forefingers deep into his temples, he said, "On this very date in 1789 George Washington ordered the creation of the Badge of Military Merit. Did you know that? Later changed to the designation, 'Purple Heart.' Think I earned one last night."

He noted my lack of golf attire and the stricken look on his face bordered on panic. "You didn't forget, did you?"

I told him not to worry, that I'd got sidetracked and would meet him on the first tee, assuming the weather cleared. He grunted, then caught sight of the invitation resting on the counter. Not one to put much stock in protocol, he picked it up, read it once, then again, then checked the address on the envelope. "You going?"

"Considering it. Might make some important contacts."

"For what purpose?"

I feigned indignation at his directness, but he kept eyeing me, waiting for details. "In case you haven't noticed," I explained, "the stock market's in freefall. My retirement may have been a bit rushed."

Billy Ray nodded, fanning the scented envelope beneath his nose. "You familiar with these people?"

Not really. I was still getting acclimated to life in Palms Away, but it seemed no more a Petri dish of rumor and innuendo than the gated community I'd called home in Chicago. As for the Whestins, I'd heard they were famous for their sometimes raucous parties, and a quick google of Mr. Whestin revealed that his billion-dollar holding company was ripe for a public offering. That was about it.

"You know something juicy?" I asked.

Billy Ray's eyes narrowed. "You'd be surprised what I know."

"I'll bite."

"Okay, then I'll tell you. I know that people with big money don't always play nice. That they step on toes to get to the top and then stomp on your neck to stay there. And I know when they get caught breaking the law, they'll dance like Fred Astaire and sing like Ethel Merman."

I yanked the envelope from his hands. "You need to get out more. It's a charity thing, for crying out loud. Shelter for Abused Women and Children. Labor Day weekend."

Enough with the third degree. "I'm going to make us an espresso. Celebrate my acceptance into Palms Away high society where I belong."

On the floor of the pantry was a deluxe, never-used espresso machine I'd given Colleen as a birthday present, just before she revealed a newly acquired love of Japanese green tea. Which started an argument.

"I'll pass," Billy Ray said. "Besides, in Italy, espresso is generally enjoyed after dinner." He raised a pinky. "You should be drinking a cappuccino."

I gave him a look, and he got the drift. "Just watch yourself, okay?" A quick glance outside, an assurance it would stop raining before our tee time, and he was out the door, mumbling something derogatory about my taste in music.

Alone again, I picked up the invitation and for the third time since yesterday read the separate note tucked inside, written in an obviously female hand. "We hope to see you on matters of both business and pleasure." Signed, "A."

Maybe it was the orange juice.

Or undigested remnants of last night's marbled rib eye.

Or maybe the stomach acid burning a hole in my stomach lining was just the result of a tendency to borrow trouble. Still, Alina and Jeremy Whestin were *the* power couple of Palms Away. Given Colleen and I had yet to set foot in their manse just two streets over, I had to wonder: why would I be the recipient of this invitation now, one addressed exclusively to me?

Unless, God forbid...had word spread about my unofficial separation from Colleen? Was "A," however prematurely, playing matchmaker?

Unattached ladies in their mid-sixties and beyond outnumber their male counterparts down here by a considerable margin. But I was only fifty-eight and still very much married, though it had now been sixty days since Colleen had taken refuge with a girlfriend until we both calmed down.

Or until "someone" in our relationship changed.

In one fashion or another, I'd heard Colleen's argument many times since she guessed how we'd built our home here despite savings markedly dented by my addiction, job loss, and the expensive recovery program. Just as I thought we'd got past the great espresso vs. green tea tiff, off she'd gone again.

"We should give the money back. Start over if we have to."

"Promise you'll show up for the conjugal visits?" Relying on prison to ignite our long dormant sex life seemed to me an iffy strategy.

"Then donate what's left to charity," she'd said. "Or"—a perfectly timed pause, affording time to ladle on the sarcasm—"are you still planning to open your own shop?"

Clearly, Colleen had no idea how little of that tainted money still existed, and I was too embarrassed to tell her. With an emotional blast-off imminent, I left the house. When I returned an hour later, she was gone.

Truth was, I didn't disagree with her. In theory, anyway.

I'd resigned in disgrace from Banefield, McDermott, Schmidt & Partners, Public Accountants, having effectively committed career suicide by literally blowing all I'd achieved up both nostrils. Then, still under the influence, I accepted a tidy sum of money from a troubled client who rightly figured that saving face would prove more compelling to me than saving my soul.

So, yes, I should have handed the money back when I came to my senses. Or gone to the authorities, blamed my actions on the cocaine and cut a deal. But I didn't. That frayed lifeline was going to finance one last chance to escape my past and make possible a better future for Colleen and me. It never occurred to me that a bribe of nearly $3.2 million would be insufficient to accomplish either.

Shoving Billy Ray's warnings aside, I checked off the "will attend" box and slipped the RSVP card into the stamped return envelope. Because despite my own admittedly conceited concerns that I'd been invited to serve as eye candy for a bevy of widowed and divorced beauties hungry for love, there was one other possibility.

Jeremy Whestin had a job for me.

3.

Fifteen minutes later, the rain stopped as Billy Ray predicted. There was no time for a session on the bongos, but I took a moment to see if Dale was still on premises. At first glance, I caught no sign of him or of Sneaky Pete.

Just then a flash of white caught my eye, a snowy egret gliding to the edge of the southernmost bank to my right. It settled ten feet from a great blue heron—and then a pleasant surprise: a spindly-legged heron chick had emerged from behind its mother, the two of them picking at the edge of the bank's soft wet ground for a breakfast of worms and insects.

The mother moved a few feet away, a vigilant eye on the shallow water where, if she got lucky, a small-mouthed bass might venture. The chick pecked hesitantly, sometimes nabbing a morsel, most often not. It stopped and squawked for attention, as if irritated by the difficulty of its task and wanting to be fed by mommy. All in all, a scene John J. Audubon himself would have admired, until Sneaky Pete ruined it all.

"*Gator!*"

It was Dale, yelling and pointing across the pond as he sprinted back along the bank. A second later the egret took to the sky in a gauzy blur as Sneaky Pete exploded from the water like a submarine-launched cruise missile, his gnarly legs and powerful tail thrusting his huge body halfway up the bank in a burst of lethal energy. My jaw went slack as he clamped down on the mother's belly, then lifted his head, turned and smashed the defenseless bird onto the water with a mighty *splat*, spun once in a classic death roll, and disappeared below, headed for deeper water.

The attack took maybe ten seconds. Already there was no evidence of violence on the far shore. No waves on the now calm water. No birds chirping in the surrounding Shady Ladies and Live Oaks. And no Sneaky Pete. Even the chick seemed too stunned to move.

I swallowed hard, trying to catch my breath. The chick, which seemed to be vacillating between staying put or getting the hell out of there, finally receded into the marsh, its fate likely a foregone conclusion. For which, I decided, it had no one to blame but itself. If it hadn't been so damned selfish, if it had just allowed its mother to fend for herself, she wouldn't have been distracted, wouldn't now be a disintegrating lump of muscle and bone and sinew rotting inside Sneaky Pete's gut, her offspring alone and defenseless.

Despite my agitation, a pang of regret for the chick tugged at my heart, but only for a moment. I learned long ago that the little guy in this world was bound to get the shaft, sooner or later. Even momma here couldn't hack it. Better to make friends with the big and powerful, I always said. Some of whatever they possess could rub off on you, assuming you could handle it.

What the—?!

Severed body parts were suddenly flying past me into a cesspool of ravenous gators sporting dark blue suits, starched white shirts and striped ties. I staggered backwards as their gaping, toothy mouths spewed one hundred dollar bills, and their cold, lifeless eyes conveyed a truth that chilled my spine: "We've got you now."

Jesus, I thought, shaking the image from my mind, *where had that come from?*

I stuffed my shaking hands into my pockets as Dale ambled up to the deck, tugging at the front of his soaked shirt. "That one bears watching," he said. "Gettin' up around eleven feet, I'd say. You throwin' food at him?"

Not a chance.

Alligator attacks on humans are fairly rare, but toss them your leftovers, and you're asking for a bad day. Even if you don't, they're due respect. Four years ago, a Sanibel Island landscaper fell prey to a monster gator just over twelve feet long. With the help of witnesses, the poor woman survived the attack but later died from massive infection.

As for me, I was still as "city" as a city boy could get. I knew enough to keep my distance from those who would do me harm.

"I'll be checkin' regular-like," Dale said, "but you have the Community Association call me if you see somethin' that disturbs you."

Too late. I was already plenty disturbed, though Dale's unruffled demeanor was having a calming effect. I decided that the heron's gruesome death had merely been a natural phenomenon of life in a community anchored by a wild preserve—and that it had nothing to do with me. What any of this had to do with gators in coat and tie sporting gluttonous appetites for greenbacks, I didn't want to know.

I glanced at my watch. Time to play golf.

4.

2:30 P.M., the next day, Friday, August 8,
Harrison Bank & Trust, St. Louis, Missouri

Jeremy Whestin paced about the executive conference room, fighting off the diffuse pain consuming his skull. He ignored the other members present for the meeting and stared out the window, his temper nearing the boiling point.

Mack Evans, his private investigator, should have called an hour ago.

Jeremy had intended to send Jack Armbruster, Whestin Group's president, to this meeting but at the last minute dispatched him to a conference in Kansas City involving the heads of his holding company's nine subsidiaries. At the time, Jeremy had been happy to delegate the responsibility, uninterested as he was in spending even two days with a bunch of nervous nellies distraught over lagging sales and gloomy forecasts. Now he regretted his decision.

What could be worse, he wondered, than sitting here answering pointed questions as if he were a snot-nosed kid just out of high school, begging for a loan to open a lemonade stand? *Fucking a-holes.*

"You okay?" asked bank president Daniel Harrison, a short, pudgy man in his late forties with an embarrassingly thin mustache and a balding pate. He kept his eyes on the financial statements fanned before him.

Just for grins, Jeremy thought about flipping him the bird. *Not a good idea,* he decided, judging by the worry lines etched into Daniel's forehead. Ralph Bartlett, executive loan officer, didn't look too happy, either, fussing about in his chair as if he had hemorrhoids. And Wallace Gerard, Jeremy's chief financial officer, seemed poised to bite off the gold-plated nib of his precious *Mont Blanc* fountain pen.

Fighting the urge to walk out on the lot of them, but not before he told them to go to hell, Jeremy waved off Daniel's concern and took his seat at the conference table, steeling himself for the balance of a grilling that had been going on for more than an hour.

Daniel ran a finger between his shirt collar and neck. "Anybody else warm?" He lowered the thermostat and retook his seat. A thin line of sweat trickled down the front of his starched white shirt as he rearranged the papers in front of him, then looked to Wallace to restart the discussion.

The CFO twirled his pen between thumb and forefinger, dropped it, placed it on the table and then took a moment to gather his papers. "As I was saying, the past two late payments were the result of an unfortunate combination of events." He held up his copies of the three most recent financial statements. "I think we've turned the corner."

Daniel shot Ralph a look.

From Mutt to Colonel Klink, Jeremy thought, as the tall, thin loan executive with the demeanor of a Nazi SS officer took the cue.

Sucking in a breath through flared nostrils, conveying grave concern, Ralph looked first at Wallace and then at Jeremy. "The Loan Committee is spooked by the general business environment and the strain it's obviously putting on Whestin Group. I don't have to remind you that we would be within our rights"—he paused, nose lifting—"to accelerate the loan if any more payments are received past due."

Jeremy bit his lip so hard, the pain cancelled out the ache in his brain. His ears burned, and he decided to blame his actions on the fact that he hadn't slept well in weeks. Or on the unpredictable, often verbal side effects of his condition the docs warned him about. Whatever the reason, he couldn't stop himself.

"You're a total asshole. You know that, don't you, Ralph?"

Jeremy stifled a belly laugh as Ralph's thick, salt-and-pepper eyebrows shot up and down like a squeegee wiping perspiration from his forehead. "Sorry, Ralph, that was uncalled for. You're not a *total* asshole."

Wallace's normally dark complexion blanched. As for Ralph, Jeremy thought he looked ready to back his customer against the wall and—

"Let's keep this civil," Daniel said, jumping in to diffuse the moment. His eyes darted about the table. "We're all in this together."

Jeremy could appreciate Daniel's position. Whestin Group's $200 million loan involved a consortium of four other banks, though Harrison B&T held the bulk of the obligation. The bank also bore sole responsibility for Whestin Group's $95 million line of credit. With that line nearly depleted and still roughly seven months of payments remaining before the loan came due in March, collars had grown tight. Ralph had just made clear that Harrison could abruptly end the party if they didn't get the assurances they needed—and those payments on time.

Daniel leaned back. "What's the latest on the public offering? How's the schedule shaping up?"

"We'll have an underwriter on board by mid-October," Wallace answered, referring to the private investment bank that would be assessing the underlying strength of Whestin Group's securities offering and then, for a share of the proceeds, would assume the financial risk in bringing that offering to the investing public. "That'll give them plenty of time to do their due diligence before we have to deal with the SEC and then start the dog and pony show. We're still looking at a mid-February launch."

"And the accountants?" The question came from Ralph, who was avoiding eye contact with Whestin Group's CEO.

Wallace wasn't looking at Jeremy, either. "We expect the comfort letter to arrive on time, no issues," he said.

There better *not* be any issues, Jeremy thought. The comfort letter was an accounting firm's statement obtained by the underwriter prior to a public offering, as required by securities laws. It was supposed to confirm that unaudited financial information included in the prospectus followed Generally Accepted Accounting Principles. Jeremy knew that as long as the underwriter accepted what Wallace fed them, there would be no problem—assuming Wallace could be trusted.

The overseer of all this was supposed to be Whestin Group's law firm, whose responsibility, among others, was to assess the possibility that key participants in the transaction—in this case, Jeremy—might be acting irrationally or under the influence of a cognitive bias.

Jeremy wondered if they were also trained to pick up on the irrational dictates of a CEO battling a deadly disease.

He chuckled to himself, confident he had the attorneys issue under control. The founding partner of their law firm was an old college buddy who understood what constituted an acceptable risk in light of the potential for extraordinary gain. He would do as he was told.

One glance at Harrison and Bartlett and it was easy to read their minds. *Six more months. Can you survive that long?* It was a question Jeremy couldn't answer, not for the company or for himself.

Wallace tapped his pen against the palm of his left hand. "We're working on an investment arrangement, a private placement that looks—"

"Cash won't be a problem," Jeremy said, cutting him off. "We'll make an announcement on that subject end of next week. You'll be fully informed as soon as we finalize the details."

Wallace kept his eyes focused on the table, and under his breath Jeremy cursed the man's recklessness. They'd agreed not to say anything about their potential new investor until Jeremy could give it more thought.

"Glad to hear it," Daniel said, "but I'm concerned about the future appetite for public offerings. Everything I read, the economy could be in this mess for a year or more."

Jeremy countered by telling him that the markets would be starved for action, pleased to see someone stepping forward with confidence in their company's potential for growth. "One way or another, we'll have a new President just before we launch. Fresh ideas, fresh optimism."

He wanted to believe it. *Needed* to believe it. But so much had to go right between now and then. If it didn't....

"That may be true," Ralph said, his voice conveying all the warmth of a tray of ice cubes, "but who's going to—"

Jeremy's cell phone buzzed in his pants pocket. *Thank God.*

"Excuse me, gentlemen," he said, removing his Blackberry.

Relief washed over Daniel's face. "Use my office," he said, pushing back from the table. "Why don't we all take a break?"

Jeremy nodded his appreciation and answered the call. "Talk to me," he said, heading for Daniel's office.

"Just sent the file to your computer by encrypted email," Mack said. "In short, your Mr. McDermott appears clean, as far as the health issue goes, but he hasn't worked in quite a while. I suspect he's hurting financially, especially given what's happening in the market. I've also picked up on a rumor that all is not well on the home front. Financially, a divorce will kill him."

"Hell, he walked away with more than $3 million of our money. Where'd it go?"

"Taxes, rehab expenses, down payment on the Florida home, furnishings, living expenses. And now the market's dying. Not a good combination."

Jeremy closed the door and leaned against Daniel's desk. "Shift subjects. What about that private equity firm, the one apparently so anxious to invest $110 million in our ailing company?"

The sound of shuffled papers, then, "As Wallace told you, they're a subsidiary of a company called *Liens Internationaux*—Links International—a business broker headquartered in Marseille. They arranged the purchase of those cell phones from a source in Southeast Asia. I'm checking into that now, but anything associated with those guys has to concern us. I know that part of the world from my days with the Agency. Those brazen Asians got piracy down to an art form."

"Wallace says they just want to get a foothold here in America, and they're willing to buy their way in."

"Could be—if you believe him. Or could be they've 'borrowed' certain software from their competitors or done something else to lower their costs. Then they just pass that along and still make a damned good profit."

As do we, Jeremy thought. "Get to the good stuff."

"Not sure I'd exactly use those words. A small, tightly knit group of Algerian businessmen owns the company. My sources say there could be something fishy there but nothing concrete they can pinpoint."

"What the hell does that mean?"

Mack's answer caused Jeremy's vision to blur, and he picked up only fragments of sentences as his P.I. recited from his notes. Something about a violence-heavy effort to overthrow Algeria's pro-Western government...going on for years...financed via dirty money from prostitution, drugs, arms smuggling.

"The Muslim population in France numbers in the millions," Mack said, "but in Marseille, something like a quarter of the city's population is Muslim. A legitimate-looking private equity company based there, even one owned and managed by Muslims, wouldn't necessarily raise eyebrows. My guess, though, is that for tax purposes, the sub is probably registered in a Caribbean country friendly to offshore financial centers."

As Mack droned on, Jeremy reached into his pocket for a pill he wasn't supposed to take for another two hours, unwilling to accept the implications of what Mack was saying. "So right now, you're telling me there's no proof they're anything more than what they say they are. Right?"

"Not based on what I've uncovered so far. But I find it hard to believe they're investing $110 million in Whestin Group just for the thrill of becoming minority stockholders. And if my suspicions prove right, the penalties for you, personally, in dealing with these people—"

"*I know.*"

Jeremy downed the pill with spit and pressed the palm of his free hand deep into his right cheek, deflecting attention from the pain that sat on top of his head like a hot frying pan. "Anything more on our CFO?"

"Still trying to connect the dots, see if there's anything revealing about his connection to this Links International."

"Why would you suspect that?"

"For starters, Wallace Gerard isn't his birth name. It's—."

A knock at the door. Wallace stuck his head inside and pointed to his watch.

Jeremy was in no hurry to return to the meeting, but he said, "Gotta go, Mack. We'll talk later. Keep digging."

"Wait—heard anything from our friend, Mr. Murray?"

"Nothing so far."

"You want me to...?"

"Not unless he makes trouble." Jeremy abruptly disconnected the call.

Wallace canted his head towards the conference room. "How do you think it's going in there?"

It was an idiotic question, and Jeremy brushed past his CFO without comment. When the meeting resumed he feigned interest in the subjects of expense and sales revenue projections, cash flow statements and profit ratios but couldn't keep his thoughts from returning to eight months earlier—New Year's Eve.

Wallace with one arm around Alina's waist.

The panic in his eyes when Jeremy found them in a back hallway on his way to an auxiliary wine cellar.

Alina's air of casual indifference, the one she'd lately been routinely affecting in her husband's presence.

She'd made a joke about a tipsy Wallace getting lost, then kissed Jeremy full on the lips. Crisis averted or at least forestalled. Now this latest news from Mack that threw into doubt his decision to authorize the purchase of one million pre-paid cell phones for the communications subsidiary, through a company possibly tied to—he couldn't say the word. Couldn't even think it.

A question from Daniel pulled him back into the conversation. "You comfortable with these numbers? Wallace here says the worst is over."

Jeremy glanced at his watch, hoping Daniel would get the message. "I'd stake my life on those numbers," he said. "And you can take that to the bank."

Daniel winced, good-naturedly. "Then I guess we're adjourned."

The four men shook hands, forced smiles belying the fact that despite Whestin Group's past successes, despite the enormous potential embodied in the initial public offering, the bank had reason to be concerned and would likely stay that way until Whestin Group went public, and they got their final payment.

Poor schmucks, Jeremy thought, *they don't know the half of it.*

Then again, maybe neither did he.

5.

In the parking lot, Wallace handed Jeremy a sealed folder containing the accurate financial statements for the past month.

"We've got a ways to go," he said. "Especially in communications. Get that turned around, we should be fine."

Jeremy tossed his briefcase and the folder into the backseat of his Mercedes S600 sedan. "Get in," he said. He started the engine but left the air conditioner off. It was fun to watch Wallace sweat.

"This private placement comes from an overseas source that barely knows us," he said as Wallace closed his door. "One-hundred-ten million bucks. Tell me again that's not going to raise Ralph Bartlett's bushy eyebrows."

Jeremy wanted to shove Wallace's face through the windshield as his CFO spoke slowly, his tone borderline condescending. "The deal calls for us to issue preferred stock, convertible to common after the public offering. Thus the value of the stock will float with the company's value. It's factored into the pricing.

The underwriter will look at it as bridge financing—completely normal."

Interesting choice of words, Jeremy thought. Nothing about this deal seemed "normal."

Wallace had calculated that an underwriter would value Whestin Group at twice its revenue. After factoring in the percent of the company they were willing to sell and allowing for some $16 million in fees related to the IPO, they could retire the commercial loan, pay down the credit line completely and still retain over $100 million in fresh cash—if the offering came off as planned.

To get to that point, Jeremy would have to cozy up to an investment company about which Mack suspected the unthinkable. A subsidiary of a firm that may already have arranged to send them tainted merchandise. The whole idea went against everything he thought he stood for. He was a Marine, for crying out loud.

But did he have a choice?

Given the present financial environment, other sources for the critical cash infusion came with enormous red tape. Due diligence taken to the extreme, usurious interest rates, demands for a substantial ownership position and spots on the board. According to Wallace, Links International had made no such demands, and their private equity subsidiary promised to transfer the money within two weeks of a signed agreement.

"Exactly how will this be handled?" Jeremy asked.

Wallace loosened his tie as a drop of perspiration meandered down his left temple. "For tax purposes, the private equity firm has accounts set up in various offshore financial centers, primarily in Anguilla and the Bahamas, but other places, too, like the Caymans and British Virgin Islands. Perfectly legit. The money will come to us from one of those accounts."

"Seems to me that alone—"

"We're talking OFC's that aren't on any watch list developed by Treasury or any other entity. This isn't like we're doing business with Iran or Somalia or the Sudan."

Or Algeria? Jeremy wanted to ask.

He bit his tongue. The last thing he wanted now was a spooked CFO in the middle of preparations for a public offering that would make or break Jeremy's company and save or ruin a reputation forty years in the making.

His head hurt like hell, and it sounded to him as if he were talking in a tunnel. "I'll let you know Monday."

Jeremy wanted to spend no further time in the presence of his CFO, who got the message and exited the car. He put the Mercedes in gear, nixing his plan to stop by the office to review Mack's reports. He'd check them on his laptop over the weekend or on the Monday flight to Florida.

It was three-thirty. He'd had enough bad news for the week. Fortunately, he knew how to reduce the pain, even if just for the weekend.

Twenty minutes later, Jeremy's key had barely touched the condo lock when the front door opened, revealing a pain reliever better than any pharmacy could dispense.

Vicky Laine—to everyone else at the office she was *Victoria*—pulled him into the foyer by his belt and pushed a maraschino cherry into his mouth. He sucked the tips of her fingers, then kissed her, leaving the plump red fruit exposed between her lips. She bit into the firm flesh, swallowed and kissed him back.

A chill raised the hairs on his chest. He looked down to see a Manhattan on the rocks pressed against his shirt, took it from her and sipped.

Vicky's black teddy clung to her shoulders by one slender strap. Jeremy set his drink down and ran a fingertip along her collarbone, then slipped the strap off to the side. He leaned in and sniffed her neck. "Whatever that is, I like it."

"Garlic, sage, and a touch of onion," she said, tilting her neck. "I'm preparing meatballs."

She moved his hand to the inside of her thigh and smiled coyly. "And for appetizers—well, we've got time enough to whip something up."

Jeremy brushed a breadcrumb from her cheek. "Nice to get the afternoon off. You must have an understanding boss."

Vicky traced a finger down Jeremy's zipper. "Speaking of getting off...."

His heartbeat quickened, not from anticipation but from anxiety. He hadn't been performing up to his standards lately, and it bothered him. But Vicky hadn't complained, pretending not to notice. He remembered the day three months ago at the condo when he'd announced the news. She'd buried her head in his shoulder, then quickly gathered herself and pushed him down onto the bed, her cheeks glistening with tears.

"No time to waste, then," she'd said, before giving him the ride of his now considerably shortened life. And here she was again, greeting him with a cocktail in hand, ready to be whatever he commanded. All the more reason he hated what he would soon have to do.

He ran a finger along her lips. "You're too much, you know that, Miss Vicky?"

"*Mistress Victoria* to you, pervert." She paused. "How'd the meeting go? And how are you feeling?"

"About as expected," he said, answering the first question. He ignored the second. "Look, I'm staying the weekend, then—"

"It's home to the bitch. Sorry. *Beach*."

Jeremy was in no mood for a confrontation, certainly not one with jealousy at its heart. And thus he decided not to mention that he'd be staying in Florida through the August 30th party and likely a week after that. A month in all, but he needed the time off before things got nuts. He'd tell her once he got down there.

"Legitimate business, baby doll," he said. "I might be adding another member to the staff, and he happens to live in Palms Away."

"How convenient."

"Hey, it's southwest Florida. In season, about as many mid-westerners there as here. And you can't do much better than Palms Away."

"It's a *he*, you say?"

Jeremy ran a hand beneath Vicky's teddy and pulled her close. "Enough with business. I'll take a minute to finish this"—he held up his glass and nodded in the direction of the upstairs bedroom—"while you get the pillows fluffed up the way I like it. I'll slip in so quiet, you won't know I'm there."

"If you mean *there* there, Mr. Whestin, I'll know it." She bit his ear lobe. "And I'll be ready."

He patted her on the ass, nudged her toward the stairs and headed for the study. Collapsing into an easy chair, drink pressed to his forehead, his thoughts weren't on what awaited him upstairs, or the possibility that Rainey

McDermott could be the solution to his most pressing problem. He was thinking about Alina. About the possibility that she was screwing around on him with the very man he'd entrusted to screw with his books. About ramifications too profound to contemplate if his suspicions were true. And about how Alina would react if she ever discovered what he'd done to her all those years ago.

He downed the last of his drink and started for the stairs, pissed he needed one hand on the wall to steady himself.

"I'm ready," Vicky called out from the bedroom.

"Coming," he said, smiling as he heard her husky laugh in response.

Two more months, he calculated, as if to give himself strength. By then, he'd have McDermott on board, double-checking the books for falsified entries and illegal transactions neither the underwriter nor the Securities and Exchange Commission could be allowed to uncover. Soon after, he would set things straight with Alina, and she would never need to know what a louse she'd married.

Then and only then would he tell Mistress Victoria he was leaving her.

6.

I sensed Colleen's presence before I'd fully awakened.

Blinking the sleep from my eyes, I smiled at her as if she'd never been away. And then it hit me. Today was Saturday, August 9. Our thirty-third wedding anniversary.

She'd come home.

I'd bought a card last week, just in case. It was in my top dresser drawer, already signed with a conciliatory inscription. I just had to find the right time to present it and reap the rewards for my thoughtfulness.

"Good morning, Rainey," she said, a formal air to her greeting. "I rang the doorbell. Thought maybe you had an early tee time, so I let myself in."

A flimsy explanation, which set my unbrushed teeth on edge. "I'm going fishing with Billy Ray in an hour," I said, yanking the sheets over my privates. "What are *you* doing?"

I could see her more clearly now, and my enthusiasm waned as I tried to understand the intent behind her distracted, wooden stare. Her hair, I noted, was longer, with new, sexy bangs angled to one side, and she wore a pale green pullover that fell lower on her chest than was the norm for her. Colleen had a nice cleavage but seldom showed it off. Not like this.

She also had a small suitcase with her. "I'm going on an overnighter to Marco Island," she said as if commenting on the weather. "By boat. I need my swimsuit and a wrap. Girl stuff."

I wasn't sure what to make of the fact she was still wearing her wedding ring. "Alone or with...?"

"Friends." She and her suitcase disappeared into her closet.

I threw on a tee shirt, shorts and ball cap, brushed my teeth and headed to the kitchen, my mind spinning. Was Colleen intending to walk right back out the door, no questions asked or answered? I poured myself a pomegranate and orange juice combo, trying to slow my pulse.

Ten minutes later, her footsteps echoed across the marble floor leading to the front door, and I scrambled to head her off. "What the hell's going on? You walked out, no telling me where you're going, when you're coming back. *If you're coming back.* And now you show up two months later—on our anniversary, by the way—just before you head off on a cruise?"

"I told you, it's just an overnighter."

She shifted her suitcase from her right hand to her left, and for a moment I thought she was actually enjoying this, which ignited the fuse attached to the dynamite of my fragile male psyche. I needed to calm down, fast. Salvage what I could. Show her a glimpse of the new me.

"I got a call from Diego. He says we're running out of money."

She nodded, her lips pursed, conveying more disbelief and aggravation than concern. Sort of like, *how could you fuck this up, too?*

"He called me," she said. "I think he just wanted to see how I'm doing, but he did say you're going back to work."

"The juices are flowing again, but"—I swallowed hard—"I could use some moral support."

Colleen curled her left thumb over the top of her wedding ring and spun the diamond to the underside of her finger, a habit whenever she was upset with me. "Been there, done that," she said. "Besides, the subject of morality is probably one we should avoid right now."

What?

She reached for the door. "I'll be back around noon Monday. If you want, we can meet for lunch. Talk things out. I know this wasn't the best timing, and I'm sorry about that."

A flicker of hope. I grabbed her hand, unable to accept even the possibility she was interested in someone else, much less sleeping with the guy. "Look, Colleen, I wanted to call a thousand times, beg you to come home. I didn't because...I'm an imbecile. Please, I love you, and I need you to stay."

Her eyes moistened, and she leaned her head against my neck. I thought I sensed her reconsidering until she pulled away and whispered, "Monday."

I stood in numbed silence as she walked to her car, the weight of the suitcase bending her to the right. "Happy anniversary, baby," I muttered and slammed the door.

The pain hurt so bad, I didn't care if I ever saw her again.

7.

An hour later, I was in Billy Ray's boat, about fifteen miles from his slip, the two of us perspiring freely in the mid-morning sun.

I watched in both amusement and admiration as my captain adroitly steered his twenty-four *Canyon Bay* alongside a stand of mangroves deep inside Estero Bay. Perched atop the boat's tower, he reminded me of an amalgam of Buddha and Captain Quint from *Jaws*.

We'd been drifting inland with the tide, idling through the shallow waters, on the lookout for schools of hungry redfish. With Billy Ray up top since getting underway, skimming the waters at around twenty-five miles per hour where allowed, our only chance to converse had been during sections of water marked "Idle Speed." Even then it was clear my friend was in no mood for small talk. He'd barely spoken to me all morning.

"See anything?" I said quietly, just being friendly.

Billy Ray, dressed in frayed khaki shorts and a chum-stained work shirt, adjusted his polarized sunglasses and pointed to a spot about thirty yards off the starboard bow. The telltale signs of redfish activity were easy to see in the clear, skinny water: silver tails breaking the surface, tiny waves pushed forward as mouths worked the sand and mud below, rummaging for shrimp and crabs.

He cut the power to the trimmed outboard and effortlessly descended the tower, his back to the railings. We'd fished together three times before, and it was obvious the man knew his way around a back bay skiff.

My job was to keep us roughly twenty feet from the mangroves and ahead of the school, using the electric bow-mounted trolling motor. Experienced anglers often waded into the water, but we'd decided to take our chances casting from the boat with spinning reels. A few minutes later we were pinging the waters with cut Spanish sardines on my line, shrimp on Billy Ray's and enjoying enough success to keep my mind off my various woes.

Still, nobody was talking.

Since reds are notoriously skittish, chitchatting was generally frowned upon, but even in the heat and humidity, Billy Ray's silence had a chill about it.

Ten minutes in, I broke down. "Everything all right? You don't seem all here."

He pressed a sleeve against his forehead, then reeled in his line, secured his rod and grabbed a Corona from the cooler. "Ready?" he asked, holding the beer in an outstretched hand.

I declined, my eyes on the water.

Billy Ray moved closer so we could talk without spooking the fish. "How long have we known each other?"

So, something *was* on his mind. "Year and a half. Pretty much as long as I've been here."

A nibble—and a rookie mistake. I jerked on the line too quickly and the biggest redfish in Florida's inland waterways history skittered away with my bait.

"Why?" I asked, irritated with myself. "You tired of me?"

He shrugged but didn't smile. "Just seems like I don't know all that much about you."

"You're scaring me."

After downing half his beer, he asked about my former profession, saying it sounded "dry as month-old potato chips." I took that as good-natured ribbing and told him to take a flying leap.

"Don't be so sensitive," he said. "Please, continue."

Okay. The initials "FBI" scrolled before my eyes as I reached into the bait well for another sardine and told him I'd always had an affinity for numbers. "In college," I said, affixing my bait, "I took the requisite accounting courses, graduated, got a job with a small accounting firm, then earned my CPA license. Four years later, I made partner. Not much to my life story, actually."

My cast kinked and fell embarrassingly short of its target. I sensed the fish laughing at me.

"That's it?" Billy Ray said. "Your whole life is wrapped up in a few sentences all directed at work?"

As a matter of fact, yes. My childhood had been a disaster, and as for my present circumstances, what Billy Ray knew about Colleen and our difficulties was all I wanted him to know. I decided to keep the conversation focused on business. If he knew more than he was letting on, I wanted to tease it out of him.

"Like most men, I am what I do," I said. "And what I do is uncover financial fraud." I readied myself for another cast with a rod that suddenly felt like a two-by-four with a rope on the end.

"Ever get bored with it?" Billy Ray asked.

"Never."

"Then what happened? Did the business go south or something?"

I shrugged in concert with a clenched sphincter muscle. *What was he after?* "Sometimes, change is good," I said. "Besides, my mother's health was deteriorating, and it just seemed like a good time to exit Chicago and look after her—and for new challenges, as they say."

"And now you want back in?"

"If the right circumstances arise."

"Like working for Jeremy Whestin?"

"Maybe. Look, I'd like some day to start a one-man consulting business. Help companies victimized by fraud, show others how to prevent it in the first place. Mr. Whestin might be of assistance—or he might not. Can't hurt to meet the guy, can it?"

Billy Ray shrugged, then informed me that he'd checked the club's automated tee time system before leaving his house and learned of the pairings set by the commissioner of our Wednesday golf group. "You're with Whestin, in case you didn't know."

Well, well. I acted like it was no big deal, but my gut told me that this pairing was no coincidence.

"You free for dinner that night?" Billy Ray asked. "I'm going to want details."

I shook my head. "Sorry, having dinner with my mother. I'm trying to make it a set date every week."

He nodded, finished his beer and began threading a shrimp onto his hook while I tried gamely to rediscover my casting mojo. Billy Ray had touched a nerve with his questions, and I gripped the handle of my rod as if choking a snake, then launched another awkward cast. It didn't help when I thought I detected a snicker as he started to move aft.

"How about you?" I asked, out to even the score. "Did you find your job with the Bureau totally satisfying? You didn't sometimes want more?"

He turned. "Meaning?"

"I dunno. In thirty years you made it to Special Agent. One of thousands of under-appreciated heroes toiling for one of the largest departments in the federal government. You didn't sometimes want to bust out, apply your expertise in the private sector? Maybe run your own company?"

"I did okay."

I could feel him staring at me, waiting for some point to all this. In truth, he'd put me on the defensive, and I was digging back at him like some catty bimbo on *The Real Housewives of Orange County.*

"I'm just saying, something in security services, maybe. Some place you could give orders instead of take them. Work with big budget companies that know how to show their appreciation."

Billy Ray shook his head. "Doesn't get much bigger than the Bu." And then he busied himself with a search for God-knows-what in his battered tackle box.

We fished in silence for another ten minutes before Billy Ray announced it was time to move on. I didn't care. His questions and my childish response had removed all enjoyment from the day. I was ready to go home.

Once underway, I stared straight ahead, my thoughts bouncing from Colleen and our tense encounter this morning to Diego's warning that I had six months to get my financial act together before I'd have to slink out of Palms Away with a bag over my head. In between I tried to convince myself that my one good friend down here had meant no harm. I mean, what could he possibly know? He was *former* FBI. Right?

Later, as we approached his slip, I moved to the bow of the boat, preparing to grab the mooring lines. But he didn't slow down and instead turned the boat west toward the Gulf of Mexico, where I'd heard this morning that the chop would be three to four feet.

"Going for the big guys?" I asked, anticipating grouper.

"Patience," Billy Ray said.

I grabbed a beer and braced myself for a bumpy ride.

Twenty minutes later, my bladder signaling signs of distress, I was about to inform *El Capitán* of my need to hang it over the side when the boat slowed to idle.

I scanned the Gulf waters for obvious signs of fish, such as other boats with lines out. Cormorants diving beneath the water from a surface mount. Seagulls plummeting into the water from great heights. Nothing jumped out at me.

Billy Ray clambered down the tower, binoculars in hand, and focused east, in the direction of a six-story, pale yellow building I knew to be the LaPlaya Beach & Golf Resort. Colleen and I had stayed there once when we were in town scouting possible locations for our home. Nice digs.

He handed me the glasses and pointed. "Second floor balcony, far right corner. Lady with the straw hat."

I steadied myself and focused on the woman, one of those for whom a quick glance compels yet a lengthier evaluation. Even this far away, with her face shadowed and her eyes hidden behind stylish shades, she had a model's air about her. Not standoffish, high fashion, New York style; more a casual, approachable sophistication, southwest Florida style.

She turned, her gaze seemingly focused on our boat, as if aware she was being watched. I nearly waved but instead asked Billy Ray what we were doing here.

He'd already settled into his captain's chair. After noting the time and jotting something in a small notebook, he peered down at me. "You're still going to that Whestin party, aren't you? Thought you'd appreciate a sneak preview of your hostess."

What a guy. I refocused on Mrs. Whestin, who was now conversing with her waiter. "How'd you know she'd be here?"

Billy Ray bumped the throttle and headed back north. "Like I said, you'd be surprised what I know."

8.

The rest of the weekend at first passed too slowly, then too fast, half of me impatient to learn where Colleen stood on the subject of us. The other half hoped she'd call to say that something had come up, and we'd have to reschedule our lunch. If she'd indeed gone to Marco Island with other than girlfriends, if her overnighter was really a sleepover with a member of the opposite sex, I wasn't sure I wanted to know.

Today was Sunday and she'd called around eleven, said "they" had left Marco early this morning and had just got in. She needed to tell me something and didn't want to discuss it over the phone. Not a good sign, and I nearly demanded answers right then. No need to waste lunch and a good fried clams basket on irreconcilable differences.

Somehow, I held my tongue, and we settled on a dive overlooking an inland waterway dotted with homes built in the 1970s and a handful of newer homes that represented the inevitable first wave of tear-downs-turned-mansions. I wondered how many would soon be available price reduced if the market delayed a dramatic turn for the better.

Colleen's BMW convertible stood out handsomely in the sparsely populated parking lot. She'd left the top down and a wave of sadness, guilt and remorse washed over me. The car had been a thank-you-for-sticking-with-me gift I'd given her just before we'd left Chicago, a make-up for the three years of hell I'd put her through. Two on coke, one in rehab.

I'd bought my BMW sedan at the same time. "We might as well ride the road to recovery in style," I'd said. A nice sentiment that in execution hadn't quite worked out as I'd hoped.

Colleen was sitting at a benched table for two on the restaurant's back deck, sipping an iced tea, sheltered from the sun by a large red and white umbrella. She wore a sleeveless dark blue blouse, khaki-colored shorts, and a pink ball cap pulled down over her auburn hair. I couldn't recall her ever looking so damned desirable.

I wasn't sure my shaking knees would hold me up as I approached the table. With my heart pounding and breaths coming in short bursts, it felt like a first date with the gal who'd just been named high school homecoming queen. Which Colleen had been.

She waved, and the sunlight glinted off a heart-shaped locket that dangled from the charm bracelet I'd given her twenty-five years ago in remembrance of the child we lost to a miscarriage. The end of what turned out to be our only shot at natural parenthood. After that, our careers had come first, and we settled into a typically self-indulgent Yuppie lifestyle.

I swallowed hard and gave her a quick shoulder hug. It was warm outside, but her skin felt cool to the touch. And if I wasn't mistaken, she'd changed perfumes.

"How was your weekend?" I asked, a pleasant smile pasted to my face.

Colleen took a deep breath and looked at me with those Irish green eyes that put to shame any emerald nature had ever created. "I'm seeing someone. His name is Steve Wannamaker."

A bold uppercut to McDermott's chin. He didn't see that one coming!

Steve Wannamaker. Teaching pro at the mid-level Eagles Nest Country Club. I'd met the guy last year at a charity golf event as a guest of Billy Ray's. He'd been assigned to our foursome. Around forty, I guessed, which would make him roughly fifteen year's Colleen's junior. Short in stature. A little thick around the middle for a professional golfer, if you ask me.

Did I say *fifteen years* Colleen's junior?

"What do you mean *seeing*?"

She took a deep breath and fidgeted with her locket. "When I left, I stayed at Angie's place"—*one of her girlfriends; maybe there was hope*—"but within three days I knew moping around there wasn't going to cut it. I had to get out, find something to do. A friend I'd met at the Art League is a member at Eagles Nest. She took me there one day, and...we ran into Steve."

"Anybody get hurt?"

"What?"

"Nothing." I began drumming on the table's edge. *Changes in latitudes, changes in attitudes, nothing remains quite the same....*

"Anyway, one day after he gave me a golf lesson, he—"

"You took lessons?" I'd never seen Colleen near a practice range, much less agree to lessons. If reconciliation was in the cards today, she was taking a roundabout way to get there.

She nodded. "He asked if I'd like to hear about an internet business he's starting. Going to name it—don't laugh—'Goofy Golf On-Line.' Sort of a clearinghouse of oddball golf merchandise. Exploding golf balls, caps with built-in fans, joke books, crooked tees. You know."

"Let me guess. He needs investors."

"I have money."

She made it sound as if she were a Vanderbilt. Around the first of the year, the last time I sneaked a peek at her IRA statement, her account had grown to a tidy six-figure sum. What the market had done to it since, I had a pretty good idea.

Still, it had been a sore spot, not just because she'd called it *her* money, but because it had been supplemented by tax-deductible gifts her parents had made every year since my "affliction," as they so charitably called it. I wanted to feel anger, rage—indignation at the very least. But I felt only an overwhelming sense of loss, of having destroyed the best thing that had ever happened to me.

It cut deeper than I wanted to admit that this lovely woman had reserved her enthusiasm, respect, money and possibly her perfumed netherlands for some PGA tour never-been who thought he could sell golf crap over the internet, instead of for her brilliant husband who might soon be helping to take a billion dollar company public.

"You two shacking up? You're a married woman, you know."

Colleen folded her arms and began spinning her wedding ring. "I don't want to argue, Rainey. It was important that you knew I hadn't been out looking. I left because I needed time to think about where we were as a couple, what we wanted out of life. You and I...things haven't exactly been"—she lowered her eyes—"I got interested in this project and...well...things just happened."

She follows with a vicious right cross to McDermott's heart! He's taking a knee!

My fingers hit the table harder as I moved from Jimmy Buffet to something more appropriate to the Stones. "You in love with him?" I asked, trying to find the beat to "You Can't Always Get What You Want."

Colleen reached across and flattened my hands against the table. I could barely breathe. "I'm attracted to his passion. He's the kind of struggling entrepreneur you were going to dedicate your career to, remember? One of the many reasons I fell in love with you."

I noticed she didn't answer my question. Or maybe she had.

"You always had a soft spot for the underdog," I said, sounding more charitable than I'd intended. "How long do we go on like this?"

She leaned back. "I'm flying to Chicago Thursday to see my parents, then head up to Traverse City, stay at their cabin a couple of weeks. I need to get away from...everything."

And then you file? I wanted to ask. But Colleen was right, this wasn't the place to get into a hair-pulling contest. I realized then I'd be having lunch alone, but I wasn't ready for her to leave.

"I'm going to a party in a couple of weeks. Jeremy and Alina Whestin." *You busy?*

She barely raised an eyebrow, then stood and fished her car keys from her purse. "You should bring something. A bottle of wine always works."

I made a mental note to pick up a nice pinot noir. Perhaps something from Oregon. Colleen touched my hand. "I'm sorry, Rainey. You have no idea how much."

McDermott's on his back, and they're bringing in a stretcher. This looks bad....

I swatted at an imaginary mosquito. "You want the espresso machine?"

She shook her head. "Still into green tea. It's something Steve"—she paused, and her cheeks flushed—"but thanks."

And away she went, leaving me alone and smiling sheepishly at our waitress, whose soft round features and sympathetic brown eyes reminded me of my fifth-grade teacher, Mrs. Gray, on whom I'd had an aching crush.

"Everything okay?" the woman asked, giving me what seemed to be the evil eye.

"Great," I said, cheerily. "Everything's just great."

I thought I detected a slight shaking of Mrs. Gray's head, as if she were thinking, *Troublemaker. I knew he'd never amount to anything.*

9.

Half an hour after landing, comfortably settled into the backseat of his airport limo, Jeremy placed his first call of the new week.

"Nice job on the dossiers, Mack."

"Good news there on McDermott. But Wallace could be another matter."

Jeremy wasn't in the mood. "Mack, listen. For better or worse, I've confided a lot in Victoria. Probably more than is prudent. We get down to the short hairs on this thing, I...I'd just like you to stay extra-close to her over the next few weeks. Keep me posted if anything doesn't smell right, got that?"

A sharp pain arced across the top of Jeremy's head, and he regretted trying to get through the morning without taking a pain pill. He wouldn't make it through the afternoon without one. "Just keep your eyes open," he said and snapped shut the cover of his cell.

His thoughts turned to Rainey McDermott. An old friend, he might say. Jeremy didn't like the idea of adding an outsider, not after the mess with George Murray, the previous freelance accountant. A blunder that could end up in a prison sentence if things unraveled. Mack had assured him they would not.

What had George been thinking, threatening him with blackmail like that? The two of them had been doing business for more than twenty years. Was no one to be trusted any more?

He had Mack slash George's tires one night, leaving an unsigned note that said his tongue would be next. To show there were no hard feelings, Jeremy instructed Mack to leave an envelope in George's glove box with $35,000 in cash inside. A security deposit. The last one he intended to leave.

This time, things would be different.

Jeremy would be working with a CFE, a certified fraud examiner whose talents he knew and respected. A man who, like most everybody else he'd ever dealt with, had his price—and, he had a feeling, an ego to match.

He cursed himself for not having gone this route before. Then again, he could excuse himself for not thinking clearly, though from here on he would have to be certain of the logic of every move he made. It wasn't going to be easy. One thing was for certain: the stakes were still too high to trust that Wallace could pull this off alone, especially if his mind was on an end game involving more than just a successful public offering.

What they'd pulled off before had been nickels and dimes compared to what they were planning now. Bringing Rainey McDermott on board would certainly cost him considerably more than he'd budgeted for George Murray. But George was gone now, and he could think of no better replacement to babysit Wallace Gerard. If McDermott let him down? Refused his offer? Then he would do what he had to do, relying on powers of persuasion that had never let him down.

One last call. To say he had a bad feeling about this was the understatement of the year, but he was out of time and out of options that made reasonable financial sense.

Wallace answered on the second ring.

"Do it," Jeremy said. Two simple words that zapped the thin reserve of energy and morality he had left.

"I'll make the arrangements today," Wallace said.

"Where's it going?"

"Looks like the British Virgin Islands."

Ordinarily he would have asked why there and not somewhere else, but that would have demanded a level of focus he didn't have in him right now. He hung up without comment, then removed from his pocket a compact humidor he'd picked out in Italy three years ago, a gift from Alina on their fourteenth wedding anniversary.

A minute later, he gave thanks for a spectacular *Bolivar Belicosos Finos*. Smoking stood at the top of the list of things not to do for a man in his condition, but *to hell with 'em all*. He was going to defy the odds—and do it on his terms.

When the limo pulled through the gates of Palms Away, he nodded at the security guard and smiled contentedly as a perfectly formed smoke ring floated though the air.

Alina had caught only a glimpse of her husband as he entered the house and headed straight for the bedroom. Now, as Jeremy exited his closet dressed in a tee shirt and swimming trunks, she thought he looked paler, the lines in his forehead etched deeper than the last time she'd seen him a month ago.

Ordinarily, she might suggest that he see a doctor. But not now. She let it go.

"Thought we'd go to the club for a late lunch," she said. "You obviously have other plans."

Jeremy grabbed a *Fortune* magazine from his nightstand and propped a pair of reading glasses on his head. "Make me a vodka tonic, will you? Twist of lime. I'm not that hungry."

He pointed to his bathing trunks. "Join me?"

The thought nearly made her gag. She'd hoped they would go to the club for lunch. With members dropping by to say hello and perhaps join them, she could present to Jeremy the dutifully caring wife without having to give him her undivided attention. She used the same reasoning when setting up dinner dates. The more guests the better, but always at least two other couples.

The rough times were the nights he insisted they dine in alone. Thankfully, with him so often absent, those evenings had been rare. Right now, the last thing she wanted was to spend the afternoon relaxing by the pool with the man she detested, but with the week just beginning, she put her annoyance aside and agreed to join him, at least for a few minutes.

Alina brought Jeremy his drink and sat down on a chaise lounge he'd pulled next to him. She hadn't changed out of her sundress, but he didn't seem to notice. "Rainey McDermott's coming to the party," she said of the man who'd occupied her thoughts for a week now. "We got his RSVP today."

Jeremy had called her from St. Louis last week to ask if she knew anything about the McDermotts. To her surprise, he'd opened up about the possibility of offering the man a consulting position with the company's accounting department, adding that he'd discussed this with no one but Mack. Which told her maybe not everything, but enough that her potentially stalled plan began to move in a new direction.

"Still think he's your man?" she asked.

Jeremy took a sip of his drink and shrugged. "I'll know more Wednesday. We're playing golf together."

Alina silently crossed her fingers. If McDermott turned out to be right for Jeremy, he had a chance to be perfect for her. At the very least, he'd be competition for Wallace, leverage to use against him if he didn't start playing ball her way.

"Florida sunshine becomes you," Jeremy said with a look she thought bordered on a leer. It made her skin crawl.

"Don't stay out here too long. We have seven-thirty reservations at Joe's Crab Shack with the Allens and McMillans. I don't want you looking like one of the crabs."

She headed for the house, ignoring her husband's muttered protests.

10.

Wallace sat heavily on the edge of his bed, tension creating knots that stretched from his upper back to his calves. He'd been rehearsing this moment in his mind for a month now, ever since he'd quietly announced to Jeremy that he'd found a financing source they could live with. At last he had the authorization to move forward. But instead of elation, he felt only dread.

How, he wondered, had it had come to this?

But he knew the answer. Waleed al-Ghamdi had *potential*, and his Muslim brothers expected him to use it now or shame would again be cast upon the family name.

It was early evening here, 11:30 P.M. in Marseille. Rashid had been alerted to expect his call.

He punched in the number on one of the dozen pre-paid, virtually untraceable cell phones he'd bought over time at local drug and food stores. The voice of his cousin cut through the 4,800 miles that separated them as clearly as if he were in the next room of Wallace's south St. Louis townhouse.

"We were expecting this call last week," Rashid said.

"Everyone can relax. It's a go."

"Your Mr. Whestin is comfortable with us?"

"I wouldn't use the word 'comfortable,' but he's aware of how well the phones are contributing to the bottom line. We'll be ordering more."

"I know you will."

Wallace said nothing. Through their private equity subsidiary, Links International stood ready to lend $110 million—at highly desirable terms—but only if Whestin Group agreed to purchase a total of one million of the cell phones manufactured by one of their "partners." He'd already taken delivery of five hundred thousand, the balance of the order to be shipped in two lots between now and the public offering in February.

He didn't know why it was so important to make the phones part of the private placement, and he wondered if there would be other special demands placed on him down the road—ones not be so easy to accommodate. But there was another reason this transaction made him uneasy: he'd accepted Rashid's terms without questioning the basis for the substantial discount he was offering.

"We want everyone to make money," Rashid had said. "That way, we'll be doing business again."

A vague response at best, but Wallace had been in no position to argue or investigate further, and Jeremy, despite misgivings, had just given his blessing. So be it.

"We're ready to authorize the next shipment," Wallace said. "The balance of our obligation will be fulfilled per our agreement. There will be a mandatory six-month lockup on redemptions. My guess is we will need that much time to get the company performing back to speed, anyway."

"And then?"

"After no more than six months, your silent partners should be in position to sell at a handsome return, as stipulated."

"Stipulated but not guaranteed," Rashid said. "These days, transacting business through the New York Stock Exchange is a less than optimal means of tidying up our bookkeeping." He paused. "We could have demanded a much higher return, you know, but it's just as well. The more we get out of this transaction, the more that finds itself lining our brethren's filthy pockets."

He spat into the phone, and Wallace grimaced. He'd been down this road with his firebrand cousin before. Corruption was a fact of life throughout the Middle East and North Africa—including their Algerian homeland—but Rashid had many times made clear his distaste of the practice.

Wallace asked how the account would be set up, hoping to head off another diatribe. Rashid told him that nothing had changed since their last communication a week ago. He'd sent a coded message over the internet indicating he would be opening an anonymous account for Wallace in an offshore financial center, likely in the British Virgin Islands. Wallace could only imagine how a wire transfer from an OFC would tighten the bank's collective scrotum.

Best of all, Ralph Bartlett would assume the wire transfer had originated directly from the private equity company—for which Wallace would have a logical explanation. There would be no way to know that he, Wallace, would have exclusive control of the account.

"I'll wire our bank in the States on an as needed basis," Wallace said. "A precaution should anything go wrong." An honest explanation, but he knew instantly he'd phrased it poorly.

"Nothing is to go wrong," Rashid snapped. "If it does, neither my father nor I can protect you."

Wallace dug the fingernails of his free hand into the flesh of his palm. *Protect me from what?* he wondered. *The authorities—or my own family?*

His throat burned, and he fought the urge to lash out at his sanctimonious cousin and his corrupt band of thugs. While they'd fully endorsed this unexpected "opportunity," he'd hated the very idea of it. But Whestin Group was desperate for operating funds, and right now, Wallace knew that his future, a life with Alina and the success of Whestin Group's IPO were inextricably linked. He'd had no other affordable options.

Still, despite the fact he was sticking his neck out for everybody, they now had the nerve to threaten him?

Fine. When Alina and he walked down that aisle one day, when he rose to head of Whestin Group *International*, he would be finished with his obligations and the restoration of the family name soiled so long ago through no fault of his own. So much had changed since then. So much of him was now *American*.

"I should have the papers to you midweek," he said. "Something to show our accountants."

"They have been persuaded?"

"Let's just say that a successful public offering is now in their best interests, as well."

"Good. It is time something came of your lofty position, Waleed. You have been in America more than twenty-five years, yes?"

"Twenty-*seven* years now. My loyalties have always been to our cause."

It wasn't the most forceful statement Wallace had ever uttered, and Rashid laughed derisively. "You have taken your sweet time proving it." Again, the spitting sound. Wallace's cousin had been more like a brother to him before they'd been so abruptly separated. Though nearing fifty, Rashid still exuded passion about everything, the consequences be damned. Not unlike the kind of man Wallace might have become had he been allowed to stay and fight. He shuddered at the thought.

"This is an opportunity to prove yourself to our new organization," Rashid said, adding sarcastically, "our new *vision*. I trust you know what you are doing."

Wallace understood. For years his cousin had worked closely with the Salafist Group for Call and Combat. The GSPC, initials of the group's French name, had become the most deadly terrorist organization in Algeria, repeatedly attacking military forces and even kidnapping Western tourists in an effort to overthrow the nation's pro-West government. Then, just two years ago, the GSPC joined forces with al Qaeda. Four months later, the group became al Qaeda in the Islamic Maghreb.

"I fear where we are headed," Rashid had said at the time. "We will become less about establishing an Islamic Algeria and more about attacking American interests and its allies."

Wallace had a fear of his own, that his adopted country could be attacked again—maybe with his unintended help.

He'd been a United States citizen for nearly three decades, bought a condo in Florida where he planned to retire one day. Even become a baseball fan. When those airliners blasted into the Twin Towers and the Pentagon, he'd been horrified and frightened. The extent of the hijackers' planning, the so-called bravery that had been so celebrated in the Arab world, made him ashamed. Many times since, he'd said a prayer of thanks that his Americanized name and American genes helped to hide his homeland.

"Did you hear me, cousin?" Rashid demanded. "We are putting a great deal of faith in you."

Wallace bristled at the innuendo but knew no good would come of a sharp reply. He offered reassurances and said his good-byes.

As he prepared for bed, he had to acknowledge Rashid's skepticism. Who, they must wonder, is Waleed al-Ghamdi but an untested, wannabe patriot living the good life in America? In truth, he was nobody in their eyes.

If only he could count on it staying that way when this was over.

Wallace needed to tell her the good news.

Many nights when Jeremy had been in St. Louis, they would talk to well past two in the morning. Flirting, plotting, testing each other. But this time, Jeremy was with her in Florida. He would have to play it safe.

He sent her a text message: "Must decline invite. But TY."

Innocuous, purposely so, should anyone be checking her calls and messages. Anyone named Jeremy Whestin. If he were ever pressed, Wallace could just say he'd lost the RSVP card. Truth was, he had every intention of attending the big Labor Day weekend party. He just needed a few things to work out in his favor. But he hoped the message would elicit a response—assuming she cared.

His phone rang a moment later, startling him. "Are you alone?" he asked, holding his breath.

"I might as well be," Alina said. "He took some pills an hour ago. I won't hear from him until tomorrow morning."

Wallace didn't know what to say, but he knew what he was thinking. She wouldn't be having sex tonight.

"What's this about you not coming?" she asked.

"Just teasing."

"Teasing—or testing?"

This woman was getting to know him too well. "I got the money today," he said, changing the subject. "I mean, I arranged it. A private placement to tide us over until the public offering."

"Doesn't sound like something necessarily incriminating. Or is it?"

Wallace hadn't told her about Links International. Or about the cell phone connection. He realized he probably shouldn't have said anything about the private placement, either.

"The evidence is building," he said, then asked if she was ready for the party.

"I can do these in my sleep."

His response was to tell her that he loved her.

No poetic set-up, no romantic sunset or flowers or card. No kiss. No hug. He felt foolish, but he'd danced around his feelings for weeks now. It was hard to reveal his emotions with Alina so focused on her hatred of Jeremy and her vow to take him down.

Still, she'd made him feel that he was more than just a means to an end. She cared about him, she'd said. Had feelings for him. Envisioned a future for herself that included him by her side and she by his. At first, it hadn't made sense. Now it made all the sense in the world. He couldn't imagine a future without her in it.

In the weeks leading to New Year's Eve, he'd sensed her feelings growing deeper. He should have just let things play out, but he'd pushed her that night—and she'd pushed back, demanding answers he wasn't ready to give.

"Too soon," he'd said. And then Jeremy showed up and scared the shit out of both of them. Nothing had quite been the same since.

"Alina?" He held his breath and waited.

"I love you, too, Wallace. But...love is based on trust."

"I know you're upset, but the less you know now, the safer you will be." It sounded like a line from a B movie, and he knew she wouldn't buy it.

"You better go, Wallace. You have a lot to do."

Typical female, he thought as he hung up. Playing manipulative games when she didn't get her way. But he could play the game, too. He would immerse himself in every detail of the public offering while maintaining his silence about what Jeremy and he were up to, certainly the details. Alina had him wrapped around her finger like so much thread, but if she wanted to tap into the only leverage he had, it would take proof of where she stood.

Of course, if she waited too long, he might just have to demand it.

Every man has his limits.

11.

8:00 A.M., Wednesday, August 13

I bought a new golf glove and a fresh sleeve of balls at the club's pro shop, convinced the stars had aligned. And I wasn't referring to the rare and dramatic appearance of Venus and Jupiter seemingly touching each other in our southwestern skies. Today, I was to play my first golf game with *the man* himself.

Until Billy Ray's announcement, I hadn't figured on meeting Jeremy Whestin until the night of his party. Never foresaw the possibility that we might first be playing a round of golf together. Certainly not that he would take the liberty of asking the commissioner of our Wednesday golf group to put him in my foursome—in *my* cart.

Now if I could just concentrate on golf.

It had been two days since Colleen revealed her involvement with Steve Wannamaker. She was flying up to see her parents tomorrow. Who knows, if something positive came of my game today, enough to warrant a call to

Colleen this afternoon, she might change her mind and stay. The odds were probably as long as Mr. Wannamaker making it big on the internet, but Jeremy Whestin was the most influential contact I had right now, and I intended to make the most of it.

Our foursome today included Billy Ray. "Wouldn't miss this for the world," he'd said. "You're going to wilt like peeled onions in a hot pan, and I want to be there to see it."

We called our Wednesday group The Kennel Club because we played like dogs and generally deserved to be boarded by the end of the round. I thought it interesting that a man of Jeremy Whestin's stature would deign to play with a mangy pack of mongrel golfers like us and decided he simply wanted to get a closer look at yours truly.

I hurried to the staging area and spotted my clubs secured to the back of a cart alongside a second set. A metal tag clipped to the bag identified those clubs as belonging to "J. Whestin." The bag was fastened on the driver's side, which meant Jeremy would be doing the driving. Fine with me.

A dozen other members of The Kennel Club were lined up at the driving range, gouging great toupees of turf from the thin Bermuda grass. I didn't see Jeremy. Fifteen minutes later, my warm-up complete, he still hadn't shown, and I began to wonder if introductions would have to wait for another day.

Billy Ray and his cart partner headed for the putting green. I joined them, and we stroked a few practice putts. "What's that flapping under your shirt?" he asked.

Actually, I did have the butterflies, a good sign. It meant I was focused on my objective today: impressing the hell out of Jeremy Whestin.

"You're up," the starter said, handing us our scorecards.

"Mr. Whestin here?" I asked, preparing myself for a letdown.

The starter pointed toward the first tee. "He walked over from the clubhouse ten minutes ago."

Damn! I hadn't made it to the first tee, yet somehow felt I'd just recorded my first bogey.

Steering the cart down the concrete path, I pushed the accelerator to the floor, turned the final corner, and there he was. Just over six feet, I guessed. Athletic build. Intimidating demeanor of a drill sergeant, albeit a well-dressed one. While the rest of us wore moisture-wicking golf shirts and unabashedly displayed our bony knees beneath ill-fitting, wash 'n dry shorts, Jeremy wore a classic yellow cotton pullover, lightweight gray slacks with a perfect break, and what looked to be a new pair of black FootJoys. Not a drop of perspiration showed anywhere.

Billy Ray pulled his cart next to me. "Nice driving, Mario." A reminder to slow down and keep my cool.

The four of us shook hands, Jeremy applying such force it bordered on a dare. The metallic chill to his skin belied the morning's rapidly warming temperature, and his pale blue eyes reminded me of the kind of glacial ice I'd seen once on *The Discovery Channel.*

"What's the game today?" I asked, discretely working the circulation back into my hand.

"The outside game is one ball or better, net, two man teams," Jeremy said, marking a "JW" on his ball with a red felt-tip pen. He pulled down his sunglasses and drilled me with his baby blues. "Of which you and I are one."

He reached for his driver, plucked a tee from the cart and added, "But I suggest an inside game among the four of us. A simple Nassau, opposites as partners this time, one best ball, twenty dollars a nine, twenty for the eighteen. Automatic one time press allowed if you're two down."

I glanced at Billy Ray, who scanned the skies as if he were searching for UFOs. I knew what he was thinking.

A Nassau was usually played for five dollars a nine at our club. Winning both the front and back nines means you've also won the overall, and you come away with fifteen bucks a man. Nobody gets hurt. Jeremy, obviously playing Mr. Big Shot, had raised the stakes to a potential total pot of sixty dollars, not counting presses. It was the kind of thing a relative stranger to the group would suggest only if he were an all-around jerk.

Billy Ray and his partner weren't going to like my response, but I was going to respect the unwritten rule that the man who makes the bet automatically gains an intangible advantage. In other words, trump his bet with one of your own.

"Fine with me," I said, "but let's count *both* balls on the back nine, high ball breaks the tie." In other words, on the back nine, it wouldn't be just one ball from the two-man team that counted; both balls would count. The last thing you wanted to be was the high ball that cost your team the hole and possibly the match.

It isn't about the money in this game; it's about performing under pressure, and I was still on a high from Billy Ray's grudge match where, to put it succinctly, we'd crushed his former FBI compatriots. In this case, I wanted to see a bit of what this Whestin character was made of. As Colleen was fond of saying, when it comes to showing their testicles, men can be such pricks.

"Okay with everybody?" I asked.

Billy Ray gave me a sly grin and nodded his acceptance. Jeremy simply grabbed his driver and headed for the first tee.

Game on.

Four hours later, I thought about contacting the Champions Tour for professional players over fifty years old. I'd shot an eighty, five strokes better than my average. If Jeremy hadn't fallen apart on the back nine and shot a ninety-three, we'd have had a real chance at big game honors. Maybe we still did. This was, after all, The Kennel Club.

As for the Nassau, where he and I were playing as opponents, Jeremy was now seventy dollars poorer, having lost all three bets, plus a ten-dollar press. He also recorded the highest score on a hole five times on the back nine for Mr. High Ball honors going away. Of course, Billy Ray was down seventy smackers, too.

I sidled up to him and offered my condolences, which he acknowledged with a stubby middle finger salute. That didn't keep my feet from floating six inches off the blistering asphalt as we headed for the clubhouse to settle up.

In the cart, we'd kept the focus on golf, politics, the market. Any thought Jeremy might have had about talking business apparently deteriorated along with the quality of his game. But there was still time.

Inside, I grabbed an open table at the back of the grillroom, hoping he and I could get some privacy. No such luck as Billy Ray plopped his sweaty frame in the chair next to me.

"God, it's hot out there!" Jeremy bellowed as he waved a hand at our bar manager. "Gino, pitcher over here and a bowl of almonds."

A wiry, olive-skinned man of sixty, Gino hurried over and nodded his head at each of us. "Pitcher comin' up, Mr. Whestin, but we got no almonds. Too expensive, they say."

Jeremy slammed an open palm onto the tabletop, knocking over the menu holder. "Three hundred fifty members paying 130 G's initiation, eleven grand a year in dues, and we can't afford almonds? The hell with that." He reached into his pocket, pulled out a C note and slapped it into Gino's palm.

"You get in your car," he said through clenched teeth, "drive to Publix, buy all the goddamn almonds you see and get back here pronto. But get me that pitcher first. And before the day's out, you place the next order of almonds, just like always. Any member of management doesn't like it, tell 'em I'm in the club directory."

Billy Ray squared his chair to the table, the rippling veins in his temples threatening to burst through his skin. I lowered my eyes and gave him the *settle down* sign. I didn't want this escalating into an opportunity lost over a silly temper tantrum about a bowl of nuts. Besides, these were my nuts on the line.

Gino turned, head held high, and walked to the beer dispenser. A minute later, he placed a full pitcher and three cups on the table, motioned to his assistant to cover for him and left. With the usual background din of boasts, bad break laments and off-color jokes suddenly reduced to library levels, several of the men in the clubroom pretended to study their scorecards; others gazed uneasily at an elevated TV screen tuned to the *Bloomberg* channel. Wall Street watching had become an ugly obsession for a lot of us who were beginning to wonder how much longer we could afford the luxury of membership at the Palms Away Golf & Country Club.

Jeremy filled his cup, then shoved the pitcher in my direction. "Alina says you're coming to the party."

"Wouldn't miss it. Appreciate the invite."

"Good. Did you know I'm taking my company public?"

Keep breathing, I told myself. "Heard rumors. Big decision."

"Maybe bigger than I figured. Might be an opportunity for a man with your background."

I tried to take the comment in stride. Jeremy had apparently done some homework and liked what he learned, but just how far had his research taken him? I filled my beer cup and downed a healthy slug.

Billy Ray was joking with a member at the next table, affecting a disinterested air, but I could tell he was using a third ear to absorb every syllable of my conversation. Jeremy gave him a quick look. "We'll talk more at the party," he said. "Give me a chance to escape all that useless party prattle."

I nodded and glanced at the television, trying to contain my excitement. Was any of this worth a call to Colleen before she headed north? Probably not. Better to wait until I had a firm offer in hand. Still....

The final foursome trudged in, threw down their thirty-dollar entry fee and grabbed a beverage, eager to see which two-man team would win the majority of what today would be a $600 pot. "Who's in charge?" Jeremy barked. "I can't screw around here all day."

For which I figured the members of The Kennel Club were mightily relieved. The man was a genuine bore, but I'd won nice money in the Nassau today, and if I got lucky, I'd win us both a few bucks more in the big game. Not bad, but I sensed a much bigger payday ahead.

Billy Ray pushed back his chair. "Gotta take a shit," he said.

I detected a not-so-subtle message there and figured he wasn't coming back. At the door he stopped and turned. "Tell your mom I said hi."

Damn!

12.

It was now 5:20 P.M., and I was sitting in my mother's private one bedroom apartment at the Bayfront Retirement Community, the two of us enjoying each other's company. A date I might have forgotten had it not been for Billy Ray.

"You feeling well?" Mother asked. "You look flushed."

"I'm fine."

She squeezed my hand and thanked me for setting her up in such excellent surroundings. "I couldn't afford this on my own, you know." I pretended to stifle a cough, hoping to hide cheeks that had grown crimson with guilt.

Earlier this afternoon I'd been collecting second place money in The Kennel Club's outside game and picking up a couple of skins to further add to the McDermott coffers. But playing well, impressing Jeremy Whestin, finding a job, the whole mess with Colleen—none of it seemed important now as I stared at the oxygen tubes clipped to my mother's nostrils and wondered what it meant that I'd reduced this charming, patient, intelligent, empathetic woman to a bunch of initials I couldn't even turn into a decent acronym.

OFHBT. Old and Failing, Hanging By a Thread.

Perhaps it was because I couldn't accept this kind of slow death after the hardships she'd endured raising her three children, working two jobs, sacrificing every personal need so that my twin sisters and I could wear decent clothes, eat decent food and sleep in decent beds in the tired old home where we'd been born.

Through it all, she somehow managed to save enough money every year to buy us a Christmas present. None of us ever complained that we didn't have a tree to put it under—except for me.

These past ten years of her life had consisted of innumerable visits to a handful of physicians and several emergency visits to the hospital. She'd endured crippling fatigue, weight loss she couldn't afford, and painful swelling of her feet and ankles. Not to forget an uncountable number of inhalers and antibiotics, bouts with bronchitis and the ever-present potential for pneumonia.

In the end—a bad choice of words—it was easier to think of my mother as parts of the alphabet. Not the whole spelling out of my life, but enough that without her, there would be no comprehending who I was or still hoped to be.

"You look more like Maureen O'Hara every day," I said, "in her early years."

Mother smiled and sat as erect as her seventy-eight year old spine would allow, hands of parchment-thin skin and brittle bones grasping the sides of a wheelchair that offered little comfort thanks to a thin vinyl seat and back strap. In truth, with a shawl wrapped around her arms and her once shoulder-length, chestnut-red hair now gray and cut short, I could imagine her playing the role of Cary Grant's grandmother in *An Affair To Remember*.

"And you'll be lookin' a lot like Spencer Tracy," she said, "in his later years."

We laughed and turned our attention to dinner.

Until about a month ago, we would have headed for the private dining room in the Care Center wing of the campus reserved for those requiring special assistance. But Mother was too weak now and preferred to dine in her room.

Tonight's fare was meat loaf, egg noodles, broccoli and a dinner roll with those little papered butter pats. There was even a wedge of key lime pie, firm and cream-colored, the way I like it.

I sat at one end of a small dining table; Mother sat in her wheelchair just to my right. A tray affixed to her armrests contained the same meal pre-cut into small bites. She didn't complain and didn't ask for assistance.

In the center of the table was a small glass vase stuffed with pink carnations, as it had been for the past month. I'd been meaning to say something. "Nice touch," I said to the attending nurse. "Your idea?"

She shook her head and whispered an answer, her eyes on Mother. "Secret admirer. In the language of flowers, pink carnations means, 'I'll never forget you.' She won't tell me who he is."

"He's not from here?"

She shook her head and then she asked if Mother wanted hot tea. I made a mental note to ask about the mystery boyfriend and then settled back to watch the upcoming one act play I'd already witnessed a half dozen times.

"Tea?" Mother harrumphed. "A British abomination, strictly for sissies. I'm Irish, woman, and you damn well better bring me my whisky this instant."

"Well, I never!" the nurse intoned, hands on her hips. She then pivoted on her heels in mock indignation and huffed her way to a serving cart just outside the door, returning with a "London Fog."

"You'll drink this, and you'll like it!" she said of the alcohol-free mixture of Earl Grey tea, steamed milk and syrup.

Mother obediently sipped her favorite beverage, her watery blue eyes twinkling. "Passable," she said and waved the nurse away.

I knew what was coming next and decided to go the route of the half-truth. I was doing a lot of that lately.

"How's Colleen?" she asked. "Don't think I've seen her since...." She waited for me to finish the sentence.

"She's investing in an internet business. Keeps her very busy. In fact, she's in Chicago right now."

"What did you call it, dear?"

"The internet. Has to do with computers. Don't let your food get cold."

Mother stabbed at her noodles and managed to suck a few into her mouth before the rest fell onto her plate. "And how are the kids? Do you stay in touch?"

Amazing.

"The kids" was the name I'd given my earliest fraud clients, entrepreneurs skilled in business but all neophytes when it came to fraud prevention and detection. It would have been nearly twenty years ago when all that started, and I remember Mother telling me then how proud she was that her son wasn't focused solely on making the big bucks. Of course, I also remember she didn't turn down the Cadillac El Dorado I bought her on her sixtieth birthday, but the dear lady was more than deserving. I just wish I'd made it a Rolls Royce while I still had the money.

"The kids are fine," I said, reaching over to pat her hand. "All grown up now."

"Do you ever call them?"

"Not really. Well...sometimes."

Mother delicately lifted a piece of meat with her fork, then stopped and asked a question that caused me to gag on my coffee. "And what about your father, dear? Do you ever call him?"

She finished her bite and smiled, all polite and pleasant, but she knew this was a subject we never, *ever* broached. I couldn't, in fact, recall the last time it had come up, but I was certain it hadn't ended well.

I stared at her with pinched eyebrows. "Why would you ask that?"

She shrugged and picked at her broccoli. "He *is* your father. And he meant well. He just wanted you kids to have a better life—especially you, Rainey. You were always the demanding one."

Hold up a sec. She was talking about the defining moment of my life, nearly fifty years ago, as if it had taken place last week. As if I was the reason for our estrangement from *Dad*.

"He walked out on *us*, Mother." But she knew that. Besides, as far as I knew, my father hadn't seen her in years. Why would she bring this up *now*? I buttered a roll and settled down when she changed the subject.

"Are you too old to have more?"

"More what?"

"Kids."

Great. I'd just as soon we'd stayed on the subject of my father given I'd been dancing around this subject for several years now, never quite sure if Mother was referring to my former clients or to the grandchildren Colleen and I never produced for her. Clarifying the point would have disappointed her either way.

"As a matter of fact," I said, readying another half-truth, "I'm giving some thought to that."

"To what, dear?"

"Having more kids."

"That would be nice." She took another stab at her noodles. "Have you discussed this with Colleen?"

"She's all for it. And she told me to tell you to eat your vegetables."

I started to ask her about Carnation Man when I noticed her eyes had lost focus, and her breathing seemed more labored than usual. "You okay?"

She formed her lips into a circle, sucked in a deep breath and nodded. What color she had in her cheeks now came only from the dab of blush she faithfully applied just before my visits. Her eyes roamed my face the way I remembered when I'd fall off my bike, and she'd check me for cuts and bits of embedded gravel and then out would come the Mercurochrome.

"Call your father," she said, a disturbing wheeze emanating from deep within her chest. "And stop blaming yourself. It's fucking up your life."

Flinching as if jabbed with a cattle prod, I dropped my fork, and it clattered to the floor. My father had been a notorious blue-streaker, even around his children. But my mother? Never! Who had she been hanging around with?

I bent down, not so much to retrieve the utensil but to hide from whatever truth Mother wanted me to acknowledge. When at last I sat upright, her eyes were fluttering—and then she slumped onto her right side. I jumped from my chair, set her upright and called her name. No response.

The rest was a blur as I ran to the hall and waved frantically at her nurse, who was talking with a staff doctor. In seconds they and a second nurse were at her side, administering medication that eventually nudged her back to consciousness. The doctor ushered me aside as the nurses helped her into bed.

"Your mother's showing signs of what we call right-side heart failure," he said. "I called her primary physician this afternoon, but there's not much we can do at an end stage like this."

I'd heard the term "end stage" before but never defined in practical terms. I only knew that I was watching Mother in her last days, and I wanted to weep for both of us.

Not much registered after that, except that the doctor suggested I begin thinking about "arrangements." He shook my hand, told me to call if I had more questions and left.

Mother seemed to be sleeping, for which I said a silent prayer. I picked a carnation from the vase, laid it in her hand and kissed her on the forehead. My preference, of course, was that she would have ended up SHSW: Spry and Happy with Sufficient Wealth to weather the vagaries of life well into her nineties and even beyond, if God willed it.

Not to be. Mother was OFHBT, partly because of her DNA—she was one of those rare cases, a nonsmoker who contracted emphysema because she lacked some unpronounceable protein—and partly because her SOB husband had left her little enough money to raise her family, much less survive a problematical old age.

If I was completely honest, there was another reason: she'd been cursed with a son whose career took precedence over all else at a time when she needed him most. Who was singularly devoted to making society pay, in cash, for a childhood he might not have survived were it not for Mary Margaret McDermott. Who waited too long to provide the assistance, both emotionally and physically, that she desperately needed when it all started to go so terribly wrong.

As I headed for my luxury car and my luxury home in my luxury resort community, I decided Mother was now ASIL ASIF.

Another Someone I Loved, Another Someone I Failed.

13.

I spent the next three weeks checking in on Mother, delicately trying to tease out her thoughts about a funeral service. Did she want to be buried or cremated, and did she have a location in mind? And who did she want presiding over the service?

My questions fell on deaf ears. "I'll think about it, dear," was the best I could get out of her. For reasons I couldn't put my finger on, she seemed in better spirits. When I ventured a question about Carnation Man one visit, she blushed and said she didn't know what I was talking about. I let it go, just happy to see her feeling better.

When I wasn't worrying about Mother, I was boning up on the latest in the field of forensic accounting and SEC rules and regulations. All the recent high profile fraud scandals were creating an ever-lengthening maze of rules and regulations. I did not want to meet with Jeremy and convey the impression that I'd fallen behind.

I figured it was time well spent since I had no guarantee of anything but an interview with the head of Whestin Group. If it failed to bear fruit, I'd have to get myself ready to scrounge up business wherever I could find it—and fast. And I'd have to do it in a still unfamiliar landscape.

In Chicago, commerce never took a vacation. You wore different clothes in the summer, spent more time outside on the weekends, and were generally in a better mood, but life—*business*—continued on as usual. Not here in Naples, a sub-tropical clime where so many people summered up north that driving down normally jammed Tamiami Trail in the middle of the day was like barreling down I-75 with hardly a car in sight. And now, with the lifeblood of the community—real estate sales—grinding to a halt and commercial space vacant by the tens of thousands of square feet, the area was beginning to resemble a ghost town.

Many restaurants had closed for the season, accompanied by speculation they might not reopen, ever. Most malls were all but deserted and dozens of smaller, independent retailers had locked their doors and thrown in the towel. At times, I'd go out to play a round of golf at the club and find myself the only one on the course.

Some place to start a business, I thought.

My accounting-related research on the Web revealed that CPAs like me could now get a new designation—CFF, which stood for "Certified in Financial Forensics." Sort of a next step up the prestige ladder from the Certified Fraud Examiner designation I already held.

I made a note of the application process and took a break to make myself some popcorn. Bowl in hand, I was about to google the Securities and Exchange Commission to review any recent rules changes when my phone rang. I didn't recognize the number, but it carried a Chicago area code.

Any number of possibilities occurred to me, but at 10:10 P.M. none included Paul Banefield, senior partner and founder of my former place of business. We exchanged stilted pleasantries, neither of us asking what the other was up to, but Paul did apologize for calling so late, which I figured meant more bad news.

Sure enough..."I got a call this afternoon from the FBI," he said. Adding "The subject was Grayson Automotive Systems" just as I tossed a handful of corn into my mouth. A kernel lodged in my throat, and I had to swallow twice to dislodge it.

Grayson had been a subsidiary of a holding company called Archway Industries, headquartered in St. Louis. Among other duties, I prepared an audited annual statement for use by Grayson's bank, vendors and other appropriate parties. Archway's internal accounting department would use these statements to file with the Department of Revenue in each appropriate state where Archway owned businesses.

Since leaving Chicago I'd tried to take comfort in the fact that awareness of my role in the sale of Grayson had been limited to a couple of their executives who had every incentive to keep quiet themselves. The president, Hank Garrett, had in fact died of lung cancer two years ago, taking his secrets with him. I'd heard the other, one of Garrett's assistants, had disappeared somewhere on Mexico's Baja peninsula.

I'd felt safe, or at least safer—until this call.

"And?" I asked, trying to sound nonchalant.

"At first, the agent asked some general questions about our involvement," Paul said. "How long Grayson had been a client, what we did for them. Then he got around to the sale. He was under the impression we handled it, but I set him straight. Told him that you made the presentation to the folks who bought it—just after you left us."

"Did you ask him what this was all about?"

"He wouldn't say, but he did ask me to verify your address and phone number." He paused. "I wasn't sure I should call you. Been thinking about this all evening. But you and I went through a lot building the firm, adding that forensics angle, thanks to you. I always thought of you as a friend, Rainey, not just a colleague."

"Appreciate that, Paul, though I can't imagine what this is about." A lie, of course, and it made me sick to think Paul would have his doubts. Given the grief I'd caused him and the ugly circumstances surrounding my departure from his company, this call was a heads up I didn't deserve.

We said something about staying in touch they way people do but never really mean and then hung up. I set the popcorn aside. Shouldn't have been eating it, anyway, as it inevitably set my stomach acids to percolating. But what I was feeling now in the pit of my stomach had nothing to do with any late night snack.

With surprising ease I recalled my last two years with Paul & Company, the 24/7 strain of working under ever-tightening deadlines for ever-larger, more prestigious clients, of knowing there was garbage buried in mountains of documents and electronic files if I could find it. Agonizing over what failure would do to my reputation and future income.

As I was to learn so often happens with driven people, one snort and I was hooked.

I'd never felt so much energy.

Never saw things so clearly.

Never got so much done.

Never saw it coming.

Four years ago, 5:45 P.M., Thursday, January 29, 2004
Chicago, Illinois

Penelope Procter, my twenty-seven year old secretary and love-struck drug supplier, stood in the office doorway, demeanor apologetic, eyes red-rimmed and worried.

"You're bleeding," she said.

A drop of blood plopped from my nose onto the leather desk blotter. I swiped at it with a finger and pressed a tissue against my right nostril.

"Mr. Garrett's on line two," she said. "Should I—?"

I shook my head and took the call. Hank left a message yesterday, said he was sorry to hear about my "difficulties," and that he was rooting for me. Then he said he wanted to discuss an opportunity I might find of interest, as soon as I was up to it.

It had been just five days since Penny found me on the floor, unable to breathe. I was embarrassed that clients like Hank might already know the depths to which I'd sunk, but I also wasn't surprised. While my fellow "seniors" would give me a second chance if I wanted it, I knew they frowned on an addiction to anything other than boosting fees. If they were honest, what they really wanted was to see me go, and I couldn't blame them.

With a smoker's huskiness to his voice, Hank got to the point. "Grayson's going up for sale in March. We've got a hot prospect, but naturally, they'll demand a hard look at he books. And, uh, as you know, things have been difficult in manufacturing for some time."

He cleared his throat. "Given you know us better than anybody, we want you to review our books, then, uh, give us a clean bill of health."

"A full audit?"

"Not...really. We've already done the hard work. Just need you to give it a look-see, then affix your John Hancock. Make it official and all. And when it's time, we want you to, uh, handle the presentation to their board."

I smelled garbage on the cusp of turning rank. Just breathing felt akin to lifting ten-pound weights with my diaphragm. "And if I find a problem?"

"We'll take care of it. Point is, we don't want *them*—"

He stopped and coughed, ugly and coarse. When he recovered, he told me the sale should fetch around $45 million and that my cut would be seven percent for helping out on such short notice, especially given my health concerns.

I did the math. I'd pulled down some handsome fees in the past, but the number Hank just tossed out bordered on the ridiculous. Thus it likely meant only one thing.

Colleen told me that in those weeks I now faced in rehab, they'd not only help me beat my addiction, they'd help me understand why it had happened, give me a fresh outlook on life and my place in it. Much appreciated, but with my reputation in ruins, my income cut at least in half, and both my bank account and my marriage on life support, what I needed was a new start.

Is that what Hank was offering me? A fresh start? If so, and I needed to break the law to get it, was I any different than the crooks who'd swindled my father? Maybe I wasn't.

In the past few years I'd abandoned the smaller, less lucrative clients, the ones who were as vulnerable to fraud as any giant corporation. Maybe more. In the process, I'd betrayed my ethics, my partners and my clients—and had perhaps damaged beyond repair the one thing I cared about most: my marriage to Colleen. I wanted to vomit, and my withdrawal symptoms had nothing to do with it.

"Interested?" Hank asked.

Justifications raced around my cranium like velodromium cyclists in full sprint.

Maybe I wouldn't find anything.

Maybe Hank was just being super-cautious.

Maybe he was talking about something other than fraud.

Then again, maybe he was unwittingly playing Florence Nightingale in disguise. After all, I could get well fast with this kind of money. Pay for rehab. Buy something nice for Colleen to thank her for sticking with me. Retire our debts and finance a whole new lifestyle for the both of us, far from temptation and defeat. And then there he was, Frank McDermott, sitting wraithlike in one of my guest chairs, a leg draped over the armrest, waiting for my answer. I glanced at Penny, whose eyes were fixed on mine, oblivious to the fact we had a visitor.

I fingered the battered ring on my right hand, a ruby-colored glass oval set in a scuffed gold band Frank had found on a street in North Chicago the day I graduated from kindergarten at St. Peters Catholic School. In front of my mother and twin sisters, he presented it to me at dinner in recognition of my "great accomplishment."

My chest had swelled, threatening to pop the buttons off the Roy Rogers cowboy shirt I'd worn to school that day. It was years before that ring fit me, and though I now despised the man—not for his business failures but for essentially vanishing from our lives when we needed him most—I hadn't taken it off a day since.

Hank coughed again, waiting for my response.

Don't blow this, I heard Frank say. I never got to know him, but Mother told me he had a wicked sense of humor.

I put the phone to my mouth. "Appreciate you thinking of me, Hank. I'm sure we can work this out." Frank shook his head and faded from sight.

We agreed to touch base as soon as I completed the required first month of in-house rehab, which was to start in two weeks. They'd told me that months of continuing therapy would follow before I got a full release, but if I couldn't beat this thing enough in that first month to take on Hank's assignment, nothing else would matter. Whatever the future might hold, it wouldn't include holding on to Colleen if we had to downsize. She deserved better than that.

I hung up, and Penny withdrew from a box at her feet a gleaming new set of bongos. After a particularly manic weekend at the office a month ago, I told her I was thinking of trading in the starter set Diego had given me for something more suitable for a man with my innate talent and tastes.

"To your potential," she said, handing them to me. "And to new beginnings."

The words caught in her throat, and we both looked away. "This is all my fault," she said, her eyes misting.

"You were just trying to help, Penny. I didn't have to go along with it."

Penny's use of cocaine had always been "social" and under control, from what I could tell, but she claimed to have given it up months ago after watching what it was doing to me. Several times, in fact, she'd tried to refuse my requests for "refills," only to succumb to threats I was now too ashamed to admit even to myself.

I thanked her for her generosity and laid the bongos inside a storage box containing the detritus of a thirty-five year career. A picture of me with members of the staff the day I made partner. Another of Colleen and me on the beach at the Maui Ritz Carlton in 1985, our first real vacation in ten years. I'd also tossed in a dog-eared file of letters from appreciative clients and a plaque from the partners commemorating the day in 1992 when I passed my exam and launched the firm into the world of financial fraud investigations.

Not much else, save for the crinkled green accountant's shade Paul gave me on my one-year anniversary with the firm. "We don't wear these any more," he'd said, setting the visor upon my head, "but to me it still represents old-fashioned values that we abandon at our own peril. Seek the truth, Rainey, and then *tell* the truth. We'll all be the better for it."

I closed my eyes, remembering the assurances I'd given Paul that he could count on me. When I opened them, I couldn't help thinking there should have been more in my little storage box and wondered if Penny had been stealing from me.

She was fiddling with some papers stacked on the edge of the desk. An age difference of twenty-seven years, three months should have been enough to keep things on a strictly professional level. Should have been but wasn't.

"I have to let you go," I said. "Nothing personal."

She nodded, leaned forward and kissed me on the cheek. "That was the problem. It never was." Then she turned and left without making a scene, and I knew I would never see her again.

Nor would I likely spend future time with the good folks at Banefield, McDermott and Schmidt. A reconciliation was out of the question. The partners would expect a cut of the Grayson fee if I stayed on board, and I couldn't afford to let that happen. Thus I would soon enter the world of the freelancer.

I buttoned my overcoat to the neck, sealed up my belongings and headed out into another frigid winter night. It occurred to me that Colleen and I should hide ourselves somewhere deep in the Sunshine State when this was all over, close to where my mother was counting down the remaining years of her sad life.

One prerequisite: a nearby beach where I could bury my head in the sand and pretend that none of this had happened.

14.

Wallace stared blankly at his computer screen and cursed under his breath. He should be in Florida, airing out his Palms Away condo on a warm Friday evening in paradise, a steak on the grill, ice melting around a triple Scotch. And planning what he would say to Alina if he got the chance to see her.

Instead he was still at the office on the eve of her party, preparing to spend yet another weekend alone in St. Louis. All because *they* didn't trust him. People he hadn't seen or spoken to in decades. Others he'd never met and hopefully never would.

It was *they* who'd suddenly had second thoughts about sending Waleed al-Ghamdi $110 million in dirty money.

They who'd delayed wiring the funds for three weeks while arguing about issues that should have been settled months ago.

They who'd forced him to cancel his airline reservations because *they'd* scheduled a conference call today. Which five minutes ago Rashid had called to cancel.

"Sorry, cousin," he'd said. "Just be lucky the funds were wired at all. It got heated here. Your father vouching for you was the tipping point, but just barely."

Father. Alim al-Ghamdi. The wise and learned one.

He'd called New Year's Day, the first time they'd spoken in three years. "Are you praying, my son?" he'd asked. "Is your life still dedicated to *Allah?*"

To both questions, Wallace had lied and said, "Yes." The night before, with his arm around a married woman's waist and their lips about to touch before her husband showed up, his relationship with *Allah* had been the last thing on his mind.

He heard a noise at his door.

"Ralph Bartlett on two," his secretary said, adding, "You're on stand-by tomorrow morning, seventh in line. Doesn't look good, but you never know."

Wallace nodded. Just as well. When he mentioned to Jeremy last week that he still hoped to attend the party, he'd received a look that required no interpreter.

Why are you going in the first place?

Wallace picked up the phone. "I take it you've seen the good news?"

"Fifteen million," Ralph said. "Congratulations."

"Just the first installment."

Would he be making more? He prayed he would, but if it all fell apart, he had a plan—and it didn't include Harrison Bank & Trust.

"May I ask who's taken such an interest?" Ralph asked. "The wire transfer came in from a bank called FirstBVI, which apparently offers the services typical of an offshore financial center. The transmittal document had the name of the bank's account rep but no other identification."

The private clients of banks such as FirstBVI were just account numbers, which, Wallace knew, was the way everyone liked it. Except the U.S. Treasury Department. For years they'd labeled OFCs havens for international money laundering. The owners of these accounts could move money in from anywhere and then around the world in seconds, with limited need to identify whose money was in the account.

"Our deal is with a wholly-owned private equity subsidiary of a company called *Liens Internationaux,*" Wallace said, showing off. "French-headquartered. We've been doing business with them in our communications division. The sub has established a fund that specializes in pre-IPO financing for small to medium companies like us, mostly throughout Europe and Asia."

"I see. Any possibility this could raise a red flag with the underwriter or the SEC?"

"The check sailed through, didn't it? That means FirstBVI isn't on any list of financial institutions banned by Treasury. I'm sure this will be covered in the comfort letter." It sounded good. Wallace just hoped it was all true.

"And the terms are...?"

"A reasonable quarterly return and preferred stock convertible to common, post-IPO. We get a healthy cash infusion, while strengthening an existing relationship that can open doors for us overseas. I'll be happy to send you a copy of the loan document."

"Yes, I'd appreciate that. Still, just wondering—why did the check transmittal come in via an OFC? Why not wire the money directly from France?" Ralph's voice was a mix of irritation and resignation. "We're supposed to verify who we're doing business with and—just wondering why an OFC, is all."

Ready, aim, *fire*. "Because, Ralph, under French law, if a company keeps its money outside of the country—in an OFC, for example—it avoids taxes. It's common practice." He felt the heat from Ralph's embarrassment shoot right up through the receiver.

"Just doing my job here," he said. "If you're comfortable with this...what did you call it?"

"Links International."

"Right. And this transaction doesn't place Jeremy's ownership status in jeopardy—"

"It won't."

"Then that's good enough for us."

"Then subject closed. Good day."

Wallace clenched a fist in triumph. The last thing Ralph Bartlett wanted was trouble with one of the bank's largest accounts, one which happened to owe them a ton of money and planned to run tens of millions of dollars through its system if all went well. Ralph had likely already followed protocol and asked his international banking department to perform a cursory investigation of Links International and its private equity subsidiary. Wallace had been confident their report would raise no red flags, and it looked as if he'd been right. As usual, Ralph was just being a pain in the butt.

It had been a good call, but his mood darkened when he again thought about the potential end game.

If all went according to projections, the powers behind this investment—the "they" that could derail his future plans and dreams—would have millions to use any way they wanted. Money that was freshly laundered through the New York Stock Exchange, sitting comfortably in a U.S. bank. And with the first installment now deposited in Harrison Bank & Trust, there was no turning back.

He glanced at his calendar.

The private placement likely wouldn't be returned to its owners as stock for months after the public offering, which itself was still a good six months away. A lot can happen in that time, he thought. After all, hadn't the Democrats just nominated Barack Hussein Obama for President? Few thought such a thing remotely possible.

He let his mind wander.

Maybe the economy *will* turn around in time to assure a successful IPO.

Maybe we'll find an answer to all of the planet's woes, and even achieve lasting peace in the Middle East.

And we won't have to raise taxes on anybody.

Right, Wallace thought.

And maybe his adopted baseball team, the lowly Tampa Bay Rays, will win the American League pennant.

15.

Wallace threw several confidential files into his briefcase, along with the thumb drive containing the two sets of books he'd been juggling for months now. He heard a noise and saw Victoria Laine in the doorway. She looked lost.

"You have plans tonight?" she asked.

Strange question. Wallace figured they'd exchanged no more than three sentences of a personal nature since Victoria had joined the company. He hefted his briefcase and grimaced. "Not much time for plans these days."

"Just a drink? I could use the company."

Wallace gave that a moment's thought, then decided, *what's the harm?* He certainly could do worse than spend social time with the likes of the attractive Victoria Laine on a Friday night. He suggested a restaurant around the corner that offered cushioned booths adjacent to a friendly horseshoe bar.

The end-of-the-week crowd of office workers had just begun to thin out when they arrived. Wallace commandeered a booth at the far end of the bar, then left to order drinks from the bartender. When he returned, Victoria seemed surprised, as if she forgot where she was.

She needed company, all right, Wallace thought, and he had a good idea why. Same reason he needed company, too.

"Staying busy?" he asked, sliding into the booth. He thought about loosening his tie but decided against it.

"You know Jeremy."

"Not the same when he's out of town, is it? My blood pressure drops twenty points."

Victoria noticed a woman she knew standing at the bar, nodded, smiled, and turned back to Wallace. "I thought you'd be at his party this weekend."

"Duty called."

"You've been to the plantation?"

"It's not quite that, but it's very nice."

Victoria leaned against the back of the booth. "Have you seen them together? At social engagements, I mean? He just doesn't seem like the partying type."

"He's not. Alina's the charmer, very at ease in a crowd."

"Jeremy told me they were like two manatees passing in the night."

Now it was Wallace's turn to scan the bar, hope he could spot someone he knew who would come over and give them something else to talk about. What else, he wondered, had Jeremy confided in Victoria Laine? Just how much did she know?

"Sorry," she said. "That was inappropriate."

He made light of it and asked if she had family here.

"Parents are dead. I have a sister, but we're—what's the word?—estranged. And an ex who lives in Tallahassee."

"One and done?"

"I'm in no hurry. You?"

Wallace shook his head. "Came close once. Pretty much married to my job now. As you probably know, I joined the company right after I got my MBA from Washington University."

"Yes, impressive. You're something of a mystery around the company, you know."

As are you, Wallace thought. Outside of the work she did for Jeremy, nobody knew much about Victoria. And given her special relationship with the boss, nobody felt comfortable prying into her...affairs.

"What about family?" she asked.

Wallace hadn't been asked this question in more than fifteen years, when he'd first joined what was then a much smaller company. He'd said as little as possible at the time and even less since. But there was something familiar about this woman that went beyond her physical attributes. A sincerity he felt he could trust, though he couldn't explain why. Perhaps it was an unspoken bond, the result of knowing what it like to survive the bruises Jeremy dealt out with regularity. Or because he knew her thoughts were where his were, about twelve hundred miles to the southeast.

"I was born in Algeria," he said. The word—*Algeria*—sounded foreign to his ears in more ways than one. "I have an Algeria-born father who still lives there. My mother was born in Philadelphia. She died years ago."

"Algeria. How exotic."

"I don't remember much about it. My mother arranged to get the two of us out of the country right after the Yom Kippur War. I was thirteen. She had to convince my father that her mother was gravely ill, that she needed to get to Philadelphia immediately. She insisted I had to go, too, since I hadn't seen my grandmother in five years."

"What do you mean, 'convince'?"

Wallace unfolded his napkin and set his utensils in place. "I am my father's only son, a place of high honor in a Muslim household, much as it is here. My father would consent to me leaving only after he threatened my mother with bodily harm if she failed to return me within ten days. He didn't so much care what she did, but failure to obey him in a matter such as this is a grave insult in the Muslim world. Intolerable without avenging...."

He stopped himself. Wallace had never told this story to any one, and the sudden, painful lump in his throat surprised him.

"What happened?" Victoria said, leaning forward.

He took a sip of his drink. "My mother never had any intention of returning us to Algeria. We moved around a lot, laying low with various members of her family, then friends. We spent some time in Canada, then came back to the States. It was hard on both of us for a while, but we finally settled into a routine, if you could call it that. Then, two years into college, just when I thought our troubles were over, she was murdered."

"Oh, Wallace, how awful!"

"The police said it looked like an attempted rape and robbery that went bad. I knew better."

Victoria stared at him in disbelief. "This sounds like something straight out of the movies. Did your father ever come after you? Try to get you to go back?"

"We had one conversation shortly after my mother died," he said. "He denied having anything to do with her death, but he was angry I hadn't tried to leave America on my own. I told him it was because I didn't want to. That I wanted to stay here, finish my education, build a life for myself in the United States. I had, in fact, changed my name to Gerard by then, which was the surname of my mother's father. That pissed him off royally. We argued a long time before he slammed the phone down."

"And that was it?"

He nodded. "We talk rarely. So it's pretty much been peace and quiet ever since. Depending on Jeremy's mood."

They shared a laugh, and he asked if she wanted something to eat. She said no and sipped her drink, the two of them people-watching for a while before she asked him if he thought things would change after the IPO.

Wallace thought about his last call with Alina. "I think they'll change a lot. For you, too, most likely. I mean, Jeremy's two years shy of sixty-five. Not old, mind you, but by then it might be time to pass the burden on to the next generation. Hard to say what a guy like that will do, but I wouldn't worry. There's always a place for someone with your talents."

You idiot! Wallace thought, avoiding eye contact. *What a stupid thing to say. No wonder you're single.*

Victoria didn't seem offended or embarrassed. Or at least didn't show it. "It all depends on Jeremy, doesn't it?" she said.

Wallace ran a hand along his chin, fighting off unsettling thoughts. Victoria was only partially right. Jeremy's wife would have something to say about both their futures before this was all over. He knew that only too well.

The bar TV was tuned to CNN, the scene behind the reporter a familiar one. Tanks and Hum-Vees. American soldiers, rifles at the ready, climbing through bombed-out rubble, searching for Taliban in some remote Afghani outpost. It reminded him. "Ronald Reagan had this saying—"

"I know, but it's easier said than done."

"True."

Wallace removed a plastic "two-for-one" appetizer menu from its holder. "Sure?"

Victoria rolled her eyes. "You pick."

They ordered and settled into conversation about the economy, the election, weather. Global warming, she said, was a crock. And Hillary Clinton wasn't through yet.

The woman had a head on her shoulders, Wallace could see. He'd been impressed by her intelligence and quick wit many times in meetings with Jeremy. He hadn't moved her up the ladder strictly for a guaranteed roll in the hay, that much was obvious.

When they were finished and the waitress brought the bill, Victoria had her credit card ready. "My idea, my treat," she said, signing the receipt. "See you Monday."

He thanked her, then headed for the bar to order one for the road. CNN had moved to a story on the rising tensions between Russia and its defiant neighbors in Georgia. Wallace again thought about Reagan and his signature phrase, the one Victoria apparently knew by heart.

Trust but verify.

She was right. It *was* easier said than done. Something he would have to consider carefully before he gave Alina Whestin everything he knew.

16.

8:10 P.M., Saturday, August 30

I headed up the steps of the Whestin manse, surprised at how nervous I felt and glad of it. It took my mind off two calls I hoped not to get: one about Mother's deteriorating health and the other from the FBI, an odd juxtaposition of problems, to say the least. But I was most obsessed with Colleen and the nuclear bomb she'd dropped three weeks ago.

Shock and disbelief, then outrage and anger, had now turned to numbed denial. According to the schedule she'd given me at our lunch, she should have been back from Traverse City by now. When was she going to call? Or did she want this torture to continue indefinitely?

Not that I was going to let those fears ruin my performance tonight. If I could get back into the game and somehow skate my way past whatever interest the federal authorities had in my association with Grayson, I might still be able to snatch my wife from the mitts of little Stevie Wonderboy.

That prospect didn't, however, calm my nerves.

If the question "What do you do for a living?" came up tonight from any of the guests, I decided to offer a vague reference to "accounting" and let it go at that. If pressed, I'd explain I'd been a partner in a CPA firm and sold my interest in search of new and more rewarding challenges.

The smart play, I decided, would be to keep the conversation focused on the other guy. Beyond that, I'd see if I could make some meaningful contacts before Jeremy whisked me off to his study to present the offer of a lifetime.

The massive oak doors that led into the Whestin home gaped open, unattended. I could hear the din of an already well-lubricated gathering coming from the great room and lanai, accompanied by the sounds of live country music. I deposited my boxed pinot on a foyer table overflowing with hostess gifts and dropped an envelope containing my charitable contribution into a basket labeled with a card that read, "Thank you for your generosity."

I ventured inside, took one glance around the great room and had to laugh. The combined net worths of the people in this room easily exceeded three hundred million dollars, spread among fifty couples who traveled the world in private jets, possessed homes in at least two states, chaired philanthropic foundations, sat on the boards of sizable corporations, vacationed in all the best places around the world and both collected and drank the best wines.

And yet no matter the function or location, and despite the fact our ages ranged from the late forties to the early seventies, the boys inevitably gathered on one side of the room, the girls on the other. The exception was a section of the lanai, off in a far back corner, where a three-piece band played music for a dozen guests who seemed familiar with a variety of country dance steps—as if I would know one when I saw it.

I passed a group of men swapping lies about their golf games and sharing tips they'd picked up on *The Golf Channel.* They acknowledged my presence, some offering quick introductions, others a nod of the head as they continued talking.

There was something unsettling, I decided, about a man who arrived at a mixed couples soirée sans date. After all, it was hard to separate from your woman, to show you were an independent man, if you didn't have a woman to separate *from.* Otherwise you were just an aging lion on the prowl. For now, better to stand on the periphery, I decided, observing, like an extra in a grand movie.

I did notice that almost no one was talking about Gustav. This afternoon it had cut across Cuba's western coasts as a Category 4 hurricane, yesterday prompting the evacuation of some 60,000 Cubans and thousands more this morning. No one wanted to think about the consequences if Gustav hit Louisiana just three years after Katrina. But it wasn't expected to make landfall on *our* shoreline, and that was all we party-goers cared about.

"Y'all care for an hors d'oeuvre, cowboy?"

I turned to see a young woman in her mid-twenties, a pretty little cowgirl in a vest and white hat, with a handsome pair of six-shooters and a rump that had clearly never seen a saddle. She held a platter of barbecued shrimp in one manicured hand, napkins in the other.

"Why, don't mind if Ah do, Miss," I said in my best southern drawl. I speared a shrimp, then another. Annie Oakley smiled sweetly, then clomped away in boots that clung provocatively to a pair of well-defined calves.

Making my way to the bar, the vice around my stomach mercifully unclenching, I got in line and took in the magnificence of the Whestin estate. It sat on a double lot at the end of a cul-de-sac in one of the more exclusive neighborhoods in Palms Away. The great room opened onto a lanai capable of hosting a political convention, or perhaps the Super Bowl. Six large clay urns, overflowing with pink bougainvillea, flanked a Roman-style swimming pool large enough to serve as an Olympics training facility.

Just outside the lanai, a variety of palm trees lit by landscape lighting and tiki torches swayed in a gentle, though seasonally muggy, breeze. Everywhere I looked, I saw so many plants and shrubs and palms I thought I was in a nursery.

Off the great room, I could see a spacious dining room, professionally decked-out kitchen and a hallway leading to the master bedroom. When I'd arrived, I'd passed a grand staircase in the foyer that I figured led to the upstairs guest bedrooms. They say money can't buy taste, but from my quick observation, the Whestins possessed both in abundance.

Just then Jeremy emerged from a walk-in wine cellar. He waved, gave me the just-a-second sign and disappeared into the kitchen. With the line at the bar having doubled, I made my way toward an hors d'oeuvres table and plucked a couple of smoked sausages. I was perusing the rest of the offerings when a tap on the shoulder caused me to turn and there she was. The straw-hatted woman from LaPlaya's balcony.

"Alina Whestin," she said, extending her left hand. "And I believe you are Rainey McDermott?"

Flattered, I bowed slightly, trying not to cock my right eye like a jeweler's glass over the blindingly brilliant yellow solitaire gracing her ring finger. "Pleased to meet you," I said, my stomach tightening again.

Her eyes, large and expressive, reminded me of Sophia Loren's. *A man falls in there*, I thought, *he might never make it out*. And not that I cared, but a hint of cleavage peeked above the open neck of a simple white blouse that accentuated her lightly tanned skin. Combined with western-style jeans, open-toed sandals and a gold bracelet on her left wrist, the outfit wasn't overtly sexy. More like *inviting*.

A waiter walked over, as if on cue, a cocktail on his tray. Alina handed it to me. "Tanqueray No. 10, yes? Olive, no vermouth?"

"Parlor trick?"

She brushed aside a wisp of her champagne-colored hair. "Just a guess."

A female guest hurried over to compliment her host on a spectacular bronze and marble fountain that dominated a corner of the massive lanai. "It's our own design," Alina said. "The inspiration came from the *Fountain of Tortoises* in—"

The lady touched Alina's arm and smiled knowingly. "Minneapolis?"

"Rome," Alina corrected politely, as if this were a mistake anyone could make. She reached back and nudged my pants leg. We were sharing our first inside joke, and suddenly I felt like a member of the V.I.C—the Very In Crowd.

When her chat ended, she leaned in and whispered, "Let's catch up with each other later. We need to talk." And then she was off, leaving me grinning like a teenager, though with a middle-aged man's bladder.

Pleased at such an auspicious start to the evening, I headed off in search of relief—and the man I sensed held the key to a promising new future for the McDermotts.

17.

I exited the first floor guest bathroom and spotted Jeremy Whestin headed in my direction, as if he'd been waiting for me to finish my business so he could begin discussing his. We shook hands, and he offered to give me the grand tour.

A man on a mission, he maneuvered us without fanfare past the step-down wine cellar and through a well-oiled crowd milling about a restaurant-grade kitchen agleam with stainless steel. We then took a set of back stairs to a softly lit study dominated by a burled walnut desk that had to be seven feet long.

"The wood comes from West Africa," Jeremy said. "Supposedly lacquered forty-five times."

"And this?" I pointed to a billiards table with heavily carved legs.

"Gift from Alina. That pool light's supposed to be genuine Tiffany, but it's all bullshit to me." He reached into a desk drawer, pulled two cigars from a built-in humidor and offered one to me.

"Cuban?" I asked, before inspecting the cigar's band. *Dominican Republic.*

"Ahhh," I muttered, feeling a special kinship with the woman from

Minneapolis.

"I smoke both," Jeremy said, already into the ritual of clipping the tip.

He handed me the cutter and a moment later, there we stood, two relative strangers enjoying a time-honored ritual, puffing several times to establish a reliable, even burn. The first expulsion of smoke, followed by the mandatory head-back appraisal of taste and aroma, then—*what?*

Jeremy sat behind his desk in a hunter green leather executive's chair. He directed me to an opposite-facing guest chair and got right to it. "I know you were a CPA in Chicago, but your specialty was fraud, correct?"

"Financial fraud," I said. "My job on those cases was to search for what they call 'indicia' or indications of fraud. If I found it, I had to gather and present my evidence in a very disciplined way—one that supported the case being presented by my client. Could be the prosecution or could be the defense. Either way, my goal was to win, but to do it 'by the books.'"

Slow down, I told myself. *Don't look so damn anxious.*

"You're talking doctored financial statements?" Jeremy asked, my clever pun apparently sailing clear over his head.

"Mostly, but I also got involved in what some call asset theft."

"Embezzling?"

I nodded. "Duplicate payments, multiple payees, shell fraud. That sort of thing. Then there was intentional defective shipment fraud, contract rigging, falsifying inventory records—a lot more than that. Ever heard of the Bill of Lading Act?"

Jeremy gave me the stupefied look I expected. "Look it up. In any event, I didn't want for work. More reporting regulations and stiffer penalties are no doubt on the way, but there never seems to be a shortage of those greedy enough—or desperate enough—to try to get away with accounting fraud. One of those human nature things, I guess."

My little speech finished, Jeremy pulled open a bottom drawer of his desk and lifted a dark bottle and two glasses. "Rum. Interested?"

I showed him the still half full glass I'd brought with me. He filled his glass and asked how I ended up in Palms Away, "at such a relatively young age." He added, "There's more to life than working on your golf game, you know."

This time I'd rehearsed my answer.

"Investigations take time, which translates into expense. Too often, just when I'd start to make headway, I'd be told to call off the hunt. Most often it was for financial reasons, but sometimes because the client figured that whoever had screwed with the books or absconded with the cash or merchandise had either stopped or moved on to greener pastures. After that it was all about minimizing expenses and keeping the potentially embarrassing deed under wraps."

I got up and walked to the billiards table, casually rolled the eight ball into a corner pocket. "I had my share of success, don't get me wrong. But I could see burnout looming. It was, as they say, time to move on."

"And now?" Jeremy sipped his drink, then picked up his cigar and flicked the ashes into a black onyx ashtray. I returned to my chair and followed suit.

"I've been here about two years," I said, "and away from the business about twice that. I'm beginning to miss it."

My host swiveled his chair to the left, and I got a better look at something behind him that had caught my eye earlier—a wall-mounted glass and chrome-framed display of handguns, three in all.

Jeremy noted my interest. "The one on the upper right is a Smith & Wesson .45 automatic. Same model I carried during my tour with the Marines."

"You saw action?"

"Damn straight. Battle of Hué with the 1st Battalion, 3rd Marine division at the time. I arrived February, 1968, right after the beginning of the Tet Offensive—and just in time for the monsoon season."

I quickly calculated that Jeremy would have been dodging bullets in Vietnam almost two years by the time I, as a sophomore in college, was participating in the December 1969 military draft lottery. My number had been well outside the problematical first one-third. A fortuitous result for which I'd always felt a measure of guilt.

I pointed to the revolver in the middle. "Is that what I think it is?"

Jeremy turned toward the display. "Smith & Wesson .44 Magnum."

"Make my day."

"Technically, it's the Model 29-6, mechanically better than Inspector Harry Callahan's. But they all hit with massive power."

He paused and made sure I was looking straight at him. "You get this relatively tiny entry point but a cone of damage out the back you could drive a truck through. You'll bleed out long before you go into shock."

I nodded respectfully, noting the choice of pronoun and tense. The third gun, the one on the left, seemed less threatening. "And the little one?"

Jeremy gave me the look of tolerant distain reserved for those who didn't know what they were talking about. "That's Alina's baby. She uses it for target practice, but it's the preferred handgun of the mob—in case you didn't know—because the bullet hits hard enough to enter your skull but generally stays inside and rattles around in your brain."

How nice.

"The nation's in for a rough ride over the next couple of years," he said, changing the subject. "Maybe more."

"Especially if we're attacked again."

Jeremy shook his head and tapped his cigar on the edge of the ashtray. "They should save their martyrs for another nation. We're doing a good job of destroying this one all by ourselves. Still, there's no turning back from extraordinary advances in communications, genetic engineering, robotics, alternative fuels—commercial space travel, too."

He pointed a finger at me. "I want to be involved in all of it. But we have to get past this IPO first."

"Date?"

"Mid-February. We've finalized our list of potential underwriters. Schedule calls for signing a letter of agreement by mid-October. I want our financials in order by then."

"Sounds as if—"

He held up a hand. "I want you to make sure my presentation passes muster. Plain as that."

The room began to spin and not just from the cigar smoke that had begun to nauseate me. I said nothing, but cautioned myself not to fall back on my specialty: borrowing trouble. This could be perfectly legit.

"Nothing official," Jeremy said. "Nothing in writing. You'll report only to me. An 'advisor,' call it. I want you reviewing our financials each month, right up to the SEC filing in November and then on through to the day we go public. Maybe beyond, if we're both happy with this arrangement."

Nothing official. Nothing in writing. Which meant no need to acquire a Florida CPA license. No need to apply for my CFF, either. That was the good news, but it left the obvious question: *why me?*

"You of course have a chief financial officer and an independent accounting firm. So...?"

"Let's just say I want back up—and I prefer to use someone whose work I know."

I held my cigar down at my side, as far from my lungs as I could get it. And then I sat perfectly still, my eyes focused directly on Jeremy's. Any movement of any body part, however slight, and the contents of my stomach would be available for public viewing.

Jeremy seemed to sense my distress when he reached into his desk drawer and pulled out a baggie, but it was only for disposing of our cigars.

"And if I find something that smells?" I managed to ask, gratefully handing over my Dominican companion.

"Let's talk about that. I suggest lunch at the private members club at LaPlaya. Know it?"

"Second floor balcony?"

"If it's not too hot. Noon, Tuesday. We'll discuss what's in this for you. In the meantime, I would ask you to keep this conversation in confidence."

He stretched his head side to side. "Now if you'll excuse me, I think I'll grab some aspirin. Been battling a bear of a headache all day."

"I think the party's just getting started. Looks like you'll be up late."

My host smiled thinly. "As the saying goes, you can sleep when you're dead."

We shook hands, and he disappeared down the hall. I finished my drink and at the top of the stairs tried to gather my equilibrium.

"...whose work I know," Jeremy had said.

The question now was, just what did he know?

18.

I returned to the party still clammy, any feeling of exhilaration tempered by a distinct sense of foreboding. My background check issues aside, near as I could tell I'd just been offered a job. But doing what? Reviewing financial statements as an "advisor"? How much could that pay?

This evening that I'd hoped would provide answers about my future had generated nothing but questions. Maybe *Mrs.* Whestin could clear things up.

Heading in the direction of the bar, I passed a dozen couples imbibing more wine, whiskey, vodka and gin than likely was prudent. One thing I'd noticed about the folks of Palms Away: they knew how to party. A few even knew how to hold their liquor.

I got to the bar, ordered another gin and spotted Alina giving instructions to the caterer. He heaped a dozen slabs of baby-back ribs into a metal warming bin, part of a block-long buffet table loaded with trays of French fries, cole slaw, baked beans, apple sauce, mini-cobs of sweet buttered corn, a huge salad bowl and the kind of hard rolls that once a few years back caused me to chip the veneer off one of my lower front teeth. Danger, it seemed, lurked everywhere.

Alina spotted me and came straight over. "Are you all right? You look a little pale."

"Guess I'm not a cigar smoker."

"Thank God for that."

She took my arm, and I couldn't help wondering if any of Colleen's friends were present. I hoped they were and that word would get back to Mrs. McDermott that her husband had been quite the center of attention at the Whestin's party.

Alina's thoughts, however, were obviously not on my domestic difficulties. "Did he bring up business?" she asked.

"You could call it that. He wants to explore possibilities over lunch Tuesday."

She walked me to a corner of the room. "He wants you to work for him. If you're interested."

"I'm flattered, but—"

"Don't go unless you're prepared to work for Whestin Group. Jeremy's very persuasive."

It started to rain, one of those sudden, short-lived showers familiar to Palms Away residents, falling mysteriously on one side of the street and not the other. It wouldn't amount to much this time of night, and the buffet had been set up under an extensive overhang. Those already in line jockeyed for position around the table, acting as if they hadn't eaten in weeks.

A strong breeze pushed the rain line close to several guests huddled at the eastern end of the lanai, crammed together under the loggia, waiting for the buffet line to thin. Everyone else took refuge at the bar, which quickly became crowded and uncomfortably warm. I felt moisture building under my armpits and across my back, but my discomfort was only partially due to the weather.

I was wondering why I, of all people, had been singled out by the CEO of a billion dollar conglomerate to discuss a possible working relationship. But also why I was getting special attention from his wife, a woman who had more than enough to do hosting her many adoring friends and neighbors. Again, I was flattered, but…?

"I'll call you after your lunch," Alina said, pulling me close. And with that she tossed me a flirty smile and left, mingling among her guests with a casual grace one would expect of the community's reigning social doyen. I set aside my concerns and wedged into line for my crack at the feeding trough.

A few minutes later, with a tastefully stacked plate of food in one hand and a refreshed cocktail in the other, I did my version of the mix-and-mingle, hoping to convey to my inebriated neighbors that I was on my way to somewhere important but would be happy to stop and chat, if they'd like. This from the guy who'd been worried about being set up for a cattle call.

Thankfully, only two women asked about Colleen. I said there was a conflict in her schedule and let it go at that. Most of the time I felt painfully alone and isolated, keenly aware that the woman who'd always been at my side at these affairs no longer was. Did I just say, "affairs"?

An hour later, Jeremy had yet to return to the party, and Alina had settled into conversation with a group of friends intent on holding her captive. By now I'd had my fill of food and liquor and small talk with people who seemed disinclined to ask me over for dinner any time soon, much less broach the possibility of needing my services. It was time to go.

I slipped out the front door unnoticed, curious why Alina wanted to call me, but satisfied I'd passed another test in the eyes of Jeremy Whestin. I was unsure, however, that he any longer represented the break I'd been hoping for.

Then again, perhaps I was just being paranoid.

19.

Three days later, I still couldn't get the taste of that damn cigar out of my mouth. Yet another reason I'd lost all appetite for lunch with Jeremy today and for serving as a "consultant" on the Whestin Group public offering.

First, I'd dealt with his kind before. Cocky, confrontational, innately intimidating. But it was more than that. If, as I suspected, this assignment entailed something beyond just reviewing the books, if it involved turning a blind eye on Generally Accepted Accounting Principles—GAAP, we call it—I wanted no part of it, no matter the financial reward.

Then what, I asked myself as I pulled up to the entrance of LaPlaya's private members club, was I doing here?

Curiosity, perhaps. Or self-preservation. I wanted to know if Jeremy Whestin was up to no good, and why, if my instincts proved correct, he thought I'd agree to be part of it.

Did he intend to buy my cooperation? He did say we'd discuss "what's in this for me." On the way up in the elevator to the club's dining room, I couldn't shake the uneasy feeling that Jeremy Whestin was a man who liked holding all the cards—and right now, I had zilch.

I gave myself the once-over in the elevator's mirrored wall and reviewed my strategy: listen respectfully, guard my answers, and learn what I could. If we had a basis for a deal, if I felt I could handle Jeremy's abrasive personality, and if the price was right, fine. I needed income, and *lots of it,* as Diego had rightly emphasized. But if my answers were in the negative, I'd request more time and take my suspicions to Billy Ray. He'd know what to do.

The elevator doors opened onto a handsome, tastefully furnished lobby heavy on mahogany. The dining room was around the corner, where Hans, the maître d', escorted me past the bar and outside to the same veranda Billy Ray had so thoughtfully pointed out to me just over three weeks ago. I glanced out toward the Gulf to the spot where we'd been, relieved not to see my good friend staring back at me.

A dozen or so privileged members and their guests were dining beneath a white canvas ceiling dotted with slowly rotating fans. Jeremy was again seated at the far south end, taking in the view below of the pearlescent sand of Vanderbilt Beach and the gentle surf reflecting a palette of teal and sea green. In a crisp white linen shirt open at the collar, lightweight beige slacks and driving-style loafers, he looked to be a man totally in command of his destiny, though I thought he could use a few more days in the sun to put some color in his cheeks.

We exchanged handshakes, and I took my seat. "Escaped another one, huh?" I said, stating the obvious.

Hurricane Gustav had made a technical landfall yesterday just southwest of a small rural town along the coast of Louisiana. It was no Katrina, but damage was extensive from the coastline well into the central part of the state. In addition, parts of Florida, including the Keys and panhandle, as well as Mississippi, Alabama, Texas and even Arkansas had been bruised by Gustav's wrath.

Media reports had been ubiquitous for the past several days, but Jeremy responded to my comment with scrunched eyebrows, looking at me as if he had no idea why I would bring up such a point now on a perfectly calm, beautiful day here in Naples. I decided not to elaborate.

A waiter offered me a menu, and asked if I wanted something to drink. Not wanting my mental acuity compromised, I ordered iced tea.

"I'm not that hungry," Jeremy said, pushing his menu aside, "but you go ahead. It's all good."

My stomach had been grumbling since mid-morning. When the waiter returned with my drink, I ordered the ahi tuna. Before I could offer a compliment on the party, Jeremy again got right to the point.

"I'm not interested in your golf game, your political leanings, whether or not you're Born Again, how many women you bedded in college, or the state of your marriage. I'm sure you're full of questions, and I'll get to them, if it proves necessary. Right now, talk to me about what an underwriter will look for when they review our financials. Will the potential for fraud be on their mind?"

The question should have sent me leaping off the balcony, sprinting full tilt down the beach. But if Jeremy had become the matador waving his red cape with the audacity of his question, I'd become the *toro bravo* preparing to plunge both horns into his groin. I wanted to make it clear I was not going to be a part of any illegal or even questionable scheme—and if necessary, I'd make sure the authorities were on to him.

Calm down, play it out, I said to myself. All he'd done was ask a question. I decided that responding directly might lead him to think I was interested, which might get him to open up. I fought to maintain a normal speaking voice.

"An underwriter will spend significant time on your business model and forecasts for sales and profits. They'll look at the way you're organized and the depth of your senior staffing. Conduct a competitive and situational analysis—essentially look for anything that could impede growth. The potential for fraud exists in any financial document, but confirming it one way or another generally exceeds the underwriter's reach."

"Then what gives them confidence?"

"What they perceive to be full disclosure. They're looking at what meets the eye and making a judgment that you're telling the whole truth and nothing but."

I casually unfolded my napkin. "Usually that means providing audited results going back three to five years, identifying major expense accruals, revenue discounts, booking practices. The existence of appropriate internal controls. Even then, the underwriter will likely take the word of the auditing firm that the company's financials reflect reality and adhere to GAAP."

Jeremy didn't raise an eyebrow so I assumed he knew what that stood for. He then asked about the SEC. I'd helped to take three companies public and knew how the Securities and Exchange Commission operated. What most people didn't know was that this government agency wasn't the watchdog everybody thought it was.

"In boom times like the late nineties," I said, "and especially during the active merger years of '05 and '07, the SEC simply didn't have enough qualified people to do the meticulous due diligence everyone assumed it was conducting. Still doesn't."

I figured Jeremy and his support team damn well knew what the SEC would be looking for. He wanted to assess something else—or he was setting me up.

"The SEC wants to see much of the same information as your underwriter," I said, "but formatted to their standards. Their primary interest is in assessing the risks inherent in the securities offering. Is there a lack of operating history? Any problems with members of management essential to the company's future success? And so on. Pretty basic, but one slip-up could screw your IPO real quick."

The sun had moved west of the veranda, its rays hitting me squarely in the face. Time to stop circling each other. "Where are you headed with all this?"

Jeremy leaned forward, the same pinched look on his face I'd noticed at the party. "I run a big company, Rainey. Usually leave this kind of stuff to my president...and...CFO. I have my reasons for getting more...involved than...normal."

He massaged his right temple and worked his jaw as if he'd just endured a bad day at the dentist. "So...if the audited statements...raise no...red flags...then..." His next words dribbled out slurred and incomprehensible, as if the Novocain hadn't yet worn off. He doubled over, clearly in pain, but then just as quickly sprang erect, seemingly oblivious to what had just happened, as if coming out of self-induced hypnosis.

Alarmed, I searched for other signs of a stroke. A drooping eye or corner of his mouth, obvious weakness in one of his arms. I almost asked him to stick his tongue out so I could see if it was crooked.

He blinked twice, then stared at me, calmly waiting for an answer.

"As a rule," I said, eyeing him closely, "neither the underwriter nor the SEC reconstructs the thousands of transactions that form the basis of the financial statements. If a reputable underwriter is involved, if the statements have been audited by an independent and established accounting firm, and the underwriter has obtained what we call a comfort letter from the accountants, that usually suffices."

"So...fraud isn't...on the SEC's mind...either?" He seemed to be recovering, but his speech was still slow and thick.

"The short answer is, 'No fraud suspected, no fraud investigated.' Uhh...you all right?"

He stood and steadied himself against the railing. "Excuse me...Rainey. Nature calls."

I watched him make his way to the men's room. His steps were deliberate but not wobbly, and I saw him offer a friendly nod to the bartender. Maybe he was just a bit under the weather. It would explain his lack of appetite, though not the gibberish and the doubling over. That was a concern but not as much as the questions he'd been asking.

What was going on here?

20.

My lunch arrived just as Jeremy returned to the table. His eyes had cleared, and he was talking normally again, eager to further our conversation. Weird.

"That night at the party," he said, "you mentioned something about clients pulling the plug on investigations that got too expensive or time-consuming. How did you do your job when you didn't know where to look and the budget was limited?"

He was persistent, I had to give him that. I took a bite of my tuna, but beneath the table my right heel was tapping the floor in nervous anticipation.

"Most fraud," I said, "is discovered by accident. Somebody—could be an outside auditor or someone in the accounting department—just stumbles onto something that doesn't smell right, and they call it to the boss's attention, or maybe the FBI or IRS. Sometimes they'll leave an anonymous message. Or walk right through my front door."

"And the other half?"

I grabbed a roll. "I mentioned at your party that there's a very disciplined methodology to forensic accounting. Still, most fraud is detected simply because we start sniffing around, asking questions of scared-stiff secretaries, pissed-off back-office administrators and neglected warehouse managers, even vendors with current contracts and those who consistently lost out in the bidding wars. When the appropriate pressure is applied to those most vulnerable or weak, then here comes Tweety Bird, especially if we promise leniency for saving guys like me a helluva lot of work."

Jeremy took a moment to give that some thought, an opening I didn't want to lose. "You've implied you know something about the work I've done. I assume that's the reason we're here."

Behind us, a bus boy fumbled a plate. It exploded like a grenade at Jeremy's feet, sending a dozen jagged pieces of china skittering across the ceramic tiled deck. I expected Jeremy to level at the poor kid the kind of tirade he'd directed at Gino that day after golf, but instead, he waved our waiter to the table.

"Tell Hans to move us to a corner of the main dining room," he said. Then to me, "You don't mind, do you, Rainey? It's getting hot out here."

No problem. Depending on where this conversation was headed, a little air conditioning might be a good thing.

Hans seated us at a corner table, well isolated from the only other tables currently occupied. The waiter placed my lunch in front of me, and Jeremy ordered another round of beverages.

"Does the name Grayson Automotive Systems ring a bell?" he asked, exchanging one troublesome topic for another. Unfortunately, this one was potentially far more damaging to my job prospects.

Blood rushed from my brain as if a trapdoor had opened. "Refresh my memory."

"Very well. You helped handle the sale of Grayson, which back in 2004 was a property of my holding company."

"You were the head of Archway Industries?"

"Founder and CEO but not the front man. At the time we were working with your company, that role was played by our president, Jack Armbruster."

I recalled meeting Jack once or twice but had had no working interaction with the man. Nor had I ever had any reason to meet Jeremy back then. "So where does Whestin Group come in?" I asked, now thoroughly confused.

Judging by the smug look on his face, Jeremy couldn't wait to answer. "I changed the name three years ago," he said. "Took us away from both the somewhat parochial and certainly industrial connotations and gave us a name we could take global. Of course, it's been suggested that my ego may have had something to do with the name change, but I deny that categorically."

Smiling at his attempt at self-deprecating humor, I realized that my research into Whestin Group should have gone deeper. What I'd read had been excerpts from recent trade reports and general business stories about Jeremy's plans to reinvent his company, speculation about overseas acquisitions and those rumors about strains on cash flow. I didn't see any reference to "formerly known as Archway Industries."

I glanced at my tuna, which now looked disappointingly over-cooked, and told Jeremy that my job as Grayson's CPA had merely been to certify the financial documents and assist the buyer with his due diligence. It was exactly the kind of response a guilty man would give who wanted his inquisitor to think that he should be above suspicion for a crime that clearly someone else had committed. When and if the FBI ever interviewed me, I'd have to do better.

Jeremy examined his fingernails. "They felt you did more than that. You not only helped pull those documents together, you handled our presentation."

Our eyes locked in the kind of childish stare-down I hadn't experienced since the second grade. I looked away first, not out of intimidation but because I'd grabbed both ends of my fancy cloth napkin and was focused on ripping the damn thing in half. Jeremy didn't have to bring me out in public to flaunt his superiority while humiliating me as if I were some lousy...*bus boy*. We could have covered all of this over the phone.

I was about to tell him what he could do with this fucking interview when he repeated what he said Saturday night. "I need you to help guarantee that my books pass muster, Rainey. Dig as deep as you think necessary. If you find something...disturbing, you bring the evidence to me."

We were back to staring at each other as it hit me that my experience with Grayson wasn't going to cost me a position with Whestin Group—it was the reason why I was the only man for the job. Again I should have been bee-lining for the door, but all I could do was ask, "And then?"

"That's my business."

"Not entirely," I said, wondering why I was bothering to respond. "It becomes *my* business in a hurry if something goes wrong. The last thing I can do is guarantee smooth sailing through the IPO process—especially if something 'disturbing' is lurking in your financials."

"All the more reason I know you'll do a thorough job."

Pompous ass. "And if I say no?"

He shrugged. "Rumors spread quickly in gated communities like Palms Away. What a waste to see all your potential destroyed over a few bad choices."

"I could go to the FBI, very likely get special consideration for heading off a scheme to defraud thousands of investors."

McDermott boldly calls with two pair....

"With what for evidence?" Jeremy asked. "Wallace Gerard, our CFO, is protecting our interests relative to Whestin Group. As for Grayson, he still has the financials we'll claim we gave you. The accurate, not-so-pretty ones. It will be our recollection that we also told you a handsome fee would be forthcoming if the sale went through. Regrettably, we thought the chances for that would be slim, because we didn't think we had a convincing story to present to our prospect."

He assumed a look of mock innocence. "Goodness, detective, it appears that unbeknownst to us, Mr. McDermott submitted false documents that painted an untrue picture of Grayson's financial status just to assure a handsome fee."

His opponent counters with a straight flush. Pot to Mr. Whestin!

I was playing now with chips I didn't have, hoping the house would give me an I.O.U. "I was in your employ, Jeremy. You inherit some responsibility for my actions. At the least, the publicity and resulting lawsuits would be embarrassing and definitely ill-timed."

"Perhaps, but there would be criminal intent to resolve first. And if you go the civil route, we'll come after you with everything we've got. It might take years to sort things out, but I promise you, *we'll* survive. And regardless of the outcome, you'll be outed. The cocaine. The bribe. The dalliance with a secretary half your age."

My vision blurred, and I balled both hands. Colleen knew about the first two. She did not know about Penny. If she learned about her now, I could hardly express outrage at her involvement with Steve Wannamaker, not without her spitting in my face and pushing the accelerator down on divorce proceedings.

Desperate to say something, anything, that would cause Jeremy to reconsider his plan to ruin my life—again—I naively turned to logic and reasoning. "The problem with doctoring financial statements is that you've got to find a way to get them back in balance. You rob Peter to pay Paul, then Luke to pay John. Before you know it, all the apostles and Jesus Himself can't save you. You'll get away with it for a while but not forever. I could give you a hundred examples."

Jeremy's blue eyes turned a shade paler. "I never said anything about you doctoring our financials."

I tossed my napkin on the table, gave him my best *What do you take me for?* smirk and pushed back my chair. But where was I going? To the FBI without evidence? Up against a billion dollar holding company prepared to put all the blame on a former junkie? I turned to the last resort of the beaten man. *"Fuck...you,"* I said, though louder than intended.

Hans jerked his head around and took a step in our direction, but Jeremy waved him away. "You haven't heard me out, Rainey."

"I've heard enough."

"No, you haven't. Do what I'm asking, and I'll pay you $80,000 a month, September through February. Slightly above what you were making in Chicago and, I'm fairly certain, more than you're making now."

If I clenched my jaws any tighter, I'd break another veneer, but goddamn if I'd give this bastard the satisfaction of seeing it. I quietly sucked in a breath and returned his self-satisfied stare with all the defiance I could muster. "This isn't about money."

"Perhaps not entirely, but it's always part of the equation."

Jeremy sipped his drink and for the first time in an hour seemed relaxed and energized, even sincere. "The bigger we get," he said, "the more we need someone like you to keep us safe." He said something else, but it didn't register, and I hated myself for asking him to repeat himself.

A second later, I fought the urge to upchuck my tuna steak all over his white linen shirt.

21.

Alina thought of dropping the top of her bathing suit but with the lawn service slaving away in the backyard, decided against it.

She'd been lying on the chaise lounge for only a few minutes, sipping lemonade and jotting notes on her yellow pad, but already she felt flattened by the humidity and a temperature in the low nineties. Still, this was better than being cooped up inside, breathing conditioned air as if she were a patient in a hospital.

She applied a second coating of sunscreen to her face, chest and arms, using the corner of her towel to dab at the perspiration between her breasts. The phone rang just as she was about to settle back with the day's *Sudoku*.

"It's official," she heard Mack say. "He starts Monday. Jeremy's quite pleased."

"He's on his way home?"

"Should be there in ten minutes."

"You've been a real friend, Mack. I promise I'll find a way to express my thanks. In the meantime, I hope you're being careful."

"You just worry about yourself. I'll be fine."

"Anything else you want to tell me?"

He paused. "I've told you enough."

"And I'm grateful. But if you need to unburden yourself further, you know how to get in touch."

She ended the call and retrieved her notepad.

There was no readily discernible logic to the scribbles on the page, nothing any outsider would understand. Just two names next to which she'd attempted to jot precise percentages. Her odds for success.

The technique, which she dubbed "OddsR," was a habit established the day she began working at Manetti Pharmaceuticals twenty-six years ago. It was simplistic, maybe even a little silly, but it helped her evaluate people from a less emotional perspective. The higher the number, the more she could trust the person to help her get what she wanted. Any number below seventy and you were more enemy than friend.

Alina contemplated the first of the two names on her list.

Wallace Gerard. Score: seventy-eight.

The number had once been significantly higher before he began demanding evidence of her feelings for him. She could have handled that, until he stopped sharing his inside information, promising only to reveal what he knew "when the time was right."

Unacceptable.

She called the shots. Which was why Rainey McDermott's arrival couldn't have come at a better time.

Next to that name she'd placed a series of question marks. If her plan to replace Wallace had any chance of succeeding, she would have to get to know this man quickly. If she liked what she saw, trusted what she heard, she would work her magic on him the way she'd worked it on Wallace. From what she saw at her party, she wouldn't have to work it too hard.

Alina thought about Mack and the chance he'd taken. She knew he was revealing only some of what he knew about Jeremy's dirty linen—and his own—but that would change in time.

Good old Mack. OddsR: 93.

22.

Jeremy pulled into the garage and switched off the engine but kept the radio on. They were playing Elvis Presley's "Burnin' Love," and he knew every word of the song that now seemed eerily perfect for the moment, though likely not in the way The King intended.

"God Almighty, I feel my temperature rising," he sang, his fist serving as a microphone. "Higher and higher, it's burning through to my soul."

He'd just finished the last half of the second verse—"My brain is flaming, and I don't know which way to go"—when what felt like a lighting strike zapped from one side of his skull to the other. His head snapped back, then he slumped forward, resting his head against the steering wheel. *How much more of this pain was he expected to take?*

Jeremy clenched both hands until the agony subsided. Maybe a minute. Maybe five. Then he took a deep breath and slowly made his way inside.

After his second cold shower of the day, he wrapped a towel around his waist and padded to the study. Alina, visible from the shadows of the window, seemed half-naked in a bikini few women over thirty would even think about wearing, much less at fifty.

He couldn't take his eyes off her as she tapped a pen against her chin, lost in thought. *Planning another party,* he guessed. When he walked outside and sat next to her, she quickly flipped to a blank sheet.

"You look hot, baby," he said, rotating his hips and curling his upper lip in his best Elvis impression.

Her response, without looking up from her pad, was to tell him the temperature was ninety-two degrees.

In other words, *I'm not in the mood.* He felt like grabbing her wrist and suggesting she get in the mood but squelched the urge.

"How was lunch?" she asked.

"Like peeling an orange. Tough on the out, pulp on the in."

"And Wallace?"

"What about him?"

"Does he know? As I recall, he wasn't too happy about that George Murray hire."

"I don't remember discussing that with you."

"Well, you did."

Jeremy couldn't argue. The last thing he trusted these days was his memory. With the exception of Wallace Gerard. And maybe his wife.

"You leave Wallace to me." He stared at the pool. "We haven't been skinny-dipping in a long time, have we?"

Alina tilted her head in the direction of the landscapers and closed her eyes. Her indifference infuriated him. He wanted to throw her into the pool, rip off her suit and make deep, hard love the way they had in the early years. The way they hadn't in a long time.

If the goddamn lawn service wants to watch, let 'em.

I'm returning to St. Louis Thursday," he said. "That'll give me a much-needed day in the office before the weekend. And then we start the final push to the IPO." He paused, staring at the outline of her nipples through ber bikini top. "It's been nice being here...with you."

"Let me know if you need any help packing," Alina said, her eyes still closed.

At that moment, Jeremy wondered why he was so worried about atoning for past sins. If he followed through with his plans, would she even care? He was too tired to think about it.

"I'll be inside if you need me."

She barely nodded.

Back in his study, Jeremy widened the slats on the shades, unable to force his eyes away from the woman whose love—and forgiveness—he thought he wanted more than anything in the world. Except maybe a successful IPO. And a few more years to live.

Until Vicky, the others had just been a way to pass the time while he was away from Alina in Palms Away. He made no excuses: he needed the touch of a woman, and he hated being alone.

The surprising depth of his relationship with Vicky made him feel all the worse about what he needed to do, but he couldn't shake the feeling that something else was going on. He couldn't articulate it, not just yet, but the feeling of uneasiness was growing stronger. For the second time in the past thirty minutes, he called Mack.

"I'm going to call Wallace now," he said. "Confirm the McDermott hiring."

"Wish I could be a fly on the wall."

"Listen, Mack, I know I have you keeping an eye on Vicky when I'm here in Florida, but...."

"Trouble?"

"Not sure. Just like you to keep tabs on Mrs. Whestin when I'm away. Quietly. You'll know what to do."

A long pause on the other end. "So...watch Ms. Laine when you're in Florida and Mrs. Whestin when you're in St. Louis or otherwise traveling?"

"Problem?"

"Just wanted to be clear. That'll have an impact on my expense budget, but if you—"

"You have no budget. Just do it." Jeremy disconnected the call and tried to focus his thoughts on the positive.

Notwithstanding his doubts about Alina and Wallace, this had been a piece-of-cake kind of day. It had, in fact, been fun to watch Rainey McDermott put up a fight. But in the end, he'd been no match for the unassailable logic of Jeremy's proposition.

As for Wallace, he didn't anticipate any trouble there, either. He'd grumble about it, see this as having his version of a spell-checker looking over his shoulder, but he'd follow orders. What choice would he have?

Jeremy punched in Wallace's number, his eyes riveted on Alina. She'd moved from her lounge chair and had seated herself on the second step of the pool, head angled toward the high sun, the water up to her waist. The languid scissoring of her legs left Jeremy nearly hypnotized, and he resented the intrusion of Wallace's voice.

"You remember our friend Rainey McDermott?" he asked. "Grayson Automotive Systems?" He could hear Wallace's jawbones grinding. "He's on the payroll, effective Monday. I want you to send him our annual statements for the past five years, the statements you worked on for the first two quarters this year and the monthly financials for July, along with the electronic data files. Express them to his Florida address for arrival Monday. Send the doctored August statements as soon as they're ready, then all succeeding monthly statements up to the IPO. Victoria has the address."

"May I ask why?"

"Mostly to assure that no anomalies escape scrutiny. And I want him to see the value of working for Whestin Group. We're going to need people with his expertise going forward. Am I clear?"

"Yes, but—"

"Give him what he asks for but volunteer nothing. And that includes information about the cell phones. If he asks, give him the story we've told everybody else."

"And if he wants a closer look?"

"We've got warehouses in Chicago, Las Vegas and L.A. He ain't going to Fort Smith, Arkansas."

"I assume he knows the schedule?"

"We agreed he'll have his report ready October 2nd. If he finds something we—*you*—need to fix, we'll push back the schedule, if we have to. Whatever it takes to make sure we're airtight on this thing."

Jeremy imagined Wallace breathing a sigh of relief. Roughly four weeks was a tall order for one man, no matter how good he was or how strong his motivation. Still, four weeks was better than nothing—and it sent a signal. "I'll be back in the office Monday afternoon. We'll discuss this in detail then."

He ended the call and turned to the window, unprepared for what he saw.

Alina was topless.

If the lawn crew wanted to peep through the palmettos, she no longer seemed to care. And neither did he. He thought of accepting her invitation, if that's what this was, but held back. Two could play this game.

Besides, he'd been in Florida since August 11, a little over three weeks. They'd tried twice to make love his first week back, both times at his initiation. The desire had been there, the plumbing had not despite doubling up on the intake of his little blue pill. They hadn't tried since.

No need to risk humiliating himself again, he decided, as Alina removed her sunglasses and stared straight at his window. For now, this would do.

23.

I hadn't checked the calendar, but I was fairly certain that today was Monday, September 8, my first official day in the employ of Whestin Group and the CFO who'd just last week threatened to blackmail me.

I set the shower nozzle on "massage" and let the jets of hot pulsing water slowly return me to consciousness. Several minutes later, I grabbed the shampoo and tried to recall what I'd done with the past five days of my life.

It rained a lot in the early afternoon, I think, which was about the time I got up each day. When I slithered out for the mail, my feet burned on pavement as hot as the Hell I would someday call home if I couldn't extricate myself from Jeremy's clutches and somehow rectify the mess I'd made of my life.

Mostly, I'd stayed inside those days, banging away on the bongos far into the night. When I took a break, I munched on anything I could find until I was down to a bag of chips and a can of chili, no beans.

I also noticed there was nothing left in the gin bottle.

That could account for my lack of memory, but more likely it had something to do with obsessing over a number that crowded out all competing thoughts.

Eyes closed I could see two guards emerging from an armored truck, each hauling bags of cash into a bank vault, every dollar to be deposited into my personal account.

Five...million...dollars, the amount of stock options Jeremy had made part of my "deal" at the end of our lunch. He'd mentioned a couple of conditions that would provide incentive for me to keep working for Whestin Group and to stay committed to its success. If I left the company too soon, for instance, the options would expire immediately.

It was a shrewd move and not without risk on my part since the value of those options was tied to Whestin Group's future success, which itself was no sure thing. Certainly not if Jeremy got caught for what I was fairly certain he had in mind. Still, the last time I succumbed to a bribe even close to the size of this one, I figured I'd never see another, if for no other reason than you don't run into "opportunities" like that very often. Not to mention that after rehab I'd sworn never to put myself in that position again. And yet it had happened, this time my reward boosted by nearly two million dollars. How lucky can a guy get?

"...help guarantee my books pass muster," Jeremy had said. "Find something disturbing, you bring the evidence to me."

No sweat, Mr. Whestin. Anything else I can do for you? Forge a few checks? Surreptitiously transfer merchandise from inventory to your garage and charge it to a vendor? Strip naked and run through the town square?

For five...million...dollars I will apparently do anything.

At least that's what I needed him to think.

The doorbell rang just as I finished dragging a razor through a week's worth of growth. It was the postman with my package from Wallace, sent registered mail.

I signed the receipt and took the package, my trepidation turning to embarrassment when I saw Billy Ray pedal up on his bicycle. He tipped his ball cap at the postman and smiled broadly as he approached the front door where I stood guard.

"Just happened to be in the neighborhood," he said. "How you doing? Haven't heard from you in a while."

"Been kind of busy. Sorry."

He eyed the package, then squeezed the rubber bulb of his Clarabelle the Clown horn. "You...uh...call me when your schedule permits, okay?"

I assured him I would and closed the door, cursing my luck. I wasn't ready to discuss with anyone that I was now working for Jeremy Whestin, and especially not with my best friend who'd already warned me to "watch yourself."

Nothing I could do about it now, I decided, and headed for the staging area I'd set up on my dining room table.

Jeremy had given me one month to review the books and make my report before he was scheduled to sign an underwriter. I didn't know what I'd find or how I'd use it, but right now my focus was on the contents of Wallace's package.

First thing to spill out among an array of potentially doctored annual reports, balance sheets, income reports and cash flow statements was an envelope marked "Personal." Inside: a check for eighty thousand dollars.

My heart raced as I set aside my first remuneration in four years. All the familiar sensations rushed to greet me as if I'd never been away.

The mental prep, readying myself for competition against those trying to break the law and fool me in the process, was no less adrenaline producing for me than as for a marathon runner waiting for the *crack!* of the starter's gun. Not quite a coke high but a lot less costly in the long run. And a lot more profitable.

I began outlining my approach.

This was going to be an old-fashioned, muck-about-in-the-haystack reactive engagement, and I had four weeks either to turn something up or at least convince Jeremy that I'd investigated everything the underwriter or the SEC could possibly be interested in and had found nothing. It was difficult to believe that a finding of zilch would still garner me those stock options, but if I could stick to my plan, it would never get that far, anyway.

The assignment was akin to being asked to supply the square root, to the nearest ten decimals, of a number that isn't a perfect square, without using a calculator, because the teacher wanted to see your math. It wasn't that difficult if you knew what you were doing—just a massive, time-consuming pain in the butt.

Two hours later, I was immersed in my first-cut review of the financial reports when I got a call from Wallace, the man for whom, for some undisclosed reason, Jeremy wanted "backup."

"Did you find the check?" he asked.

Something about the man's tone rubbed me the wrong way. Professional competitiveness, perhaps. I said yes, thanked him for his assistance, and then asked if he had a minute to answer a few questions. My request was met with silence, but at least he didn't hang up.

"The balance sheet for August reflects a private placement of $15 million," I said. "May I ask who the booster is?"

He said something about a private equity firm owned by a company in France they were already doing business with. He then volunteered the terms of the deal, explaining that the money would give the company some breathing room leading up to the IPO and that the transaction would not have an appreciable impact on the value of the company's stock. Given they were fortunate even to find someone willing to loan that kind of money these days, the terms seemed exceptionally generous.

"Another question, if I may. What use were you making of your line of credit in the first quarter, before the private placement?"

A simple phone call to the bank would reveal where Whestin Group stood on use of its corporate credit line. I hoped Wallace would guess I was asking the question just to irk him.

"We were approaching a maxed-out condition," he said, quickly adding, "but that was due to a number of unusual circumstances, including some problems with customer late payments."

"No problem," I said, smiling to myself. "Just trying to get a feel for the playing field here." Dislike him or not, I was going to have to work with Wallace Gerard, maybe even get him to reveal secrets without knowing it. "Will you be in Florida anytime soon? If it works out, we should try to meet up."

"The underwriter interviews begin late this afternoon. We have much to do before making a selection—after you submit your report."

Apparently he didn't care to shake hands any time soon, and I didn't blame him.

A beep alerted me to another call. I told Wallace I'd be in touch and hit the "flash" button.

"Hello, Rainey," I heard her say. "Congratulations on joining the company."

"Thank you."

"I was hoping we could meet soon. I have something to show you that I think would be helpful in your work with us."

"Jeremy's in St. Louis, isn't he?"

"Point being...?"

"Nothing." I cleared my throat. "Name the date."

"Tomorrow, eleven-thirty, LaPlaya. On the beach. And let's keep this between the two of us."

24.

My cursory review of the Whestin Group documents ended last night just shy of eleven. After getting back to it early this morning, I still hadn't found a suspicious rise in sales in any division but no dramatic declines, either. Nor, from what I'd seen, any unusual expense items. Overall, the numbers painted a moderately attractive picture during a time of severe downturn.

My task, however, wasn't to be impressed by the numbers, or to make sure everything balanced. My task was to find evidence of fraud, persuade the FBI I hadn't done the doctoring—and then convince Jeremy, out of the kindness of his heart, to keep quiet about my past as he headed off to jail. Nothing to it.

As for discovering fraud, it seemed on the surface a formidable task for a one-man gang like me. But then, even a full-blown audit wasn't designed to uncover fraud. That was an entirely different thing, with an entirely different set of rules and procedures. Why Jeremy felt the need to hire me was still a mystery, but clearly his distrust of Wallace had a lot to do with it. Maybe everything to do with it.

I was mindful of what was at stake for him. He never said that the company he founded—and perhaps his personal fortune—were in any trouble. But I was fairly certain that if the public offering fell through, or if Whestin Group defaulted on its loans in the next six months, the bank wouldn't hesitate to vaporize his equity in the company. And then, if necessary, they'd go after his personal assets.

It would be a last resort action for the bank but better than holding millions in uncollected debt. Jeremy likely would have few options other than to sell off at least some of his holdings at whatever price he could get to meet his obligations. It would be an expensive and humiliating experience. No wonder he was taking every precaution.

But if the public offering did fail, either legitimately or because his scheme was uncovered, where would that leave me? I was prepared to live without the five million dollars in stock options, but could I be certain Jeremy would keep his mouth shut about my past? The thought sent me back to the financial statements strewn about the dining room table.

I was about to take a harder look at the income statements when I noticed the time. Immediately I set aside my files and headed for the shower. I had one hour and twelve minutes left before my eleven-thirty rendezvous with Mrs. Jeremy Whestin, and I was not going to be late.

"This way, please."

The attendant grabbed a blue and white beach towel from a stack inside his service hut and led me across the hot sand to the south end of LaPlaya's beach. We were well into the off-season and only a handful of the lounge chairs were occupied, mostly by pale-skinned Northerners headed for a painful evening spent applying copious amounts of aloe.

The cloudless sky was bright cerulean, the temperature already in the mid-eighties. With no breeze and a trickle of perspiration meandering down my back, I wished I'd opted for shorts instead of slacks, especially when I saw Alina relaxing on her lounge chair. Dressed "resort casual," she wore ivory-colored shorts that ended just past her knees, a crisp tan safari-style shirt with the top two buttons undone, and gold sandals. A floppy straw hat lay over a canvas beach bag at her side.

Some business meeting this is going to be, I thought.

I took the towel from the attendant and handed him a tip. Alina turned and lowered her sunglasses. "Enjoying the view?"

Her eyes took hold of me like a tractor beam from the *Starship Enterprise*. "Doesn't get much better than this," I said.

Behind me was the second story verandah where I first laid eyes on this woman and where one week ago, inside, her husband had threatened to expose my darkest secrets if I didn't cooperate—and to make me a very rich man if I did. Scanning the water for Billy Ray's boat, I wondered how life would change for Mrs. Whestin—and for me—if her husband ended up behind bars.

"So," she asked, "how does it feel to be working for Whestin Group? These are exciting times for us." She applied lip-gloss, dropped the tube into her bag, and began toying with the second button of her shirt.

"I've got about four weeks to do what could be ten weeks worth of work," I said. "That part's not so exciting."

"You're not complaining, are you?"

I assured her I was not.

"Good. And how are things with Colleen?"

The answer must have registered on my face because she quickly apologized. "Sorry, personal question. Back to business—other than the timeframe, how do you feel?"

"Anxious to get started," I said, relieved I didn't have to explain where Colleen had gone. And with whom.

"What if you find something that doesn't smell right?" she asked.

Where had I heard that before? "You mean, like—?"

"Something that smacks of fraud."

At the edge of the beach I saw Billy Ray's mirage shimmering in the heat, arms folded, his face one big fat *I-told-you-so* frown. He was waiting to hear my answer, and so was I.

Alina, apparently, had more pressing matters in mind.

"Hold that thought," she said, grabbing her beach bag. "Let's get lunch, then we're going to take a short trip to North Fort Myers."

To...*where?*

An hour later I was fumbling for my seatbelt as Alina accelerated a new head-turning Corvette away from LaPlaya and headed north along Vanderbilt Beach Road, top down.

She told me the car's color was "velocity yellow," and I didn't have to look at the speedometer to know we were going considerably faster than the posted speed limit. The wind promptly whipped my hair into a disheveled mess.

Once on northbound I-75, Alina guided the convertible effortlessly through the mid-afternoon traffic, cruising at eighty-five as if she were on a Sunday afternoon drive to her grandma's. World-class power growled under the hood, but it didn't seem to intimidate the driver.

We drove for almost forty minutes before she got off the highway and turned right. A mile down the road, we veered into an industrial park of mostly nondescript, concrete block buildings. After several more turns she stopped in front of a handsome gray granite building with heavily tinted windows and a double front door of polished aluminum.

A sign above the door read, "Manetti Pharmaceuticals."

Below, in smaller type, I could make out, "A Whestin Group Company."

"My father founded this business," Alina said. "He died Christmas Eve, 1986, of a heart attack. I took over the next day." She continued staring at the building, remembering.

From the materials Wallace sent me I'd learned the company made a variety of chemicals for hospital use, mostly for anesthesia. There'd been no mention of prior ownership.

"I had big plans for that company," Alina said. "But ten months in, 'Black Monday' hit, and the stock market crashed at exactly the time our toughest competitor cut its prices. Still, I was handling it, until the rumors." Her voice trailed off.

"About...?"

"Our quality controls. All bullshit, but I was only twenty-eight and inexperienced compared to my father. And a woman, so what did I know, right? Some of our older clients jumped ship when we couldn't identify the source of the obviously false accusations. Didn't matter that we'd never had a screw-up before and didn't have one then. We were in deep trouble—until six months later, and in he swooped."

"He...?"

"Jeremy. The man who planted those rumors." With the look of a woman recalling the man who'd raped her, she reached over and squeezed my knee. "And why am I telling you all this?"

Beats me, lady.

"Because, Mr. McDermott, Jeremy used those rumors to steal my company. And with your help, I'm going to steal it back."

I looked down and saw my hand resting on the door handle.

Why, I wondered, *does everything have to be so complicated?*

25.

Alina dropped me off at LaPlaya around two-thirty. I had the door open before the car stopped moving, but she grabbed my arm and handed me her business card.

"I've put a great deal of trust in you, haven't I?" she said.

The answer was obvious. The question was *why?*

Her answer did little to quell my uneasiness over this bizarre afternoon. "I know I've put you in a tough spot, Rainey, beyond the one you've created for yourself already. But I also know you want to do the right thing, if you can find a way. I'm telling you, there is a way—but you have to trust me."

"No offense, but why would I want to get involved in this? My life is fairly screwed up as it is."

"Fair question. For now, I just want you to think about what I said, and what it implies about the man you're working for. Then"—she pointed at the card in my hand—"call me. I promise you won't regret hearing me out."

We'll see. I thanked her for lunch but made no commitment other than to try to stay away from this woman. Too many downsides to "hearing her out," I decided, and not enough up.

I already had a good take on Jeremy Whestin's character if based on nothing more than what he'd sucked me into with Grayson and what he was threatening me with now. What he'd apparently done to his wife didn't seem all that shocking. I'd seen worse, though Alina understandably saw it differently.

On the way home, I had the radio tuned to the one major news station we have down here. The talk continued to be about Treasury Secretary Henry Paulson's unnerving announcement Sunday that the government needed to take over twin mortgage giants Fanny Mae and Freddie Mac, or the U.S. economy would be toast.

Surprisingly, the stock market rallied yesterday, the Dow ending up 236 points. But it was barreling downward today as financial markets around the world began to question just how bad the whole sub-prime mess might turn out to be—and just how much a "bailout" might cost.

Just what I needed: more bad news, for which I decided to blame Diego.

A few minutes after driving through the welcoming gates of Palms Away, I pulled into what should have been an empty garage. Instead, Colleen's car was there, parked in the spot it hadn't occupied in three months.

I hadn't heard from her since our lunch, but if she'd kept to her schedule, she would have been back from her visit north a week now. I held my breath, hoping against hope she'd come home for good.

But it wasn't a *she* I saw sitting quietly at the outside bar, sipping on a Diet Coke. It was a *they*.

Colleen smiled pleasantly as I approached, playing the loving wife and daughter-in-law, acting as if she'd never been away deciding our future on her own sweet schedule. "We've been catching up," she said.

"Hello, son." Frank swiveled on his bar stool and held out his hand.

I ignored it and stared at Colleen. "What's going on?"

"Your father called me this morning. He needs to talk to you."

"You're looking well," I heard Frank say. I couldn't return the compliment.

My father seemed smaller than I remembered. The once wiry muscles in his arms had given way to pale, splotchy, undefined flesh. His thinning hair was a mix of dark brown and gray, more the latter than the former. But his eyes were clear, and his prominent jaw reflected the cocky, ambitious Irishman he'd been before risking the family's meager savings on a small tool and die manufacturing plant on Chicago's north side.

It was a gamble that blew up in his face as he immediately discovered a mountain of undisclosed debt and an angry lineup of vendors looking to be paid for invoices months past due. He ended up with roughly half the number of loyal clients he'd been promised, and when most of them cancelled their contracts or stop placing new orders, he had no choice but to file for bankruptcy a year later. And then he moved out.

To this day I wondered why Frank hadn't at least provided the hope of better times to come by gutting it out with the rest of us. Fathers make mistakes, sure, but they don't abandon their family. They don't leave their first-born and only son to grow up on his own, his only role model a father who showed him how not to handle disappointment and temporary defeat. It had all led to an estrangement I had no idea how, after all these years, Frank could fix.

But I had new questions now, like what was so important, so urgent, that he needed to talk to me about it today? And was Colleen ready to come home for good?

She'd given Frank her cell phone number as soon as we moved to Florida—mostly for emergencies, she said, but I knew she called him from time to time to make sure he was all right. Which had been fine with me as long as she kept any news to herself.

Colleen was seated to Frank's right. I picked a stool to her left. Staring at Colleen out of the corner of my eye, I asked if this was an emergency.

Frank leaned forward on his forearms and shrugged, as if to say, *I'll let you decide.* "I've got a buddy—a close friend in Cape Coral. Name's Pete Patterson, but we call him 'Pintail.' Loves to hunt ducks. Get it?"

I continued staring at Colleen, who was wearing a watch I hadn't seen before.

"Anyway," Frank continued, "Pintail thinks he's got himself involved in one of those"—he looked at Colleen—"what did I call it?"

"Ponzi schemes."

Frank touched her hand. "Yeah, that's it. He's out about twenty grand, and he doesn't have that kind of dough to lose. Who does, huh?" He scanned the lanai then turned to face me. "I thought maybe you could talk to him."

I took a moment to compose myself. I hadn't talked to this man since the start of the New Millennium, and only then because Colleen forced me to call him. I'd waited for an apology but none had been forthcoming, and that had been the end of that. Now here he was eight years later, not to express regret for ruining his son's childhood, but because he was concerned for someone who wasn't even family.

"I'm sorry about your friend," I said, "but he should go to the police."

Frank slapped his knee. "That's what I told him! But he's scared and embarrassed. Bad enough if his friends find out, but his wife? He told me she'd kill him. He's so distraught, he's thinking of leaving her before she finds out."

He leaned forward to get a better look at me. "I'm thinking maybe you could track down this shyster, see who else got scammed. If Pintail knows he's not the only one, he might come forward and maybe bring some others with him. You could help him get his money back, maybe save a lot of heartache for others."

I came halfway off my stool. "Let me see if I've got this straight. You're concerned about somebody who 'can't lose that kind of dough.' Who might just skip out on his wife. Who might be more concerned with saving face than facing up to the consequences of his stupidity. And *now* this upsets you? Do I have that right?"

Frank looked away, but I wasn't sure he got the message. I was about to zing him one more time when Colleen turned and fired eye daggers at me. Fine. But I wasn't going to apologize.

"I've just taken on a big assignment," I said—Colleen thrust her jaw forward, looking a lot like a barracuda I saw while fishing with Billy Ray one day; not the look of a woman who'd come home to work on her marriage—"and I just wouldn't be able to give this the attention I'm sure it deserves." I ran a finger along the edge of the bar. "Sorry."

No one spoke for several moments until Colleen helped Frank to his feet. "Come on, Dad. Time to go."

He crooked an arm inside hers and the two of them walked slowly to the door. I followed at a distance. When Colleen left to back the car out of the garage, Frank turned and hitched his pants. "Nice seeing you again, lad. I know you'd help if you could. And...say hello to your mother for me."

I stopped just short of cursing him. "Do you know that Mother's dying of emphysema, spending her last days all alone at a nursing facility in Cape Coral? The doctor says—"

Frank closed the space between us, enough that I could see his eyes watering. "She's not alone, son. I visit her every Tuesday morning."

I recoiled in disbelief. And then I remembered the pink carnations. Before I could force words past the sudden lump in my throat, Colleen was out of the car, grabbing Frank by the arm and buckling him in with the efficiency of a NASCAR pit crew. Without looking my way or taking time to fasten her own seatbelt, she put the car in gear and sped off.

If I had to guess, I'd say she wasn't coming back to unpack her bags and cook me dinner any time soon.

That night I sat at the club bar, nursing a cocktail, in no hurry to return to the home that would soon be the key and maybe only asset in the divorce case of *McDermott v. McDermott*. And try as I might to ignore it, I could still see the tears in Frank's eyes, which left me feeling hollow and angry at my juvenile performance.

I also couldn't ignore the obvious: he was Carnation Man. If Mother was up to it, I was going to call her tomorrow and get the truth.

A tap on the shoulder. I turned and saw Billy Ray smiling self-consciously, shifting his weight, waiting for an invitation I didn't trust myself to offer. "You want to set up a game?" he asked, executing an imaginary golf swing.

I gave my arm a stiff rotation. "Shoulder's acting up. I'm taking a month off."

He grabbed a handful of pretzels from the bar. "Sorry to hear it. You know the number." He headed off towards the rear of the dining room, out of sight.

Alone again, I ordered another drink and later polished off a fried grouper sandwich with French fries. I swiped up the last vestige of ketchup and thought about what it meant that I'd just lied to my best friend. That four years after making it out of rehab in one piece, after walking away with a multi-million dollar payoff, after promising Colleen things would get better, I was right back where I started: running out of money, blowing off friends and family, disappointing my wife and lying to myself.

Only this time there was no Colleen to prop me up. Not even Penny, the latter thought immediately souring my stomach as if the grouper had been a day past fresh.

It was only eight-fifteen.

I decided I could go home and sleep off my depression or put in another hour or two dissecting the Whestin Group financials.

Or....

Emboldened by the last of my second gin, I pulled out my wallet and searched for Alina's card.

26.

Alina stepped from the shower, wrapped herself in a towel, and sat down at her vanity, both excited and nervous. She'd hooked her fish. Now all she had to do was reel him in.

She had just enough time to apply the creams and lotions essential to projecting the appearance of a woman far removed from the start of her sixth decade. *If only men knew what it takes,* she thought.

Rainey's decision to see her had been one she'd expected, just not this quickly. That she'd scheduled her facial, manicure and pedicure for late this afternoon was pure coincidence but one for which she was thankful. Tonight was going to be an important step in her plan to woo a new partner to her side, and she wanted her appearance to be just so.

Most men, she remembered reading years ago, were sexually aroused by visual stimuli, but others were more aroused by sounds, touch or fragrance. She wondered where Rainey's proclivities lay and decided that tonight she would cover all the bases.

Her touch-ups complete, including a final spritz of *Light Blue* in all the strategic places, Alina slipped into a white terry cloth bathrobe that extended two inches above her knees. She wore nothing underneath but a leopard print thong.

The doorbell rang, and her pulse quickened. She made one final assessment in the mirror. The effect was just so.

Stopping long enough to grab Rainey's drink from the freezer, Alina cracked open the front door and peeked at her guest. "Now that's what I call dedication," she said, glancing at her watch. Flashing a coy smile, she handed Rainey his drink and directed him to a sofa in the sitting room just off the foyer.

After pouring herself a glass of merlot, she took a seat on an opposite-facing chair and tucked her legs beneath her. "To a lucrative partnership," she said, hoisting her glass. The top of her robe parted ever so slightly and not by accident.

Rainey clinked her glass and sipped his drink. "I'm here to ask questions. Starting with who told you what Jeremy had done to you."

"A rare man with a conscience, someone who'd been part of the plot to discredit me and decided I needed to know. That's all I'll say."

"You didn't think about divorce the second you found out?"

"Maybe that was my first thought, but—" she tugged at the hem of her robe—"I'm afraid I might have misled you, Rainey. I intend to get back control of my company, yes, but as part of a much more ambitious plan."

"I'm listening."

"It's simple, really. I want the IPO to be a huge success that brings Jeremy all the accolades he thinks he deserves. Then, just as he's basking in his glory, I will threaten to expose what he did to falsify the company's books unless he steps down, turns his stock over to me and gets the hell out. He can claim ill health, old age, a bad hair day. By any practical definition, his life will be over and that which he covets most will be mine."

Rainey was about to take another sip of his cocktail but stopped. "I suppose I admire your guts, Alina, but you keep talking about fraud. What makes you think—?"

Alina pursed her lips, as if to say *please, let's be serious*. "When Jeremy let slip last year that the company was in trouble and then told me a few weeks later that they needed to go public, I figured he wouldn't just go out there naked and hope for the best. It's not his style. He'd do whatever it took to swing the odds in his favor, no matter the risk. Which, I figured, meant playing around with the books."

Rainey tipped his glass in her direction. "A reasonable guess."

"Which then pointed me in the direction of Wallace Gerard. I could tell he was attracted to me. Two months—and a few promises—later, I had an insider as a partner and confirmation that he was indeed involved in doctoring the financial statements. Obviously, with Jeremy's authorization."

"Promises?"

"What?"

"You said you made Wallace a few promises."

"Oh, that," she said, running a hand just inside the top of her robe. "Yes, well, I said that in time I'd use my influence to see that he be made president. Jack Armbruster isn't happy about going public. Eventually he'll want out."

"That's it? Wallace took the risk of a lifetime on the hope you'd hold sway over the board of directors? Why do I suspect you promised more than that?"

Alina shrugged. "It's irrelevant now. He's playing it *too* close to the vest. Won't reveal anything to me, he says, until the time is right. Sorry, this plan is to be executed *my* way."

Rainey suggested she'd been spending too much time in the sun, and her temper flared. "Do I need to tell you what it feels like to know that Jeremy schemed to bring me to my knees, and then knowing full well how it had affected me, *proposed* three years later? It makes me want to soak in a bleach bath every time I think about it."

She hadn't meant to get so emotional, but she could see Rainey looking at her in a different way. At least he was still listening.

Her robe had parted another half inch, and she made a point of closing it, as if she had a chill. "Anyway, Wallace is on the outs with me right now, and it's his own fault. When you came on board, I saw a way of increasing my odds from a sixty or seventy with him to maybe a ninety or more with you. At least that's what I'm hoping."

He gave her a look, clueless.

"Never mind," she said. "I'll offer you the same deal Jeremy's offering: same salary, same stock options and a guaranteed senior position within the company after the IPO, if you want it."

Rainey slowly shook his head. "All this assumes a successful public offering and that your gun-loving, ex-Marine husband reacts to your threat the way you anticipate. Oh, and that a likely very jealous, loose-cannon Wallace Gerard doesn't cause you big trouble when he finds out he's been replaced by the man hired to look over his shoulder. Namely, me. And God help us if Jeremy uncovers your little scheme without you knowing it. Remember that scene from *The Godfather*, the one with the horse's head in the Hollywood producer's bed? Well, this time it won't be a dead horse bleeding in your bed—it'll be *you*."

Alina sipped her wine, enjoying the challenge. It was getting her wet. "I would say that's a bit overblown, but you are entitled to your opinion. I'm just saying this is something I need to do. It's important to me, and I know we can pull this off."

Placing her wine glass on the table, she moved to the sofa, amused as Rainey tried to maintain a professional demeanor, his eyes looking everywhere but at her robe that was now hiked halfway up her thigh.

He finished his drink, then picked up a magazine and scanned the cover. "I can make it so those financial statements pass scrutiny," he said, thumbing through the pages. "It's possible Wallace already has. But if it's ever proved you knew what was going on and used it to blackmail Jeremy, this house of cards could blow right down on top of your pretty head. Mine, too."

He tossed the magazine on the coffee table and with a quick glance at Alina's bare legs, stood and faced her. "Find some other way to exact your revenge. I'm assuming the stock, if it isn't already jointly held, is bequeathed to you as part of Jeremy's estate. Somewhere down the road, if you'll just stay patient, it's all going to be yours anyway. And again, if you can't wait, divorce him." He sat down in the same chair Alina had just left.

"I told you," she said, "divorce is too easy. And as for the stock, it is *not* in my name, nor is it bequeathed to me. It's promised to his son, Kevin."

It was obvious from the blank stare on Rainey's face that this was news to him. "He was ten when his mother ran off with another man," she said. "She apparently wanted nothing to do with Jeremy or her son. I guess Jeremy did his best, trying to raise him and a company at the same time. He was good at the latter, not so good at the former."

"Where is he now?"

Alina shrugged. "Kevin tried to work for Jeremy a couple of summers before he headed off to college. He hated the experience, and the two of them got into terrible rows, from what I've heard. I think Kevin lives in North Carolina now, works at an ad agency. The two of them haven't spoken to each other in years."

"All the more reason Jeremy should have made some changes by now. I mean, you've been married how long?"

"Seventeen years this November," she said, shaking her head. "Long enough for him to know whether or not he trusted me and—I don't care. I told you, my motives have nothing to do with money. Nor, by the way, with the little tramp he keeps in St. Louis."

Rainey's eyebrows shot up as Alina waved a dismissive hand. *"Victoria* Laine, executive whore. And please don't look so shocked."

"Sorry. Look, Alina, you've taken a huge risk tonight. What makes you think I won't warn your husband that his wife and chief financial officer have turned on him? I might even get a bonus."

Alina pouted in mock disapproval. "Not exactly the way to endear yourself to your new employer. I mean, pointing an accusatory finger at his loving wife? With no evidence?"

Her hand moved to the sash loosely holding her robe in place. "Some risks are calculated, Rainey. I believe you'll do the right thing. And I believe it now more than ever."

"Because...?"

"Because you're still here."

She untied her robe and in two steps stood before him. When she leaned down and rested a hand on his belt buckle, she paused to give him a chance to reject her advances. He didn't move.

Rainey had been without his wife for at least three months, she knew. How long it had been since they'd made love was likely a lot longer than that. And now he was inches from a nearly naked woman who clearly wanted him, who was going to make it easy. She knew few men who would say no to an offer like that from a woman with a body like hers, especially after they'd had a few drinks.

She kissed him, and he kissed her back, just as she expected him to. Then she stepped out of her thong and placed it in his hands, something to fondle as she unbuckled his belt, slid his pants down and took hold of him. Their eyes met, and Rainey flashed her a Rhett Butler smile. *I know what you're doing and frankly my dear, I don't give a damn.*

Did she have a partner, one she could trust?

She couldn't be certain, but right now, at this moment, she didn't give a damn, either.

27.

Three hours after ringing Alina's doorbell, I fell into bed exhausted from the kind of sex I didn't think the gods bestowed upon forensic accountants who were nearing sixty and occasionally needed reading glasses. Sex that had included a leopard skin thong fit for Sheena of the Jungle.

Mostly I was in shock.

What the hell had I just done?

Alina and I were both in failing marriages, and yes it had been several months since I'd even been with a woman, much less one who wanted me. And yes, my wife was shacking up with another man. Why then did I feel so guilty?

Or was this fear coursing through my veins?

Alina Whestin was hitched to the man who'd threatened to expose my secrets if I didn't do as he requested. Or, just for the heck of it, blow a hole out the back of my head and then drive a truck through it. And if she'd wanted to match her husband's threat to blackmail me with one of her own, I'd just given her the perfect opportunity.

Forget my tendency to borrow trouble; I was now actively *creating* it just as I had in Chicago. One of these days I'd have to figure this out.

I was pondering my latest unconscionable misstep when the phone rang, causing my heart to stop at exactly 12:47 A.M.

"Mr. McDermott, this is Cheryl Donner from Bayfront Retirement Center. I'm afraid I have bad news...."

Five days later, I found myself fidgeting in the front pew of a non-denominational chapel serving this morning as the site of my mother's memorial service. Refuge for fallen Catholics like the McDermotts and the fulfillment of the directive Mother gave me during what was to be our final date together just last week. A grand total of about thirty seats were occupied.

Behind me, spread across six rows of metal folding chairs, sat Billy Ray; the seven remaining members of Mother's bridge club; two nephews, sons of her deceased brother; a half dozen of the ambulatory friends she'd met during her years at Bayfront; the nurse who'd faithfully prepared her "London Fog," and a dozen or so of the other miscellaneous souls she'd met along her journey through a rotten life.

To my left sat my two sisters, Kelly and Kathy; their husbands; and three grown children, all down from Chicago. I couldn't say I was close to any of them, and in fact, we hadn't seen each other since the day Colleen and I departed for Naples.

"Nice to see you," I must have said a dozen times. "Yes, it's a shame, but she's in a better place. Need a lift to the airport? Wouldn't want you to miss your flight home."

Next to that troop sat Colleen, thankfully without Steve Wannamaker. With the exception of a brief condolence call Wednesday morning, we hadn't spoken since she sped away from the house with my father buckled in at her side.

The passing of my mother, the death of my marriage, the crossing of a line with Alina into territory I couldn't yet define—it had been a hell of a week. And the wrestling with unfamiliar emotions apparently wasn't over yet, because next to Colleen sat Frank.

He'd arrived on the arm of a tall, weathered, seventy-something woman with jet-black hair and high cheekbones. A black tee shirt, apparently purchased at the local Harley motorcycle shop, only partially hid a tattoo etched just above her left breast. Frank introduced her as "my friend Dolly," who was now seated at his side, patting his hand.

The officiate said a prayer, gave a brief sermon I didn't hear much of, then began reading anecdotes from family and friends. I glanced at Frank and his companion, or whatever the hell she was. What nerve! Who would dress like that for a funeral? And why would Frank allow it?

I thought again about the sacrifices my mother had made during my childhood. She'd worked as a secretary for an administrator at Chicago's Rush University Medical Center, out of the house at six-thirty, home just before seven. I don't remember missing a single breakfast or dinner, and somehow three brown lunch bags never failed to appear on the kitchen counter as we kids headed off to school.

Her job would have provided a decent wage for a single woman without children, but for a mother of three, shouldering debts bequeathed by her absentee husband and little money in the bank, there was precious left over for the niceties of life—for any of us.

A poke in my side. "He's asking if anyone wants to say something about Mom," Kelly whispered.

Before I could react, Frank rose and shuffled to the podium. I felt like yanking him back by the collar and telling him to wait in the car—and to take his bimbo with him. If he said one word out of line....

"Mary Margaret McDermott was the finest woman I've ever known," Frank began, obviously secure in his relationship with his girlfriend. "I didn't deserve her the day we walked down the aisle, but instead of making the most of my good fortune, I took this blessing from the Lord and put her through hell."

Someone at the back of the room coughed as Frank glanced at his two daughters and then at Colleen, before settling his eyes on me. "She forgave me for everything," he said, "because that was the kind of woman she was."

He turned and looked at the row of family pictures, hastily arranged by the twins, that sat on a cloth-covered card table positioned next to the podium.

"God bless *you* now, Mary," he said. And with that he pulled a pink carnation from his jacket and laid it on the table next to a picture of Mother posing with her high school diploma on the day before she married Francis Patrick McDermott. Two months after she was pregnant with me.

I suppose I should have helped him to his seat, but he hadn't needed my help before, and despite a slight limp, he apparently didn't need it now.

He had *Dolly*.

By 10:30 the officiate was accepting congratulations for delivering a moving eulogy and, I assumed, for doing so in less than thirty minutes. I'd managed to say a few words, most of which I'd expressed to Mother last week. I'd have said more if I'd known I would never see her alive again.

The subject of her Carnation Man never came up, primarily because I couldn't make myself ask the question. If Mother had wanted me to know, I told myself, she would have said something. At least that was my rationale.

Billy Ray, my ride home, put a hand on my back. "Car's out front," he said.

I scanned the small crowd at the door. In the rush of sympathizers who'd crowded around me after the service, I'd lost track of Colleen. "Have you seen her?" I asked.

Billy Ray canted his head toward the parking lot. "I think she's left."

I wasn't sure what I'd expected. A kiss or hug. Maybe a suggestion we meet for coffee. *Something*.

Every muscle in my body ached, and all I wanted was to sleep for the next seventy-two hours—or days. I put a hand on Billy Ray's shoulder and should have kept walking for the door when I spotted Frank in an anteroom just off the lobby, leaning against a window that overlooked a small garden of purple and pink pentas. Instead I asked Billy Ray to give me a second.

My first thought was to barge in and challenge Frank face-to-face. I didn't care anymore why he'd left us. I wanted confrontation and any excuse would do.

I cleared my throat. Frank turned, and straightened but said nothing, a man ready to face his firing squad of one. In the few minutes since admitting he didn't deserve the kindness of the woman he'd deserted, he seemed further diminished, no spark discernible in his dispassionate eyes. It hit me then that not only was my mother dead, so was my father. Suddenly, I didn't know what to say.

Frank looked at me as if he'd heard the gun jam. His eyes softened. "Don't be so hard on yourself, lad," he said. "It wasn't your fault."

The words exploded from my mouth. "Why does everybody think *I'm* at fault? If it weren't for the care I provided, Mother would have died years ago of the broken heart *you* gave her!" I shook my head. "You've some nerve."

The sadness and regret in Frank's thin smile forced my eyes to the worn carpeting. "If I had any nerve, lad," he said, "none of this would have happened."

Dolly entered the room, shoved me aside with a purposeful elbow to my ribs and took Frank's arm, averting a not very respectful end to Mother's memorial service. I stepped aside and turned my back as the two of them headed for the door.

Frank got to the threshold, stopped and turned. "I wasn't talking about your mother's passing, Rainey."

I couldn't move, unable to make the leap across a Continental Divide of hurt, disillusionment, smoldering anger and guilt I was just beginning to understand. The lump in my throat also made it impossible to talk, which I wouldn't have anyway, not until I figured out what had just happened and what he'd meant by that last comment.

As had been case for most of the past decades when the subject was my father, I said nothing. But as I watched him leave, Dolly by his side, I envied the man. Whatever his demons, he seemed to have made peace with them. And whatever his new life had become, he had a woman to share it with, tattoos and all.

28.

I pulled into the Perkin's Pancake parking lot the next morning, risked a peek in the car's vanity mirror and winced.

After a night of trying not to cry over the loss of my mother and losing the battle, I'd garnered no more than four hours of restless sleep as I also kept thinking about a possible call from the FBI. The resulting bags under my eyes looked more like luggage suitable for a *Samsonite* commercial.

As I thrashed about the bed last night, I was also keenly aware that after a week of searching for evidence of fraud inside Jeremy's company, I hadn't found much that would be of interest to the authorities, with the exception of some suspicious numbers related to the company's communications division. If I didn't strike pay dirt soon, I'd be on my own with the authorities, relying on a plea of temporary insanity that was maybe not so temporary.

Alina waved at me from a booth by the window, but I was too tired to wave back. She'd called last night before I dozed off, asked if I wanted to talk. There was no need to put off what I had to say, and so I took her up on her offer.

"I'm so sorry about your mother, Rainey," she said as I sat down across from her. I noticed her flinch slightly when I removed my sunglasses.

"You've been through this?" I asked.

She nodded. "I lost my mother when I was very young."

I could see she wanted to lean across the table and give me a kiss, but that was one of the things we needed to get straightened out.

Under the influence of alcohol, self-pity and an overload of eye candy, I'd made love to her, but we weren't "lovers." Not officially. With one no-excuse exception five years ago that came after twenty-eight years of marriage, I'd never cheated on Colleen, never even flirted with another woman. And yet I felt something for *this* woman.

My feelings weren't difficult to analyze. I could recite the psycho-babble "logic" as well as any psychologist: just lost his mother, separated from his wife, compensating for a childhood without a father-figure present, vulnerable, stressed out, desperate to love and to be loved.

But as my rehab counselor told me, "feelings are feelings, no matter the rationale." *That'll be thirty thousand dollars, please.*

The waitress arrived, and we each ordered a cup of black coffee. Alina passed on breakfast, and I ordered a raspberry muffin, the special of the day. I wasn't sure I could keep anything else down.

I looked at Alina, trying to figure out where to start. I'd crossed the line with this woman about as far as one could cross it. I didn't want it to happen again, at least not until this engagement was behind me, and I knew where both of us stood with our spouses—not to mention whether or not I'd end up in a federal penitentiary.

"A favor?" I asked.

She nodded in the way of an unsuspecting woman eager to please her new beau.

"Allow me to do my job," I said. "If there's fraud involved as you say there is, I'll find it. It's what I do."

"And then?" Still earnest, still trusting.

"I don't know. It's all just a little confusing right now."

She sat back, the first evidence of wariness flitting across her face. "You think this is normal behavior for me?"

Good question.

I thought of her "partnership" with Wallace, the promises she'd made, her readiness to jump my bones our first night alone because Wallace wasn't cooperating. I could easily see adding to her résumé, "professional manipulator," albeit a beautiful one. Still, if Alina had the potential to make my life with Jeremy that much tougher if I didn't cooperate with her, if somehow she could become my enemy, then it made sense, as *Sun Tzu* would advise, to keep her close until I could get a better handle on just what I was facing.

"I didn't mean that," I said. "It's just that my life is nothing but complications and obligations right now. And at this point, I don't know what my investigation will reveal. Maybe I won't find anything. Maybe you'll be back to relying on Wallace."

"And maybe you'll be back with Colleen?"

I let that pass as our coffees arrived.

Alina pushed hers aside and reached across the table to squeeze my hand. "Don't you hold out on me, too, Rainey."

For some reason, right there in a Perkins Pancake House full of vacationing families and senior citizens reading the morning newspaper, my mind flashed back to her leopard skin thong, soft and slick in my fingers as she bent down and—*Good God, man, get a grip!* I jerked my hand away as if I'd just touched the top of a hot stove, knocking my cup off its saucer and spilling coffee across half the table.

I grabbed my napkin and started sopping up the mess as a waitress arrived with her rag and helped me out. Alina, I noticed, didn't move, but just stared at me, no longer looking so eager to please or so trusting.

"Are we partners?" she asked when the waitress left.

I didn't know how to answer that, and I didn't like being pushed, not when I was uncertain about everything right now, including myself. Even though what I'd committed with Alina technically was adultery, I wanted it to mean something, to have been more than just a tipsy nod to my neglected testicles. Otherwise....and yet I had no idea what it meant.

"Let's find another word," I said. "Partnerships have a nasty habit of ending badly."

She smiled and pulled a small yellow writing tablet from her purse. "I'll work on that."

I left her sipping her coffee and jotting notes. On the way out of the parking lot I realized that I'd driven over here wondering how this very determined woman would react to my need for distance, especially coming so soon after our naked night on her couch. Apparently I needn't have worried. She just wanted a little reassurance and not much at that.

It seemed too easy.

Back within the relative sanity of my dining room office, after an antacid worked its magic, I called Greg Aronson, vice president of sales for Whestin Group's communications division. He acknowledged he knew I was serving as a special assistant to the CEO and encouraged me to "ask anything."

"I see sales have been slumping," I said, scanning the notes I'd made on the division's first and second quarter balance sheets.

"Demand's kind of flat right now," Aronson said. "In fact, it stinks. You see what's happening today? Lehman Brothers filed for bankruptcy. The market's in free fall. I think it touched 10,800-something on the DOW. This is killing me. I've got two kids in college and a wife who doesn't work. If you saw my credit card bills—."

I felt the earth move as if I'd been standing on the San Andreas fault in the middle of a Richter 8.8. "It'll recover," I said, more to hold at bay my own fears than Aronson's. "Now back to your balance sheet here. Sales are flat to down, but the profit you're reporting seems unusually healthy."

"I don't see the monthly financials," Aronson said. "Just the sales figures, so I'll take your word for it. But as the old saying goes, 'It's not what you sell it for, it's what you buy it for that counts.'"

"Meaning?"

"We've been selling prepaid cell phones for about three years now, out of various retail outlets. Been good sellers for us. But then recently we committed to a million phones from a new vendor out of Southeast Asia. Got them for well below what we'd been paying. I was told they wanted to get a foothold here, and they were willing to buy their way in."

My internal antennae began sparking, and I expected to smell my hair burning. "These phones any different from the ones you'd been selling?"

"Not that I can tell. Minor differences, maybe. They're fairly stripped down models."

"Any of the older units still in stock?"

"Yeah...something like fifty-thousand. I don't think they're scheduled to move out for another couple of weeks."

"And these phones are warehoused in...?"

"Fort Smith, Arkansas. Entertainment capital of the world."

Here goes. "I'd like to give the folks there a visit, look around some. Probably won't be able to get there for another week or so. That sound okay?"

"Suit yourself. Fort Smith isn't the easiest place to get to, but they'll roll out the red carpet. I'll call the manager this afternoon and clear the way."

I thanked him and checked my notes: a million cells phones from a new vendor—in Southeast Asia. At a substantial discount. Who was this new resource? And could Aronson's explanation for the deep discount be trusted?

Again I detected that nasty odor of deceit and knew this was at least something that the accounting firm would need to include in its comfort letter. I'd be most interested to see what due diligence they'd done to arrive at a favorable judgment.

But the most pressing question now, did this merit a quick trip to Fort Smith? It would at least be an excuse to get out of town and clear my head. Why, I wondered, couldn't those phones have been warehoused in Las Vegas?

I had to assume that someone in the communications division might alert Jeremy to my call. If nothing were amiss with those phones, I'd be given full clearance. But if I'd stumbled onto something, he'd likely try to convince me there was nothing in Fort Smith worth investigating—or at least make sure to restrict my access on premises. I wasn't going to give him the chance.

If I arrived at the warehouse a few days earlier than expected, the manager would likely be surprised and hesitant. At which point I'd launch into an exasperated rant, surmising that a temp in the home office had screwed up and failed to forward the message of a last minute change in my schedule.

It had been my experience that lower-level supervisors nearly always caved, happy to save a bad situation, especially for someone from headquarters who'd come a long way just to pay them a visit. After all, I wanted no more than a quick tour, and then I'd be on my way.

Getting into the warehouse would be the easy part. Deducing which were the old phones and which were the new, then pilfering a sample of each, would take a little doing, but I'd accomplished similar feats of derring-do before.

I booked the last seat on a Wednesday morning flight and got back to work.

29.

Victoria slumped against her dresser, hands pressed tight to her ears. The harsh, pitiable sound of dry retching accosted her body, threatening to nauseate her, as well.

She couldn't let that happen.

From the moment Jeremy revealed his death-sentence prognosis, she'd found an inner resolve to be there for him, no matter how bad things got. If only he knew how many nights she'd cried since, never letting him see how his illness was destroying her, too.

The pale light seeping in from the bathroom cast a sallow, ghostlike aura over the bedroom furniture, as if she were observing them in a dream. She could just make out the cover of the latest *Architectural Digest* resting on the seat of a stuffed chair where she'd been reading the past two nights until Jeremy fell asleep. This wasn't her furniture, her bedroom, her condo; it was theirs. They were a couple, and if ever a couple needed to stick together, it was now.

At the sound of another hacking cough, Victoria crept to the edge of the bathroom door and cringed at what she saw. Jeremy hunched over the toilet.

Naked. One white-knuckled hand clenching the edge of the seat, the other pressed against his right temple. Wordlessly, she entered the room, dampened a washcloth and draped it across his neck.

"Give me a minute," he said. She patted his back and left, gently closing the door behind her.

From the beginning she'd known there was no real future for the two of them. Jeremy had possessed mistresses before, the longest one, she'd heard, lasting just under six months. That she'd beaten that by a factor of four gave her no joy. And certainly not hope. Not now.

Her first priority had been to get hired, then see what developed. If she got lucky, even if it was only a one-night stand, she'd make certain Mrs. Whestin knew. It might get her fired, but it would be worth it. One not-so-small way to let the woman know she would never find peace, not until she confessed her sins.

When their first night of reckless abandonment turned into two before she could catch her breath, she'd held her tongue. There was more to the man than bravado. And whatever he needed, sex or otherwise, he wasn't getting it at home from a wife who didn't even live here.

Two whirlwind months later, when he'd asked her to become something more in his life, she'd been both shocked and elated. At the time, the home office staff consisted of Wallace Gerard and Jack Armbruster, three vice presidents, a couple of assistant number-crunchers and a handful of secretaries, all with longer tenure and more impressive résumés. When she rose so quickly to become the CEO's executive assistant, no one said anything. Perhaps they'd seen this act before.

It didn't matter. She was where she wanted to be. Only now, she lived each day wondering when Jeremy would learn the truth—and what his reaction would be.

Taking his wife's phone call had been an accident, though perhaps inevitable. The shock from Alina's end had been palpable, but so far, there'd been no repercussions. By not responding, by ignoring this double breach of fidelity, she seemed to be saying, *take him, but you will never get it all.*

Jeremy emerged from the bathroom, smelling of mouthwash. His towel encircled a waist that wasn't so much washboard flat as it was shrinking.

Staring at her with those brilliant blue eyes that even now displayed no fear, he pushed her onto the bed and asked if she wanted to get laid.

"I don't know," she said. "My boss is a real bastard when I'm late."

Jeremy didn't seem to mind the rebuff, and she understood why. He took her left hand and rubbed her naked ring finger. She wondered if he noticed.

"McDermott wants to visit the Fort Smith warehouse," he said. "He called Greg Aronson yesterday."

Which, she understood, meant that his mind was somewhere else. It also meant the cell phones were in play. Since Jeremy had shared Mack's concerns with her, she immediately grasped the worrisome implications.

"I knew he'd see the up-tick in profits," Jeremy said, "ask a few questions for which we'd have answers. I didn't think he'd want to visit a fucking warehouse in the middle of nowhere."

"When?"

"Sometime next week."

He sank onto the bed, and Victoria began massaging his shoulders. His skin felt clammy. "I thought you were looking for that kind of due diligence," she said.

Jeremy rolled his head to one side. "I am, but the phones were supposed to be off-limits. If he discovers anything amiss in our books, we can always do a *mea culpa*, tell him we'll make things right. He wouldn't necessarily need to see those entries again. But the phones...*shit*."

He leaned back against Victoria's chest, and she put her arms around him. "You think he suspects something?"

"He called the warehouse, didn't he? If there's a problem and he somehow discovers it, I can hardly tell him I'll make things right unless I'm willing to pull those phones out of circulation and call the goddamn FBI. If I don't, all pretence that I just wanted to assure a successful, above-board presentation blows up in my face. And then *he's* got the leverage, or at least a measure of it."

"But you haven't heard anything more from Mack, right?" Victoria asked, hoping to ease his mind. "As far as you know, those phones might be perfectly legitimate. I mean, they've been on the market for months now, and no one has brought a complaint."

Jeremy nestled his head against her breasts. "Mack still has his doubts and that's good enough—or bad enough—for me. All I know is, I don't want McDermott snooping around down there. No underwriter's going to do it and certainly not the SEC. He's going beyond what I asked him to do."

Victoria didn't want to argue the point, but Rainey McDermott appeared to be doing exactly what he was being paid handsomely to do.

"Wallace knows?" she asked, running her fingertips across Jeremy's belly.

He didn't say anything for a moment, and she wondered if he'd dozed off. She repeated the question and felt him draw a breath. "I'm returning to Florida on the 26th," he said, "but I can't wait that long to see what McDermott's up to. I told Wallace yesterday to get down there this week and head him off."

Victoria thought that Wallace would find that an odd request, and that Rainey would have to figure he was on to something if Jeremy had sent an emissary to foil his plans. But those were Jeremy's issues to deal with. *She* was more concerned about the nine days they had left before her lover returned to Florida, not to mention the obviously deteriorating state of his health. He seemed barely able to get dressed in the morning, much less keep up this pace of flying back and forth between St. Louis and Florida while supervising preparations for the public offering.

"When's the next doctor's visit?" she asked.

"Mid-October. Another MRI. Then I bargain with the devil for time."

His shoulders sagged, and Victoria could feel him succumbing to the powerful painkillers that were now a part of his morning ritual. She knew he'd either force himself off the bed, or he'd be asleep in minutes.

She ran her fingernails lightly across his biceps, tracing little circles down his arms. Her fingers had just touched his thighs when he pushed himself away, turned and kissed her on the forehead. "It's getting late."

As he walked to his dresser and rummaged for his underwear, Victoria had to give him his due. At a time when most men's bodies would have long ago surrendered to the effects of age and gravity, forty years behind a desk and the ordeal of the past six months, Jeremy was still a handsome man. A man who still had the power to turn her on.

But it wasn't his physical presence she needed now. What she wanted more than anything she'd ever desired in her life was the totality of his emotional commitment. It was not to be shared or divvied up. *She'd* won this engagement. He belonged to her now, and all that went with him.

Jeremy stood at the dresser with his back to the bed, motionless for a moment before wobbling and catching himself against the open drawer. "It's a bad one today, Vick," he said. "Maybe I'll rest a minute."

Victoria thought her heart would split in two as she got him settled into bed, propped a pillow behind his head and covered him with the bed sheets. In a couple of hours, he would call the office, tell them he'd be in around noon, and everything would appear to be fine.

That was her job now, to keep up appearances as she bolstered the spirits of her man in the process. She swiped at a tear that edged her eye. *Just put me first,* she whispered. *Don't falter now!*

If she could count on Jeremy to do just that, then he could count on her, no matter how bitter these remaining weeks might be. But if he failed her, she vowed at that moment to exact her revenge even if there was but one day left in his wretched life.

30.

Wallace couldn't suppress a self-satisfied grin. He'd put in a productive eight hours, had his calendar lined up for another busy day tomorrow, and then he'd be off to Florida on Thursday.

His first order of business would be to meet Rainey for lunch. Bring up his call to Fort Smith. Try to talk him out of what surely would be a wild goose chase. Or, failing that, arrange to accompany him, per Jeremy's orders.

With that accomplished, he'd have the evening open for dinner with Alina. Given Jeremy's directive yesterday, he was to book a return flight the next day, Friday, unless circumstances dictated a quick trip to Fort Smith as McDermott's official escort.

"He can look, but he can't touch," Jeremy had said, setting off alarms in Wallace's already frayed brain.

As far as he knew, Jeremy had no reason to suspect those phones, other than his own uneasiness over dealing with an unfamiliar foreign source. When Wallace asked him why he was suddenly so concerned, Jeremy had merely said that he wanted to know what McDermott was up to, and that he wanted him focused on the financials, not traipsing all over the country poking his nose into Whestin Group warehouses. But, Jeremy had said, "If he insists on going, then shepard him there and back—and tell him the idea was mine."

Wallace had to admit he was impressed at the speed with which McDermott had apparently caught the scent. Whestin Group companies had warehouses all over the country. That McDermott had picked up on one in Fort Smith, where they were most vulnerable, gave him something to think about.

Still, he wasn't going to argue with Jeremy just to find out what he did or didn't know about the legitimacy of the phones. Too risky. And while this sounded like a babysitting job, something the warehouse manager could handle without help if properly forewarned, it was an opportunity to see Alina. He'd said nothing.

"If he starts asking about those improved margins," Jeremy had added, "just tell him what you told me: we found a resource looking to open a new market and unload an overrun in the process. Then get your butt back here Friday, if you still can. I want us to meet with Armbruster, see where he stands on nailing down an approach to the marketing. It's turning into a giant cluster fuck, from what I see."

Which meant no more than one night with Alina. It would have to be enough for now.

He'd missed her party and had barely spoken to her in the three weeks Jeremy had been in Florida. He now had a legitimate reason to call, and he needed to do it now.

It was six-fifteen here, an hour later in Naples. Jeremy had called in around noon, complaining of a severe headache, and hadn't come in all day. A couple of secretaries were still here, but otherwise, Wallace was alone.

They exchanged pleasant hellos, and Alina seemed to be relaxed and pleased to hear from him. "I was going to call you," she said. "I've missed you."

A good start. "What are you doing Thursday night?"

"Prearranging our phone sex, are we?"

All apprehension melted. "I have to take care of a little emergency business at lunch with Rainey McDermott, in person, per Jeremy's orders. But afterward, I'm planning to take you to dinner."

"Emergency?"

"He might be trying to get a look at some cell phones we have warehoused in Fort Smith. Jeremy wants me to dissuade him, if I can, and to accompany him to Fort Smith, if I can't. Sorry for the short notice, but this is my first opportunity to call."

Wallace could hear Alina riffling through the pages of what he assumed was her datebook. "What's wrong with the phones?" she asked. "What's the big deal?"

He paused, but knew he'd trapped himself. "Maybe nothing. We're checking on some issues...I was going to tell you about that Thursday, if you're available."

"So happens I am. And, by the way, my compliments to you on your restraint. Obviously, you are confident McDermott poses no threat to us or you would have called me when Jeremy hired him. And I agree. This can work for us, if we play it right."

Wallace didn't share her sentiments. When that freelancer hadn't worked out—George...Something-Or-Other—he'd felt vindicated. But now someone with much stronger credentials had taken his place. What was Jeremy up to? Should he be taken at his word, that he just wanted backup, or was he, Wallace, under suspicion? He decided he would probe Alina for her take on the matter Thursday, assuming he wasn't preoccupied with probing other parts of her body.

He waited for her good-bye, but there was only silence. Then she asked him what he was wearing.

Alina had made this question part of their early ritual, and he knew she delighted in catching him off guard, in places that were not so private. "A white shirt," he said, "with that silver silk tie you bought me."

"Good. I want you to use it to tie my wrists together."

"Alina, this isn't...."

"Has Jeremy left?"

"Didn't make it in today. Bad headache." Jeremy had missed several days in the past month due to illness, but Wallace figured his wife knew.

"Too bad," she said. "It would be fun to think of him there, just down the hall...."

A part of Wallace wanted to end this before it got out of hand. The other part, the part he knew would win, wanted to see just how far this woman would go. They'd never tried this in the office. "Seriously, Alina...."

"Leave your door open. I'm going to move outside to the loggia."

Wallace glanced at his door and shuffled some papers, waiting. A minute later, she told him, "I'm naked now, Wallace. This won't take long, unless you'd like it to."

He heard her move the phone closer to a buzzing sound that alternated between clear and muffled, signaling where she'd placed the instrument that moved at her pleasure.

A sound at his door. Victoria Laine.

Wallace flinched. "I'll be a few minutes," he said, his hand over the phone. Victoria gave him an odd look, said it was nothing important, and left. The encounter aroused him all the more.

"What are you doing now, Wallace?" Alina asked. "Where are your hands?"

He closed his eyes, spun his chair away from the door and lowered his voice. "I'm holding the phone with my left hand...and...signing checks with my right."

Alina's breathing grew louder and more ragged. "I need you to do this with me, Wallace. Tell me...tell me where your hand is. I'm close now...."

"It's there."

The words had barely left his mouth when he heard her moan, softly at first, then louder, in three short bursts. A mix of exquisite-sounding pain and ecstasy that made him feel like the most desired man on earth.

He waited, listening to her breathe.

"I told you it wouldn't take long," she whispered. "Thursday, you said?"

"Yes."

"Don't be late."

A blanket of goose bumps covered Alina's damp skin. The sweet chill, combined with the still rapid beating of her heart, left her feeling like a ball of static electricity. One touch, in the right place, and she'd explode all over again. She turned on her side, brought her knees to her chest and punched in Rainey's number.

"Wallace just called," she said when he answered. For the first time she noticed the tenor of his voice. Deep, unhurried, intelligent and self-confident.

Not Gary Cooper, exactly. More like Gregory Peck. "He's flying in Thursday on Jeremy's orders. Said it's emergency business, and it involves you. He hasn't called you?"

"I'm avoiding his calls."

"And why is that?"

"If I told you, I'd have to kill you."

"Over a few cell phones? He mentioned your interest in the Fort Smith warehouse."

"What else did he say?"

"He wants to see me. I said it would have to be dinner only. He didn't sound pleased. It's been so long since he and I...I'm just a little on edge."

"Then why did you accept?"

She would have to handle this carefully. "If I reject him completely, he'll get suspicious. You'll just have to trust me. If you go to Fort Smith, with or without Wallace, call me when you get back, okay? We can work this out."

She noted Rainey's split-second hesitation before he said, "I'll keep you informed." The tension in his voice remained.

"Are you going somewhere now?" she asked.

"Why?"

"I was just wondering what you're wearing."

"Slacks and a nice shirt. I'm meeting a friend for dinner."

"Are you in a hurry?"

"Actually, yes. Why?"

Alina waited for Rainey to get the signal, but he said nothing. She thought about making her desire more obvious but instead asked if she could see him tomorrow. He hesitated, then told her he'd be especially busy the next two days. Alina decided he was either deeply distracted or playing it cool. She chose to accept the latter possibility and smiled, contemplating the moment when she could turn the tables.

Something told her she wouldn't have to wait long.

31.

It was two days after my somewhat odd call from Alina and a day after my visit to the Fort Smith warehouse. My flight had landed twenty minutes late, which meant I was going to have to break a few speed limits on the way to my destination, or Wallace was going to be even more pissed at me than he likely already was.

I called Alina from the car. She sounded relieved to hear from me but nervous.

"Wallace called. Told me about your message."

"I'm headed for The Ritz Grill as we speak," I said. "Looking forward to a delightful evening with your friend."

Wallace had called from St. Louis yesterday, left me a message while, unbeknownst to him, I was already winging my way to Fort Smith. He said he needed to meet me for lunch, and that he'd be in town today, Thursday. Apparently he expected me to drop everything to accommodate him.

Wrong.

I'd left a reply at his condo in Palms Away, the message Alina was referring to. Told him I couldn't make lunch, but that I'd reserve a table for dinner at The Ritz Grill off Vanderbilt Beach Road and hoped that would work. And then I turned off my cell until now.

"My *friend*," Alina said, "isn't happy. And neither am I. He was planning to have dinner with me. Now I'm stuck having a drink with him at the house afterwards. Thanks a lot."

I muttered a quick *shit-damn-fuck* under my breath. That Wallace would end up visiting her late in the evening hadn't occurred to me. And here I thought I'd solved a problem, not created a worse one. "Relax," I said, trying to convince myself that we both had everything under control. "I'll call you when he's on his way."

Thirty minutes later, I made my way to the hotel's dining room bar and ordered a drink, relieved to see that Wallace hadn't yet arrived. "What'd the market do today?" I asked the bartender.

He rolled his eyes and told me the DOW had dropped 447 points, which meant the index was now down more than 2,600 points for the year, and it was only September. This was adding up to real money. And from Diego? No word.

I tossed down my drink, ordered another and thought about my dinner companion tonight.

Perhaps it was just professional competitiveness, but I couldn't wait to see the look on Wallace's face. I'd made it to the Fort Smith warehouse before he could head me off, which, if my suspicions proved correct, would infuriate him *and* his boss. *And* he'd just been forced to change dinner dates. I tried, unsuccessfully, to block out the thought that it would be Wallace, not me, who'd be enjoying a nightcap with Alina, the woman he still considered his partner.

As the first taste of my drink hit my lips, a hard tap on my shoulder shoved the glass into my front teeth. I turned to see the thin-lipped face of Wallace Gerard. After a quick check for chipped enamel, I stuck out my hand. "Nice to see you, Wallace."

He returned the handshake, barely. "I suggest we be seated," he said. Then he ordered a Scotch and soda and left to find the maitre d'.

I settled up with the bartender and wandered into the dining room. "Hope I didn't screw things up for you tonight," I said as we settled into our seats.

Wallace declined comment, took a sip of his drink, then another. "So, how did you find the fair city of Fort Smith?"

"Word travels fast, I see."

"It does, indeed. Jeremy thought it would be a good idea for us to meet. He wants to know what, if anything, you've...picked up. And why the rush?"

I shrugged. "I don't have a lot of time to discover what you've been up to. Besides, occasionally an engagement requires getting out from behind the desk and into the field."

"So you picked Fort Smith—and had to get down there yesterday."

"Seemed as good a day as any to get a feel for your warehouse operations and inventory controls. Fort Smith just happened to be the closest of your major warehouses."

"Impressions?" Wallace casually scanned the dining room, as if my answer didn't matter one way or the other.

"Obviously, a full inventory analysis wasn't possible," I said. "But from what I can see, everything seems to be in order. Your new cell phones are moving out at a nice clip."

I reached for a cracker from the breadbasket. "One thing, though. Plant security isn't my area of expertise, but you might tell someone up there to tighten things up a bit."

"And why is that?"

"Your warehouse manager, Scott Thornton, gave me three hours of his time. He was very helpful. But just before lunch, he got a call that he had to take in his office." I bit into my cracker, enjoying the moment. "I'm afraid he left me alone with those cell phones for nearly fifteen minutes."

"Point being?"

"It wouldn't have been that difficult to swipe a phone or two, if I'd been so inclined. And I didn't pass through any security checkpoint, coming or going. Probably because I was with Scott, you think?"

Wallace looked as if he were stifling a yawn. "I'll make a note to pass that along. We're upgrading security throughout our manufacturing facilities, but we haven't made it to Fort Smith yet. Otherwise, you would never have made it out the door."

We locked eyes, but I said nothing. I'd made my points: I don't take the easy way out, and I'm not stupid. Unfortunately, all I had now were two cell phones tucked into my luggage in the trunk of my car and no proof of wrongdoing. Yet.

"Must be quite a stressful job, this forensic accounting thing," Wallace said. "I mean, given what happened to you."

I made a mental note that Wallace wasn't above hitting below the belt when he was put out. "Ancient history. Next subject."

"Okay...how are you coming along with your review? Anything we need to address?"

"Nothing yet, but I'm coming at this from at least a cut deeper than your underwriter will. And the folks from the SEC. What I see now is the picture of a company whose financial state is almost too good to be true, given the economy."

"In other words, you haven't found shit."

"Was I supposed to?"

"You tell me. Jeremy hired you to do more than take up space, certainly given your financial arrangement."

Wallace was fishing for more than answers to what I'd been doing in Fort Smith. He wanted to know just how much Jeremy had confided in me. I knew I should keep my mouth shut, but I was tired and irritable and probably not as sharp as I needed to be. And I didn't like thinking about where he'd be ending his evening tonight. I also didn't like him thinking I didn't know what was going on.

"Let's put it this way, Wallace: I haven't been hired to dot the I's and cross the T's on those financial statements. Jeremy's got you for that. I've been hired to uncover fraud before anyone with the authority to send the two of you to prison does. Jeremy hasn't come right out and said so specifically—I think the guy enjoys playing head games—but I know I'm right. Otherwise, why would you be here?"

Wallace, weighing his response, showed more restraint than I'd just displayed. He caught the eye of our waiter. "Let's order."

Not yet. I owed this jerk for the reference to my troubles in Chicago. "I know there's a lot at stake here, and I guess I can see Jeremy's logic in bringing me in. But, really, it seems like overkill, don't you think? This prepping for the

IPO seems like something you should be able to handle on your own."

He scanned the menu. "Jeremy's his own man. Sometimes he consults with me, sometimes he doesn't. His instincts are usually reliable. But then, nobody's perfect."

"Except for perhaps his wife."

Wallace put the menu down and picked up his Scotch. "What does that mean?"

"I'm just saying, she's beautiful, intelligent, has a great sense of humor, contributes to charities. Impressive."

"You two have been getting acquainted?"

"I talk to as many people as I can on engagements like this. Secretaries, loan officers, vendors—"

"—Warehouse managers."

"And the wife of the CEO when it makes sense." I swirled the ice in my drink. "Will you be seeing Alina—Mrs. Whestin—while you're here?"

"Perhaps. As a courtesy."

"That's nice."

We ordered and made small talk throughout dinner. I expected it to be the longest hour of my life, but it was going by far too rapidly, Wallace's assignation with Alina growing closer with each passing minute.

He kept checking his watch, growing more sullen and distant as the wine he'd ordered, on top of the Scotches, worked its way through his bloodstream. I regretted setting up a dinner where he had the opportunity to get blitzed, then toying with him the way I had. Alina would have her hands full tonight.

I fell into a funk but tried to tell myself that she was partly to blame, too. After all, she'd been the one to agree to a rendezvous with Wallace in the first place. Maybe she'd think twice the next time he came to visit.

An hour later, following a cursory handshake at the valet station, Wallace gunned his car down the hotel's driveway. My jaws felt wired shut, and I punched the numbers on my cell phone hard enough to bruise the tip of my forefinger.

"He's on his way," I mumbled and slammed shut the phone's cover.

I did not want to hear her voice.

32.

Wallace arrived just after ten-fifteen, the smell of alcohol and Gorgonzola sauce heavy on his breath. Alina knew his drinking could either make it easy to pull information out of him or encourage him to take liberties with an entirely different goal in mind. If she played this right, they would both get their way tonight.

She'd dressed conservatively—a cotton blouse and jeans—just to throw him off. It was fun to play around with Wallace, offering him the occasional hors d'oeuvre before the spectacular main course.

A powerful lover, he unfailingly put her needs first, never starting until she gave the word, never finishing until she allowed him to. Jeremy had once been that way but no more. Age? Disinterest? Maybe he was in love with his executive assistant live-in. She couldn't be sure, and she didn't care.

As for Rainey McDermott, it was too early to tell. She'd been unusually gentle with him last week, and yet he'd brought her to climax, something she hadn't expected. But he'd politely rejected her attempt at phone sex and that left her slightly unbalanced. It also left her wanting him with an intensity that surprised her.

In the kitchen she fixed drinks and didn't protest when Wallace came up behind her and placed his hands around her waist. She turned and handed him his drink. "How was dinner?"

He ran a hand lightly across her collar. "We talked about Fort Smith, if that's what you mean. He implied he might have snuck out with a sample of the merchandise. I'll be reaming somebody a new asshole tomorrow."

"You concerned? I mean, I take it Jeremy sent you down here to keep this from happening."

"So maybe he's got a sample of a cell phone—big deal. What's he going to do with it, call the cops?" Wallace downed most of his drink. "He really didn't say much, and I didn't expect him to. Unless he's bluffing, he's no nearer to uncovering what I've been doing than the day he started."

He set his glass on the counter and undid the top button on Alina's blouse. "I'm more concerned with why he was hired in the first place. What's your opinion? He implied he's talked to you. Says you're—how did he put it?—'an impressive package.'"

"Oh, please. We bumped into each other at the club once." She guided Wallace's hand to the second button. "All he mentioned to me was that Jeremy wanted you to have backup on such a complex and important assignment. I don't think we have anything to worry about. Not if you've done your job."

"If he wanted me to have backup," Wallace said, staring at Alina's now exposed bra, "then why isn't the guy reporting to me? Why all the secrecy?"

"You know Jeremy," she whispered, pulling him close. "Mr. Control Freak."

Wallace kissed the top of her bra, and she purred her approval. She needed to keep this man on her leash, in case Rainey McDermott proved a disappointment, but tonight was also for gathering information—and sending a signal that *she* was still in charge.

Alina took hold of Wallace's hand and led him to the living room couch. "Let's slow it down a bit. We have plenty of time."

He sat next to her, his eyes focused on her chest. "It's been too long," he said, crudely forcing a hand inside her bra.

"I know," Alina said, letting him have his fun. "Now tell me, what have you been up to? It's been a long time for that, too. You can start with those phones."

Wallace withdrew his hand and sat back. "You want to talk *business?*"

"I want to talk about the plan. *Our* plan. I want to know what's happening. You've been so secretive lately."

"I wasn't sure we still had a plan. You've been a little distant, yourself."

"Don't be ridiculous. I told you, we just needed to be careful. Jeremy's acting very strange lately. It's not like him to call in sick so often. Makes me wonder if it's an excuse to be away from the office."

"Doing what?"

"I don't know...."

Wallace dismissed her vague innuendos with a wave of his hand and shifted his gaze to her waist and the promised land below. "I thought you weren't concerned," he said, running a hand inside her thighs.

"I don't trust him, and you know I have my reasons."

His hand was nearly to her crotch. "You leave the numbers—and Jeremy—to me. We pass the underwriter's review, which we will, and we're home free. And I'll give you everything you need to destroy your husband."

"I want you by my side, Wallace."

"Count on it."

"Then humor me," she said, squeezing her legs together. "What news do you have? I need to know what Jeremy knows. I want to hear that we're making progress."

Wallace left his hand where she'd trapped it. "We're in good shape, trust me. But I don't want to talk business, not tonight."

He reached up with his free hand and made a move to unclasp the front of her bra, but Alina pushed his hand away. If it was hardball he wanted to play, so be it. She'd accommodated his childish obstinacy long enough. What she was about to do would send a signal that if he wanted her, he would have to play by *her* rules.

"Give me a second," she said, closing the front of her blouse. "And stay right where you are."

Escaping to the powder room with her handbag, she removed her cell phone and dialed Mack's number. "Five minutes," she whispered into the phone. If things were going well when she got the callback, she would ignore it. If not....

When she returned, Wallace had kicked off his shoes, removed his shirt and loosened the top of his trousers. She laid her bag on the coffee table. "Where were we?" she asked, snuggling into his arms. "Oh, yes, you were going to tell me about those phones."

The intensity of his response caught her off guard as he grabbed her by the shoulders, spun her around, and pulled her blouse over her head before she could mount an effective defense. She was about to protest when he pushed her bra straps off her shoulders and commanded that she "Get rid of this."

Alina convinced herself she was still in control, that the closer Wallace got to his objective, the more memorable the lesson she was about to impart. She unclasped her bra and Wallace attacked, biting her nipples, pushing her down, forcing his weight upon her. He moved to her stomach. "Lose these," he said, lifting her body off the couch as he tugged at her jeans. An order, not a request.

She'd been looking forward to having sex with Wallace tonight, and there'd been a time in their relationship when this kind of aggression turned her on. But this was more than alcohol at work, she could see, more than the actions of a man out for long-delayed sexual gratification. Wallace was out to make a point of his own, to assume the dominant position in their relationship. Her nostrils flared as she screamed to herself, *Come on, Mack. Where are you?*

She fumbled with her belt, stalling. When it came free, she pretended to tease Wallace with a playful fingering of the top button of her jeans. "I'm serious," she said. "I want to know what you've been—"

"Shut up!" He slapped her hand aside, undid the button and began pulling on her zipper. She pushed herself away and smiled flirtatiously, as if she were still playing hard to get.

Wallace was in no mood to play along. Grabbing at the waistline of her jeans, he yanked her back toward him. Alina pushed at his hand, but he batted it away with his fist, hurting her. He was now someone she didn't know, a man whose singular focus at that moment had nothing to do with romantic passion and everything to do with sex, power and the male ego. It was time to call a halt.

Slap him hard across his face if you have to, then scream so loudly he'll have to—they both froze.

"Let it go," Wallace said as Alina tried to reach for her phone.

"I can't," she hissed. *"It's Jeremy."*

Wallace sat up in disbelief as she pushed herself free of his weight. "He left a message this afternoon, said he might need to call me tonight. You've got me so distracted, I completely forgot."

She retrieved the phone from her handbag and checked the caller I.D. Confirming the caller's identity with a roll of her eyes directed at Wallace, she spoke quietly into the phone, pretending to be listening to the caller, then a minute later disconnected, shaking her head.

"This is terrible timing, Wallace, but you have to leave. Jeremy wants me to retrieve some personal papers from his office and then call him back. There's something he wants to discuss, and he's expecting to hear from me immediately."

She quickly retrieved her blouse, foregoing her bra. *Let him think about that.* "I can't talk to him with you here. He'll know something's up. He's on edge as it is."

Leaving Wallace with his mouth agape, she rushed out of the room to Jeremy's study where she grabbed a file she'd earlier placed on top of his desk. Maybe she hadn't been able to play Wallace the way she'd hoped tonight, not yet anyway, but at least for the moment she'd thwarted his crude attempt to put her in her place.

She hoped he'd agree to leave for a few minutes, calm down, and she could persuade him to come back. They could talk first, then make love, just as she'd planned all along—assuming he cooperated. The sooner this tug-of-war ended in her favor, the better.

Alina returned to the great room, and the color drained from her face. Wallace was staring at her cell phone, the cover flipped open.

"I have one just like this," he said.

Her throat tightened. Without thinking, she'd tossed the phone into her purse after Mack called, leaving it easily accessible to prying eyes.

Wallace flipped the cover down and returned the phone to her handbag. While she pretended to scan the contents of the bogus file, he dressed in silence, walked to the door, turned and waited.

He was looking at her differently now, a man wondering if he'd just been played for a fool. Expecting the question for which she had no answer, Alina decided against suggesting he return in a few minutes. She leaned in and kissed him lightly on the lips. "I'll make this up to you soon. I promise."

He did not kiss her back.

When he'd gone, she opened the phone and hit the caller ID key. First name up: *Mack Evans.*

She could make an excuse for that, if Wallace decided to call her on it when he'd sobered up. Say something about Mack having placed the call for Jeremy. She was even prepared to make something up and tell him what they'd talked about.

But if he'd scrolled down further, the call at 9:43 P.M. would be a lot harder to explain.

33.

The next morning, I got right to work on the financial statements. But by eleven my concentration was shot, and I knew why. Alina hadn't called, and I'd run out of patience.

On the third ring it occurred to me she might still be entertaining last night's guest—Wallace. I slipped into a foul mood that didn't dissipate when she answered and claimed she was about to call me.

"Just wanted to make sure you're all right," I said. "How'd it go?"

She told me what happened. "When I got back to the room, Wallace had my cell phone, and the top was flipped up."

I put down my coffee. "Did he say anything?"

"No. He's on his way to St. Louis now, as far as I know. I left an apology, told him it was just bad timing. I didn't say anything else."

This was hardly comforting news.

It was one thing for me to purposely get under Wallace's skin as I had at dinner, to pull his chain, make him wonder what I knew about his relationship with Alina. But it was another thing entirely to be calling her right after I left, leaving hard evidence that he now had reason to be suspicious of us both.

"Even if he saw my name on the caller ID," I said, "he won't say anything to Jeremy. Explaining his late-night presence at your home—*Jeremy's* home—would cause more problems for him than it would solve." I should know. "If he wants to let his imagination run wild, let him."

"And if he asks?"

"Tell him I hit the wrong number on my speed dial."

"You have me on speed dial?"

"No comment. But it sounds like the less contact we have with Wallace, the better. For both of us."

Was I concerned about lessening his suspicions, or did I simply not want him hanging around Alina? A little of both, if I were honest about it, but she brought up a point we couldn't ignore.

"He and I are supposed to be partners, you know. More than that, really."

I acted unperturbed. "You'll know how to handle it." I then asked if Wallace had mentioned Fort Smith.

"He knows you went, suspects you might have walked out with one of the cell phones. He didn't seem all that concerned."

Smug bastard.

"Are you on to something?" she asked.

I figured I owed her that much. "I've got some questions about the legitimacy of the inventory."

"And what do dashing forensic accountants do in such cases?"

If I weren't careful, flattery would get this woman everywhere. Still, one more crumb of information might cheer her up. "Does the name Billy Ray Hammonds ring a bell? He lives in the Spring River villas, on the north side of Palms Away."

"Let me think...yes, I think so. Stocky, big nose. And his wife's Mary or...?"

"—Millie. She died in a car accident a couple of years after they moved here."

"Yes, I remember. Such nice people. They helped me with a charity function a few years back. He has some heart issues, I think. I recall Millie saying something about that and worrying about his weight. Why do you ask?"

"He used to be a special agent with the FBI until the heart thing forced him into early retirement. With his background, he might be of some help, at least steer me in the right direction. I'm going to meet him for lunch at the house today."

That was enough. "Anything else we need to talk about? I've got to get ready for Billy Ray."

She paused. "I think Jeremy's keeping tabs on me, for what reason I'm not sure."

Tabs? As in secret cameras hidden throughout the house where I'd just had sex with his wife? Sound-activated tape recorders? Bugged phones?

"When did this start?"

"Right after your luncheon, he—"

"My God, that was over two weeks ago!"

"Take a deep breath, Rainey. The man he's got tailing me is on my side. That's how I know about all this."

It hit me that if I had evidence of anything, it was that Alina Whestin knew how to cover her pretty little tail. First Wallace, then me. And now she apparently had some P.I. doing her bidding, too. Mack Evans, maybe? Whoever he was, I wondered what perks came with *his* contract.

"Could he possibly know about Wallace and you?" I asked.

Alina sidestepped the question. "We just need to be careful. Right now I've got to think what I'm going to say to Wallace." She wished me good luck at lunch, blew a kiss into the phone and hung up.

It was mid-morning, but already I had a strong desire for a stiff drink. Or two. Something to lower my heart rate, dry up the sweat on my brow, and send me off to a nap where I wouldn't have to think about what this woman was doing to me.

In therapy, I'd been told I had a borderline addictive personality. It played out in the long hours I spent obsessing over what *had* to be foolproof investigations. I'd forgone vacations, passed on social outings that weren't tied to clients or prospects, put off work that needed to be done around the house.

I'd also been too busy to attend to Colleen's needs or visit my ailing mother in Florida. And as for reconciling with my father, I seldom gave it a thought. In the end, my love of the work, the void it filled, the order it brought to my life—or should have—led to an addiction of an entirely different kind.

Now, as I realized how much I didn't want Alina having anything to do with Wallace—or Jeremy or God knows how many others in her string of contingency partners—I wondered if my condition had resurfaced, this time in a far more dangerous form.

34.

Billy Ray arrived at noon, and we sat outside at the bar while the grill got hot.

My friend didn't talk about the "old days" very often, but I knew him to be a man of high character, his penchant for spending quality time with a single malt Scotch notwithstanding. I was certain he'd play it by the book.

We popped the tops on a couple of Coronas, and he asked about my shoulder.

I'd forgotten about that night at the club and felt like shit all over again. "Better," I said, then excused myself while I retrieved the hamburger patties from the refrigerator. When I returned, I handed Billy Ray the two pilfered cell phones.

"See anything different about these two?" I asked, seasoning the burgers.

He examined each. "Look about the same to me. Mostly some cosmetic differences. One's got a camera. Why?"

"You know anything about the guts of these things, the electronics?"

He looked at the phones again, one in each hand. "Difficult to trace, I know. No contract required. You can buy them with the minutes already loaded or add them afterwards. We can track them better these days, but it still requires a lot of coordination."

I noticed the use of the word "we." Once FBI, always FBI.

"These things run on different software technologies," he continued. "Complicated business. Mucho competition, domestic and foreign, but that's a little out of my league. I was mostly insurance fraud there at the end."

I nodded, playing it cool. "You hungry?"

Billy Ray patted his belly, and I threw the burgers on the grill, adjusted the heat and began sorting out the buns, condiments, chips and tomatoes. He stared at me with expectant eyes. "You going to tell me why all the interest in prepaid cell phones?"

"Research. I'm working for Whestin Group, did I tell you?"

He downed a swallow of his Corona. "No, you didn't tell me. How'd that come about?"

I waved it off as no big deal. "Jeremy mentioned something about it after our golf game, brought it up again at his party. Invited me to lunch at LaPlaya a couple of days later and told me he could use my help. Turns out they're going public in February, and they might have a little problem with one of their products."

"Meaning?"

My palms grew wet as I prepared my next lie.

"One of their divisions sells these phones by the boatload. Recently, a Southeast Asia manufacturer trying to get a foot in the door offered them a substantial price cut, but a sales rep suspects Whestin Group might have bought compromised merchandise."

"Counterfeit parts?" Billy Ray asked. "I hear they're good at that."

I grabbed a bottle of barbeque sauce and slathered a glob on each patty. "Or maybe pirated software. Without having to invest in technology, the bad guys don't need to recoup that cost, so they can sell competitive models at a deep discount. Anyway, I've had some experience in fraud investigations, including compromised inventory, and so here I am."

Billy Ray continued staring at the phones. I cleared my throat. "They're not ready to take this to the FBI and get all immersed in an investigation. Bad publicity with the IPO coming up. Which is where I come in. I'm quietly trying to assess the company's vulnerability to shenanigans."

Clouds moved across the sun, darkening the bar and Billy Ray's face. The burgers sizzled on the grill, and I gave them a too-quick flip.

"Let's see," he said, "Jeremy Whestin lives in Palms Away, and so do you. He's got a company we've all heard is in some trouble. Decides to hire a fraud investigator and, voilà, there you are, just down the street, nothing but time on your hands, looking to make 'contacts,' as you called it. What are the odds, huh?"

I rotated the burgers a quarter turn. "You got a problem with that?"

"Maybe I do. And maybe I especially don't like to think what he'd do if he found you messing around with his wife."

I flinched, and my spatula clattered to the floor. When I bent down to retrieve it, my back went into spasm, and it was all I could do to bend myself upright and affect an air of mild disinterest.

Billy Ray was a notorious needler but always in fun. I never saw him intentionally try to get under someone's skin—as he appeared to be doing now. "What does that mean?"

He looked down, likely disappointed in both the dishonesty of my response and recent behavior. "That night when you told me about your shoulder, you looked pretty down. Didn't sound like yourself. Kind of gave me the brush-off, as a matter of fact."

"Sorry about that," I mumbled. "I'd had a bad year that day."

"Uh-huh. Anyway, when I left you, I went out to the patio, ordered a sandwich and a beer. A little later, about to go home, I'm thinking maybe you could use some cheering up. I started to go back inside, and that's when I saw you leave. You remember where you went?"

I didn't remember being followed that night, but then, I hadn't been thinking about sneaking away to screw Jeremy Whestin's wife. I was just doing my job. At least that had been my plan. A nifty new tag line for the residential sales staff leaped to mind. *Palms Away, where all secrets are eventually exposed.*

"You need some food in your stomach," I said, flipping two medium rare patties onto a platter. We made our sandwiches, neither one talking for several minutes.

"You don't have to tell me what you were doing at Alina Whestin's house—

at night," Billy Ray said, breaking the silence. "It's none of my business. But as a friend, I'll feel better when you're clear of this thing. And remember, the FBI isn't in the habit of issuing warnings."

"You're *former* FBI. You're my friend now."

"Then maybe you should listen to your friend."

We finished lunch, neither of us saying much. Billy Ray pushed aside his plate and picked up one of the phones.

"Like I told you," he said, "I'm no expert, but there are lots of ways to screw with these things. The system software could be duplicated without permission, of course. Then you got your semiconductors, integrated circuits, flash memory chips—a whole bunch of technology I bet could be copied pretty easily."

I was right to be suspicious—it's what I'd been hired to be—but unless these phones could be analyzed by experts, there was no way to know if they were legal or not. "How would the FBI investigate something like that?" I asked, wishing I had the nerve to add "quietly."

Billy Ray gave me a quick glance, downed the last of his beer and pushed the phones in my direction. "I've got friends in the department that owe me favors, but...."

His hesitation said it all. He'd help me if I pushed him, but he'd rather not. "Thanks," I said. "I'm just exploring possibilities."

One of which was that these phones weren't counterfeit or didn't contain pirated software. Despite Jeremy's attempt to head me off at the Fort Smith pass, maybe all this really was as simple as a supplier willing to cut his prices to get into the U.S. market. But to look into it further, to get the FBI involved officially or otherwise, would put the wrong kind of spotlight on Whestin Group, the last thing *anybody* wanted.

"Any more questions?" Billy Ray asked. "Because I've got one of my own."

"The floor is yours."

He adjusted his frame on the barstool. "You remember working with Grayson Automotive Systems?"

As my seared ground beef flipped in my stomach, I could see that inviting my former FBI buddy to lunch had been a very bad idea.

35.

"Grayson was one of my clients," I said. "Why?"

"Were you the point person?"

The words hung in the humid air like an anvil suspended over my hapless head. "You could say that. Why?"

Billy Ray rubbed a hand across his chin. "Seems the Bureau has its eyes on your Mr. Whestin, mostly related to fraud connected with that sale of Grayson. Did you know that?"

"What do you mean, 'fraud'?"

"Suspected fraud. The new owners believe the books must have been cooked before the sale—assets overstated, liabilities understated. Something. They never got the P&L results for which they'd paid a handsome price."

He grabbed his reading glasses from his shirt pocket and pulled a crumpled note from his pocket. "Close to forty-five million, says here."

"How do you know all this?" I scanned the shelf under the bar for anything that could serve as a barf bag.

Billy Ray stuffed the note back into his pocket. "I'm doing some extra set of eyes and ears work for my old partner, Anthony Crain—Tony. We worked together in New York. He's heading up the Fort Myers field office now. What are the odds, huh?"

"You're tailing Jeremy?" He was headed somewhere I didn't want to go, and the anticipation prickled my skin.

"Kind of a know-nothing assignment, really," he said. "Throwin' a bone to an old dog. By coincidence, I was at LaPlaya the day you two met for lunch."

I reached for my beer. Coincidence? No such thing.

"I didn't see you."

"Didn't want you to."

What's the big deal? I wanted to ask, but I didn't trust my voice. My heart was beating like a metronome set on max speed.

"Anyway," he said, "after Grayson changed hands, it took the new owners two years to figure out something wasn't right and then a few months more to decide what to do about it. The market was beginning to soften by then, which I guess made it harder to know what really was going on. They wasted another six months working with an accounting firm to try to get to the bottom of things but ran out of patience and money. I guess you know how that is."

"They couldn't find *anything?*"

"You sound surprised. You certified those books, right?"

Watch it, you idiot, I screamed at myself, then choked out an explanation that maybe it had all just been a case of bad timing. "This isn't the best of times for anyone associated with the car business, you know."

Billy Ray shrugged. "You might be right. In any event, one of the owners is friends with a prosecutor in the United States Attorney's Office. Given the amount of money involved, it took just one call to set the wheels in motion."

Something didn't make sense. "Whestin Group is based in St. Louis," I said. "So is Grayson. Even if evidence of fraud is discovered, wouldn't the new owners be looking at filing a civil suit?"

I'd participated in dozens of local fraud cases in Chicago, prosecuted under state law. I knew there would have to be extenuating circumstances of a serious nature to warrant the involvement of the FBI. I normally wasn't a heavy perspirer, but my shirt was so drenched, I thought maybe I'd left the burners on. I hadn't.

The wall-mounted temperature gauge behind me registered ninety degrees with humidity approaching sixty per cent: warm, but fairly typical for a September afternoon in Naples. I grabbed an extra napkin and mopped my brow.

Billy Ray, I noticed, was flapping the front of his shirt.

"You forget," he said. "Grayson's new owners are headquartered in Cleveland. If fraud was involved, and communications between the two parties included information related to the sale—information later proved to be false or intentionally misleading—you could be looking at mail fraud, or fraud by wire if emails were used. Federal offenses.

"And that's not all. The owners got a phone call from an anonymous source who told them to start looking inside their manufacturing facilities."

"Grayson was always a tough client for me," I interrupted. "Very technical business. Design, grinding, welding, fabrication—"

"And subassembly work," Billy Ray interjected. "In this case, related to automotive transmissions. According to the informant, one of the parts that comprised this subassembly was stolen. One hundred thousand of them, stored pretty as you please at Grayson's warehouse outside of Chicago, where they were then shipped to St. Louis for assembly."

I remembered certifying the value of Grayson's various parts inventories, but I'd had no reason to suspect then that any of it was hot. At the end, my sole concentration—if I could call it that—had been reviewing Grayson's books and preparing a case that presented a financially attractive picture. Unfortunately, my case may well have been built on tainted numbers—surprise, surprise.

My sweat glands accelerated to overdrive, but the blood in my veins suddenly ran cold. If I'd been doing my job the way I'd been trained to, I might have checked that inventory, but would it have mattered? Would I have found a way to overlook that, too?

"We're just getting started on this," Billy Ray said, "but we could, at the very least, be looking at an ITSP case."

Interstate Transportation of Stolen Property. A Federal offense. Enter the FBI.

Billy Ray pulled the top of his shirt away from his body and gave it a couple more flaps. I thought about suggesting we move inside, but I didn't want to prolong this ordeal. Billy Ray apparently did.

He got up from his seat and pointed to the loggia. "Let's sit under the fans." When he'd settled into an oversize wicker love seat, he asked how well I knew Wallace Gerard.

Before today, the question would have merely raised my curiosity. But now, it felt like one more nail in my coffin.

"We've talked a time or two," I said, standing at the edge of the loggia. "Why?"

"We've got a file on him, too."

"Grayson?"

"Partly. But he—and Mr. Whestin—could be up to their ears in shit for something far more serious. And so, by association, could you."

"Wait a minute. I'm just checking over their books and responding to special requests. That's all."

My friend drummed his fingers on the side of the love seat.

"Right after you left LaPlaya," he said, "I called Tony, told him what I saw. Sorry 'bout that, partner, but I was concerned for you. I did warn you, remember? Anyway, turns out I was a little late. Our Chicago office already had you on their radar screen. They sent Tony a full report, and he shared it with me a couple of days ago because he knew you and I were friends."

A burst of white heat sprinted up my spine. To their list of Islamic militants, hardened criminals and God knows who else, the Federal Bureau of Investigation now had a file on one Rainey J. McDermott, retired accountant, recovering addict.

Billy Ray tugged on an ear lobe. "Tony thought you might be able to shed some light on all this, given you apparently resigned your firm to handle Grayson's books personally. He asked me to ask you if you wouldn't mind talking to him."

I felt what I thought was a raindrop and looked heavenward. But it wasn't rain. It was the sweat of a guilt ridden man.

Somewhere, tucked away in a private safe, Jeremy kept a second set of Grayson's books—the real ones, he'd said. The ones he claimed would nail me to the cross if I did something stupid. From the day he'd leveled his blackmail threat, I'd wondered about that second set of books. Would they alone constitute evidence I'd been a part of a conspiracy to mislead the prospective new owners? Could I argue my way around that with the help of a savvy lawyer?

I hadn't, in truth, ever seen evidence of fraud in Grayson's books because I wasn't looking for it. The hard work had been done by someone else—Wallace, most likely. Which wouldn't be a good thing, either, if the FBI discovered evidence I'd missed but should have caught.

Part of me wanted to chuck the whole thing and ask Billy Ray to escort me to Tony's office. But I had no evidence to use as a bargaining chip. All I'd do is call more attention to myself, with no guarantee anyone would go to jail—except possibly me.

Plead ignorance, I decided. "I don't remember much about the Grayson assignment. I was a cokehead back then, lucky to be alive. I'm not proud to admit it, but I freelanced that job so I wouldn't have to share my fee."

We stared at each other for a moment, long enough for me to remember the call from Paul Banefield. I asked how long the "investigation" had been going on.

"A couple of months," Billy Ray said. "Tony's got his hands full with other cases right now, so there's nothing official at the moment. He just wants to talk, see what you know. I couldn't tell you all this stuff about an investigation with you maybe being a part of it if he hadn't given me the okay."

He got up and stood next to me, his gaze across the pond. "Maybe you're being tailed, too," he said.

I turned and spotted a figure of indistinguishable age and sex leaning lightly against a culvert. He—or she?—wore a dark green nylon windbreaker zipped neck high and long pants that looked like those Gore-Tex weatherproof jobbies professional golfers wear on foul weather days.

At this distance and with binoculars covering his face, I couldn't discern any distinguishing physical features, especially since whoever this was had pulled the bill of an electric blue ball cap down low on his forehead. Alina's comment about Jeremy keeping tabs on her flashed through my mind. Had the scope of surveillance widened?

"A handful of people come back here to check out the occasional sunbathing alligator," I said. "Or to bird watch. Blue heron, egrets, ibis. Even saw an eagle fly over one day. But whoever that is has got to be roasting in that get-up."

Billy Ray removed his sunglasses and squinted at the figure. "I wouldn't be too concerned," he said. "A professional would dress to fit in—'hide in plain sight,' we call it. Maybe it's one of those widow ladies scoping you out."

Seconds later, the figure turned and disappeared. Billy Ray shrugged and headed for the door. I touched his arm. "What did your FBI buddy tell you about Wallace Gerard?"

He snapped his fingers, as if I'd just reminded him of something he'd forgotten to mention. "You do any work in money laundering?"

"I ran across it a few times." I thought of my conversation with Wallace and the private equity firm in France. Did Billy Ray know about that, too?

"Good," he said. "We've got nothing concrete, just suspicions. Maybe you'll come across something helpful."

We got to the front door and shook hands. "What should I tell Tony?" Billy Ray asked.

"Can he give me a week?"

He nodded. "I'll tell him. He's maybe looking at you as a cooperating witness down the road. Wait too long and…like I said, the FBI doesn't issue warnings."

But Billy Ray just had. I thanked him without specifying for what. I figured he knew.

He drove off, and I slumped against the door. That Whestin Group had likely doctored its financials was one thing. Selling illegal merchandise to boost its bottom line was no small matter, either, especially if the parts in question were in any way defective and thus dangerous.

But money laundering?

I started to shiver, and I knew it had little to do with stepping out of the heat and humidity and into the air conditioning. My investigation had just taken on a new urgency. There was now a lot more work to do and, according to Billy Ray, it wouldn't be long before the hot breath of the FBI began scorching the back of my neck in earnest.

36.

I headed for the dining room and the growing stack of folders I'd created. It took me a minute, but I located the entry for the private placement on the August balance sheet.

My questions were obvious: If Whestin Group was involved in money laundering, were they laundering their own funds, somehow obtained from their own illegal operations? If so, it might take the resources of the entire FBI and the Treasury Department to expose it, especially if highly secretive offshore banking entities were involved.

Or, I asked myself, was the company laundering funds for someone else?

If that was the case, it didn't take much of a leap to point the finger at Links International and the millions they'd just agreed to pour into a shaky Whestin Group in the middle of what was shaping up to be a severe recession. Maybe a deeper look would turn up other suspects, but I didn't have that kind of time.

Even so, suspicions weren't evidence, and while I might have my doubts about Links International, what was I supposed to do with them?

I was about to google the company when a chime sounded on my computer, alerting me to an email from Jeremy. He was returning to Florida next Friday, the message read, and he wanted to set up a meeting the following day.

Then my phone rang. Busy day—and an interesting coincidence: a call from Alina. "Jeremy just called," she said. "He's returning Friday."

"I know. I just got the email. Details to follow."

"He's taking you to a gun range in east Naples."

"Say again?"

I hadn't shot a gun since nailing a robin with a friend's air rifle when I was thirteen. I'd had nightmares for weeks.

"Another of his many intimidation tactics," Alina said. "Let's just say he wants to reinforce the importance of staying on the straight and narrow. He figures to reinforce the message by showing you how good a shot he is."

Or maybe, I thought, Jeremy had just learned about the FBI's interest in him—and he wanted to assure my lips were sealed. Accidents do happen.

"You think he'd shoot me if he found out I'm thinking of double-crossing him? Oh, and by the way, conspiring with his wife, to boot?" I left unsaid the *sleeping with* part.

"I'd put nothing past him."

"That's reassuring."

"Enough. How was your lunch with Mr. Hammonds?"

"I was going to call you, remember?"

"Sorry. I'm feeling a little neglected these days—unless you count Jeremy spying on me."

Alarm bells rang in both ears. Who was spying on who? Or whom? I could never get that straight.

What a lovely marriage these two had. More to the point, if Alina now had Jeremy's spy working for *her*, maybe I was under surveillance, too, at least until she was absolutely sure I was on her side. Reassurance I wanted to give her but couldn't just yet.

For all my roiling emotions, I knew nothing about this woman except what she'd told me. Had, in fact, already taken things far beyond professional decorum. I could clam up, I decided, or try to induce her to provide information I might not otherwise get. Of course, I'd tried that approach with Billy Ray on the boat and look where *that* got me.

Billy Ray said he wasn't sure, but thought it would be fairly easy to counterfeit the hardware on those cell phones," I said. "Or pirate the software that runs it. He's offered to call in a favor, get the experts in the Bureau to lend some assistance. All on the QT, of course. I think I'm going to give him the go-ahead."

A long pause. "You don't need to pursue this, do you—except to impress Jeremy?"

"It's in my blood."

"I don't know. If you won't have anything in time for your meeting, anyway, maybe you could take a few extra days to think about this."

"Don't worry. I trust my buddy."

Alina's reluctance to involve Billy Ray and the FBI was understandable but nothing that would imply she knew more than she was letting on. Like the fact that her husband and Wallace were the subject of an FBI probe. Or that I was, too, and might soon be testifying against both of them to save my own sorry ass.

"Look," I said, "I understand that blackmailing Jeremy at the height of his success might prove personally satisfying, but if the underwriter or the SEC or some disgruntled employee somehow found something they shouldn't, something I missed—let's just say that from my perspective, the sooner you force Jeremy to give up his stock, the better. And garnering Billy Ray's help might be one of the ways to make that happen."

"And, by the way, ask Jeremy to drop his threat to expose your past?"

"That would be nice, but I'd think he'd do that, anyway. I mean, what would be the point?"

"For Jeremy, you're probably right. As for me, I guess it would depend on just what I was getting, given the public offering wouldn't have happened yet."

Good point, but... "I thought this was about revenge."

She paused again. "You're right. Do what you think best."

When Jeremy had leveled his threat, my first instinct had been to tackle the assignment head-on, see what I could find, then take my evidence to the FBI, consequences be damned. But did that make sense? Was that "best"?

The money Jeremy promised could set me up for good this time, if I was more careful with it. And Alina, like Jeremy, had promised me an opportunity to stay on at Whestin Group and put the books back on firm footing. Where Wallace would fit into all this was a topic for another day. I didn't have to make my decision this minute—go to the FBI, stake my future on Alina, or turn my back on both of them and trust Jeremy—but that day of reckoning was fast approaching.

"How about dinner tonight?" I asked, well aware that over the past few years I'd thrown caution to the wind more times than I'd tossed grass into the air on the golf course to see which way the wind was blowing. If I wanted to see Alina again—and I *did* want to see her—I'd take my chances. Besides, she had a private eye watching over us. Maybe Mack Evans or maybe somebody else, but at least someone who was watching out for Alina and who would have put me, at her direction, on the "all clear" list. For now anyway.

"Sounds wonderful," she said. "What should I wear?"

An opening. Should I take it this time?

The light bulb had come on as I'd headed for my dinner with Billy Ray Tuesday night. I'd thought about calling Alina when I got home, offer my apologies for missing her much-appreciated signals. But I talked myself out of it. What if I'd been wrong? It wasn't even that I wanted to get into phone sex with her now or any sex at all, but my lack of sexual "awareness" the other night still left me feeling like a blockhead.

"I dunno," I said. "What are you wearing now?"

Her response was immediate. "Are you mocking me, or is this your version of foreplay?"

Nothing wrong with *Alina's* sexual antennae. "Neither. I just thought—"

"Then aren't you forgetting something?"

"Pardon?"

"I call the shots. And right now, *dinner* sounds lovely."

Touché.

We settled on a nearby steak and lobster joint and agreed on a time. Alina said she preferred to meet me there, which meant we weren't going to end the evening at either of our homes except by an invitation I wasn't going to extend and which I knew I shouldn't accept if offered.

It was times like this, when I was about to succumb to the craving, sweating one moment, chilled to the bone the next, that I was supposed to call for support. But that had been for cocaine, a hell I'd never once in the past four years ever really seriously considered revisiting.

What, then, was this?

37.

Through the condo's kitchen window Victoria spotted a cardinal perched on the back deck railing, taunting her with its scarlet body and black face. She'd wanted to go bird watching with Jeremy during this latest three-week visit, but it had never happened. Now it was Friday, September 26, and he was heading back to Florida again.

Not that the two of them had done anything particularly exciting while they'd been together. He'd been immersed in IPO details nearly every day, getting to the office as early as his health would permit, arriving home often past eight at night, several times too exhausted or ill to even join her for dinner.

Last weekend, she'd cooked in every night, but he hadn't exhibited much of an appetite. The rest of the time they'd spent reading together or watching movies. Sunday he'd gamely agreed to walk with her along the nature trail behind the condo, but an especially violent headache nixed that.

No matter, they'd been together, and that was all that mattered.

The red bird flew off, as Jeremy would be doing soon in a couple of hours. He promised he'd return right after McDermott gave him the thumbs up or down next Thursday. He was heading back now, he explained, because he wanted the two of them to meet ahead of time so he could lay some intimidation on the man, to succeed where Wallace had failed. At least that was the reason he'd given her. She prayed he was telling her the truth.

She spotted his vest pocket travel valet on the kitchen counter next to his car keys, sunglasses and briefcase. By force of habit, she checked to see that it included his airline tickets, license, and reading glasses. Before he walked out the door, she would make sure he also had his wallet, cell phone and pills. Especially his pills.

Jeremy's voice carried in from the study where he was finishing up a few last minute calls. Pushing aside her fears and suspicions, she pulled open the top drawer of the kitchen desk and removed the card she'd picked up yesterday at the Hallmark store.

"Thinking of you…" the outside said. The personal note inside, more sentimental than most she'd left him, expressed how much he meant to her and how she would count the seconds until his return. Mushy, but so what? She was a woman, and she'd remained resolute far longer than most would have.

His briefcase was locked, but she knew the combination, since for most of the past two years she'd been the one to organize his trip materials, even labeling his folders with colored tabs. She clicked the numbers into place, opened the lid and tucked the card halfway down the top pocket.

By habit Victoria straightened the folders Jeremy was taking with him, each related to the pubic offering. She gave them a quick scan, stopping at a thin, unmarked file near the bottom. Had she forgotten to label one for him? That wasn't like her, and especially now he deserved her very best.

A quick, silent rebuke to herself accompanied the opening of the file. Inside she found a letter from Jeremy addressed to the board of directors. She read it twice, then a third time before she doubled over and slid to the floor, her stomach cramping as if she'd just got The Curse.

The letter, not yet signed, was dated Monday, October 13, the week after the decision was to be made on an underwriter. It stated that Jeremy desired to sign over his stock to Mrs. Alina Marie Whestin, effectively immediately.

Jeremy was the sole stockholder and could do whatever he wanted with his stock. This letter was just a formality—and a concrete way, she guessed, to show his wife that this was no empty promise. It referenced health concerns and the need to get this change in stock assignment as well as leadership out in the public as far ahead of the IPO as possible. It included several references to Jack Armbruster's experience and capabilities.

Victoria didn't recognize the initials of the person who'd typed the letter. Nor did she fully understand what this decision meant for Whestin Group's future. But as far as what it likely meant for her, personally, there could be little doubt. Unless…wasn't it possible that Jeremy might be offering his stock as a peace offering to Alina for telling her he wanted a divorce? Yes, surely dear God, it *was* possible.

But did it make sense? Would Jeremy need to give his wife *all* of his stock? And why didn't he propose to his lover first? Or at least discuss his plans with her? Was he that cocksure of himself?

Jeremy walked in, saw the open briefcase. He knelt beside her and took the letter from her hand. "We have a lot to discuss, Vicky. I promise we will when I return."

The blood rushed from her head as she straightened and grabbed his arm. "Just tell me, is this good news for us or not?"

He gave her a comforting smile, but it smacked more of a ploy than a sincere effort to calm her down. She saw no reassurance in his leaden eyes, no indication that this was just a misunderstanding, that he still loved her and would make everything right.

For a moment she saw herself on the cover of *Star* magazine, tears staining her mascara, Jeremy trailing at a distance, a hand shading his face from the paparazzi, the two of them cowering beneath a headline that read, "Betrayed!"

The breath suddenly rushed from her diaphragm as if a mugger had elbowed her, and she staggered towards the hall bathroom. Jeremy reached for her hand, but she pulled away, barely making it to the toilet before she vomited.

When she had nothing left to spit up but bile, she returned to the kitchen. Jeremy was gone, the spot where his briefcase had been now replaced by a note. *Don't do anything stupid.* Victoria shook her head. She already had.

She picked up a notepad from the kitchen counter and made out a quick shopping list. First item: a bottle of Jack Daniels for the long weekend ahead.

38.

By 7:30 P.M., I couldn't keep my eyes from crossing after three more hours of poring over Whestin Group's numbers. What a way to spend a Friday night.

Bad enough what our politicians were doing to perforate my intestines. Last Saturday the Treasury Department submitted draft legislation to Congress for authority to purchase billions of dollars worth of "troubled" bank assets. The next day the Federal Reserve granted a request by Goldman Sachs and Morgan Stanley, the nation's last two remaining investment banks, to change their status to bank holding companies.

But scariest of all was President Bush holding a prime-time television address Wednesday to urge Congress to quickly pass the Treasury's bailout bill. What did he know that the rest of us didn't? Was the whole world about to collapse?

And yet for all of that and the impact it was having on my dwindling stock portfolio, I had more pressing concerns, beyond even the ones raised by Billy Ray over my involvement in the sale of Grayson Automotive Systems.

Like the FBI's interest in my current employer—and me.

Like Wallace and the possibility that somehow, money laundering was involved in Whestin Group's operations.

On top of which, tomorrow afternoon I'd be on the firing line with my blackmailer, whose intent would be "intimidation." As if I needed any.

I couldn't face another minute of reviewing Whestin Group's financial documents, but I wasn't in the mood to sit around and fret. I flipped open my phone and dialed information, rationalizing again, as I had so many times before in my career, that for all my accounting expertise, for all my forensic experience, suspicions and skepticism, I couldn't count on coming up with evidence of fraud on my own within the timeframe allowed. I needed someone to squeal.

"City and state, please," the recorded voice intoned.

"St. Louis County, Missouri."

"What listing?"

"Victoria Laine."

An operator came on the line. "I have a listing for a V. Laine on Dogwood Court."

"Any others?"

"No, sir."

I called the number and got "V. Laine's" answering machine. After introducing myself, I left a message I figured she couldn't ignore.

"I'm trying to reach a Victoria Laine who works for Whestin Group. If I've reached the right number, I'd like to talk with you confidentially, by tomorrow morning at the latest. Again, I stress this is confidential."

If this didn't bear fruit, I'd move on to the next name on my "sweat" list. Someone in the Whestin Group food chain knew something, a potential shortcut to answers I needed and didn't have much time to uncover. It was a long shot, but I'd been on the job three weeks and now had just one week left before informing Jeremy of what I'd found—or hadn't.

His assistant might well break a leg in her haste to tell her boss that I'd called. But to get a call like that from a fraud investigator, on a Friday night, might catch her just enough off guard to give me an opening. I had no idea where it might lead, or how Jeremy might react if he found out, but Victoria Laine was worth a shot.

Bad choice of words.

Tomorrow I'd be playing cowboys and Indians with the CEO of Whestin Group at a gun range in east Naples. And I'd be the Indian.

The next day dawned ideal for an outing at the gun range, I thought. Gentle breeze, a little humid but no rain. I'd spotted two Mourning Doves perched on the gutter above the garage and vaguely recalled something about their *coos* meaning someone had just died. I hadn't thought much about it at the time, which made me wonder why I was thinking about it now, an hour before Jeremy would be loading his .44.

I pulled into the club parking lot ten minutes before he was to pick me up, then walked to the porte cochère and waited. At exactly noon, as specified, Jeremy arrived, driving his black Mercedes. It reminded me of a well-appointed hearse as I opened the passenger door and got in.

He was on his phone, talking via a hands-free headset. I couldn't tell who was on the other end, but Jeremy sounded irritated. We were almost to the I-75 exit, a fifteen-minute drive, by the time the call ended. He yanked off the headset. "That guy gets on my nerves, you know? How's he been to work with?"

No *"Good to be back in Florida, how have you been, what are you up to, how's the golf game?"* And, thank God, no *"How's my wife?"*

I guessed he'd been talking to Wallace. "No problem, so far."

"He thinks having you check his work is an affront to his manhood. A waste of time and money."

That Wallace might be pissed—even vindictive—didn't surprise me, especially if he'd seen my name on Alina's caller ID. But I also hadn't come up with concrete evidence of fraud. *I told you so,* I could hear him saying.

"And that's not all," Jeremy said. "He thinks you're interested in my wife."

He stared straight ahead, his face reflecting no emotion behind his sunglasses. His hands held the steering wheel in the relaxed manner of a man who knew he had a solution for every problem—and enjoyed watching the people who caused it guess what it was.

"He hasn't come right out and said it in so many words," Jeremy said, "but he's dropping hints. Weird, huh? Unless, of course, you've been sneaking around behind my back."

I looked directly at him. "Definitely weird," I said, deciding that the less I protested, the better. Still, it set my teeth on edge to think that Jeremy's question might be the result of Wallace's justified paranoia and jealousy. I wanted to put my fist through the windshield.

He said nothing for several minutes, then, "If anyone is interested in my wife, Rainey, it's Wallace. Don't ask why I have my suspicions, but I don't trust him. You know that."

As he massaged his right temple, I was reminded of the nonsensical sentence he'd uttered that day at LaPlaya. "Headache?" I asked, gathering my thoughts.

"Head*aches*. Guess I was a little naïve when it came to this IPO business."

"How's it going?"

"Maybe *you* should answer that question."

I thought about just how much I should tell him at this stage. It irked the hell out of me that Wallace was sitting up there in St. Louis confident he'd defeated my best efforts—and maybe he had. What I'd uncovered in the books so far hardly warranted a five million dollar payoff. And as for the cell phones, it was all conjecture at this point.

But forget Wallace. What had *Jeremy* expected of me? Call it pride or just being pragmatic, I didn't want him second-guessing his decision. Time for a no-answer answer, the same one I gave Wallace.

"Everything your accountants, the underwriter and the SEC are going to want to see is all there, neat and tidy. But just to be sure, I'm looking a layer deeper than the norm."

"So you're ready to throw in the towel?"

I thought about the call I'd made last night to Ms. Laine. Throw in the towel? Not yet.

"I'm in the process of wrapping up. You'll have my report on your desk the end of next week, as promised."

"Nothing in writing. You have something to say, you say it to me directly."

I assured him I would, but at this point, it looked like we were heading for a very short meeting.

A few more miles down I-75, Jeremy took the Marco Island exit east. A series of turns and bends later, we were on a dirt road that led to a long wooden structure with a dusty, corrugated metal roof. I heard the reverberation of pistols and the occasional *crack!* of rifle fire from behind a building that looked as if it had been around since the days of Wild Bill Hickok.

We pulled into a parking spot between two late model pickups with gun racks clearly visible through the back window. "Too bad I couldn't talk Alina into joining us," Jeremy said. "She's the shooter in the family."

He opened the trunk and pulled out a stainless steel gun case. "First we buy ammo, then we kill some targets."

"Can't wait," I said, my thoughts drifting to his wife, a woman of many and varied talents.

39.

It was only four in the afternoon, but Alina was ready for a drink

"It's 5 o'clock somewhere," she muttered, trying to keep her mind off what Rainey might have had to endure at the gun range—and what it was Jeremy wanted to talk about when he got home.

He'd arrived from St. Louis yesterday, immediately taken a nap, spent the rest of the day on the phone and then surprised her by announcing he wanted to grill salmon steaks for dinner.

"You're in charge of the wine," he'd said, giving her a kiss on the cheek that made her skin crawl.

For an appetizer she'd prepared chilled shrimp with rémoulade, which they ate at the outside bar as Jeremy prepared the grill. The sun had sunk just below the horizon by the time they sat down to eat, leaving the sky a mix of brilliant yellows and oranges, with touches of rose and robin's egg blue. She could easily make out Venus in the southwestern sky.

In any other circumstance, Alina would have appreciated the romantic possibilities, but this was Jeremy. She despised the man. Fortunately, he got another severe headache that shortened the evening, forestalling an awkward bedroom encounter. He'd apologized, as if he were letting her down.

"After my session with Rainey tomorrow," he said, "I need to talk to you," then he disappeared into the cabana. He didn't leave this morning until it was time to pick up Rainey.

Alina grabbed a handful of ice cubes from the kitchen icemaker and dropped them into her vodka tonic. She was about to head for the lanai when she heard the garage door open.

Ninety minutes on the range with Rainey McDermott, firing both his service revolver and the big .44, had left her husband exhausted, she guessed. What resembled a ring of ash encircled his eyes, and there was a slight forward bend to his posture. It looked as if it hurt to turn his head.

"I'll be back in a minute," he said, heading for his study. He said nothing about his time with Rainey.

A moment later, he returned to the kitchen with a manila folder. Alina noted that he hadn't bothered to shave that morning, something he never neglected, even on weekends.

"You don't look well," she said, glancing at the kitchen clock. She'd made reservations at a restaurant in Naples, the plan being to meet friends from St. Louis first for drinks, then move on to dinner. Something told her they would be dining at home tonight, if at all.

Jeremy rested his elbows on the glass tabletop and massaged both temples. "I have brain cancer," he said, as if telling her he'd caught a cold. "Inoperable."

Alina waited for him to smile, an indication that he'd just made a very bad joke. When he continued to stare at the folder, she waited for him to amplify his absurd statement, clarify what he really meant. A number of times lately he'd said things that hadn't made sense.

But Jeremy sat quietly at the kitchen table and as the impact of his words ricocheted around her skull, a seething rage welled up in her chest.

Not because the man she'd once hoped would erase the emotional void in her life had turned out to be such a bastard.

Not even because Jeremy's impending death was a reminder of how much of her own life she'd wasted.

But because any attempt to humiliate him following the public offering would now have little meaning and certainly no lasting impact. He'd taken away even that.

Jeremy raised his eyes and from the look on his face she could see neither hope nor fear but simple resignation. He was dying, and neither of them could do anything about it.

"How long?"

"Maybe a year. Maybe a lot less."

"What have they told you about—"

Jeremy let loose with a string of expletives and began slamming an open palm against his forehead, over and over until a red welt appeared above his right eye.

Alina took hold of his arm and held it tight against her side. "What about treatment?"

"I told you, the fucking thing's inoperable. They could try to remove what they see, but I could wake up an imbecile. Besides, they can't get it all. It'll come back. They're giving me something for the pain, but that's about it."

"How long have you known?"

"A few months. I got a second opinion, but the diagnosis was the same. The pills were a help at first, but now...." He stopped and rubbed his head against Alina's side.

"Does any one know?" she asked, not bothering to ask why he'd taken so long to tell her. She thought he was about to give her a name, but he fell silent and shook his head. She wasn't buying it.

"I'll have to make a public announcement soon," he said, "convince everyone that the company's in capable hands with Jack. Hardly the news we want coming out ahead of our public offering, but it is what it is." He motioned for her to take a seat.

Alina complied as Jeremy removed a single typewritten sheet of Whestin Group stationery from the folder and handed it to her. She forced her eyes away from her husband's tormented face and read the document at normal speed. After reading it a second time, more slowly, concentrating on each word, she placed the letter on the table.

By God, she thought, she *would* get something for all the pain she'd suffered, for all the wrongs that had been done to her—and she wouldn't have to lift a finger to get it.

What had she told Rainey? That this wasn't about the money? *Bullshit.* In the end, it was always about money. And power, of course. Which meant the public offering still had to go through but now for a very different reason.

"I'm going to call Rainey," Jeremy said, fumbling for his Blackberry. "We spent the afternoon together and never confirmed a time for our meeting next week." He gave her a wry smile. "I must be losing my mind."

Alina reached across the table and squeezed Jeremy's hand. The gesture summoned a wan smile. "Maybe we could take a boat ride this weekend," he said. "It's been a long time."

She nodded and watched silently as her husband placed his call, relieved he didn't explode when Rainey failed to answer. But her thoughts weren't on her dying husband; they were on the man he was trying to reach.

Everything now rested on Rainey McDermott's decision to cooperate. When—not if—he found evidence of fraud, there would be no IPO if he decided to go to the FBI instead of to Jeremy or to her. She needed to improve the odds, scare some sense into him. Or at least remove one of his weapons.

Her thoughts drifted to Billy Ray Hammonds.

As good a place to start as any, she decided. Better, actually.

The man had a heart condition.

40.

I thanked the flight attendant and squeezed into my seat, amazed at the events of the past twenty-four hours.

Late last night, following my Saturday afternoon at the firing range with Jeremy, I'd received a strange call from Victoria Laine. Her words had been slurred, as if she were drunk. She'd agreed to meet me, she said, thick-tongued as if she were drunk, but only if I got to St. Louis immediately. Borderline belligerent, she added, "And don't try scarin' me about being involved in some questionable shit. I'm plenty involved, and somebody's gonna regret it."

Promising I'd meet her deadline, I'd packed for an overnight stay and driven to the airport early this morning to put myself on standby for a flight to St. Louis that would have me landing mid-afternoon.

Two seats had come available, and I didn't mind that I'd been assigned the middle seat in the last row. I was on my way to meet with Jeremy Whestin's secretary, in her condo, on a Sunday afternoon. No intimidation from surrounding office workers—or from Jeremy. Exactly as I'd hoped. And I apparently wouldn't have to play any games. Victoria Laine had dirt on her lover and seemed prepared to spill it just for the asking. I couldn't help but wonder why.

During the flight, I alternated between checking the questions I wanted to ask and catching up on my sleep. Something told me I wouldn't be getting much of it with the deadline for my meeting with Jeremy now four days away.

The plane landed on time, and I checked my messages. Jeremy had called twice, once last night and once this morning while I was in the air. I decided not to respond until I knew why Ms. Laine had agreed to meet me.

It was nearing 4:00 P.M. as I parked the rental car in front of Victoria's condo in West St. Louis County. My eyes widened as the door opened and a strikingly attractive brunette I guessed to be in her mid-to-late forties motioned me inside. From the way she'd cut her hair to the overall shape of her face, to the fullness of her bust line, I could tell even from a distance that there was something familiar about this woman. It would come to me.

Briefcase in hand, I entered the condo, introduced myself and liked what I saw. Frayed, bleached out jeans. A man's chambray work shirt, untucked, sleeves rolled up to just below her elbows. The top two buttons, undone. My guess, she had a trainer. A silver bracelet with turquoise insets, like something she might have picked up on a trip to New Mexico, dangled from her left wrist. Her large hazel eyes were a bit puffy, as if she'd been crying lately—or, like me, hadn't been getting much sleep.

"Water, soda, beer?" she asked. "I'm out of the hard stuff."

I chose water. When she returned with two bottles I made a point of complimenting her on an antique secretary desk that occupied a corner of the living room. "French?" I asked, showing off.

She nodded, clearly impressed. "Solid oak. I got it when my father died. We'll talk more about that later."

A nod of her head directed me to sit in a love seat. Framed pictures of various sizes rested on the coffee table, on the lamp tables to each side of the sofa, and on the three glass shelves that bordered the left side of the entertainment center. Victoria was in most of the pictures with what I assumed were friends. None of the pictures included Jeremy. Perhaps those were reserved for the bedroom.

"The condo's mine, you know," she said, handing me one of the waters. She sat down at the far end of a large sofa to my right and stretched her legs across the cushions. "Maybe not in my name, but I earned it. Believe me."

I decided to let that one go and focused my attention on an unframed, unsigned oil painting—a portrait—that hung on the wall behind the sofa. The subject was a woman whose features bore an uncanny resemblance to those of my host.

"Self-portrait?" I asked, thinking I was just being friendly.

To my surprise, she said she'd painted it three years ago, when Jeremy had been in Italy. "It's a lift of Henri Matisse's *Portrait of Lydia Delectorskaya, the Artist's Secretary*. My hair was longer then."

I knew nothing of art, but the painting had a professional look to it, and I figured another compliment couldn't hurt. "You have talent."

"Then you are easily fooled, Mr. McDermott. But aren't we all?"

She reached for one of two folders she'd placed on the coffee table. "I'm glad you called. Then again, I'm thinking a crack investigator like you should've contacted someone like me, in my position, long before now. You just phoning this in?"

I might have been taken aback, or at least concerned that I might have a hostile interviewee on my hands. But Victoria's arched eyebrows and the way her lips curled upward slightly at the edges said, *I'm just pulling your chain, mister.*

That relaxed me, and I was ready to go toe-to-toe with this woman of obvious intelligence and good taste. "A matter of priorities," I said. "I first had to get the lay of the land."

She gave me a deadpanned stare. I cursed myself over the unintended pun and scrambled to recover. "Given where I am in my investigation, you are now a priority. That's why I called. But I would ask you to relax. I'm not here to sweat the boss's secretary."

"Executive assistant."

Strike two.

I shouldn't have, but I gave the painting a quick glance. "My apologies. And please, call me Rainey."

"Thank you...Mr. McDermott. And be thankful for your timing. Two days ago, you wouldn't have got to first base with me."

She broadened her smile and sipped her water. "So tell me, is it part of a fraud investigator's routine due diligence to traipse across the country snooping around in client warehouses?"

"Our version of sightseeing," I said. "Fort Smith was actually quite a pleasant town, what I saw of it."

"And was your visit successful?"

Victoria Laine was a looker; that much I could see. And sharp. I'd have to be careful. I was here to learn what *she* knew, not the other way around. It occurred to me then that Jeremy could have arranged this meeting to see what I knew—and what I intended to do with the information. "By successful, do you mean—"

"Oh, relax, will you. No one knows you are here. This isn't a trap, and I'm not wired. You can check if you'd like."

What I liked was this woman. "That won't be necessary. No need to get personal."

Fire danced in her eyes, reminding me of the way Alina looked when she told me what Jeremy had done to her. "Guess what?" she said, leaning forward. "My personal life is exactly the reason you're here."

She sat back and composed herself. "You gonna write this down or what?"

I opened my briefcase and took out a pen and legal pad. "First question: why did you invite me here? I'm sensing hostility."

Sadness replaced the anger in her eyes as she handed me the first folder. "We'll get to that. But first things first. Let's start with the numbers."

41.

I scanned the contents of the folder and listened intently as Victoria explained what Wallace had been doing to enhance the recorded sales and revenue numbers in the communications division. I figured in due time she'd tell me *why* she was ratting out her boss.

"I made those notes from memory," she said. "I sat in on the meetings Wallace had with Jeremy when they began discussing this stuff last year. At first, they thought they might have to doctor the books of more than half the subs, but they decided that the real eyesore was in the communications division—the one they thought held the key to getting everybody excited about the company's future. That's been Wallace's priority."

I'd come to this assignment with a good idea of how Wallace likely would doctor the books. Off-loading expenses, paying for them through a shell company, would be too easy to spot in any serious audit. My guess was, he'd simply been padding sales and receivables, but I'd only made my way through a cursory review of the supporting documents of half the subsidiaries. With Victoria's notes to work from, my job just got a lot more focused.

"Tell me about the cell phones," I said, placing the folder in my briefcase.

Victoria gave me a look of respect. "Mack Evans has been looking into this for Jeremy. Hasn't come up with anything concrete yet, but he suspects they're tainted. He's got sources in Malaysia quietly spreading money around for information. Somebody in the chain hinted at pirated software. Mack's trying to get it verified."

I got a chill, partly because I'd been right to suspect those phones, but also because the company that set the deal up—Links International and perhaps one of its key subsidiaries—could be into something far more dangerous. And thus, so could we all. For a moment I wished Billy Ray were here to feed me the right questions.

Victoria shook her head. "Jeremy's a sick man running a sick company. He's made decisions I think are irrational. But after a while, you learn to keep your mouth shut."

I thought of my afternoon with Jeremy. He'd started off full of energy, enthusiasm and bravado—much as he had during our golf game—but thirty minutes later gave every indication of being a man in a great deal of pain. Disoriented, even, as he'd been at LaPlaya. The last hour, I'd done most of the shooting. If intimidation had been his motive for our get-together, he hadn't pulled it off.

"How sick?" I asked.

"Brain cancer. He's got less than a year. My guess, a lot less."

Her words hit me like a bomb blast. *Brain cancer?* Why hadn't—? "His wife knows, of course." Probably an odd thing to blurt out but I couldn't stop myself.

Victoria's eyes turned frosty. "She does now. I guess he's held off until he could get his *affairs* in order."

I held up a hand. "Let me get this straight. You're Jeremy's executive assistant and"—I looked around the room—"you're living in a very nice condo for which you readily admit he fronted the money. Now he's dying of cancer, and you're revealing company secrets that could bring him down just months before his company goes public. What am I missing?"

"Alina hasn't told you?"

"Told me what?"

"That we're sisters."

My head jerked back, jolted by the now obvious physical similarities. "You're having an affair with your sister's *husband?*"

Why? I wanted to ask. *Are you insane?*

"Past tense," Victoria said. "As of two days ago, he and I are no longer an item."

"And Alina knows Jeremy and you—?"

Victoria nodded. "She discovered it by accident over a year ago. Didn't seem to faze her. She's never said a word to Jeremy that we're related, as far as I know—and believe me, I would know. And I haven't said anything, either."

"Sounds kinky to me, lady, but if you're both okay with it—"

"I'm not okay with it, Mr. McDermott, but I never felt secure enough to demand he divorce Alina and devote his remaining years to me."

"So what's changed?"

"He's turning his stock over to her, that's what. All of it, the fucking generous asshole." She turned and stared out the window, arms hugging her waist.

My mouth fell open. So much for Jeremy's son's inheritance and so much for Alina's desire for revenge. Did she any longer need Wallace? Not that I could see, though Alina could still have a lot to say about his future with Whestin Group. As the controlling stockholder and wife of the founder, she could make just about anything happen.

More to the point, did she need me? Her pursuit of evidence with which to blackmail Jeremy was over now. In fact, she needed any evidence of fraud buried.

"You can close your mouth now," Victoria said.

I did and shook my head. "I'm sorry, it's just that—when did you learn about this stock transfer?"

"Friday morning, by accident. God knows when he was going to tell me. I spent the rest of the day and most of Saturday on a bender." She pinched the bridge of her nose. "I won't do that again. He's not worth it."

"And Jeremy was going to tell Alina this weekend?"

"That's my guess."

I saw a tear at the edge of her eye, ready to spill. "You okay?"

She waved a hand. "You don't understand."

"Enlighten me."

Victoria ran a finger under her eye and curled her feet beneath her. "Very well. Let's go back to the beginning: twenty-two years ago, Alina murdered my father to get control of the family business."

I couldn't move, as if my whole body had been injected with Botox. "Sorry, for a moment there it sounded like you said 'murdered.'"

She cocked her head, as if to say *see who you're dealing with here?* "They said he died of a heart attack. No autopsy, no investigation. I accepted it at first, but when the shock wore off, I became convinced otherwise. I've been trying to prove it ever since."

In my time as a forensic accountant, I'd conducted countless interviews in search of the truth. I'd seen greed, revenge, jealousy and lust cause people to do some crazy things, but I'd never dealt with murder. "How can you be so sure?"

Victoria seemed relieved I hadn't upped and walked out the door, that I was willing to hear her out.

"My father summoned me to his office at the end of the previous day," she explained, "before he headed home. He told me that he no longer intended for Alina to inherit the company. Instead, he said he was going to designate me, his younger daughter, as the heir. Period, end of story. I was then to immediately find Alina, give her the news and tell her to be in his office the next morning to witness him making the change in the Revocable Living Trust. He even wanted her to notarize the damn thing."

"Sounds harsh, but how does all that lead to murder?" I kept waiting for her to change her story, to tell me that she meant to say "manipulated," or "mangled," or "manhandled." Anything but "murdered."

Victoria tapped her fingers on the edge of the sofa. "Think about it. My father had me tell Alina at the end of the day, so that she'd spend the rest of the evening and half the morning on Christmas Eve, for God's sakes, stewing over it. I've always said that when it came to his first-born, dear old dad was an evil man."

"Sounds like it."

"Anyway, what he didn't count on was that it gave Alina time to put together a plan to stop him. Not a lot, but enough. And she knew he'd do nothing official until she was present."

I rubbed my chin in classic Bogart fashion. "I dunno. Seems a little far-fetched if that's all you've got."

She stood and grabbed the second file off the coffee table. "Let's go outside. I'm not done yet."

How could that be?

I'd just learned that Jeremy had inoperable brain cancer.

That Victoria was sleeping with her sister's husband, who happened to be my boss.

And that Whestin Group's CEO and controlling stockholder intended to turn his stock over to Alina, the woman Victoria had just accused of murdering their father.

What else could my star informant possibly have to tell me?

I got up and followed, a bad feeling germinating in my gut.

42.

We each sat in white plastic chairs with a small white plastic table between us on which Victoria placed her folder and water bottle. Both sides of the brick-paved patio were heavily landscaped with thick shrubs that provided a decent amount of privacy and shade. There was still plenty of late September steam in the air, but it felt good to be back in the Midwest.

It also felt good to be working, involved in a full-blown engagement, thoroughly immersed in an interview with a key witness to behind the scenes illegality. Still, for my first rodeo in four years, I'd drawn one hell of a bull.

Victoria cleared her throat. "You asked why I thought Alina killed my father. I'll tell you why—because he believed she was responsible for the premature death of my mother."

"Dear God, another murder?"

"In his eyes. You see, Mom couldn't get pregnant early on. She was thirty-nine by the time she had Alina, after a brutal labor that nearly killed her. The doctor said that a second pregnancy was out of the question. But did my father listen? No. What he wanted more than anything was a son, someone he could trust to run the company. Alina, after all, was a *girl*. Sooner or later, he probably would have found a way to replace me, too."

She shook her head. "Just two years later, he forced the issue, you could say. Nine months later, I was born to a mother who died three days after delivering me. My father immediately blamed Alina for ruining his wife's health. I sometimes think he blamed her for everything bad that ever happened to him."

I thought back to the Whestin's party and the charity they were supporting that night: the Shelter for Abused Women and Children. I should have left a bigger check.

Victoria blew out both cheeks and took a sip of her water. "He made her the scapegoat for his own feelings of guilt and suffering, Mr. McDermott. I get that. But he was still my father. He was going to turn the company over to me. Maybe I didn't deserve it, but it was his decision to make. He didn't deserve to die for it."

"I understand," I said, thinking, absorbing. "But why would Alina agree to work for a man who'd been so mean to her?"

Any sympathy Victoria had left for her sister seemed to show now in faraway eyes and slumped shoulders. "She told me once it was her last chance to prove him wrong. She relished a challenge, always did, and I really think she felt she was making progress. Then—I didn't even want the company, to tell you the truth, and I told Alina that when I went to see her that afternoon. I felt sick about my father's decision, and I told her we could work this out. She said not to worry. It seemed a very odd response to very bad news. Next day, not thirty minutes after their meeting started, there's an ambulance in the parking lot. Doesn't that strike you as amazingly coincidental?"

"What did she tell you?"

"That he grabbed his arm, pitched forward and hit his head on the conference table. She claimed he died almost instantly. For a while, in shock, I bought the heart attack diagnosis. But months later, when I noticed Alina couldn't look me in the eye, something clicked in my brain. I can't describe it, but I knew somehow she'd killed him, only by then it was too late. She'd had him cremated."

"And that brought you to Whestin Group?" I had no idea what revelation would come next. I just knew I needed to keep asking questions.

"How I ended up here," she said, her eyes suddenly ablaze, "was part of a not-too-well-thought-out plan to piss off my big sister. Let her know I would never rest until the truth came out. That I got as far as I did still amazes me. I didn't expect to fall in love with Jeremy, that's for sure. I was an idiot to think he felt the same way—and now I want him to pay."

Get in line, lady.

"What do you expect me to do now?" I asked.

Victoria opened the folder and stared at what looked like a single piece of paper. Then she looked at me and said she expected me to upend the public offering and in the process help her send a message to the man who'd just jilted her.

"He's blackmailing you, Mr. McDermott. And just to be on the safe side, he figures he can buy your cooperation, which should piss you off if you're even half a man. I'm also hoping you don't like the idea of helping a company like Whestin Group sell misrepresented stock to thousands of unsuspecting people, and in the process add to the treasuries of scum like Jeremy Whestin and Wallace Gerard."

I waited for her to calm down, but she was in no mood to extend mercy toward a fraud examiner in the process of confirming once again that he was the biggest fraud of all. I mean, if there's one kind of person we all find off-putting, it's a slow learner, isn't it? Let's all say it: Rainey McDermott. S-L-O-W L-E-A-R-N-E-R.

"I know you helped Jeremy commit fraud once before," Victoria said, "and I know about the cocaine. But what's your excuse this time? The preservation of a privileged lifestyle? The protection of secrets that will come out eventually, anyway? They always do, you know. Where does it end?"

She turned her head in disgust and stared into the yard. If I'd had a shovel, I would have gone out there and dug my grave, then jumped in and asked her to bury me alive.

Instead, with my phone vibrating in my pocket, I asked, "Why don't *you* go to the police? Why put this on me?"

She scoffed. "Whistle blowing is a noble endeavor but professional suicide. I'm going to need a job. Being labeled a snitch is considered sort of a black mark, okay? Not to mention appearing in the paper as 'the other woman.' You, on the other hand, are a whistle blower by profession. Or you're supposed to be."

I started to protest out of embarrassment alone but stopped when she tossed the folder into my lap. "My guess is you think you've got everything under control, think you can use your expertise to steer this investigation to suit your priorities. Guess again, Mr. Big Shot Fraud Examiner. Nobody controls those two. And if you doubt me, read what's in that folder. If it doesn't stir your conscience, you are beyond redemption. Maybe we both are."

She glanced at her watch. "You'll have to go now. I've got some urgent packing to do."

I tucked the folder under my arm and grabbed my briefcase. "Where will you go?"

"Relatives in Santa Fe. By the way, I jotted my phone number inside that folder. Call only if you absolutely must."

We stopped at the front door, and she touched my arm, as if adding to the gravity of her closing remarks. "Do what I'm asking, Mr. McDermott, and there will be consequences."

"I'm not the only one in trouble, you know."

She smiled, but I saw no joy in her eyes. "I know what I'm dealing with. Jeremy's a ruthless bastard, but Alina is a killer. You would be wise to remember that."

43.

My return flight to Florida wouldn't depart until early the next morning, which meant I'd be spending Sunday night at the Airport Marriott. I didn't expect to get much sleep, not if I spent any time thinking about Victoria and her game-changing disclosures, assuming they held water. I thought about the mysterious contents of folder number two, and every muscle in my body seemed to tighten simultaneously.

Arriving at the hotel around 6:30 P.M., I checked my phone for messages. Two calls: the first from Jeremy. I'd return that one when I got back to Florida. The second call, from Diego, arrived while I was returning the rental car. Though he likely had more bad news about my finances, I relished the thought of talking with an old, *grounded* friend I knew I could trust.

Besides, our conversation would delay me having to discover whether or not I was beyond redemption. If I was, there was no need to rush the confirmation.

Diego answered on the first ring. "You have good news for me?" he asked.

"I was about to ask you the same, but if you're asking do I have a job, I am pleased to answer in the affirmative." I spent a minute bringing him up to speed on my engagement with Whestin Group and managed to drop in a reference to both my salary and potential stock option windfall. No need to tell him that it would all be blown skyhigh if, as Victoria had reminded me, I lived up to my professional ethics before my morally-challenged backbone disintegrated altogether.

Did I say...*professional ethics?*

Diego whistled softly. "I'm impressed. And here I was calling to warn you not to get upset."

My stomach growled, and I realized I hadn't eaten since grabbing a coffee and a Danish at the airport this morning. "About what?"

"The bailout bill goes before Congress for a vote tomorrow. I'm not sure what the reaction will be if it passes, but if it fails...."

"You finally ready to throw in the towel?" I asked, borrowing from the very same question Jeremy had asked me—the one that led me to Victoria. "I'm thinking we go to frozen pork bellies and flaxseed oil."

"I am not ready to throw anything," Diego said, full of what seemed to be genuine conviction. "The markets might go down tomorrow—a lot. But they will make their way back. To bail now would be shortsighted and foolish. I just want you to be prepared. In fact, I suggest you avoid all media tomorrow."

Easy enough. I'd been sticking my head in the sand for years now. What's one more day?

We ended the call, but not before I extended an invitation to Diego to visit me before the Christmas holidays. It was an act of faith. I had no idea where I'd be a week from now, much less in a couple of months. I just hoped wherever I landed, I'd still be a free man.

After a quick run to the ice machine and a raid on the courtesy bar, I called room service and ordered dinner. My last act of procrastination was to scan the complimentary copy of *USA Today* I'd picked up at the front desk. Ten minutes later, I opened the last folder while standing up, too nervous and too exhausted to lie down on the bed.

A minute into my read, my head began to spin in one direction, my guts in another. I sunk to my knees, read the contents again and drew the same conclusion: the public offering was dead.

It had nothing to do with "redemption" or "patriotic duty" or even lingering thoughts of "cutting a deal." But it did have everything to do with what it meant to be a human being with a functioning conscience.

Victoria had been right. There would be consequences, but it shouldn't have taken this last piece of information to see how low I'd sunk to sate my own pathetic ego and save my own pitiful hide. Neither of which mattered now. I just had to figure out how to play it from here so I didn't screw up what had to be done.

All I had were Victoria's notes and this report from Mack Evans I still couldn't fully comprehend, much less confirm. Instinct, years of training and a couple of painful experiences with two bullheaded prosecuting attorneys told me I needed to build a better case than the one I had now before calling the FBI.

I also wanted to do this on my own, if for no other reason than to keep Victoria clear of suspicion. Jeremy might suspect her involvement, but he couldn't prove it if I did my job, and she stayed out of sight.

But what about her sister?

Did Alina know about the content of this report? If so, could she possibly still want to be a part of this scheme? With what for rationale?

Of course, if she didn't know and learned the truth from me, she'd want the IPO killed as much as I did. *Wouldn't she?*

I had to be certain.

It was enough to deal with the sibling rivalry craziness, Jeremy's cancer and the wild accusation of murder. Once Jeremy passed, I could walk away from all that and pick up the pieces of my life as a janitor at the local high school, if I had to.

But if Alina was still willing to let the IPO go through and expected my cooperation, then I'd been screwing—literally—with the wrong woman. And she had to be stopped.

44.

I'd called Alina's cell Sunday night, after pulling myself together, intending to leave a message since I knew Jeremy was in town. Instead she answered on the first ring, said she was anxious to see me and suggested a late lunch run Monday to Marco Island. Where had I heard that before?

We'd be traveling on her yacht, she said, a forty-two foot Sea Ray named *My Guy*. "Come straight from the airport to the Marina Bay Yacht Club in North Naples—and be dressed appropriately." I'd heard that before, too.

She said Jeremy was under the weather again and likely would be sleeping most of the day. Further, the maid would be in doing odds and ends, so someone would be around if he awoke and needed help. In other words, the coast was clear, and tomorrow was supposed to be a lovely day for cruising.

Marco seemed a bit far to go, a trip that likely wouldn't have us back home until nearly six. But Alina said she needed the diversion and in response to my question that Jeremy might ask where she'd been, she'd merely replied, "You worry too much."

If you only knew.

After a restless night and a bumpy flight from St. Louis, I arrived at the marina both overly tired and full of nervous energy, trying to set aside for the moment Victoria's well-deserved stinging rebuke. I was also questioning the wisdom of agreeing to meet Alina before I'd had time to fully digest Victoria's "evidence." It didn't help that my first instinct upon pulling into a parking spot in front of the docks was to scan for signs of a private investigator lurking in the bushes. I saw only Alina waving at me from the helm. I'd expected to be greeted by a chartered captain, though in her yellow fisherman's windbreaker, khaki shorts, and blue reflective sunglasses she certainly looked the part.

I climbed aboard, and she handed me a mimosa. Twenty-five minutes later, the champagne doing little to calm my nerves, we were into the Gulf, headed south for the ninety-minute cruise to Marco. Alina put the boat on plane and angled her body in my direction.

"Jeremy's been trying to reach you," she said, kicking off her deck shoes.

"Been busy."

"On a Sunday?"

"I don't have much time."

"You pulling a Wallace Gerard on me?"

You mean a Waleed al-Ghamdi?

"A secretive nature goes with the job," I said. I'd too quickly dispensed with my mimosa and desperately wanted a beer or stronger.

Alina opened the middle section of the windshield and a strong wind whipped through the cockpit. The Gulf waters lay as flat as the stomach I last had in high school and the humming of the engines, combined with the mimosa, ordinarily would have lulled me to sleep in seconds. Not today.

"So, what did she give you?" Alina asked, casually. "And don't be coy. I know where you've been."

It took everything I had to hide my anger at not at least considering the possibility that Alina might have had me tracked. Still, she'd felt it necessary, whatever her reasons, and it pissed me off. It was one thing to lie naked in her arms, quite another to be stripped of my privacy by a nameless, faceless Peeping Eye she'd hired to expose not just Jeremy's every move, but apparently mine, as well. Just what was this woman's game?

"Let me guess," she said. "She told you about Jeremy's cancer."

I gave her my best poker face and said nothing.

"No big deal," she said. "You were going to find out about that sooner or later. I only found out myself Saturday." She put a finger to her lips. "Now let's see, what else? Oh! Did she also tell you that we're sisters? I'm sure she did. Which leads me to believe she also told you that I'm the sinister force responsible for the death of our father." She held bent forefingers to each side of her head, imitating the familiar cartoon image of the Devil.

"She didn't appear to be joking," I said. *"Did you?"*

Alina tossed off a dismissive hand, as if discounting the inane ramblings of a psyche ward patient. "I did not, and I'm a little irritated you would even ask. But then, I'm somewhat used to it. Vicky's tried this story before. I think she's actually come to believe her lie. But tell me—what did she offer as proof?"

I said nothing, and Alina shook her head. "It's so obvious, Rainey. She's been jealous of me all her life. Now she's jealous that Jeremy still cares about me, so much so he even wants to give me all of his stock. I don't trust her, and you shouldn't, either."

There was some validity to that. Victoria Laine was just shy of a complete stranger to me. I'd yet to check out the information she'd handed over, and as for that murder accusation, it was a fantastic yarn but thin on substance, to say the least.

"What about you?" I said. "How in the hell have you handled this...sleeping arrangement? Victoria said Jeremy doesn't know, but obviously you do."

Alina steered the boat to starboard to avoid a row of crab pots. If any of this angered her, it didn't show. "Vicky was divorced from her husband five years ago," she said, "but she used her married name on the employment form and never said a word. Jeremy doesn't much discuss with me what he does with the company, or whom he hires. You were an interesting exception, as if he suddenly cared about my opinion."

She gave me her half-finished mimosa and asked me to get her a beer. I gratefully disappeared into the galley below, returning with two lagers. I handed her one, and we both took a long drink.

"I found out about this arrangement by accident," she continued, "two years ago. I'd called the office to confirm Jeremy's availability for a party I wanted to throw. Normally, the receptionist screens his calls. This time, she answered."

"And?"

"We talked briefly. Of course, she didn't come right out and state what she was up to. She didn't have to."

"You never said anything?"

Alina looked at me, askance. "And give her the satisfaction of thinking I was upset?"

Silly me. "So...?"

"I told her I wasn't going to tell Jeremy because it would mean so much more when he gave her the boot on *his* terms, which I knew he would, sooner or later."

Sooner has arrived, I thought. Did Alina know that, too? "You think it was the stock transfer that set her off?"

She gave me one of those *poor Rainey* sighs, which fired my nerve endings like fine cactus needles stuck in the end of one's thumb. "I'm guessing you know the answer to that, too," she said. "But since you asked, I'd say it's more than just the stock that's got her so riled. I'd say he's leaving her. Am I right?"

I took an extra moment to polish off my beer. "That's for you to discuss with your husband, the man who apparently wants to make amends."

Alina gave me an *I thought so* nod of her head. She held the cool beer can to her neck, parting the top of her windbreaker as she did. "Just so you know, I didn't see this coming. And for the record, Jeremy's confessed nothing. I'd say that in light of his condition, he's just trying to ease a guilty conscious before he meets his maker."

"Perhaps, but if this IPO goes through—"

"What do you mean, *if* it goes through?"

Part of me screamed to keep my mouth shut, the other part demanded the truth. "There's a good chance Jeremy and Wallace are involved with Algerian terrorists. Or do you know that, too? Regardless, when information like that leaks out, it tends to put a damper on investor enthusiasm."

Her jaw stiffened. "I have no idea what you're talking about. What do you mean *terrorists*? And if this is another Vicky Laine revelation, you would be wise to check your facts before potentially making a fool of yourself."

Her response was worthy of an Academy Award if Victoria was right, and Alina knew it. Maybe she didn't. Wallace, she said, had been tight-lipped from the beginning, the very reason I was now *her* backup. If that were the case, how would she react if I could at least plant a few seeds of doubt?

The Marseille-based business broker, its private equity subsidiary, the mention of a suspected terrorist connection by name and location, the whole rotten stock-for-dirty money arrangement—I described it all, convincing myself of the validity of Victoria's claims with every "fact" I recited.

The boat started to come off plane, and Alina bumped the throttles forward. "Wallace never mentioned anything about money laundering and certainly nothing about terrorists," she said. "I told you, he's been very secretive. *If* what you're saying is true, it makes me sick, as well. Jeremy must be a desperate man."

"Or not in his right mind."

"Obviously. But I know he'll stop at nothing to protect this IPO. Which means you have to go right now to the police or FBI or whomever and give them what you know."

I hadn't expected that.

"Except…"

Oh-oh.

"What do you really know? What would constitute evidence? If you've purposely been misled, or Vicky's mistaken, where does that leave you? You've had less than a day to think about all this, much less evaluate it. Maybe, now that I think about it, you need to proceed with caution."

Good points, all. "So what are you saying?"

"Take what you know to Jeremy. He might surprise you."

For a moment I thought the sun had gotten to her. "Are you serious? Jeremy authorized this scheme, even after he got that report, verified or not. That's how badly he needs money—and how badly he wants this public offering to go through. What do you think he's going to say to me, 'Thanks, now go away and be a good little boy'?"

Alina steered into the wake of a north-bearing yacht as it passed to port, and *My Guy* effortlessly sliced through the waves. Just then a sleek, silver-sided fish with a jutting jaw arced out of the water to my left, then sliced beneath the surface and disappeared.

"Barracuda," she announced, unimpressed. "Look, Rainey, I'm just hearing about all this terrorist business. I need time to absorb what you're telling me—and so do you. But I have to believe there's still a way to give us both what we want."

She was no more than four feet from me, but suddenly nothing about her looked familiar. "In other words," I said, "you haven't given up on the IPO."

I didn't want to hear her answer, fearing what she might say. "Did you know Wallace was born in Algeria?" I asked. "Did you know his last name used to be *al-Ghamdi*? That was in Mack's report, too. Maybe the next time the two of you are smooching it up, you might try whispering 'Waleed' in his ear. Hell, maybe you already do."

The stereo had been blaring away above the din of the engines and the wind that buffeted the cockpit, but I hadn't noticed until Alina reached over and turned down the volume. "Tell me that wasn't jealousy I just heard," she said, a playful grin tugging at the corners of her mouth.

I wasn't in the mood. "Don't push me, Alina. And no, that wasn't jealousy. It was just...I just don't think you realize what we're involved in here."

She lost the grin and nodded in what I hoped was sincere agreement. "Let's not argue," she said. "I'm just asking for a little time. Let me confirm that report, see if Mack has any additional information. I trust him to keep any communication between us confidential."

"And why is that?"

She gave me a *calm down, will you?* look that made me feel about thirteen years old. "Trust me, he hates Jeremy as much as I do. If everything checks out, then you can blow the whistle on the IPO any time you want—and I'll support you."

"Better make it quick. I report to Jeremy in three days."

"What are you going to say?"

"Whatever buys me time to keep digging. But I won't mention Victoria. Or anything that Jeremy would suspect came from her or from Mack. I probably shouldn't have said anything to you."

Alina reached over and squeezed my hand, but I pulled free and made my way to the head. When I returned, we both agreed to make small talk the rest of the way and to enjoy a non-confrontational lunch.

It wasn't easy.

Everything we discussed seemed trivial and forced in light of the decisions we would soon be forced to make and the inevitable consequences to follow. I tried to imagine Alina as a murderess. A seductress, yes. But a murderess? Of her own father? It didn't seem possible. But if I couldn't believe Victoria about that, then could I trust anything else she'd told me?

I didn't need the whitecaps we encountered on the return trip, but somehow the contents of my stomach stayed put. It was nearly six by the time we returned to the marina, and I was able to step foot with great relief on terra firma.

"Let's talk after my meeting," I said, climbing into my car.

Alina leaned in and kissed my cheek. "Promise me you won't do anything rash?"

You talkin' to me? Hell, lady, I was a forensic accountant with an old-fashioned accountant's green shade buried in a box somewhere in the attic. I never did anything rash.

Right.

On the way home, I dialed Jeremy's number, figuring I'd get his answering service. I was right and explained I'd been on a quick fishing expedition with friends in Sarasota yesterday, and that I'd see him Thursday, afternoon, per his message. I also thanked him again for the lovely afternoon at the gun range.

What a difference forty-eight hours makes.

By the time Jeremy had packed up our firearms two days ago, I'd convinced myself that a plan I'd been toying with might work: I would make a presentation focused solely on my assessment of the financial statements, leaving out any mention of the cell phones, save maybe for the security issue. I would then keep myself immersed in Whestin Group's books until the IPO, at which time I'd collect my stock options, keep my past a secret, and afterwards do what I could to cover everybody's tracks, especially my own. If Alina pursued a divorce down the road, well—who knows?

All this assumed, of course, I survived the scrutiny of the FBI for my role in the alleged Grayson fraud. Admittedly a giant presumption.

But the events of this weekend changed all that—especially if Alina tried to keep the public offering alive. If Mack's report checked out, I couldn't let that happen.

Back home, I forgot Diego's warning, switched on CNBC and caught sight of a number that nearly threw me into cardiac arrest. The House did indeed reject the Treasury bailout bill and, as Diego had predicted, the DOW took it hard, down an unfathomable 774 points for the day. In a span of less than a year, we were now nearly four thousand points from the all-time high. I thought about calling my Congressman to demand that somebody go to jail.

I poured myself a double gin on the rocks and settled into a lounge chair on the back deck. I had a lot to sort through, but exhaustion overtook me.

The sun was still well above the horizon in the early evening sky; the air, warm and still. An occasional insect—a beetle, a wasp, a fly—lit upon the unruffled water, creating tiny ripples that caught the attention of a still hungry bass below. Through heavy eyes I slowly scanned the pond and—wait, had I just caught a glimpse of Sneaky Pete's submerging tail? I couldn't be sure. The possibility that Dale might not have removed him in my absence gave me hope. The gator and I had been friends of a sort, until he got a little too full of himself. Still, I thought we should be given the opportunity to say our good-byes.

Otherwise, was nothing in my power to control?

Was *everything* slipping away?

45.

Wallace flipped the page on his desk calendar, another day of subterfuge behind him. He rubbed the back of his neck and tried to convince himself that eight months of covering up operating shortfalls would put anybody on edge.

He already kept one set of corporate statements that complied with GAAP, the set that lately only Jeremy was allowed to see. The set that would singe Ralph Bartlett's eyebrows if he ever got his hands on them—and make the day for any federal investigator comparing them to the set he would soon be presenting to the underwriter and then the SEC.

The doctored financials that now occupied his every waking hour represented an enormous commitment of time and mental energy. Altering the numbers to reflect impressive sales and receivables, with corresponding expenses and support documents, was difficult enough, even with the help of modern accounting software.

Still, he knew that for all his meticulous efforts, it remained a possibility that a zealous member of the underwriting team might decide to look where

Wallace didn't want him to. He had to admit that, personal pride aside, it probably was a good idea to have Rainey McDermott checking his work—assuming he could trust Jeremy's stated motive.

But it was more than this complex, high stakes juggling act that bothered him this evening, that had been a festering preoccupation since the night Alina so abruptly asked him to leave her condo. As Wallace disconnected his thumb drive and locked it in his briefcase, he knew exactly whose face occupied the knot in his stomach: Rainey McDermott's.

He wasn't so much concerned about McDermott acting alone as a one-man consulting firm, intent on earning his enormous reward. He didn't even mind if he found something and waved it in Wallace's face. After all, by McDermott's own admission, he was looking deeper than any underwriter or the SEC likely would.

No, it was far more than that. It was what the man could be persuaded to do under the spell of Alina Whestin that ate at his gut like termites on rotting wood. She'd certainly done a job on *him*, ever since another of her silly parties last fall, when she'd asked the question that launched their partnership: "Why settle for CFO?"

Ever since, he'd risked his career and perhaps his freedom for this woman. But now, as he sat here alone in his office at eight-fifteen in the evening, it all felt like betrayal. Why, he couldn't stop wondering, had McDermott called Alina that night after The Ritz dinner?

She'd called the next day, left a message of apology. Said she couldn't wait to see him again. The usual female bullshit. He hadn't returned that call or the several others she'd left in the past eleven days. None of which mentioned a call from McDermott.

Let her sweat, he decided.

Wallace turned off his computer and glanced around the office. Satisfied everything was as secure as he could make it, he turned his attention to dinner and the likelihood he would, yet again, end up ordering carryout. Briefcase in hand, he flipped off the lights and was about to start toward the elevators when he heard noises coming from Victoria's office. Probably the cleaning service; she'd called in ill today.

He passed her open door and stopped short. Victoria was on her knees, stacking files into a yellow plastic box with wheels and a long pull handle. Three other boxes next to her desk looked to contain an assortment of books and folders and a few personal items. If he didn't know better, he'd have sworn she was cleaning out her office.

"I thought you were sick."

Startled, Victoria steadied herself on a desk drawer handle, then coughed loudly, a hand over her mouth. "I am, and I'm taking the rest of the week off, too. Doesn't mean I can't be productive."

Wallace took a step closer, hoping to get a better view of the contents of the boxes. Victoria put up a hand, turned her head and coughed again. "I wouldn't do that. Doc says I might have the flu."

He took a step back, eyeing a crystal desk clock in one of the boxes and the back of a chrome picture frame in another. "You're coming back, aren't you?"

Victoria cleared her throat, a pained look on her face as she swallowed. "Jeremy's authorized some redecorating for his prized executive assistant. I'm just getting this stuff out of the way."

"I hadn't heard."

"Relax. It won't blow the budget."

Wallace stared at Victoria, who wore black jeans and a baggy gray sweatshirt that somehow still managed to accentuate her obvious physical attributes. She was Jeremy's plaything, but that didn't mean he couldn't admire from afar.

"Need any help?"

"I can manage."

Wallace nodded. "Then good evening. Hope you feel better soon." A minute later, he stood facing the closed elevator doors, his hand not yet ready to push the button that would send him to the parking garage.

If it had been anybody else cleaning out their office, he'd have called Jeremy or someone in security to check out their story. Everything the home office did these days involved sensitive information pertaining to the public offering. Any employee activity out of the ordinary warranted scrutiny.

But Victoria Laine wasn't going to do anything to upset the IPO, not when the man for whom she cared deeply was so close to realizing his dream. And not with a fat bonus check just months away. He pushed the elevator button and decided that tonight he would settle for pizza.

46.

Jeremy awakened Tuesday at 9:00 A.M., far later than the usual predawn start to his day that had been his habit since his time in the Marine Corps. But that habit was slowly disappearing under the influence of painkillers that, if he could believe the date on his watch, had apparently knocked him out for most of the past seventy-two hours.

He didn't remember anything about yesterday, or how he ended up in the detached cabana, but then he didn't remember much of anything at the moment, except telling Alina about the stock transfer. Was that Saturday? Or Sunday?

Making his way to the bathroom, he stopped at the sink and stared at his beloved pill bottle, the only thing that stood between him and a bullet to his temple. Better living through chemistry, he thought. Better dying, too.

The prescription had been refilled several times since the diagnosis back in…in…he couldn't remember. He did know that the pills made him sleepy but were doing less to alleviate the pain while he was awake. If he opted for a stronger dosage, they might as well put him in the coffin and close the lid.

He decided to forego taking another dose and instead grabbed a quick shower. He'd just finished toweling off when Alina opened the door. She wore a white blouse and black slacks with a brown leather belt and fashionable sandals. A delicate gold necklace with a tiny gold sand dollar hung from her neck. Jeremy's first impression was that he looked as if she were about to pose for the cover of *Gulfshore Life*.

A look of relief spread across her face. "Thank God. I was about to call the coroner." She straightened the bed sheets as Jeremy steadied himself against a bedpost. "Can I fix you breakfast?" she asked.

"Dressed like that?"

"This old thing?" she said, batting her eyelashes. "I've had it since …yesterday."

"In that case, toast and a grapefruit." Jeremy touched Alina's hand. He'd been hoping to spend time with her today, but she obviously had other plans. "Big luncheon?"

She shook her head. "Just errands. How about you?"

"If it really is Tuesday, I've got some catching up to do."

Alina handed him his cell phone from the nightstand. "I turned it off so you could get some sleep."

She kissed him on the cheek and left. He watched her disappear into the main house, no memory of how she'd reacted to his announcement that she would soon be Whestin Group's controlling stockholder. It couldn't have gone too badly, he decided. She hadn't volunteered a kiss in…again, he couldn't remember.

He turned on his phone, scanned the list of messages and punched in the one from Rainey McDermott confirming their meeting Thursday. His next call was to his CFO.

"We've missed you," Wallace said. "We're getting heat from Ralph Bartlett. The news yesterday has the bank worried about the viability of the public offering."

"What are you talking about?"

"I thought you would have heard. The House rejected the proposed Treasury bailout bill. The Dow dropped nearly eight hundred points."

"What's it doing today?"

Wallace started to answer, but Jeremy cut him off. There was only one thing on his mind now. "You talk to McDermott lately?"

"Not since our dinner. Why?"

Jeremy glanced out the window. "Put Vicky on."

"She's still out sick. Called in yesterday and apparently this morning, too. You haven't...?"

Jeremy did remember trying to reach Vicky at the condo Saturday night, before he'd taken the extra dose of pain pills that sent him to la-la land. There'd been no answer. Checking his phone now, he found no return message.

"I don't know if this means anything," Wallace said, hesitating, "but I saw her here last night boxing up files and personal stuff. Said she wanted to take some work home while she got better. Thought maybe she had the flu."

Then why hadn't she returned his call?

"She also said she was getting ready for her office to be redecorated," Wallace said. "It's pretty cleaned out now."

What felt like a nest of red ants came alive in the pit of Jeremy's stomach. He picked up a pencil from the nightstand and twirled it in his fingers. "Must have slipped my mind," he said. "How's your week look?"

"Booked solid. I'll be—"

"Change your plans. I want you here when McDermott makes his presentation Thursday. Catch the morning flight. Be at the house by three. I know it's short notice, but do what you have to do."

He ended the call before Wallace could respond, then placed another call to Vicky's cell. He got no reply and called the condo's direct line. When he again got no answer, he called Mack. "Get over to the condo," he said. "Use the spare key if you have to. Call me when you get there. If I don't answer, leave a message. I want to know who and what you find."

He laid the phone on the bed and sat very still. His eyes never flinched as the pencil snapped in his fingers.

47.

Alina grabbed a serrated knife and separated the sections of Jeremy's grapefruit as a late morning rain shower erupted from patchy clouds moving northeast to southwest.

September was the time of year in southwest Florida when even the full-time residents wanted out. Torrential rains most afternoons, humid as hell, black mold growing on sidewalks and pool decks. And always the threat of a hurricane—which was just the way she liked it.

More tropical storms and hurricanes hit Florida than any other state, but so far, in a storm season that officially started June 1, only tropical storm Fay had hit the area. Heavy winds, buckets of rain, some flooding, damage mostly to landscaping—and lots of tedious, overwrought publicity.

Her Northern friends kept asking, "How can you live down there in the summer? I'd be scared to death. And the *heat!*"

"It's difficult," she would answer, hoping to convince yet another retiring snowbird to look elsewhere for permanent residency. "You are lucky to be where you are."

She heard Jeremy enter the main house, but he didn't visit the kitchen. A moment later, she found him leaning against a desk chair, staring out the window of the downstairs study she'd converted into a small library. "Lost your appetite?"

He nodded, smiled weakly and sat down. "Maybe later." He gave her a sideways glance. "You look like you've got something on your mind."

Alina sat down on an adjacent couch. "Rainey didn't go to Sarasota. He went to St. Louis to meet your executive assistant. At her invitation."

Jeremy crossed his arms but said nothing.

"Rainey and I met yesterday. He said he went to—"

"What do you mean, *met?*"

"If I may finish...he said the trip was part of his due diligence. I asked him what he learned, and he said nothing he didn't already suspect, at least from an accounting standpoint. But thanks to your assistant, he now knows about your overseas benefactor, and that's got him spooked. He's thinking there's no way he can let the public offering go through."

"Why?"

"She showed him a report from Mack, something about a possible connection between your source for the private placement and—"

"I instructed her to keep her mouth shut."

"That was before she found out about the stock transfer."

Jeremy's body stiffened. "What's going on? Why is Vicky spilling her guts to McDermott? And why did he call *you?*"

"Me first. What was her reaction when she found out about the stock?"

"What do you mean *reaction?* She's a secretary...."

"Cut the bullshit. She's your lover, who happens to be my sister. Or didn't you know?"

Jeremy's lips parted, his body recoiling as his face lost all color. He looked cemented to his chair. "I...I'd never even seen a picture of—. You said she was out of your life long before we met."

"She was, until I found out she was—let's see, what shall we call it?—*working* for you."

"Alina, you have to believe—."

"What, if it had been anyone else, no problem?"

Jeremy slammed his fist against the armrest. "You tell *me!* How long have you known about this? What game are *you* playing?"

She rolled her eyes. "Me! Oh, that's rich."

"This is getting us nowhere. You want a divorce? You'd be better off waiting until I keel over. Or maybe you'd prefer to shoot me now."

It seemed odd to Alina that at that moment she remembered the first time they'd made love, two middle-aged adults screwing like teenagers in the back of Jeremy's car, celebrating their newfound partnership in her driveway at two in the morning. The next day, they found the imprint of her bare feet against the back window. Jeremy had told her then that he would never let any car wash attendant touch it. He'd been lying, of course, as he'd been lying from the beginning. Now it was her turn.

"I do not want a divorce, Jeremy. In fact, if ever we needed to stick together, it's now."

He exhaled, like a man suspected of murder who'd just been told the district attorney wanted to cut a deal.

She stood and nodded in the direction of the kitchen. "I'm going to make myself a Bloody Mary. We've got a lot to discuss."

Alina dropped an olive into her drink and sipped quietly in the kitchen, gathering herself. *He thinks we're in this together now.* Perfect. She swirled the ice in her glass, straightened her shoulders and returned to the study.

Jeremy looked up as she sat down on the couch. His hair, thin and dry, needed a trim, but his erect bearing still bore evidence of his time with the Marines. Alina knew he would never walk away from a fight. Especially if he thought he'd been double-crossed.

"Want some?" she asked, holding out her glass.

He shook his head. "You said you found out by accident."

"A random call to the office. Vicky told me everything, but I decided I wouldn't be the one to reveal the secret to you. If she wanted to say something, that would be her decision. I think her knowing I didn't care took the edge off her gloating, which is just what I wanted."

"Why wouldn't she have told you the day I hired her?"

"I suppose she had to be sure you wanted her badly enough to make her your mistress—and maybe something more—before letting me know. To have been laid by the boss, then discarded"—*like all the rest*—"would have been the ultimate humiliation."

"What was her motive? Why do this to you?"

Sipping on her cocktail, having more fun than she'd had in months, Alina recounted her sister's "irrational accusations" about what had caused their father's death. "Becoming your confidante and lover was her way of getting back at me. She just didn't figure on falling for your irresistible charms."

It began to rain harder. Jeremy swiveled his chair and stared out the window. "You still haven't explained McDermott. You two fucking me over—or just fucking?"

Both, Alina wanted to say, but she knew the stock hadn't yet been transferred. Jeremy could still change his mind. "We have enough pressing issues without manufacturing more," she said. "Nothing sexual is going on between Rainey and me."

Jeremy swung around. "I want to know everything—and I want to know it now."

Alina spoke her lie without emotion. "Wallace told me about Manetti Pharmaceuticals. He said you were the one behind the rumors that nearly destroyed me."

She held her stare as Jeremy's pale complexion flushed again. "That's when I decided to use Wallace's inside information to blackmail you, to force you to sell my company back to me on, shall we say, favorable terms."

She'd just taken a huge gamble. If Jeremy decided to confront Wallace, she'd have to win the battle of his-word-against-mine. But she also couldn't afford to reveal her true source, a man she was certain had a lot more to tell her.

Jeremy shook his head. "There had to be more to it than that. If he doesn't fuck things up, Wallace is set to become chief financial officer of a publicly-traded, potentially multi-billion dollar company."

"I realized that, so I raised the stakes. I decided we wouldn't stop at Manetti Pharmaceuticals. We would use what Wallace knew to force you to step aside and turn your stock over to me. All of it."

"And Wallace would get...?"

"I said I would use my influence to move him up the ladder."

"Does this have anything to do with New Year's Eve?"

"Really, Jeremy, this is all a moot point now. Wallace decided to keep me at arm's length until he was sure he could trust me. That's why I turned to Rainey. But thanks to your generous decision, Wallace is nothing to me—to us—but a potential problem. As is Rainey."

Alina set her cocktail aside and took her husband's hand. "Your offer to give me controlling ownership of Whestin Group means a great deal to me. I just wish we had more time to...." Her voice trailed off as she ran a finger across his wedding ring.

Jeremy slid his hand to Alina's upper arm and squeezed it until her flesh turned white beneath his fingers. "I'm going to ask one last time—why did McDermott call you? What did you promise *him?*"

"I told him what you did to me," Alina said through clenched teeth. She pushed against Jeremy's wrist, but he wouldn't relinquish his grip. "I told him I'd match your offer if he helped me."

"Not buying it. What else?"

"You're hurting me—"

"Answer me!" Jeremy shouted, tightening his grip.

The dying, blood-dotted eyes of Leonard Manetti flashed into Alina's brain, his bony, spastic fingers clutching her arm, pulling her toward his heaving chest. She'd spent the first twenty-eight years of her life under her father's thumb, taking his verbal abuse, only to be "saved" by a husband who was now cutting off the circulation to her arm, demanding she do as she was told.

Something snapped, and she sprung forward like an uncoiling cobra, jabbing the thumb of her free hand into the hollow of Jeremy's neck. She pressed two fingers hard against the side of his carotid artery and hissed, *"Let go."*

The words barely passed her lips when Jeremy clamped onto her fingers and with military efficiency bent her thumb straight back. Alina screamed and collapsed to her knees.

He could have sent her to the hospital with any number of wounds—or killed her on the spot. But in the next instant his grip slackened, and his head slumped against the back of the chair. Alina pushed herself away and crumpled onto the couch.

Jeremy sat upright, and for a moment Alina thought he was gathering his strength for another attack. She braced herself, but he didn't move save for the rapid blinking of his eyes.

"Rainey has never been anything more than a means to an end," she said, massaging her arm. "At first he turned me down. Said he just wanted to fulfill his obligation to you, collect his pay off and start life over—Jeremy! *Are you listening to me?*"

He blinked twice more and nodded. "And now?"

She could see him gripping the sides of his chair as if willing himself to stay conscious. "He knows you're dying, knows about the stock transfer, the doctored books, the phones and the possibility you're mixed up with terrorists. He doesn't see any way he can let this IPO go through."

"Which leaves us where?"

"I've asked him to do nothing until he makes his report to you Thursday."

"And you trust him?"

"I'm not sure. He's got a friend here in Palms Away, a former FBI agent." Alina let the words sink in. "His friend offered to look into the cell phones, see if he can spot anything. I don't think we can take the chance—do you?"

Jeremy rubbed the side of his neck. The effort seemed to return energy to his body, and his fingers began tapping rapidly against the side of his chair. No doubt the thought of the FBI messing around with those phones had something to do with igniting his engines, too, Alina thought.

She asked what he was thinking, and her heart leaped at his answer. "Just that we have some work to do."

"Let me take care of Rainey," she said. "I need to confirm his intentions. For now, at the meeting, just go along with him."

"And after?"

"I'll try to persuade him to see things my way. If I can't, he'll leave me no choice."

Jeremy stared at her, a look of just-found respect in his eyes. "And Wallace?"

"Not sure yet. He might be getting nervous, but he's not ready to do anything stupid. He's in this as deep as the rest of us."

She finished the last of her Bloody Mary. "There's still Vicky to deal with."

Jeremy grabbed her glass, plucked the olive from the ice and tossed it into his mouth. "You leave that to me. Anything else?"

"What do you know about security at Manetti Pharmaceuticals?"

Jeremy eyed her and frowned. "Why?"

"As Whestin Group's soon-to-be controlling stockholder, I need to be aware of such things, don't you think?"

She leaned over, brushed Jeremy's hair behind his ears, and coaxed an amused grin. "We're upgrading security at all our warehouses," he said. "I think Manetti goes live with an upgraded system in about a week. As far as I know, it's still pretty much just entrances and exits."

He pushed himself off his chair and placed both hands on her hips. "Be careful, Alina. I'd hate to see you in trouble."

Not a chance, she thought. The only one about to end up in trouble for sure was her sister. And poor Billy Ray Hammonds.

48.

The rain had stopped and shafts of sunlight sliced through the broken clouds. Alina checked the time. She could still make both of her stops, after which, if everything proceeded as planned, at least one of her concerns would be eliminated. Permanently.

She fanned the pages of the Palms Away resident directory until she came to the two numbers she sought. She dialed the first number and introduced herself, pleased that Mr. Hammonds remembered her.

"What can I do for you?" he asked.

Alina detected the kind of easy smile in his voice reflective of a man with a clear conscience. Too bad this had to happen. "Your dear wife, Millie, helped me on some charity work for the Guadalupe Center a couple of years ago before she...it's still a shock, isn't it?"

"I think of her every day."

"I'm sure you do. Anyway, I'd like to count on your help this year for the upcoming auction."

There was a pause, then Billy Ray gave her the answer she'd anticipated. "I send a check every year."

"That is so nice of you, but it's your time I desperately need. Would you mind if I come over? This is difficult to explain over the phone."

"You mean now?"

"Later today. Say, around five? I really do hate to bother, but this has been on my list of responsibilities, and I'm afraid I've taken too long to get to it."

After another moment's hesitation, Billy Ray gave in, as she suspected he would. "One more favor. Please keep this between the two of us. There can be so much silly jealousy over who gets asked to help with these sorts of things that...well, I know you understand."

"Say no more. Millie used to grumble about it all the time."

Alina expressed her appreciation, said good-bye and then punched in the second number. She got an answering service. *Perfect.*

"Maggie, this is Alina Whestin. I think I might have secured our MC for the auction. His name is Billy Ray Hammonds, a big supporter of the school and a wonderful gentleman. I'm going over there this afternoon to discuss it with him. I'll be in touch."

She grabbed her purse and car keys from the kitchen counter. Next item on her "to-do" list: an unannounced visit to the offices of Manetti Pharmaceuticals. It would be good to see old friends.

When your back is to the wall, you do whatcha gotta do.

Jeremy Whestin slumped at his upstairs desk and smiled at the memory of some prick Marine combat training instructor who'd seared those words into his brain more than forty years ago.

Not that you've got a chance against me, boot.

He'd been four weeks into his training at Camp Pendleton, learning how to kill in any way necessary to save himself and destroy the enemy. Fighting "fair" wasn't part of the equation; worrying about it was how you got killed.

Contrary to the instructor's boast, Jeremy had defeated the man in two blindingly quick moves, drawing on Russian martial arts experience gained through high school training sessions with his Ukrainian-born grandfather. It was experience no one in boot camp knew he had until they saw the arrogant prick of a staff sergeant sprawled in the dirt, Jeremy's fingers pressed against their tormentor's jugular.

He'd been on the fine edge then, balancing gratification of an unexplained bloodlust against a life of incarceration—or worse. He smiled again, recalling how he'd debated the pros and cons while the instructor blinked back at him, cockiness replaced by respect and resentment.

It had been an exhilarating moment, the catalyst that loosed his risk-taking nature. All these years later, those words never failed to comfort him, confirmation of his personal ethic.

When your back is to the wall, you do whatcha gotta do.

Given what was at stake for her, Alina had just made Rainey McDermott her responsibility, and he trusted his wife to do what she had to do. His responsibility was Vicky. Beautiful, competent, erotic and doomed Vicky.

He punched up Mack's number, but the phone fell from his hands as he lost vision, pain electrifying his skull. If his head had been a grenade at that moment, he'd have pulled the pin.

Clamping both hands to his ears, he pressed as hard as he could, his fingers clawing at his scalp. He wasn't sure how long he sat at the desk that way, fighting to stay conscious, before retrieving the phone and calling Mack. He heard a voice that might as well have been Martian.

"I just walked in the door," Mack said. "She's not here, and her closet appears half empty. I do see a couple of suitcases in the foyer. Does that sound right to you?"

Jeremy knew what he wanted to say. *Find her Mack. Scare the hell out of her if you have to. But tell her I need to talk to her. Tell her I'm sorry. Tell her we can work this out.* He could hear himself talking, but the words weren't coming out right. He tried once more, and again nothing made sense.

"What's wrong?" he heard Mack say. "You can't mean that. Say again. I couldn't understand you."

A wave of nausea crashed against Jeremy's brain, knocking him off balance. Suddenly it was the fall of 1964. He was nineteen, in a leaking LTV, somebody's puke covering his boots as his squad practiced amphibious assaults in heaving seas off the coast of Southern California. He mumbled an order he couldn't understand, and he wasn't sure who received it. The kid clutching his stomach next to him? Or—the pain was easing now, enough that he heard a response from Mack, but he couldn't make it out. "Don't fuck this up. Do your duty," were his last commands before he ended the call.

The fog in his head lifted, and he caught sight of a framed photograph Alina had hung on the wall across from his desk. The two of them white water rafting on the Colorado River. His fifty-fifth birthday.

Alina. Only two other men knew what he'd done to her. She'd said it was Wallace who'd revealed his sin. If so, Wallace's days were numbered, too.

When your back is to the wall—*or a trust betrayed*—you do whatcha gotta do.

49.

Since returning from my boat ride with Alina, I'd been unable to dismiss Victoria's unnerving disclosures and Alina's almost nonchalant response to her accusations and assertions. I wasn't just losing sleep over this war of words and wills; I was on the edge of losing control over my life.

For most of last night and this morning, I felt as if I were living in a black hole of allegations, deceptions, lies, and threats whose gravitational pull might soon be too powerful to resist. My only refuge had been focusing on what I now knew were Whestin Group's contaminated financial statements. I'd passed on dinner last night and had nibbled on a blueberry muffin this morning. Frustrated, worried and with a stomach rumbling loud enough to warrant earplugs, I headed for the kitchen to make myself a quick PB&J.

When I finished, I grabbed the binoculars for a look-see at the pond. Sure enough, Sneaky Pete had returned, floating closer than usual to the edge of my property. We locked eyes for what seemed a long minute before he turned and swam to the other side.

I returned to the house intending to call the Community Association to find out what had happened to Dale from "Gator Done." Instead, I found Billy Ray in the kitchen carving out an apple wedge with his pocketknife. A bright red golf cap was pushed back on his head.

"I knocked first," he said. Then, calling on a passable British accent, "On my way to the store to pick up a wedge of *Comté,* old chap. A very expensive French cheese, in case you didn't know."

"You making a pizza?"

Billy Ray popped the apple slice into his mouth and licked a finger. "As a matter of fact, I have a date with Mrs. Alina Whestin, if you must know. Of the Palms Away Whestins. Perhaps you've heard of them? She wants to come over around five to discuss me helping her out with a charity do. I say, what are the odds?"

Indeed. "I thought you warned me to stay away from that woman."

"I'm a bit skeptical myself," Billy Ray said, dropping the accent. He gave me a look. "She told me not to tell anyone. You two aren't still—?"

"Jesus, man!"

He held up a hand. "Relax. Maybe, using my finely honed investigative techniques, I'll learn something Tony can use. Women like that in the hands of men like me morph into *Silly Putty,* trust me."

"Uh-huh. Forget that charity stuff. Maybe she hates her husband and wants to hand over a box full of evidence. Case closed."

"Only happens in the movies."

I forced a smile, debating if I should let him know that somewhere along the way I might have somewhat carelessly dropped his name in a conversation with Mrs. Whestin. And that this past weekend her very own sister, the one whose identity I was determined to protect, had told me that she suspected Alina had murdered their father to get control of his company. Stuff like that.

"You look anxious," he said. "If you knew some of the nefarious and not-nearly-so-attractive characters I'd faced in my illustrious career, you wouldn't give this a second thought. It'll be fun."

"Call me when she leaves. We'll compare notes. I've got some things to tell you."

"I might catch a flick tonight. Join me?"

I shook my head. "Work."

"Your loss." He smugly sucked a bit of apple from between his teeth and debonairly tossed the core into the trash.

"Just remember what you told me," I said.

"What's that?"

"People with that kind of money don't always play nice."

He gave that a moment's reflection, then tapped a two-finger salute against his forehead and headed for the door, still full of himself.

As Alina walked up the short driveway to Billy Ray's home, her heart raced with the kind of nervous excitement she hadn't felt since that fateful morning when she taken control of her life—before Jeremy conned it away from her. She had it back now, and no one would ever take it away again.

An odd thought hit her as she wondered what the official time of death would be. Maybe not so odd, she decided, the T.O.D. on her father still etched in her mind. Ten-thirty in the morning, they ruled, about six minutes off. It hardly mattered.

Today, just for fun, she put her money on five-twenty.

Billy Ray was at the door before she could push the bell, his smile as infectious as she'd last remembered. He led her to the living room where he pointed to a plate of cheese, grapes and crackers. "Very nice," she said when he made a point of singling out the cheese for special recognition.

He asked her what she'd like to drink, then mentioned he'd just placed an order for a pizza. "Plenty for both of us if you can stay. Should be here in about twenty-five minutes."

Alina's heart stopped for a second, but she decided she could still make it work, if nothing went wrong. She politely shook her head. "I have dinner plans, but a club soda and lemon would be nice."

"Comin' up. Can I take your jacket or—?"

Alina clutched her purse to her side. "I'm fine, thank you."

As soon as Billy Ray left to get her drink, she scanned the room and spotted the base unit for his mobile phones resting on a lamp table next to the sofa. She also saw his cell phone on the edge of the coffee table. And, as good fortune would have it, something else: the diversion she needed to set up Billy Ray's death.

Glancing at her watch, she used the handkerchief in her purse to pluck the cell from the table, turned the unit off and dropped it into her purse. Next, also using the handkerchief, she reached below the lamp table and pulled the telephone cord from its wall jack. "When did you say your pizza's coming?" she called out.

"Maybe twenty minutes now, give or take," came the reply.

Enough time but not much to spare.

To be polite, she cut a slice of the *Comté*, placed it on a cracker and sat down on the couch. When Billy Ray returned with her drink, she held up the cracker and complimented him on his good taste. His single arched eyebrow and debonair nod of the head, the unintentional affectations of James Bond dressed in shorts, sandals and an island print camp shirt, almost made her laugh.

"How can I help you?" he asked, taking a seat in a leather recliner with a seam split down the cushion's left edge.

Setting her drink aside, Alina opened her purse and pulled out a small yellow pad. Pretending to clear space in her purse in search of a pen, she carefully unwound a wad of tissues she'd wrapped around a nearly full syringe.

She looked up and smiled at Billy Ray, feigning embarrassment. As she appeared about to apologize for being so unorganized, she looked past her host to the room's entertainment center. In the middle of the unit was a wall-mounted high definition television screen, surrounded on either side by three shelves of accessories likely bought by Millie. Placed among them were a few items she guessed Billy Ray had added on his own: a model-sized replica of a '50s era hot rod, what looked to be an autographed baseball and several framed pictures of men posing at various golf functions.

She'd been here close to ten minutes. It was time. "Is that a Remington?" she asked, pointing at the middle shelf on the right side of the entertainment center.

Billy Ray seemed surprised by her interest, and she guessed she didn't exactly come off as a Remington kind of gal. Still, he got up and waved her over to the sculpture, admiring it as if he were seeing it for the first time. "Actually, it's a James Earl Fraser."

Alina, the syringe palmed in her left hand, told him she'd heard her husband mention Mr. Fraser before, then casually positioned herself to the side and slightly behind her host, as if giving him room to describe his prized possession. She thought she heard a noise at the front door and froze, but it was nothing.

He told her the sculpture was called "End of the Trail." With seemingly great fondness he ran a finger along the back of the slumping bronze Indian astride his exhausted steed. "My buddies at the FBI gave it to me as a retirement present. Said the Indian looked a lot like me. Here, let me—*hey! Ouch!*"

Billy Ray slapped at the back of his neck with such speed, he knocked the syringe out of Alina's hand. It clinked to the marble floor, half its contents still inside the vial. Not as much as she'd hoped to inject but enough.

She moved backwards as a fresh release of adrenaline coursed through her arteries, preparing her for the reactions of a man who would soon have the same powerful hormone raging through his. Her task now was to stay out of Billy Ray's reach long enough for his muscles to seize and his lungs to empty—and before he found a way to get help. She positioned herself behind the sofa, a cat ready to spring in any direction to avoid being cornered.

With one hand against the back of his neck and an eye on his attacker, Billy Ray picked up the syringe by the tip of the plunger, then eyed Alina with the uncomprehending, self-conscious grin of someone who knows something bad has just happened but with no clue as to what or why.

What's this?" he asked, holding the syringe to the light. "What did you just do?"

"I suggest you sit down, Mr. Hammonds. It will be easier that way."

Billy Ray carefully laid the syringe on a shelf of the entertainment center. "I don't know what you just did, Mrs. Whestin, or what you're up to, but we're going to find out." He edged toward the telephone. "You stay right there."

Alina moved along the back of the sofa away from the phone. Half the vial was enough succinylcholine to kill even a man of Billy Ray's size, especially since by picking the back of his neck she'd bypassed the layers of fat usually involved with intramuscular injections. The paralytic drug would start to show its affects quickly, but she needed to stay clear of Billy Ray for at least another five minutes. For a few minutes after that she would watch him die, hopefully before that damn pizza delivery van showed up.

He picked up the phone and pressed the "talk" button, but got no dial tone.

He tried again, then cursed and flung the receiver against the back the couch. Glancing first at the coffee table for his cell phone, he stuffed both hands into his pants pockets, searched around the room and then took on the look of a man who'd had enough. Who knew *he* had no time to waste.

Alina saw it coming. The hardening of the ex-agent's jaw, the clenching of his fists. She feigned left, then lurched to her right as Billy Ray lunged for her shoulders. He tried to correct his aim mid-leap but his trailing leg caught the base of the coffee table, and he crashed to the floor, slicing his head on the edge of the table lamp on the other side of the couch. Alina couldn't believe it was happening all over again, though this time her victim was going to be a lot harder to subdue.

Even as he was falling, Billy Ray managed to grab her right ankle, bringing her down hard on her elbows. She kicked at his wrist until he was forced to relinquish his grip. On all fours she made it back to the center of the room, separated from Billy Ray only by the coffee table and his recliner.

He rolled over on his back, holding his head and breathing hard. Struggling to his knees, he swiped a shoulder across the left side of his face as blood dripped into his eyes.

Alina watched him assessing his next move. There were likely other phones elsewhere in the house, but with the base unit unplugged from the wall, none of them would work, either—and by now Billy Ray probably knew it. She saw his left arm twitch as he opened and closed his fingers with obvious effort. It was beginning.

He mumbled something and looked toward the front door. Panic was his worst enemy now, and Alina knew he would try to use his training to fight it. It wouldn't help.

Billy Ray struggled to one knee, but when he tried to push himself upright, he stumbled, again winding up on his back.

Alina didn't have time to wait for him to go catatonic. *Lay the cell phone back down on the coffee table. No! On the floor where it would have fallen.*

A quick check on Billy Ray. He'd rolled over onto his stomach, trying to push himself up to his knees, but he was twitching more noticeably now and sucking for air.

Retrieve the syringe's cover from your purse. Grab the syringe from the shelf.

Slip it into the cover and the cover into your panties.

Next step: she inspected the floor for droplets that might have escaped the syringe. She got down on all fours and with her handkerchief swiped across a patch of flooring where she thought the syringe had landed.

She was about to get back to her feet when a sharp pain to the back of her knees sent her sprawling head first into the entertainment center, her shoulder bouncing painfully off a decorative door pull.

Alina spun to her right, prepared to kick Billy Ray in the groin or chest or face or wherever necessary to keep him off her. But his kick had been a last gasp effort. He was on his back now, rocking side to side, his face a frozen mask, his body growing rigid. Given the man's size, the succinylcholine seemed to be working unusally fast. Unless he really was having a heart attack. How lucky could she get!

One minute more, maybe two....

The doorbell rang, like a four-alarm siren.

She lurched to her feet and staggered frantically toward the telephone base where she bent down and reinserted the cord in its wall jack. She then grabbed the phone from the couch where Billy Ray had thrown it and crawled to his side.

The doorbell rang again, followed by knuckles rapping against the doorframe. *Brush the blood from his eyes. They'd expect you to do that. Dial 911.*

Billy Ray wasn't dead yet, but he would be by the time the ambulance arrived. She grabbed the phone, then flung open the door. Grabbing the startled teenager by the arm, she tossed aside the pizza box and yanked him into the house.

"Do you know CPR?" she screamed, pointing at Billy Ray's prostrate hulk. "I think this man's had a heart attack! He fell and—please, *do something!*"

The stunned teenager felt for a pulse, not sure what to do next. Alina stood behind him and calmly dialed 911. The time was five-twenty four. Not bad.

50.

I left my message about Sneaky Pete with a staffer at the Community Association, who promised me she'd send Dale out to have another look.

"When?" I asked, feeling back in control. If Sneaky Pete was about to leave the neighborhood, I wanted to be there to pay my respects.

"Hard to say," was the answer. *Great.*

I returned to the case I hoped to present to the FBI, which would rest on three obvious points: first, the communications division's financial statements, which I was confident I could handle without additional input from Victoria.

Second, there was the private placement, which might or might not generate hard evidence of money laundering. I'd have to leave that to the Treasury Department and the FBI.

Finally, I could point to Victoria's statement that the cell phones contained pirated software, a fact of which both Jeremy and Wallace, according to Victoria and my own suspicions, were aware.

Proving that could be a challenge. I didn't have a clue how the FBI might work it, but turning my samples over to Billy Ray would be a start, Alina's request for more time notwithstanding.

Hours later, surrounded by two-dozen documents and fifteen pages of notes, I had a splitting headache, in part due to the fact that I'd worked right through cocktail hour *and* dinner. It was now eight-fifteen, and as I headed for the kitchen to microwave a plate of frozen pizza rolls, it struck me that Billy Ray hadn't called to tell me about his visit with Alina. I made a mental note to chastise my buddy when he got back from whatever movie he'd decided was more important than a call to his best friend.

It wasn't until after I'd eaten that my phone rang. Certain I'd hear the big man's voice on the other end, I picked up the phone without checking the caller ID, which left me completely unprepared.

Sadness, joy, hope and then apprehension pulsed through my body at the sound of Colleen's voice. "I thought you might want to talk," she said, sounding as if somebody had just died.

"I didn't think we had anything left to say."

"You haven't you heard?"

The question sucked the air out of my lungs. "Heard what?"

"Oh, Rainey, I'm so sorry to have to tell you this, but Billy Ray...he died this afternoon, apparently of a heart attack. I thought you'd have heard by now."

Damn, lousy cell phone connections.

"What are you talking about? I saw him this afternoon. He...he looked great."

No response. "Colleen? Are you...*oh, God, no.*" I closed my eyes and tried to choke down the boulder in my throat. And then I stopped breathing.

Billy Ray. This afternoon. With Alina. The woman who'd told him not to tell anyone of their get-together. The woman I'd told of Billy Ray's offer to help me investigate those phones. The woman who may have murdered her father.

And what had I done? Neglected to tell my friend about any of it. I wanted to vomit. After getting what particulars I could, which were very few, I cleared my head and laid it all out. "Colleen, there's something I've got to tell you. I've been hired by Jeremy Whestin to help get his company ready for a public offering in February, to make sure his filing passes muster. If I find anything out of the ordinary, in his financial statements or anywhere else, I'm supposed to take my evidence directly to him."

"And then what?"

I could imagine her shoulders stiffening, wedding ring spinning around her finger.

"It's not what you think. Not any longer. I'm trying now to prove that Jeremy and his CFO are out to commit securities fraud. Billy Ray is...was...going to help me."

No need to tell her that I'd uncovered a money laundering plot involving foreign terrorists. Steve Wannamaker notwithstanding, I was pretty sure she still cared about me and would worry herself sick that I'd find a way to fuck this up even further. And she was probably right.

Somewhere out there in the FBI's heavenly green pastures, I hoped Billy Ray was giving me the finger. Suddenly the thought of disrupting the distribution of funds to terrorists who might use the money to kill thousands of innocents on American soil paled in comparison to the sorrow and disgust I felt over the loss of one person, a best friend whose death I might have prevented if I'd just left him out of all this. Or had warned him to be extra-careful.

"So you had a pretty good idea of what Jeremy was up to when you decided to work with him?" she asked.

"I had my reasons, Colleen. And it wasn't just for the money, though we could certainly use—." I stopped and started again. "I was trying to protect our reputation here. Jeremy was going to expose my past if I didn't cooperate with him." How petty that sounded now.

"How would *Jeremy* know what you did?"

I explained it all in the CliffsNotes version, which I figured was all either of us could handle.

"But *now* you don't care about the truth getting out?"

Colleen was getting warmed up, and I wasn't in the mood. "It isn't that I don't care. It's just that—look, it's enough for now that you know I'm concerned that Alina Whestin might have been with Billy Ray this afternoon. That she might even have had something to do with his death."

"What are you saying?"

"I can't explain now, and you absolutely must say nothing until I can prove my suspicions. We could make a bad situation intolerable if we aren't careful, okay?" I wouldn't have been surprised if Colleen accused me of having climbed back on the horse. It sounded crazy even to me.

"What are you going to do?"

"My job."

"You're alone on this now?"

"Pretty much."

Colleen paused a long time before I heard her say, "Be careful, Rainey. Let me know if I can help."

You could come home! I wanted to scream but mustered only a feeble, "Thanks," just before she said good-bye.

I walked outside to the bar, poured myself a stiff gin and sat on the same stool where less than two weeks ago Billy Ray offered his help. From here I could see my bongos perched on their chrome stand in a corner of the great room where they'd been gathering dust, the skins turning to mush. They were beckoning me now to take refuge from my shock and grief and guilt, but I could only stare at them in disbelief, unable to comprehend the incomprehensible.

I wanted to throw my glass against the wall, but it wouldn't have changed the truth. There was nothing left but to do what Billy Ray would have done, what he'd been hoping I'd have the courage to do all along.

51.

In minutes, the sun would edge above the tops of the Shady Ladies that bordered the eastern edge of the back yard. I'd seen dozens of spectacular sunsets since moving to Florida but not a single sunrise. And this one I owed to a sleepless night agonizing over Billy Ray's death and my own culpability, Victoria's allegations and my fears about Alina—it was all too gut wrenching to absorb.

I also remembered Billy Ray cautioning me that the FBI didn't issue warnings, and that I had an unofficial appointment with his pal, Tony.

It was the first of October, and the hot weather likely wouldn't break for another two or three weeks. I wandered into the lanai, then out onto the upper deck. Sneaky Pete, looking as if he'd been working out, was sunning himself on the far bank. I'd seen nothing of the blue heron chick since its mother had been murdered and didn't know if that was a good sign or bad.

"Rainey?"

Startled, I spun around, my eyes falling upon an Alina Whestin I hadn't seen before. She wore a wrinkled gray sweatshirt and red flannel pajama bottoms.

A white plastic band held back most of her hair, but a few loose strands fell over her forehead above puffy eyes filled with tears I couldn't trust.

What was she doing here? How was she going to explain her visit with Billy Ray? And when I told her I was going to the FBI with evidence of fraud in Whestin Group's operations, how would she react? Should I fear for *my* life? Who the hell was this woman?

Alina fell against me, burying her head in my shoulder. I wondered if she could feel me shudder.

"It all happened so fast," she said, sniffling. "There was nothing I could do."

I listened in silent agony as she relived each horrific moment: Billy Ray clutching his chest, falling against her, pushing her into the entertainment center, then staggering forward and hitting his head on the coffee table. I thought her distress seemed excessive. Was it all a game?

"Was anyone else with you?"

She shook her head. "Only the pizza boy, poor thing. I wanted to call you last night"—she stopped, her voice choking—"but the police came over, and Jeremy never left my side."

"What were you doing there?"

She hesitated, sniffling. "I wanted him to MC the Guadalupe Center auction. When you mentioned his name the other day, I thought, everybody knows him, he's a friend to the Center—."

When I mentioned his name. How lucky Billy Ray was to have had a friend like me.

Alina dabbed at her nose with the sleeve of her sweatshirt. "There was nothing I could do."

Twice she'd said that.

I led her to a lounge chair, and we sat down. "Why didn't you just call him? Billy Ray, I mean. Why didn't you just call?"

Another sniffle. "I thought seeing him would be the polite thing to do. And I wanted him to see our itinerary for the evening."

She raised her head off my shoulder and looked at me, her lower lip trembling. "Why the third degree?"

"Sorry. You shouldn't take this so personally. Like you said, there was nothing—"

"When you see a person die right in front you, it's just such a shock."

I wondered if it had been easier the second time and hated myself. We sat in silence for a minute as the rising sun warmed our haggard faces. A butterfly flitted above a bed of salmon-colored geraniums that bordered the lower patio. I noticed that Sneaky Pete had left the bank and was now floating in the middle of the pond, staring at us.

"What does this do to your case?" Alina asked.

I'd been expecting that question, but I still couldn't suppress another involuntary shiver. "I haven't had time to think about it."

Truth was, I'd thought about it plenty last night.

If I was going to hang Jeremy and Wallace, it would be on the basis of proving they'd doctored Whestin Group's financial statements to enhance the prospects of a successful public offering. The money laundering evidence would have to be uncovered by someone with a lengthier reach than I.

As for the cell phones, the thought that Billy Ray might have died for what amounted to little more than grandstanding on my part left me with what felt like a perforated ulcer and a heart heavy with remorse.

Alina slipped her hands between her thighs and cuddled closer. "I should be getting back, but I don't want to."

Tough. I took her hand and helped her up. "If Jeremy's awake and you come in dressed like that, he'll guess you weren't at the 7-11."

"He won't be up for hours. In fact, if he doesn't rally soon, he won't be in very good shape for your meeting."

Which, I thought, might be just the way she wants it.

Nothing in my training had prepared me for any of this, except to maintain a healthy skepticism of every fact and figure, no matter how positive I was of what I thought I knew. In this case, I didn't yet have all the facts, and I'd never run across a figure quite like the one nestled against me now.

We got to the door and Alina's face brightened. "Jeremy's flying to St. Louis Friday morning. Why don't I bring something over for dinner? I've been thinking about your—*our*—concerns, and I might have a solution. We'll just talk."

"He's not staying the weekend?"

Alina shrugged. "He says he wants to get those stock transfer papers signed.

Of course, we both know who still lives there."

Victoria had pushed me out of her condo last Sunday, saying she needed to start packing. Had she, please God, by now left for the safety of her friends in New Mexico? I'd been honest with Alina about what Victoria had told me, but that had been before Billy Ray's death. Had I put another human being's life in jeopardy?

I held Alina by both wrists. "You didn't say anything to Jeremy about Vic—?"

"Of course not. This has been a bad time for everybody, Rainey. But everything's going to work out if we stick together. Besides, I'm just talking lasagna. How about it?"

I was prepared to spend the weekend alone with my guilt and self-condemnation and away from whatever threat Alina might pose to my well-being. But she said she had a "solution," and my professional curiosity couldn't let that pass. At least that was my rationale. "What time?"

"Let's say seven. And good luck tomorrow with Jeremy."

Victoria closed the door to her condo for the last time, her excitement warming the ice cap that had been building across her heart.

She'd felt all along that one day the truth about Alina would surface, although her faith had been tested mightily as the years passed. She didn't have actual proof even now, but what she'd just learned might finally be the break she'd been hoping for. She gathered her purse, peeked out the window at her ride and shook her head, still not believing the events of the past three hours.

First, there'd been the not completely unexpected visit this morning from Mack Evans. She knew Jeremy would try to reach her, and when he couldn't, he'd send his runner. Victoria had hoped to be long gone by yesterday, but there'd been too much to pack, too much to get organized and arranged. It was Wednesday now, and she was supposed to be leaving on a connecting flight to New Mexico later today.

She'd been surprised it had taken this long for Mack to show up. "Jeremy's been sick," was his explanation. "I didn't get the word until yesterday afternoon."

"What word?"

"You need to leave now, Ms. Laine. Leave the state, if you can. And so do I."

Victoria's packed bags had been lined up in the foyer, waiting to be stuffed in her trunk for the ride to the airport and the flight to Albuquerque. But she wasn't going anywhere until she'd heard why Mack was so worried about her. He seemed confused, borderline incredulous, as he told his story, pacing the floor.

"I sat in the parking lot most of last night, trying to convince myself that Jeremy hadn't really ordered me to...."

"What, Mack? What did he say?"

His answer stunned her. *"Find her. Then take her out."*

She'd spent the next hour sitting in silence, trying to get those words to register, when she received the call that promised to change her life. Or at least her plans for the next few days.

She took one final glance around the condo so full of memories and high drama, hope and, ultimately, betrayal and humiliation. Then she locked the door and left for what she knew would be forever.

"You don't have to do this, you know," she said as she got into Mack's car. "I told you that."

The private investigator checked his rearview mirror and pulled away. "I can't say how he's been with you, but Jeremy has never been what I'd call a teddy bear. Only now he's someone I don't know. Or want to. I do know that based on that call you got, we need to get you to Florida."

Victoria couldn't get Mack's earlier words out of her mind. *Find her. Then take her out.* She shuddered at how close she'd grown to the man who now wanted her dead—if Mack had heard right.

Maybe he hadn't.

She'd been around Jeremy several times recently when he suddenly babbled irrelevant, sometimes unintelligible statements, using ugly words and pronouncements that frightened her. Afterward he would claim not to remember any of it. Still, if Jeremy somehow knew what she'd told Rainey McDermott, it was conceivable that in his condition he could do something unthinkable.

She watched the familiar landscape zip by for the last time. The pin oak, silver maple, eastern redbud and white ash that lined the county road were still various hues of green. In a week or two, they would transform the countryside into a kaleidoscope of rich fall colors, a far cry from the desert-influenced climate where she would soon be hiding.

"I can never repay you, Mack."

"No need. He's gone too far. They both have."

Victoria said a silent prayer of thanks to her guardian angel and sat back for the ride to Mack's apartment where they would be spending the night. Tomorrow, she would return home for the first time since leaving Florida a year after her father's death. She tried to temper her excitement. After all, if she got the evidence she expected to, she still had to figure out how to present it to Alina.

The options were many, one too deliciously ironic to contemplate.

52.

The start of the flight from St. Louis to Fort Myers had been a harrowing one. When she'd arrived at her gate this morning, Mack at her side, she'd been startled to see Wallace, a carry-on bag slung over his shoulder, handing his ticket to the desk attendant. He'd glanced in her direction, but she'd turned her back to him just in time, before he disappeared down the jet way.

Getting herself seated had nearly been a disaster.

She'd quickly stopped at a gift shop and bought a ball cap, which she'd pulled low over her eyes. Entering the plane, she'd turned her head and positioned herself close behind Mack's body, praying her seat would be far distant from Wallace's.

It was, but just as she passed Wallace's seat, he'd turned to put his bag in the overhead compartment, bumping Mack in the process. The two men had looked directly at each other, and Victoria's heart had come up in her throat. Luckily, they'd never met, and she'd hurried to her seat, unnoticed.

Hanging back upon landing, they'd avoided Wallace as he disembarked from the plane. Now, as Victoria stopped at the entrance to the offices of Manetti

Pharmaceuticals and made a mental note of the time and date—3:30 P.M., Thursday, October 2nd—she prayed that today would mark the beginning of the end of her quest to bring her sister to justice. The air hovered hot and humid above the asphalt parking lot, but Victoria's body shivered with anticipation. She turned back toward Mack, now sitting alone in the rental car she'd put in her name. He stuck out his arm and waved, his fingers crossed.

In the lobby, a tall, curvy receptionist asked her to take a seat. Jeremy put a premium on first impressions, and it hadn't taken Victoria long to know how he defined what he called his front desk "hood ornaments." This one was no exception.

A minute later, the president of Manetti Pharmaceuticals entered the lobby through a door marked "Restricted." If the call yesterday morning had come from anyone else, Victoria would have ignored it, as she'd been ignoring Jeremy's calls all week. But something told her that the call from Robert Billings was a call from God.

Joe Reardon, director of security, accompanied him. Both gentlemen acknowledged her with polite but nervous smiles. After an exchange of introductions, they escorted her to Reardon's small but neatly appointed office. He closed and locked his door, pulled the shades and asked Victoria to take a seat opposite his desk.

A large monitor had been positioned on a metal stand so everyone in the room could see it. Victoria saw nine split images on the screen, each representing what she guessed to be a live camera scan of different areas of the building complex. An occasional forklift moved about inside each image.

A separate laptop computer sat on Reardon's desk. He pulled it toward him and glanced uneasily at his boss. "Go ahead, Joe," Billings said.

Reardon unlocked a desk drawer from which he pulled a compact disk. "I was brought in six months ago, Ms. Laine, to overhaul the security systems here. A month ago, we completed the initial installation of a digital recording system that covers every sensitive area of operations, including shipping and delivery, materials storage, manufacturing, final inventory and other areas I won't bore you with. Up to then, I'm afraid security was pretty basic, to say the least."

"Joe's done a helluva job for us," Billings said.

Victoria smiled patiently. "I'm sure he has."

Reardon shot his boss a nervous smile. Despite his best efforts, a security breach had apparently just occurred on his watch, involving the no less a prominent visitor than the wife of the company's owner and chief executive officer. Victoria imagined that poor Mr. Reardon hadn't garnered much sleep last night.

Reardon rested a hand on the top of the laptop. "Naturally, we've tried to keep as much of this as secret as possible, with most of the actual installation of cameras and recording equipment completed after hours. I believe only three other execs and myself fully understand all that we've done."

Billings shifted his weight. "We aren't supposed to go fully active for another week or so, but Joe's been running tests—to fix the bugs, so to speak."

Get on with it, man! Victoria wanted to scream.

"Anyway," Billings said, "as I told you over the phone, we got an unexpected visit yesterday from Mrs. Whestin. She used to own this company"—Victoria nodded and bit down hard on her lower lip as Billings cleared his throat—"said she was in the area, got nostalgic, and thought she'd just drop by to say hello to some of the employees."

Victoria turned toward Reardon, pleading with her eyes. "You saw something on the security tapes that concerned you?"

Billings cut him off from answering. "When Mrs. Whestin asked if she could take a look around, I thought no big deal. Frankly, she'd caught me on a very busy day, so when she declined my offer to escort her, I was a little relieved."

Victoria turned back towards Reardon. "Later that afternoon," he said, turning the laptop to face her, "I was reviewing the day's recordings, and I saw this."

He inserted the CD and the laptop's screen revealed a three-quarters overhead shot of a concrete walkway with stock shelves on either side. The shelves were lined with rows of small white cartons.

A few seconds later, a lone figure entered the scene. Victoria stared at the screen, mesmerized, as Alina walked to the end of one row, looked both left and right, then returned to a spot roughly halfway between both ends of the walkway.

"This is what Bob was telling you about," Reardon said as he walked from behind the desk to watch the video over Victoria's shoulder. Robert Billings joined him and the three watched in silence as Alina reached deep into the back of a shelf at eye level and removed two small cartons. Reardon froze the video image as both cartons disappeared into Alina's purse.

"Succinylcholine?" Victoria asked.

She'd picked up more about her father's business than anyone had ever given her credit for. "Succ," one of their consistently solid sellers, was used to paralyze the airway so the anesthesiologist could more easily get a breathing tube down the patient's throat. That she'd missed something this obvious all these years stabbed at her heart.

Billings gave her a look of respect. "Apparently Mrs. Whestin persuaded one of our employees assigned to the area—and old hire of hers—to grant her access. That should have raised a giant red flag, but she's the CEO's wife and, well….it's just weird."

"I thought about calling the police," Reardon added, "but that's against company procedure, as you know."

"You did the right thing," Victoria said. Any suspected breach of security was to be brought to her attention, which she was then to forward to Jeremy. It was to be his decision alone how best to handle what could be potentially embarrassing revelations about security shortfalls.

Reardon continued. "If you know about this drug, Ms. Laine, then you know that if there's an overdose, it could paralyze the patient's breathing apparatus. Without an external forced oxygen source, the person dies of what often just looks like a heart attack."

Victoria knew that wasn't all that made succinylcholine so appealing to someone intent on doing evil. Not long after injection, the drug broke up in the body and disappeared, leaving virtually no trace of its existence, unless through a sophisticated brain scan used only in extreme cases when foul play was suspected.

That, of course, was when it was given intravenously. When the cause of death was unknown or needed to be confirmed, medical examiners routinely searched for injection sites where concentrations of a potentially lethal drug would be greatest and trace residues thus more easily identified. But if the victim's treating physician believed the cause of death to be related to a preexisting condition—and signed off on the death certificate—the case would never even get to the M.E.'s office.

"What happened after this?" Victoria asked, fixated on the computer screen.

Reardon restarted the CD, but it ended seconds later as Alina disappeared from the screen.

"I wasn't away fifteen minutes," Billings said, "but when I returned, she was nowhere to be found. The receptionist said she'd left not five minutes earlier. No good-byes, nothing."

Victoria mustered as much authority in her voice as possible. "Mr. Whestin will want me to bring him a vial. I'll wait."

Reardon looked unsure, but Billings jumped in. "Just give us a moment to pull together the appropriate paperwork."

"Well, of course," Victoria said, implying she expected such careful security measures, especially now that the proverbial horse had left the barn.

Billings looked somewhat relieved and jerked his head at Reardon, who began flipping through his files. A few minutes later, the last of the papers signed, Billings handed the CEO's executive assistant a sealed carton of succinylcholine.

"Thank you, gentlemen," she said, dropping the vial into her purse. "I ask that you keep this confidential until I meet with Mr. Whestin, and he calls you."

Victoria smiled inwardly as both men nodded, clearly relieved that fingering the boss's wife hadn't so far cost them their jobs. Two minutes later, she settled into the front seat of the rental car, her mind racing.

"Success?" Mack asked.

When she nodded he told her that Jeremy had called a few minutes earlier.

"He wanted to know if I had any leads on your whereabouts. He didn't sound too pleased with me—or too lucid, to be honest—but at least he didn't reiterate his orders."

A momentary tug at her heart told Victoria she hadn't yet got over the man who now apparently wanted her dead. But right now, she had a more important relationship issue to resolve.

"He's meeting with Mr. McDermott as we speak," Mack said. "Wouldn't you like to be a fly on the wall for that one?"

Victoria wondered just how Rainey intended to deal with his newfound information, though none of that was at the top of her mind right now.

"We have a stop to make," she said.

"Where to?"

She handed him a piece of paper with an address on it. "An old friend works there. I called her before we left your apartment."

"Because…?"

"I'm cashing in a favor I did for her years ago."

"Was she happy to hear from you?"

Victoria snuck a look inside her purse. "Not exactly."

53.

I'd been working for one—or was it both?—of the Whestins for nearly four weeks. It had been both the fastest and the longest month of my life, considering that most of my days on cocaine I either still couldn't recall or had managed to bury deep inside what was left of my brain.

I pushed the front door intercom and noticed the security camera mounted above the Whestin's front door. I was about to give it a friendly wave when I heard Alina's voice.

"Just a moment," she said, and my heart flipped. The last time I'd been on this doorstep, I'd had the option to go or to stay. I had no such option now. This was "Report Card Day," when I was to reveal what, if any, evidence of fraud I'd found in Whestin Group's books and operations.

"String Him Along Day," was a more appropriate title, I thought, though if Jeremy had any inkling I was preparing to go the authorities, "String Him *Up* Day" would be more apropos.

Alina opened the front door, and I froze. Her thin smile, taught jaw and unblinking eyes signaled trouble as Jeremy appeared at her side.

"Come in, Rainey," he said, a hand firmly on Alina's shoulder. "We've been looking forward to this."

We?

I followed Jeremy into the living room and sat on the same couch where I'd been so easily seduced by the woman who was now offering to make us sandwiches. She gave me a furtive smile, then disappeared into the kitchen.

Jeremy switched off a television that had been tuned to FOX. "World's going to hell in a hand basket," he said, sitting down in an easy chair. *The* easy chair. I couldn't help wondering what piece of furniture Alina had used to have her way with Wallace.

"Terrible news about Mr. Hammonds," he said, his eyes constricted, as if making a conscious effort to focus. "I understand you two were friends."

I nodded.

"He worked for the FBI, I understand."

"Retired a few years back."

He stared at me a second, then asked how the fishing was in Sarasota. I was ready. "The 'fishing' was great," I said. "The 'catching' was another story."

Jeremy nodded several times, as if counting off the seconds before his next question. "If you've got time to go fishing, then I assume we're ready?"

"To...?"

"Air our laundry before God, the underwriter and the SEC."

The man still had a sense of humor, I could see, though I dared not acknowledge the pun. My goal today was to make my report, impress him enough to put his mind at ease, then get the hell out of here.

"Clear sailing, from my view," I said, setting him up.

Jeremy cocked his head. "I'm disappointed in you, Mr. McDermott. Wallace is going to be insufferable—aren't you, Wallace?"

I thought Jeremy might be experiencing another weird brain event—until I heard a snicker behind me. I turned and saw that Wallace Gerard had entered the room from the kitchen where he'd apparently been sequestered.

The CFO placed both hands on the back of a chair and stared at me, all self-congratulatory. "I think you overpaid, Jeremy," he said, but with less enthusiasm than I would have expected.

I noticed that Wallace's eyes avoided Jeremy's, and that he kept his distance, stiff and distracted, no happier to be here than I was.

Given my grandson-of-Irish-immigrants status, I'd never considered myself racist, more the influence of my blessed mother than of Frank's absentee parenting. But I couldn't help seeing Wallace in a different light now and jealousy, professional or otherwise, had nothing to do with it.

Was he just carrying out Jeremy's bidding? Or was he in bed with terrorists, playing his part to once again bring death and destruction to American soil?

And what was he doing here now? Why hadn't Alina warned me? Jeremy had either set Wallace up to be embarrassed today—or he'd set me up. I'd relish the former, but I hadn't signed up for the latter.

"You didn't let me finish," I said, looking at both men. "It's clear sailing if you follow my suggestions. If you don't—well, I'm just hired help."

With one eye partially closed and a hand pressed to his temple, Jeremy looked first at Wallace, then at me. "Well, that's better," he said in a voice too loud for the setting. "You should have found *something*, given how much time you've spent with my wife."

He flashed a bemused grin, as if ribbing an old friend. I failed to see the humor. My chest muscles tightened, and I wondered if Jeremy's private investigator had been less taken with Alina's charms than she'd thought.

Wallace's eyes were now riveted on mine, his head down and shoulders canted forward. I half expected him to start pawing at the carpeting.

I decided my best tact would be to forge ahead and in broad terms tell my audience of two everything I'd found in the financial documents before Jeremy got any weirder or took another pill and passed out on me. If they asked how I got so smart in so short a time, I'd chalk it up to proprietary techniques, superior genes and a smidgeon of dumb luck. A little humility never hurts.

As for the cell phones, I would say nothing unless they asked, and then I'd confess that my trip had just been a sideshow with nothing to show for it. With no Billy Ray to help me, that was the truth—for now.

Nor could I say anything about what was essentially a bridge financing arrangement with Links International. I wasn't a private investigator with international connections and thousands of dollars to throw around for favors. Discovering the true intent of this alliance could have happened only because someone snitched, and I wasn't about to reveal that someone's name.

Alina entered the room and held a tray of the promised sandwiches in front of me. "Pimento. Just like they serve at The Masters."

With her back turned towards Jeremy and Wallace, she leaned down and mouthed, "I've said nothing." She handed me a sandwich and a napkin, then offered the tray to Wallace. He declined.

"Don't be rude," Jeremy said. "Alina slaved over those little sandwiches for hours. Didn't you, sweetie?"

I winced, expecting Alina to toss the tray into her husband's lap. But she remained calm, refusing to give Jeremy the satisfaction of a reply. She offered him a sandwich, but he looked past her. His pale lips curled into a narrow smile, but his eyes had gone cold. "Now be a good boy, Wallace, and take a sandwich."

Wallace and Alina locked eyes and no one spoke as she again offered him the tray.

"Perhaps I'm hungrier than I thought," he said, lifting a sandwich.

A look of relief spread across Alina's face. She smiled politely, then handed Wallace a napkin. "Are you sure?" she said, turning again toward Jeremy.

He bent over, as if he were going to vomit and waved her away. After a quick nod toward Wallace and me, Alina returned to the kitchen. I'd never seen her like this. So...subservient. It was unsettling.

Jeremy seemed lost in another world, and Wallace had returned to giving me the evil eye. Nothing to do, I decided, but present my verbal report and hope Jeremy could comprehend what I was saying.

"You hired me to make sure Wallace had buried any possible evidence of fraud deep enough to withstand scrutiny." I gritted my teeth. "By and large, I believe he has. But I'm only a month on this assignment, and I've already found discrepancies between the supporting sales receipts and the communications division financials—discrepancies I believe we can hide with a little more creativity."

Wallace's eyes narrowed. Jeremy didn't look particularly impressed.

"I haven't fully examined the preliminary September statements," I said, "but I'll complete that review within a week. And I assume I'll continue to receive monthly statements and the electronic data files right up to January, as we agreed."

"That...was...our deal," Jeremy said. "Don't wan' any las'-minute screw-ups 'cuz Walz here sud'ly got...." He stopped, then closed his eyes and his head fell back against the headrest. He seemed simply to have dozed off.

I started to call for Alina, but Wallace was already heading for the kitchen. "Our business here is finished," he said, glancing at me over his shoulder. "If Jeremy wants to keep you on, that's his call."

"We need to go over those statements."

He turned and took a step in my direction. "Call me Monday, but I wouldn't wait much longer than that. I've been checking Jeremy's desk lately, making sure he's not leaving sensitive information lying about. I came across a report from his doctor. Correction, *neurosurgeon*."

I did my best to act dumb. "And?"

"Let's just say his days are numbered—and so are yours."

Jeremy's eyes fluttered open. "I'm not...through with you people yet." The effort consumed his remaining energy, and he again drifted off.

Wallace shook his head in disgust and continued on into the kitchen. A moment later I heard the murmur of a conversation dominated by a male voice. The tone intensified, then subsided. I heard nothing more until Alina emerged, alone. After propping a pillow behind Jeremy's neck, she guided me to a far corner of the living room.

"What the hell's going on?" I demanded.

"Don't be angry," she whispered. "Wallace showed up ten minutes before you did. I got no warning, myself."

I heard thunder outside and noticed through the foyer windows that it had grown dark outside. "What was that crack of Jeremy's about you and me spending time together? You don't think he knows we've—?"

Alina scoffed. "You wouldn't be standing here if he did."

"Then...what?"

"He enjoys making people sweat, Rainey. Surely you've picked up on that. That's why he had Wallace show up today. Since New Year's Eve, he's delighted in putting him in his place. And by having him show up unannounced, he threw a zinger at me, as well."

"Why didn't Wallace alert you?"

Alina squeezed my hand and glanced towards the kitchen. "Wallace and I have been on shaky ground for some time now. What happened here after your dinner with him didn't help. As much as he despises Jeremy, I think he enjoyed surprising me. It shows he's still not under my control."

I thought about that for a moment. "He just told me he knows about Jeremy's cancer."

"Yes, and he's pissed I didn't tell him."

"Does he know about the stock transfer?"

"I don't think so. At least he hasn't brought it up."

"But if there's a chance—"

Alina escorted me to the front door. "We'll talk about all of this at dinner tomorrow night. Tell me, how far did you get in your report?"

"Not very. I'm supposed to call Wallace Monday to discuss what I think he needs to do. Won't that be fun."

I could tell Alina was listening with half an ear as she watched Jeremy's head slowly roll back and forth against the headrest.

"I have to get him in bed," she said. "Next week he signs over his stock, and I'm going to make sure he's rested and on that flight in the morning if I have to carry him to the airport on my back."

The emotion Alina showed over the death of Billy Ray, a man she barely knew, seemed completely absent as she faced her husband's imminent and likely gruesome passing.

"What's the deal with Wallace?"

"He'll be leaving right behind you, trust me."

My ears burned. Why should I trust anything I heard from any one of these people? And, for that matter, why should any one of them trust me?

A lightning flash greeted me as I opened the front door, followed by the sound of bass drum thunder reverberating against my chest. Raindrops began to fall, and I held a hand over my head as I raced for the car.

54.

Alina returned to the kitchen. "Can I get you anything?" she asked.

Wallace was leaning against the refrigerator, staring out the window. "How's your husband?" he asked.

"Resting."

"He ought to be in a hospital."

"Which is where I'm recommending he go—after he signs the company over to me."

Wallace turned. "What are you talking about?"

Alina reached for a recipe book she kept on the counter near the microwave. She hadn't prepared lasagna in years. "I wasn't going to tell you this until it's official," she said, flipping through several pages, "but you're looking at the majority stockholder of Whestin Group—at least after Jeremy signs the papers Monday."

Wallace walked over and spun her around. "When were you going to tell me?"

Alina glanced toward the great room. "I didn't find out until just this past weekend. I didn't want to say anything until it was legal, but I really do think it's going to happen."

She found the recipe she was looking for and made a note of the page. "It's silver platter time, Wallace. Very soon, Jeremy's going to announce that he's stepping down as chairman and putting Jack Armbruster in control. Everything we've been hoping for."

Wallace's mouth fell open. "This isn't making sense."

"I'm sure not, but it's too complicated to discuss now." Alina moved to the edge of the kitchen and peeked out at her husband, who was snoring in fits and starts.

"How was your meeting?" she asked, turning to put the lunch dishes into the sink.

"Monumental waste of—don't change the subject. What's going on?"

Alina thought she heard a sound from the next room, but Wallace had a hand around her bicep, demanding an answer. She wasn't in the mood for a second bruise and pried his fingers off her flesh. "All right then," she said, "after you meet with Rainey and learn what you need to do, can you pull this off? Will your numbers pass inspection?"

"The meeting will be another waste of time, but yes, they'll pass inspection."

"And if he were no longer around?"

"What does that mean?"

"Answer me."

Wallace squared his shoulders. "I can handle it."

"We'll see. What are you doing tonight? I thought we could—" She stopped, saw the alarm in Wallace's eyes and felt a presence. She turned at the sound of Jeremy's voice.

"Well, well, what have we here?"

Affecting a look of surprise and concern, Alina quickly propped a shoulder under his arm. "C'mon," she said, "we need to get you to bed."

"Need any help?" Wallace asked.

Jeremy waved him away. "You've done...enough."

Alina, guiding her husband toward the master bedroom, spoke to Wallace over her shoulder. "A limo's taking him to the airport tomorrow. You're headed back, too, right?"

Wallace nodded.

"Good. Just make sure he's on the plane and then stay close. A driver will be waiting in St. Louis." She nodded in the direction of the front door, indicating it was time for Wallace to leave.

A few minutes later, she pulled the covers over her husband and watched him drift in and out of consciousness. A primal hatred of this man seethed deep in her heart, blurring her vision but not her objectives. She needed to keep him alive just a few days more. After that, she might—for humanitarian reasons, of course—put him out of his misery herself.

Jeremy's eyes fluttered open. "I couldn't let you have all the fun."

He closed his eyes and fell silent.

Alina waited a minute more, then headed for her jewelry case where she kept her key to the gun case. According to Jeremy, no one knew where Vicky was. She'd tried to reach Mack herself this morning, but he hadn't returned her call, which was disturbing. Still, Vicky was Jeremy's responsibility. If he weren't up to it, she'd borrow a page out of his playbook and do what she had to do—after she'd completed *her* obligations.

She hadn't fired her Ruger in months and wasn't going to get a chance to before her dinner with Rainey tomorrow night. But hefting the pistol a few times this afternoon and tomorrow—aiming it, squeezing the trigger—would bring back the old familiarity. She might even sleep with it under her pillow tonight.

Of course, her own powers of persuasion might head off a deadly confrontation. She genuinely hoped so.

OddsR, she decided: 50/50.

55.

By the time I drove to the end of Alina's driveway, the torrential downpour had limited my vision to about ten feet of roadway ahead. I intended to drive straight home to sort out the events just past until I spotted a steady orange warning light glaring at me like a tiny sun next to the "E" on the gas gauge. Cursing, I drove across to the service station just outside of Palms Way, filled up and then stopped in the food mart for a pastrami sandwich that would serve as my dinner tonight.

Heading back across the road, my grip tightened on the steering wheel as I thought about Alina's insistence that I leave the house first while she dealt with Wallace. She'd put me on her agenda for tomorrow night, but with Jeremy now obviously out of commission, I couldn't help wondering with whom she'd be dining tonight—and how the evening might end this time.

For a moment I thought about executing a drive-by to see if Wallace's car was still in the driveway. Mercifully, I was saved from the ignominy of such foolishness by the sight of Tom Jenks, the gate guard, flailing his hands at a big-boned woman standing next to her car in the visitor's lane. She was getting soaked but giving as good as she got, obviously refusing to budge until she got satisfaction.

The resident's private gate lifted, and I crept through—then stopped a few feet in and rolled down my window. Through the cascading rain I shouted, *"Dolly?"*

The fifteen-minute dash to the emergency entrance of Naples Community Hospital could have been a Disney ride, so many times did the BMW hydroplane down the flooded road before I regained control.

I'd left Dolly behind, hopefully freed from Tom's threats to call the Sheriff. She'd had time only to blurt out that she thought Frank had suffered a seizure and hit his head on the toilet bowl, and that she'd tried to reach me at home, but the phone number wasn't available. She hadn't finished saying "hospital" before I'd spun the car around and sped off.

I was at Frank's side now, perched on the edge of his emergency room bed, staring at a bandage over his left eye. He was under a blanket, both hands resting on top. When I squeezed his hand, he opened one eye and winced. Just then Dolly bustled in and plopped herself on a chair opposite me, drying herself with a towel she'd apparently got from one of the nurses. With her long, straight hair wet and disheveled, her mascara dripping onto her cheeks, I decided she must be one helluva cook. Either that or she gave a good—never mind.

"How do you feel?" I asked Frank.

He shrugged. "They've already done an EEG and now they want to do a CT scan, whatever the hell that is. God knows when they'll get 'round to it."

Dolly leaned over and kissed his cheek.

"Appreciate you comin', lad," Frank said, as he squeezed Dolly's hand. "I thought maybe if this turned out to be somethin' serious, we ought to have a man-to-man, you know?"

He looked purposely at Dolly. She reached into a pocket of her jeans, withdrew something I couldn't make out and slipped the object into his hand. He turned back to face me, his eyes full of concern. "What's eating you, son?"

"What do you mean? I'm just worried about you."

"Sure and I appreciate that, like I said. But there's something else. Seen it the other day at your mother's service. You steal someone's *Guinness?*" Frank adjusted his body and the effort seemed to weaken him. "Better get on with it. I'm not sure how much time I got left."

I swallowed hard. "I need to make some things right—." I almost said "Dad," but stopped myself before I gave both of us a seizure.

Frank looked at me a long while, then opened his hand to reveal a small, multi-colored coat of arms, the kind one might find at a tourist shop.

"What's that?" I asked.

"The McDermott coat of arms, that's what. *Mac*Dermott, to be accurate." He spelled out the first three letters. "Before we got Anglicized."

He handed me the object. "I carry that around with me as a reminder of what I could have been and might yet become, but since your mother died, I've been thinkin' maybe you need it more than me. Or is it I? I can never get that right. Besides, I got a dozen of 'em."

I stared at the object, not knowing if I should be taking this conversation seriously. Frank smoothed out the part of the bed sheet covering his chest. "You know what the family name stands for?"

I'd never thought about it. "The 'Mac' means 'son of.' That's about all I know."

"Everybody knows that," he said, snatching the coat of arms from my fingers. "Now listen. 'Dermot'—I think 'twas one 't' way back, but it don't matter—that's a personal name with two meanings, got it? 'To be a free man, free of envy and jealousy,' that's one of 'em."

His breathing stopped, and I watched him closely. When I thought he was up to it, I asked about the other explanation.

He handed the tiny shield back to me. "'A man of arms,'" he said, the wisp of a proud smile crossing his face. "'Signifying a great warrior.'"

I ran a finger over the red chevron with its three gold crosslets on a white argent. There were also three azure blue boar's heads sporting bristling tusks. At the crest, what I think they call a "demi-lion" held a scepter crowned with the motto, "Honor et virtus." Another motto at the bottom read, "Honor probataque virtus."

"My Latin's a bit rusty. What does 'probataque' mean?"

"Proven," Frank answered, his voice barely audible. "'Honor and proven virtue.' It means you can do anything, lad. Never forget it. Not like I did."

A commotion to my left kept me from uttering words I had no idea where to find. "Time to go for a ride," the orderly told the room.

Dolly gave Frank another kiss, and I stepped back from the bed but not out of the room. No matter how long the evening, I would be here for the duration. When Frank got back, if he was up to it, we had a lot more to discuss. Mother. His leaving us all those years ago. The apology he owed me.

If now wasn't the time, then tomorrow would do. Or the day after. There was a big difference between finding the right time to at last face the music and putting off indefinitely a discussion of the demons we should have dealt with long ago.

The orderly unlocked the bed wheels and Frank grabbed my hand. "Something I've got to say, lad. I might not be makin' it back, you know."

"It's just a brain scan. They probably won't find a thing in there."

Frank didn't smile. "You know for sure nobody's ever died in one of those things?"

"I'm pretty sure—"

"Never mind. Bend down here so I only have to say this once."

I obeyed, and he squeezed my hand tighter. "You were just a kid, Rainey. A bit of a demanding brat, sure, but so were the lot of you."

I was a *what?*

I'd waited a lifetime to hear Frank's guilty plea, imagining the two of us sulking obstinately in the corner of a dimly lit Irish pub, disconnected fifty years by deed and ego but bound by blood and pain and love, confessing our sins over the holy water of an Irish whiskey, hold the whipped cream.

But having nearly given up on my fantasy ever coming true, I didn't want the air to be cleared now while Frank was recovering from a seizure, saying things that only the fear of dying with a guilty conscience would force out of him. I mean, was he about to blame *me* for this mess? I was willing to accept my deserved share, but the hell with him if he expected me to accept it all.

"Let's discuss this later," I said.

Frank shook his head. "We all make mistakes, lad, at every age. That ain't the point. The point is what you do next."

He took hold of my hand. "I don't regret buyin' that company, though God knows I fucked that up royally, didn't I? But I was wrong to bail on the family.

To bail on you and the twins and your blessed mother. To take this long to say I'm sorry. I only wish I had a better excuse than to admit I was a coward. A goddamn stubborn coward."

I glanced at the orderly, who pretended to check his watch, and then at Dolly, who was wiping tears from both of her mascara-blackened cheeks. Frank eyes, I noticed, burned with clarity and purpose.

"You're no kid now, Rainey. And you're no coward. You got things to face up to, do it."

His eyes drifted off, as if he were remembering something important he had to get off his chest. Then he smiled and nodded his head and looked me square on. "You got two kinds of people in this world, lad: those in trouble and those heading for it. Nothing in between. Heard a preacher say that on the radio awhile back, only I think I was a little looped at the time. Anyway, I think he was saying that trouble is God's way of giving you an opportunity to grow as a man—but each time you gotta face the Devil and give him the finger. I'm hoping it's a lesson I can still learn."

"The price could be high," I said. "Like...Everest high."

"Better than potato famine high, and we got through that."

I decided not to remind him that in the process roughly a million of our ancestors had died of starvation and disease. Instead, I slipped the coat of arms into my pocket and gave the okay sign to the orderly. As Frank disappeared down the crowded corridor, I could hear him loud and clear.

"You *sure* nobody's died in one of them things?"

56.

I'd left the hospital last night around eleven, much relieved.

Frank hadn't cracked his skull, but the CT scan confirmed that he'd indeed suffered a minor seizure. He was going to be on medication for a while and, as he'd feared, wouldn't be allowed to drive a car for at least six months. State law.

The doctor wanted him kept overnight for observation. Dolly had told me not to worry, that she'd check him out, and then settle him in at "their" place, Frank's modest two-bedroom bungalow somewhere in North Fort Myers. She was to call me if there were any problems. Otherwise, I promised to stop in first thing tomorrow, though I was ashamed I'd need directions. There obviously was much I didn't know about my father, but we'd made a connection last night. It couldn't have been easy to label himself a coward. In time we'd sort out who did what to whom and who got hurt the worst. But for now, this was enough.

I reached into my pocket and felt the sharp metal edges of the McDermott coat of arms. Just touching it boosted my resolve to listen politely to Alina tonight, then forcefully tell her I was going to the FBI.

She'd be bringing the entrée tonight, which left me responsible for the wine and hors d'oeuvres. I could handle the wine, but much beyond crackers and cheese, I was lost.

I told myself to relax, that Alina wouldn't be too hard on me. After all, yesterday I'd kept my promise not to tell Jeremy that I was prepared to blow the lid off his precious public offering. But after tonight, all bets were off.

I thought of Colleen and wondered how she'd react if she knew the stand I was prepared to take. Saving my marriage was a long shot, to say the least, but I needed her to know there was still some semblance of a conscience in the man she was planning to divorce.

A minute later, I was on the phone.

"Sorry to bother," I said. "Thought you'd be interested to know I'm dining at the house tonight with Alina Whestin, the soon-to-be majority stockholder of Whestin Group. She's going to try to talk me into accommodating her new priorities, but I'm turning her down and turning in her husband. I just wanted you to know."

Colleen was about to say something—probably about how proud she was of me and how wrong she'd been to leave—when a male voice on her end intruded from the otherwise quiet background. I ended the call before she could respond or explain herself, feeling like an idiot and wondering what the hell I'd hoped to accomplish.

I had the phone above my head, ready to hurl it against the wall, when it occurred to me that Colleen wouldn't be the only woman interested in my dinner date and impending heroics. Did Victoria get out of St. Louis without incident, I wondered? Did she know where she'd be staying? Did she have a plan to steer clear of Jeremy's clutches? I remembered what she'd said about calling only if there was an emergency, but I wanted her to know she wasn't alone if she needed someone to talk to and that her rather stern evaluation of my ethical backbone or lack thereof had paid dividends.

After retrieving the folder with her phone number, I got her voice mail. "This is...Mister McDermott. Just wanted to make sure you're okay. Wrapping things up here, but Alina wants to meet with me first, probably to talk me out of going to the FBI. But my mind's made up. Jeremy's going down. Wallace, too. I promise you I'm going—." *Beep.*

Dammit!

This time I couldn't control myself and flung the phone onto my desk, actually relieved as it slid past a gauntlet of papers, pencils and notepads, none substantial enough to keep it from disappearing into a crevice between the desk and wall. It made a lovely clattering sound as it fell to the floor, out of sight.

Screw it. No phone, no bad news.

I returned to the kitchen and opened a bottle of wine to let it breathe, hoping I could do the same as I got ready for the most important dinner date of my life.

57.

Jeremy Whestin knew it was a mistake when he directed the airport limo driver to take him to the office instead of home to the condo.

Now, as he sat at his desk at 6:15 P.M., trying to focus on the mail stacked to the side of his desk, he cursed his decision—and the reason for it. He wasn't ready to walk into that condo without Vicky there to greet him.

He cursed that Mack hadn't yet located her.

That his mail hadn't been sorted the way she'd always arranged it.

That he'd missed lunch and no one cared, though just the thought of food nearly made him wretch.

And now a temp dared to appear at his door.

"A call, sir."

"Not in!"

"It's your wife."

Jeremy clenched his teeth. "Tell her I'll call her back."

The woman nodded and left, her place taken in the doorway by Wallace. "One of our underwriter candidates has backed out. Said they're nervous about pulling off a public offering with so much turmoil on Wall Street."

"It's fucking four months away!"

"I know, but they—"

"Anyone else?"

"Not yet."

"Then we meet with Jack and the board Monday and make our selection. *Jesus H.*"—he paused and motioned for Wallace to take a seat across from him. "I was a little under the weather yesterday. You and McDermott come to some kind of understanding?"

"He mentioned some 'discrepancies.' No specifics."

"Goddamn it, man, we're running out of time. The underwriter will be reviewing our statements in—"

"I'll discuss this with him first thing Monday. I'm not worried."

Jeremy reached for his briefcase. *You should be, you lying, cheating bastard.* "By end of the day Monday I want to know what he found out and what you intend to do about it. Now tell that woman out there to call me a cab."

Wallace left and for the third time in the past hour Jeremy tried to reach Mack, and for the third time he was forced to leave a message.

Mack was on call 24/7. No excuses.

Where the hell was he? And where was Vicky?

Victoria had awakened in Mack's spare bedroom just before noon, exhausted and tense even after ten hours sleep.

She couldn't imagine having had to get up this morning and fly all the way to Albuquerque. Besides, she still had to decide what to do about her stroke of good fortune, and Mack had been kind enough to tell her to take her time.

He'd left her a note about him needing to "make arrangements." She could only imagine how Mack's life was about to change, all because—perhaps for the first time ever—he refused to follow orders.

It was now approaching six-thirty, and without a car she'd been forced to spend the day watching whatever news and movie channels she could find on basic cable. She did find a few conservative magazines like *American Spectator,*

Human Events and *The Weekly Standard,* but those were offset by *Mother Jones, The Nation* and *The New Republic.* All were apparently purchased off the newsstand; they didn't carry an address label.

The front door opened and a hollow-eyed Mack Evans announced it was cocktail hour. He pulled a bottle of vodka from a brown paper bag. She requested a vodka tonic, adding "You look beat."

He told her it had been a long day and let it go at that.

While he made their drinks, Victoria asked a question that had been bugging her all day. "Why haven't you invested in a condo? This is like—"

"I know, pouring money down the drain." He offered her a rueful smile. "In my line of work, one can't afford encumbrances like a permanent residence. If I need to pull up stakes quick, I can just pay the landlord my remaining rent and be outta here. Hell, I even buy my booze by the pint."

Drinks in hand, they made their way to the living room, though given its size, Victoria thought "sitting room" was more appropriate.

"Did you talk to Jeremy," she asked, taking a seat on the couch.

Mack shook his head. "I imagine he's about to erupt."

Victoria thought about telling him that Jeremy was dying, but he would hear the news soon enough. Besides, she was more interested in this man who'd made it his responsibility to keep her safe.

"If I may ask, how did you hook up with Jeremy?"

Mack handed her a bowl of mixed nuts he'd brought with him from the kitchen and sat down across from her. "I was on post with the CIA in the late '80s, southern provinces of Thailand. Home to a large population of angry Muslim immigrants from Pakistan. Violence and corruption everywhere, all directed against a Thai government they felt was oppressing them. It was especially nasty in the city of Haad Yai, where I was assigned."

He stopped and sipped his drink. "We were working undercover with the Thai military and police counterparts, providing training for border security. My job was to pay the colonel who commanded the government's forces. His job was to disperse the funds to his men."

At around 5'10" with a medium build, close-cut brown hair graying at the temples, and no striking physical marks or features, Mack was the kind of man Victoria figured to be ideal for CIA work, where the less one stood out, the better. She guessed he was around fifty years old, still fit, a man who could take care of himself in a pinch. But judging by the profound sadness in his eyes, a man who was very much alone with his regrets—like her.

"Go on," she said.

Mack stared at his drink. "I was married, away from home for months at a time. And then I met a local woman, fell in love—I thought—and got her pregnant. Suddenly, I had two more mouths to feed. I knew the colonel would take a lot less than we were paying him, so I started my own withholding plan. Turns out the colonel didn't like that and snitched on me."

Victoria could see where this was headed.

"It was bad enough that I got into a relationship with a foreign national. *Really* bad that I got nabbed for misappropriation of funds. Before I knew what hit me, I'd been relieved of my duties, suffered through an ugly divorce and lost track of my baby son and his mother. I started drinking, angry at the world. I wasn't my mother's son in those days, believe me."

"And Jeremy...?"

"He got wind of me through a mutual acquaintance, knew I was a desperate man with certain useful skills. He asked if I'd do some investigative work for him, and I jumped at it. It sort of grew from there."

Victoria leaned forward and waited.

Mack smiled, apologetically. "By training, I'm not a talkative guy, Ms. Laine. I've said more here than I have to anyone in years. Let's just say Jeremy's demands have escalated. This latest, about you...I just can't believe it."

He plucked a cashew from the bowl. "Years ago, Jeremy had me play a role in soiling the reputation of your sister's company so he could take it over at a distressed price. That was, obviously, before he fell in love with her—not that he's been a saint ever since, as you know."

He brushed a hand across his pants legs. "My hatred for the man finally got the better of me. Or maybe I just needed to do something I could be proud of. Last year I told your sister everything I knew about that scheme, thinking I was doing something nice for a good woman who deserved to know the truth. But given what you saw on that security tape and what you told me about your father—"

"Why didn't you tell Alina about me?"

A shrug. "I figured you two would cross paths sooner or later. Besides, you seemed a decent sort. I thought maybe the man had something on you, too, or you wouldn't be with him. And I swear I never knew you two were sisters until you told me on the way to the airport. I'm ashamed to say I didn't know."

"I was always surprised that Jeremy didn't request a background check on me."

"He did, but base level only. We checked out your references, and we knew about your divorce. That was good enough for Jeremy. I don't think he wanted me to find out anything bad." Mack gave her an ironic grin. "I guess every man has his blank spot."

Victoria took a sip of her drink. "About that tape…it's all the proof I need that Alina murdered my father—*our* father—to get control of a company that was supposed to be mine. And then Jeremy tells you to kill me. These are bad people, Mack. I've known that about Alina for a long time. I guess I didn't want to see the obvious when it came to Jeremy. What was that you said about blank spots?"

Deep furrows creased Mack's brow. "You told me in St. Louis about the impending stock transfer. Which means Jeremy and Alina are now partners. Which means…."

"She knows I'm on your hit list and is apparently fine with it."

"Don't forget, we've got to be concerned for Mr. McDermott's safety, too."

Victoria nodded. "Jeremy's in St. Louis now. I think I'll pay my sister a visit."

"Not the police?"

"All I have now is a tape of the former owner of the company—the wife of the CEO—blithely walking out of the warehouse with a sample of the company's product. What are the police supposed to do with that? As far as they'll be able to tell, no crime has been committed—at least not yet."

"Then…?"

"Maybe I can't get Alina to pay for what she's done, but I want her to know I'll never stop trying—and that at long last, I know exactly what she did. For now, that will be enough."

Mack finished his drink. "How do you plan to get into Palms Away?"

"I'll call Rainey, have him meet us at the gate, then lead us to Alina's house."

"He'll cooperate?"

"If not, I'll find another way."

Victoria had left her phone in the bedroom where it had been charging. She retrieved it, returned to the living room and stopped short. "I've got a message from Rainey." She gave it a listen, returned the call and got his answering service. She asked him to call her as soon as he could, surprised and relieved that this man with whom she'd entrusted her secrets apparently had a soul worth saving, after all.

"What?" Mack asked as she ended her message.

"He's going to the authorities, but Alina's asked to meet him first."

"When? Where?"

"He didn't say."

They looked at each other in silence, words unnecessary to express the obvious fact that Victoria's quest to confront her sister might have just turned into a rescue mission, with time working against them.

Mack spoke first. "Call her—let her know we're on to her. If she's got something bad in mind, she needs to know we'll point the finger at her."

"You're supposed to have killed me, remember? Besides, a threatening call might work against us, give her time to work up an alibi—and decide what to do about me." She pointed a finger at Mack. "And guess who she's going to call first?"

Mack ran the back of his hand across his five o'clock shadow. "Rainey's a big boy—and not exactly a candidate for a surprise heart attack. He'll call when he gets your message." He patted his stomach. "In the meantime, I've got to put something in this tummy of mine. Grab your purse. Dinner's on me."

58.

Alina opened the refrigerator door and appraised the lasagna she'd prepared earlier in the day. Not bad, she thought, as she tucked the casserole dish into a wicker basket along with the makings for a Caesar salad.

She hadn't displayed her considerable culinary skills for Jeremy in quite some time, but she assumed the old adage still held true: the way to a man's heart was through his stomach. As for Rainey, she hoped a good meal and a few glasses of wine would also soften his defenses.

In truth, she wasn't optimistic. She'd tried sex and had then offered him money and power and an opportunity to make amends for his sins against all those poor, unsuspecting stockholders. She'd just about had him, too, until that bitch of a sister went and ruined everything.

Jeremy had said he'd take responsibility for eliminating Vicky as a threat to their plans. Which likely meant he'd turn to Mack Evans, unless he had someone else in reserve for the more violent stuff. Somehow she couldn't see Mack agreeing to end Vicky's life, even by orders from his meal ticket. On the other hand, if Mack were capable of that kind of violence, he might prove even more valuable to her down the road.

In fact, if she could track him down, she might just try to find out if Mack had indeed been given the assignment—and then try to beat him to it. Or arrange a trade. Something of value for him in exchange for allowing her the opportunity to deliver the ultimate payback.

After placing the basket in the trunk of her car, she returned to get her tote bag where she'd placed the Ruger and the chunks of raw, rotting chicken she'd sealed inside a large-sized baggie.

It was now six-forty. Still no callback from Jeremy. She thought about checking with Wallace, but she didn't want a call like that on the phone records, not tonight when all hell could break loose.

She stopped at the kitchen phone and tried once more to reach him. If he didn't answer this time, she'd call him tomorrow with the news that Rainey McDermott was either alive and on board or dead and in pieces.

Jeremy had gone straight from his cab to bed, stopping just long enough to down a double dose of pain pills.

He had no idea what time it was or how he was going to make it through the night without Vicky by his side, comforting him, making sure he took his pills. He just knew he had to get to the bedside phone before it stopped ringing.

It could be Mack calling to tell him he'd found Vicky and asking what he should do now. Even after knowing what she'd done to him, Jeremy didn't know if he had the guts to give the orders that would end her life.

His head hurt more than at any time since his diagnosis, as if a hydraulic press were about to squish him open like a pumpkin, top to bottom. He fumbled for the phone, his teeth chattering, heart about burst from his chest like a scene out of *Alien*. A wave of nausea washed over him, and he jerked himself upright, vomiting onto the carpeting.

Then, without warning, the pain that had been his constant companion for months stopped.

Jeremy scanned the bedroom through half-opened eyes.

"Vicky? Alina?"

No answer.

"*Sweet Jesus, not now!*" he whispered as the phone stopped ringing and the room turned the color of chalk.

Wallace Gerard placed the thumb drive containing a copy of the September financial statements in his bedroom safe and collapsed onto the bed, lost in thought.

Under his guidance, preparations for the IPO were proceeding as planned. He'd reviewed the schedule this morning with Jack Armbruster, and the two of them agreed they were ready to sign a letter of agreement Monday with their preferred underwriter, pending Jeremy's final authorization and a further deterioration of the market that could throw cold water on the entire endeavor.

Assuming a mid-February date for the public offering, they had four months left for the underwriting team to complete its due diligence, prepare the SEC filing, and complete any requests for additional information. Concurrently, they'd have to prepare marketing materials for an early December "dog and pony" to just over a dozen securities analysts.

It was a lot to accomplish, but Wallace had confidence in the company's strategy and support staff. Why, then, couldn't he shake the premonition of impending disaster that had been dogging him for days, even in his sleep?

Before Rainey McDermott's hiring, everything had been set. Alina and he knew what they needed to do. A plan had been put in place. They'd been in love, he was certain of it. Now, he could count on nothing.

Jeremy's illness and the odd meeting at his house.

The stock transfer.

McDermott's as yet unexplained call to Alina from The Ritz.

The mysterious disappearance of Victoria Laine.

Perhaps each on its own could be explained. But all of them together?

He sat up, loosened his tie, and reminded himself of the one thing he hadn't yet lost: the balance of the private placement money still under his sole control. In truth, Wallace could move the money anywhere, at any time, in any amount, and no one could trace its movements to one Waleed al-Ghamdi. Because Whestin Group was still a privately held company, with one shareholder, the bank required only one signature on file authorizing such transactions—and that one person didn't have to be Jeremy Whestin.

Wallace knew that such carte blanche authority would never be permitted once the company went public and had to put in place much tougher financial controls. But for now, he was in charge. If his arrangement with Alina went south before the IPO, if there was any hint the authorities might come after him, he'd go underground. And take tens of millions of dollars with him.

The phone rang. "Peace be upon you," Wallace said in English.

"Peace be upon you and the mercy of God and his blessings," Rashid responded in kind. "I could use some good news."

"Problems?"

"There is a cancer here that needs to be cut out—and soon."

Wallace knew that his cousin was referring to Wallace's uncle, Rashid's own father. To be talking this subversively about one's closest blood relative only heightened the tension that had been building for months between the two cousins.

"We've done everything possible to assure a successful public offering. There is still much to do, but so far, no red flags." Assuming he could get past his phone conference with Rainey McDermott.

"Let us hope so," Rashid said. "We can ill-afford to lose $110 million. On the other hand, Waleed, neither can we afford to have that money wasted on short-sighted, petty tyrants bent only on lining their pockets and maintaining their rank. I will do whatever it takes to keep that from happening. I trust I can count on you should the time come for us to take bold measures."

With no appetite for confrontation at this late date, Wallace offered his full cooperation, though the pain from an increasingly nervous stomach made it hard for him to breathe. When the call ended and the vice-like pain subsided, he disrobed, showered and dressed in fresh clothes that would convey the proper humility and respect for the man whose counsel he needed now—and whose protection he might require at some point in the future. The thought sickened him but better to be prepared than caught with no options at all.

His appointment tonight would be with a man he'd never met, who toiled at a place of worship Wallace had never visited, and who presided over a community that he would by now have been expected to join—all of which would likely make things uncomfortable, at least at first.

Even so, if something went wrong with the IPO or if Alina were to betray him, if he were then to need a safe haven—even a new identify—the remaining multi-million dollar reserve he intended to maintain in the account ought to buy a great deal of cooperation from the imam. It had already bought him this meeting.

Wallace left his townhouse and strode out into the warm October evening. He made his way along the sidewalk for maybe five minutes before a dark blue Buick sedan pulled up along side of him. He got into the backseat and exchanged greetings with the imam, a fit, middle-aged man with a full head of hair and a neatly trimmed beard. In a white dress shirt, dark tie and conservative business suit, he looked every bit the part of an ordinary executive, not—as most Westerners would envision—the leader of one of the several Muslim communities flourishing throughout the St. Louis metro area.

The imam spoke softly, with just a trace of Arabic accent. "Drive around the block, Husam," he said to the driver, a younger, taller man who wore a lightweight black leather jacket despite the eighty-degree temperature outside. Wallace had a good idea why.

"I have a previous engagement this evening," the imam said, gazing out the window, his hands in his lap. "This meeting must by necessity be brief. And, of course, I must return to the mosque for *Isha'a*."

He glanced at Wallace, who feigned understanding. The imam turned back to the window. "It is the last of the five daily ritual prayers, the *Salah*, required of all practicing Muslims in supplication to *Allah*."

Wallace bowed his head. "I appreciate you meeting me."

"I have been thinking about our conversation and have some thoughts for you," the imam said. "First, it is true that we could assist you in returning to your homeland. There are good reasons for you to reunite with your family. Much is happening in Algeria and not all of it good. They could use your able-bodied assistance. But I believe there is a better path for you, Waleed." He leaned forward and tapped the driver on the shoulder. "Turn here, Husam, then return us to our friend's home."

"I am grateful for your guidance," Wallace said.

The imam waved a hand across his field of vision. "Times are changing here in America, Waleed. The ways of Islam appeal to many and will soon appeal to many more as America seeks to deal with its insurmountable troubles. We will need soldiers in the fight that someday will surely be played out here on American soil."

He reached into his coat pocket and pulled out a business card. "Even if your new venture goes through, you will sooner or later need the guidance of *Allah*, which you have so far neglected to seek. Do not wait too long."

"And if there is trouble?"

The imam handed Wallace his card. "Call Husam. He will keep you safe."

"Until when?"

"Until it is time, Waleed. Until it is time."

59.

I'd decided to have dinner in the lanai where the fresh air would, hopefully, clear my head. Though it wouldn't be dark for at least another hour, I lit two tapered candles anyway and fluffed up the mixed flowers I'd arranged in a glass vase.

Next step: fix myself a strong gin and try to calm my nerves. Billy Ray's funeral was Sunday, and tonight I'd be hosting the woman who'd been with him the afternoon he died.

I decided to move the vase to the kitchen. Whatever Alina thought this evening might turn out to be, I didn't want to convey the wrong impression. This definitely wasn't a date.

We had a lot of ground to cover tonight, and while I hoped we could start with the subject of those Algerian terrorists, I wanted Wallace to be high on our list, too. From what I witnessed yesterday, he was a wild card whose actions I couldn't predict, whether I kept my evidence quiet or didn't.

How much had Alina told him? And what was the nature of their relationship now? What, for that matter, were her true feelings for me? And did that any longer matter? Forgetting the whole Whestin Group mess, it was very likely this woman was a killer, twice over.

I detected her perfume and turned. Maybe it was the simplicity of her pale yellow summer print dress and open-toed sandals that got to me. Or tousled hair that looked minutes from the shower. Or maybe the fact she was wearing no bra. Whatever it was, she radiated a sexual energy that seemed to shimmer the air around her.

"You look lovely," I said, giving her a kiss but only on the cheek. "What can I fix you?"

"White wine, for starters. Dinner's in the trunk. Would you mind?"

Stay alert, I told myself as I walked to the car. In the back, I gathered up the wicker basket and in the process snagged the sleeve of a dark green windbreaker that had been lying in a corner of the Corvette's cramped trunk. The movement of the garment in turn uncovered a ball cap, the sight of which ordinarily wouldn't freeze my attention like this.

Except that this ball cap was a familiar electric blue.

Victoria returned from the restaurant's powder room and took her seat across from Mack. She stared at her half-eaten sautéed grouper, her thoughts on Rainey McDermott and her sister.

"It's not the company, is it?" Mack asked, looking at her plate.

She shook her head. "I just keep thinking that if Rainey doesn't say the right things...."

"You tried calling his cell again?"

"A minute ago. Apparently he doesn't have a land line."

"Maybe he's in the sack by now, the two of them going at it like—"

"Damn!" Victoria hit her forehead with an open palm. "Mack, sorry to do this to you, but you need to get the bill—now. I'll meet you out front."

In the parking lot, after scrolling through her phone's address list, she placed a call to Rainey's wife. Victoria had the number from a routine "contact" sheet Rainey filled out the day he officially became a Whestin Group consultant. It had been so automatic for her to add the number to her address book that she'd forgotten she had it.

The phone rang three times before she heard a female voice. "Is this Colleen McDermott?" she asked.

A pause on the other end. "Who's calling?"

"This is Victoria Laine, assistant to Jeremy Whestin, CEO of Whestin Group. Your husband's doing some work for Mr. Whestin, and I need to reach him, but he's not responding to my phone calls. Is he with you or do you know how I might reach him?"

"Is this an emergency?"

Victoria bit her lip. She'd count to ten, but she didn't have time. Again she asked, "Do you know how I could reach him?"

"He's at home. As a matter of fact, he's having dinner with Mrs. Whestin."

Victoria quickly moved past the awkward moment. "Please call your gatehouse. Tell them you're authorizing me to go through. I'll ask the guards for directions. Will you do that for me?"

"Yes, but is this a—?"

"Thank you," Victoria said and disconnected the call as Mack returned, car keys in hand.

"You owe me half a steak dinner," he said. "What's going on?"

She grabbed the keys, opened the back door and motioned for Mack to get in. If the evening ended as she suspected it might, he'd be glad no one had seen him come through those gates. "I'll explain on the way. How long to get to Palms Away?"

"About twenty minutes."

Victoria put the car in gear and shoved the accelerator to the floor. "Let's make it fifteen."

60.

"Stay put," I said to Alina, clearing the dishes from the table. "I'll be back in a second."

I headed for the kitchen, thankful for the break. More than an hour had passed since we sat down to dinner, the tension growing with each attempt at small talk. Enough that I'd already opened a second bottle of wine.

"How do you keep your bougainvillea so lush?" she'd asked, admiring a trellis heavy with thorny vines covered in pink blooms.

"Colleen says it has to do with getting plenty of sun and not a lot of water. Tell me, how long did it take you to get used to this St. Augustine lawn grass down here? It's like walking on twigs."

"I prefer walking the beach. We should do that some time."

It had gone on like that, each of us waiting out the other. But I wasn't going to reveal my cards until she played hers.

When I returned, slightly buzzed, I was full of "maybes." Maybe, as Alina declared on her boat, she hadn't known about Wallace's involvement with Links International and the potential for laundering millions of terrorist dollars, though she certainly knew it now.

Maybe Victoria was just a jealous, vindictive younger sister, obsessed with her elder sibling's success and, for a while, anyway, with her husband.

Maybe Billy Ray's clogged arteries had finally waved the white flag for good before having to suffer through another extra-large, four-cheese, thick-crusted pizza.

And maybe that electric blue ball cap was no big deal, either. This is a golf community, for crying out loud. Everybody wears caps.

I returned and filled her wine glass.

Bathed in soft, amber candlelight, she reminded me of Julie Christie's "Betty Logan" in the movie *Heaven Can Wait*. I wanted desperately to be her fated lover, Warren Beatty's "Joe Pendleton," a forgiving angel about to offer me yet another chance to achieve my destiny.

Then I heard the grinding *screech* of a phonograph needle dragged across spinning vinyl, interrupting my pleasant little fantasy to signal that my plot was scratched and littered with crap. Whereas poor Joe hadn't known what was going on, I knew only too well. And I knew the price was too high.

I patted my stomach. "I hope you didn't bring dessert."

"No, just me."

A gentle breeze carried her perfume to my nostrils, engendering what I could only describe as the beginning signs of panic. I began to both sweat and shiver and my vision fuzzed. *Where had I put that business card, the one with my Chicago counselor's phone number on it?*

Alina apparently sensed my distress. "I think we've stalled long enough, don't you?"

"The floor is yours, madam."

Hands folded in her lap, she suggested we talk business first, which was just what I wanted to hear. "I shouldn't even have to express this to you, Rainey, but I want nothing to do with terrorists."

She pursed her lips and looked away. After taking a sip of her wine, she said she'd conferred with her source and admitted that the information Victoria had given me checked out. "I knew Wallace was holding out on me," she said, "but I thought it was limited to the financial documents and those cell phones. This...this is so outrageous, so frightening. And I hardly know what to say about Mack, either"

Which left me wondering who her "source" was. I stopped shivering. "So you agree we go to the authorities?"

She leaned forward, a pensive look on her face. "Hear me out," she said, causing my stomach to flip-flop. She took my hand, hitting me with the classic doe-eyed model's stare. A wisp of hair fell onto her forehead, completing the effect. "At some point," she said, "the general partners at the private equity firm are going to want to sell their stock. Right?"

"Probably six to eight months in, if the company's doing well. We can't let that happen."

"Agreed. So, what if, say, four months in you tell the FBI you undertook an internal investigation on your own. Tell them your brilliant instincts led you to suspect something funny about the source of the private placement—and executive management's role in the whole thing. Tell them you quietly started asking around and then one day, someone with a conscious who figured you could be trusted to do the right thing, left Mack's report on your desk. After a subsequent investigation by the FBI, you'd be a hero and national news overnight. *Inter*national news."

"You're not thinking clearly. I finger Jeremy and Wallace, they finger me."

"Jeremy will likely be dead before the FBI concludes its investigation."

I saw no hint of sadness in Alina's eyes. Like she'd said, we were talking business. I started shivering again. "And as for Wallace, you'd sell him out"— I snapped my fingers— "like that?"

She cocked her head and frowned. "I thought you'd like that."

Uh-huh. And who's next?

"Besides," she said, "neither Jeremy nor Wallace would be foolish enough to bring up anything related to doctored financial statements. This would be about using the New York Stock Exchange to launder money for terrorists in exchange for a private placement they desperately needed. Let the two of them point fingers at each other, but they wouldn't point them at you without opening themselves up to a raft of additional charges. At the very least, the FBI would freeze the stock transfer. Under Jack Armbruster's leadership, Whestin Group survives the bad publicity, the company will be seen as having cooperated fully with the authorities, and you come out a hero."

Alina played with a gold medallion fastened at the bottom of her necklace.

It glowed in the candlelight, and I wondered if she was using it to hypnotize me. Because though loaded with risks, her idea sounded good, even plausible.

Technically, Jeremy was my client and no one had been privy to our conversations, not even Wallace. I was under no legal obligation to do anything other than inform Jeremy of what I knew. I could be seen as going to the authorities simply because it was the right thing to do without, I presumed, violating any confidentiality agreement. And, as Alina had just reminded me, Jeremy would soon be dead, and Wallace would have only his speculations to throw at me.

"You know, of course," she said, "I'll see to it those stock options are honored; your salary arrangement, as well. And afterward you'll get the chance to quietly straighten out our books and upgrade our internal controls."

This was exactly the opportunity I was looking for, to show my former friends and associates I could once again play on the big boy's field, proof that I was better than the addicted crook who'd left Chicago in humiliation and disgrace. I'd be, in fact, a *celebrity*.

Maybe....

I caught a reflection in my wine glass as I paused to take a sip. But it wasn't my likeness staring back at me. It was Frank's. The wine caught in my throat, and I spit half of it into my napkin.

"You all right?" Alina asked.

I swallowed some water, felt in my pocket for the coat of arms, and said, "I understand what's at stake for you, Alina, but all things considered, I like my plan better."

"Which is?"

"I get my information organized best I can and drop it into the hands of the FBI. You're clear because I won't say anything about what you know or were planning to do. Jeremy's too sick to be a factor. Wallace deserves whatever the Feds throw at him, and it will be his word against yours and mine. And if it comes to it, I'll cover for Victoria. I might do some time, but thousands of investors won't be placing a bet on a company that lied to them. Oh yeah, and millions of dollars stay out of the hands of extremists who might want to use it to destroy us."

Alina gave that some thought. "Putting an end to the IPO could hurt a lot of hard-working employees at Whestin Group. There'd be layoffs in an economy that can't absorb them. And you'll end up with a prison record."

"Maybe, but I'd rather be laid off than blown up. Or be responsible for more death and destruction. There are worse things than digging ditches."

"You won't need to dig ditches, Rainey. We can make things right and keep you *out* of jail."

She leaned forward and took my hand. "What Jeremy has done with his stock assures a fabulous life for me. I'm thinking it would be nice to share that life with you. Someone I could grow to love and trust."

"Alina...."

"I know, it's only been a month. But you've been willing to hear me out, to understand what I've been through and what I want to achieve. Maybe this isn't love, not yet, but I have feelings for you I've never truly felt for anyone. I can't explain it, it's ridiculous on so many levels, but I also can't walk away from the possibility that you and I are two of a kind, that we have a future. Not without fighting for you."

The response that should have come easily to my lips stayed lodged in my throat. I glanced up as raindrops began to hit my skin. When I looked at Alina, about to suggest we move inside, her demeanor turned sultry, as if she'd been waiting to capture my full attention before beginning the final act. The rain was a prop, appearing on cue.

She lowered her eyes, took hold of her skirt and hiked it half way up her thigh. And then her signature move: running one finger inside the strap of her dress until it rested lightly at the top of her braless cleavage.

As surely she must have done with so many others before, she was toying with me. Apprehension, bordering on a healthy fear of this woman, should have prompted an immediate end to the evening. But it was my pride, and irritation at being so blatantly played, that got the better of me. "Don't sit like that," I said. "It makes you look like—"

My first instinct was to scrunch down in defense, like a prizefighter about to be hit with a right cross. Alina had sat bolt upright, her jaw set, nostrils flaring, hands balled into fists. Her skin seemed to turn a shade darker, as if one of the candles had been blown out. "I don't appreciate your tone," she said, lips barely moving.

Time out.

I apologized and waited for her to calm down. "I have a wonderful cognac in the study. Care to join me?" I looked skyward. "I think we're about to get wet."

Alina pointed to her wine glass, still obviously put out with me. "Give me a moment. I'll meet you inside."

She closed her eyes and took a deep breath. The rain felt good on her skin, calming her, though she was still unnerved by her visceral reaction to Rainey's admonition and the memory of that fateful day twenty-two years ago. When, she wondered, would Leonard Manetti die?

Rainey McDermott would never understand. It wasn't his fault. In fact, she liked him enough to come here tonight to knock some sense into him. But if he couldn't appreciate that she was offering him a life—and a companion—most men would kill for, then maybe he wasn't the catch she thought he was.

She watched him disappear into the house, then grabbed her tote bag and walked briskly down the slick patio steps and across the yard to the edge of the pond. Glancing over her shoulder toward the house, she pulled out the plastic bag and tossed the chicken pieces into the water, a few feet from the shoreline.

It was not a huge amount of food, less in fact than she'd been discretely feeding her accomplice each night for the past two weeks after Rainey turned his lights out and went to bed. The gator would still be hungry—and aggravated.

She heard Rainey call out from the house. "You coming?"

Returning the empty baggie to her bag, she removed the Ruger and flipped off the safety. She couldn't be sure in the dark, wet night, but she thought she heard a pronounced *splash* just off the far bank.

61.

I found the cognac on a bookcase shelf in the study. I'd placed it there some time ago, next to a snifter, mainly for effect. Everything in hand, I was about to leave when I heard the muffled ringing of my cell phone.

"*Shit,*" I muttered, remembering.

I thought about ignoring the call, but there was that interrupted message I'd left Victoria. I hurried to my desk, hissing expletives as I forced my arm down into the crevice as far as I could, then—*yes!* I brought the phone up, saw it was Victoria and flipped open the cover.

"Wasn't sure I'd hear from you," I said.

"This is Mack Evans, Mr. McDermott. I work for Jeremy Whestin. Are you all right, sir?"

Hearing Jeremy's private investigator inquire about my well-being, on Victoria's phone, at well past ten in the evening, prickled the hairs on my neck. "Why wouldn't I be?"

"We've called several times tonight."

"We?"

"I'm with Victoria Laine. We've just arrived at the entrance to Palms Away. Is Mrs. Whestin still there?"

Thoroughly confused, I asked how he knew. "My message never got—"

He cut me off. "We're on our way, sir, but watch yourself. We think Mrs. Whestin murdered—."

Cold steel, as they say in the dime store thrillers, jabbed the back of my neck. Before I could react, an arm came up from behind and jerked the phone from my hand. *What in the...?*

Turning, I saw Alina snap the phone shut and toss it to the floor. Her eyes, moments ago in full seduction mode, were now hard, flat and emotionless, her face cool and detached like a mannequin's. Even the way she held the pistol seemed mechanical, as if placed there by a store designer for effect. I recalled Jeremy saying, *"That's Alina's baby..."* and that she knew where to place the shot.

She canted her head toward the door. "Do as I say, Rainey. I'm guessing we don't have a lot of time."

My first thought was how to wipe this stupid *are-you-kidding-me?* grin off my face. No way this was happening—but it was. Alina curled a second hand around the pistol's grip, and my knees began to shake like ice cubes in a blender.

"To the pond," she said. "Somebody's hungry."

She was too far away to be bull-rushed before she squeezed off a shot. If I was lucky, I might get a chance to talk her out this insanity or, as they used to say in the old Westerns, get the drop on her. If I didn't....

"We can end it here, Rainey," Alina said, "or we can go outside where you'll have a sporting chance. And maybe, if you're smart, you'll let me talk some sense into you. I told you I wouldn't let you go without a fight."

I couldn't comprehend any of this, but until Victoria and Mack arrived, I was willing to accept any opportunity to prolong this—what? Debate? Negotiation? Last rites?

"You first," I said, pointing the way.

Her response was to cock the pistol's hammer. So much for levity.

With Alina keeping her distance, we made our way out of the house, through the lanai and past the table where she had all but proposed to me minutes ago. I wanted to believe that she intended only to scare me, but what was that Mack had said?

"We think Mrs. Whestin murdered—"

Oh, baby, I was in deep shit now.

The rain was falling harder, pelting my head and shoulders as I descended into the darkened yard. I slipped on the wet grass and nearly fell. Catching myself, I hunched over against the rain and thrust my hands into my pockets. My right hand struck the coat-of-arms.

"Far enough," I heard as I got to within a few feet of the pond. I'd never ventured this close before once the sun had set. Rats. Snakes. Armadillos. The occasional eleven-foot alligator. No way.

Alina wanted me to face her. "I prefer you shoot me in the back," I said. "The sight of a gun pointed at my head gives me hives."

For that I got a hard, joyless laugh.

"No one is going to find a bullet in that handsome body of yours, Rainey. Or anywhere else, I suspect. In fact, I doubt anyone will even find your body. Or at least much of it. Now turn around. So we can…talk."

An impenetrable hedge of tightly packed saw-toothed palmettos blocked any escape to my left. Ahead was the pond; behind and to my right, Alina stood ready to end my life with a pistol preferred by the mob. And the only reason she'd directed me to this very spot had to have something to do with my pal, Sneaky Pete.

How, I wondered, did she know he'd be here on this side of the pond, ready to play his part? I pulled the tiny heraldic shield out of my pocket and held it at my side, hoping it would instill in me superpowers capable of propelling me to another universe.

Alina stood about fifteen feet away, wet hair falling into those incredible eyes, her dress clinging to a body that had once sent me to a place this forensic accountant had never before visited. But now, with the Ruger's barrel pointed at my forehead, she was ready to send me to another place far less appealing.

"You want to talk?" I asked. "Then put down that gun, and let's talk about the fact that two people know we're together tonight. Here, at my house. And they have evidence you—"*what the hell*—"murdered Billy Ray."

Her body stiffened for a second before she offered a bemused smile. "Good try, but I'm quite certain they found no evidence of foul play on poor Mr. Hammonds. Who, I understand, will be cremated tomorrow morning, poor man. No, Rainey, I'm afraid there will be no reason to suspect anything here tonight but carelessness, or perhaps despondency, in the sad, tragic death tonight of disgraced fraud investigator Rainey McDermott."

I pressed the edge of the shield hard into my palm, as if the pain might give birth to an escape plan. "The police are on their way, Alina. You'll never get away with this."

How lame did that sound? Still, where *were* the police? Where was Mack Evans? Victoria? *Anybody?*

Alina pushed a strand of matted hair off her forehead and leveled the Ruger. "I can see you're not in the mood to negotiate, Rainey. I'm sorry, I really am."

A man of arms, a great warrior! Don't just stand here and—the shield suddenly slipped from my wet fingers. I lunged for it without thinking.

It had no monetary value, no mysterious, powerful, spiritual ability to ward off evil or make me a better man. I knew that, but it was a gift from my father, and he said—

62.

A moment later, Alina gave herself a silent pat on the back as her victim fell among the palmettos as if he'd been a tree expertly felled to land in a pre-designated spot.

Hitting stationary paper targets on the firing range was a lot easier than shooting at desperate human beings at night in the wind and rain, but her intended victim had clearly been hit and now lay dead or unconscious and within easy reach of her trained prehistoric garbage disposal.

She wasn't the kind to gawk at car crashes, just as she didn't care for blood and guts thrillers, but she needed to hang around long enough to make sure the gator tidied up her mess.

What might have been, she thought, staring at Rainey's wet, bleeding, motionless body. And then she remembered his last words. Apparently she was about to have visitors.

Alina had anticipated the possibility that Rainey might have told others about their rendezvous tonight. If questioned about her evening, she would say they'd had dinner to discuss company business, that throughout the evening he'd seemed distracted, even depressed, confessing to serious financial pressures and seemingly morose over his impending divorce and the loss of his good friend, Billy Ray Hammonds. When she left him, he'd said something about going to the pond to say farewell to an alligator that had become like a pet to him and was about to be removed. She'd tried to dissuade him, she would say with tears in her eyes, but apparently he hadn't listened. An awful tragedy.

But *company*? That she hadn't counted on.

Alina checked the pond, impatient for the approach of her gator's hungry eyes. Then she heard a rustling behind her, and her heart came up in her throat as she saw a man bent low to the ground, shuffling sideways toward Rainey's body. He held a gun, and it was pointed in her direction.

"Drop your weapon," she heard him say, full of authority, but the command didn't register. Reflexively, she brought her pistol to bear on—could it be?—Mack Evans. What was *he* doing here? And why had he just ordered her to drop her gun? He was supposed to be on her side.

For an instant, she thought of his OddsR rating. Ninety-three? How wrong had she been about that?

Buy time, she thought, aware she was in the sights of a handgun clearly more powerful than hers. At this distance, her shot would have to be perfect; his not nearly so. Still, she guessed he'd let her get off the first shot.

"Switching allegiances again, Mack?" she yelled. "Who's the lucky girl this time?"

"I am."

Pivoting sharply, Alina felt her cheeks flush and chills rack her soaked body as she saw Vicky standing at the top of the patio stairs. Slowly she raised the Ruger and pointed it at her sister, trying to figure out what was happening.

Mack stopped and took a step forward. "I can take her. Just say the word."

Vicky told him to check on Rainey. He hesitated, then resumed making his way along the pond's edge. Alina knew she should *do* something, somehow get Mack to freeze. But she couldn't tear her eyes from her sister and the evidence she brandished in smug triumph.

"Is this how you killed dear old Dad?" Vicky asked. From the needle's tip, a spurt of clear liquid arced into the air.

Lightning pierced the murky night sky and a prodigious clap of thunder caused Alina to flinch. She didn't know how her sister had learned of her *modis operandi*, and she didn't care. She was wet, cold and dizzy with fever. Her little sister had been a thorn in her side far too long, always hovering, threatening. It was time to put an end to it.

She decided to kill Vicky first, then take her chances with Mack. If she survived, she could fill in the holes later, centered on self-defense. Easy enough with no one alive to refute her story.

Alina took a step back and centered her aim on Vicky's forehead. "Tell *Daddy* I said hi."

63.

Alina figured the commotion behind her was just Mack's attempt to distract her. But she could see that her sister wasn't staring at *her*, or at the Ruger about to end her life. She was focused in the direction of the pond, her eyes wide with horror.

Turning, she saw Mack kneeling at Rainey's side, shouting into his ear. Twenty feet to the right, in the water, she caught sight of her accomplice as another burst of lightning illuminated the surreal scene before her.

She could explain Rainey's death-by-gator tonight but not Mack's. Nor could she afford to have Mack snatch away Rainey's body before Sneaky Pete's massive jaws and toxic digestive juices could perform their duties. That was not part of the plan.

"*Stop!*" she screamed, as she fired a warning shot into the ground, just ahead of her target. But Mack never wavered. He placed his hands under Rainey's armpits and began pulling him up the muddy bank. The giant alligator was now ten feet away, a late night feast there for the taking.

Alina had no choice. She aimed at Mack's head as the private investigator suddenly let loose his grip, dropped to one knee, pulled his gun from his waistband and aimed toward the bank. A shot—the gator stopped, jerked his head to the right, then immediately turned and disappeared below the dark water.

Blocking out the sound of Vicky's screams, Alina drew in a breath and steadied her aim. *Third time's the charm*, she told herself. *Too bad.*

She fired, and Mack jerked backwards, grabbing his neck. His fingers instantly turned red with spurting blood as he landed DOA across Rainey's thighs.

As Mack fell, Alina cursed that the gator might be too frightened or too injured now to finish the job, that she might have to clean up this mess herself. She'd worry about that later.

First, a more urgent piece of business demanded her undivided attention.

Shouts from the darkness...searing, torturous lightning bolts of pain piercing my upper left arm. Something heavy on my legs, unmoving—a man, eyes closed, blood pooling beneath his neck. Is that a...gun? What's happening?

Feels like a branding iron burning the flesh and muscles of my chest. Nickel-sized hole in my shirt, inch below my left collarbone...filling with a dark liquid.

Must try to free myself. Who is this man sprawled across my thighs? What's he doing here? What am I doing here, on the ground, bleeding, fighting to stay conscious?

Others arguing. Two women...wrestling? Can't tell. Every breath a stiletto thrust to my chest. Shoulder feels bolted to the earth.

More screams.

Must do something...want to vomit from the pain.

A muffled gunshot.

Another scream.

Seconds after killing Mack, Alina had turned to confront her sister one last time, but she'd been too late. Vicky had landed on her at full sprint, legs kicking, her left fist jammed viciously into Alina's chest. An inch lower and it would have landed squarely in her solar plexus, incapacitating her. As it was, the blow knocked her off her feet, sending both women tumbling towards the pond.

She squeezed off a wild shot. Vicky screamed but somehow managed a one-armed bear hug that pinned Alina's pistol to her side.

Rolling onto her stomach, Alina grabbed the arm that encircled her and twisted it violently, loosening Vicky's grip. But she couldn't break free from the arm now pressing hard against the back of her neck. Vicky was behind her now, and Alina knew why.

Desperate, spun to her left, and then—a stab, like a wasp sting.

Instantly Alina whirled to her right as a surge of adrenaline flooded her body. Enraged, half-blinded by mud and rain, her body weighed down by her soaked dress, she dropped her gun and thrust an elbow into Vicky's ribcage.

The air rushed from her sister's lungs. Vicky doubled up and rolled away, clutching at her mid-section as blood flowed from a bullet wound just above her ankle.

Scrambling to her knees, Alina searched for the Ruger. She found it—next to a syringe that no longer had its needle. Chills overtook her body as she gingerly touched the back of her neck, her fingers edging across a stainless steel splinter protruding half an inch from her skin.

She could feel it beginning, all the debilitating symptoms she'd watched so intimately twice before. Bent on revenge, she lunged at Vicky, catching her flush across the chin with the barrel of her gun. Vicky's head jerked sideways blood sprang from a split lip. She collapsed, at her sister's mercy, but Alina's body was beginning to twitch, and it was already taking concentrated effort to breathe.

The punch had thrown her off balance, and she'd slipped down to the edge of the pond, losing her grip on the Ruger as she tried to slow her momentum. She willed herself upright, fighting muscles headed inexorably toward paralysis. The effort left her within one desperate lunge of her gun.

It shook in her hands as she pointed the Ruger one last time at the woman who'd ruined everything. At least if she had to die, she wouldn't be alone.

"Alina, *no!*"

She had to turn her entire torso to assess this newest potential threat, though even seeing wasn't believing. There was Rainey, staggering to a knee, one arm pinned to his chest by the other. She wasn't sure how many shots she had left, but if only one, Vicky's name had to be on it.

With her muscles firing a half-beat behind her commands, she blinked away the rain, trying to make sense of what she saw. Not Vicky, not Rainey, but her father, close enough she could feel the nap of his favorite blue wool suit. The one he'd been wearing the morning she murdered him.

He looked just as she'd last seen him, dying beneath his conference table, spasms jerking his frail body as if he were a marionette, his eyes brimming with blood, fear, hatred and defiance.

Leonard's ghost offered a fleshless hand, but Alina recoiled as it morphed into the massive, bleeding head of Billy Ray Hammonds. Silly, trusting soul, flailing about on his living room floor. Men are so stupid.

"Alina!" she heard again, but her attention was on Vicky, who'd come back into focus. She aimed the Ruger. If she could just get her fingers crooked around the trigger....

I was fully conscious now, the pain sharpening my eyesight, but could I believe my eyes? Alina had her gun aimed at Victoria's head.

Shockwaves of pain exploded from my shoulder, splintering downward throughout my torso. A separate, throbbing pain made it hard to breath. I tried yelling again, but Alina didn't hear me, or didn't care. *Please, God, no!* I prayed. These people had come to warn me. Now one lay dead and the other—

Mack's pistol. It didn't look like the service revolver Jeremy had brought to the range, but I figured the safety had to be off. "Just point and shoot," he'd said. I had, in fact, hit the paper target ten times in two dozen shots. Or was it three?

Pointing the gun in Alina's direction, I hoped there'd be enough space between the two woman to accommodate the likely errant aim of a wounded, semi-conscious amateur. If I missed my target, I prayed I'd miss Victoria, too, and at least buy time to get off another shot—though I had no idea how many rounds were left in *Alina's* gun. After that, it might just come down to a last second rescue by the Collier County cavalry.

The trigger, more sensitive than I'd anticipated, fully depressed before I could steady the gun with my one good arm. I watched in disbelief as Alina grabbed at her right arm and spun to her left, falling backwards into the water. It flashed through my mind that what constituted a "lucky shot" was entirely dependent on one's point of view.

Victoria was still on the ground, clutching at her ankle. With the pain in my shoulder and chest pushing me toward unconsciousness, I crawled on my good side toward Alina, and what I saw sickened me.

She'd landed in the pond nearly prone, the lower half of her body submerged in two feet of water, the upper half held at roughly a forty-five degree angle by what looked more like paralysis than conscious effort. Her cheeks, sunken with the effort to draw in air, had forced her eyes shut.

"Alina, get out of there!"

She'd been hit only in the arm and seconds ago had been able to get to the top of the embankment and aim her gun at Victoria. Why wasn't she getting up? *Why couldn't she move?*

I edged closer, prepared to offer her my one good arm, hoping that adrenaline would overcome my own dissipating strength and numb the pain. At that moment, Victoria screamed, diverting my attention for no more than a second. When I turned back to Alina, I faced a nightmarish scene I knew would haunt me for the rest of my life.

Cringing in horror, I saw her body pulled violently from the shore, whipsawed into the air at a grotesque angle no human body could survive. I thought I heard another gunshot, but realized it was the sound of splintering bones. Spun hard to the left and slapped straight down into the water, caught vice-like by one thigh in Sneaky Pete's powerful jaws, Alina had been doomed the moment she collapsed into the water.

I scanned the water, hoping for a miracle, but the pain and blood loss overtook me. My last thought before passing out: *My God, man, what have you done?*

64.

12:10 P.M., Friday, October 17
FBI field office, Fort Myers, Florida

"Here, let me," Colleen said.

She adjusted my shirt, the right side of which had fallen off my shoulder. I'd stubbornly tried to pull it up with my left hand but succeeded only in eliciting a searing pain from my fractured left collarbone. The docs said I'd be in this damn sling for another six weeks.

The bullet had ricocheted downward, nicking a piece of my lung. It was now lodged in my chest cavity, close enough to my heart that the doctors had opted not to operate. I still found it difficult to breathe.

"Let's keep an eye on it," the surgeon had said. "We don't want to open you up if we don't have to."

The irony of ironies: I might be carrying around a memory of Alina Whestin, near and dear to my heart, for the rest of my life.

"You ready?" Colleen asked, inspecting me as if I were about to go on a job interview. Truth was, if my appointment didn't go well today, I could be out of the job market for a long time.

I'd been in the hospital a week since the shooting and out recuperating at home for a week after that. I was still moving gingerly. This afternoon's meeting with Special Agents Anthony Crain and Greg Bell was the last thing I needed.

Colleen grabbed my briefcase. She'd visited me several times in the hospital, nursed me when I got home, and had stayed in the guest room while I recovered. With me under sedation a good part of the time, she'd been left alone with her questions and her nightmares. Through it all, she never asked me how it had come to this. She didn't have to. In turn I never asked about Steve Wannamaker. Maybe one day we'd all spend the holidays together.

As for the authorities, I'd already faced questioning from two Collier County detectives, once at the hospital, then again during a follow-up at home yesterday. They'd seemed satisfied, though I was sure I'd face more questioning ahead. At least no charges had been filed. Yet.

Victoria had called me first chance she got, ironically from an untraceable, prepaid cell phone she'd purchased at a grocery store. She'd endured four hours of questioning at police headquarters, she said, while hobbling along with a cast on her fractured ankle.

I'd been sedated at the hospital, so we'd been able to talk only briefly. Her only advice was to tell the truth or "something close to it."

We both knew there'd be an investigation, but she wasn't worried. Alina had started it all, firing first at me. Then at Mack. Then at Victoria. As for me, I hadn't said much to the police while I was in the hospital. A few days later, at home, I'd been ready to tell them my version of the truth. Today, it was the FBI's turn.

Special Agent Crain motioned for me to take a seat at a small rectangular desk in a windowless interrogation room. He was smiling in a friendly, knowing way, as though he understood how difficult this whole ordeal had been, and he was going to help make things better for me.

"We have just a few questions, Mr. McDermott. Should have you out of here and on your way home within the hour."

Right.

His partner was leaning against a wall in full glare. Special Agent Bell gave the impression he wasn't going to believe a word I said and that he'd be only too happy to use his middle linebacker build and what I sensed was a Dick Butkus temper to flatten me against the wall if I didn't cooperate *fully*. Physically he resembled Billy Ray as he might have looked twenty years ago, though I couldn't see my friend playing the Bad Cop in the classic scenario to which I figured I was about to be treated.

Crain, by contrast tall, fit and trim like a point guard in the National Basketball Association, handed me a bottled water, took a seat across from me and asked about my wound. I told him I was doing fine, I wanted to put all this behind me as soon as possible—"I'm sure you do," he interjected—and what questions did they have for me?

He started by asking how I began working for Whestin Group, and that he assumed Mr. Whestin had been aware of my "considerable skills" as a forensic accountant. It was an innocuous, flattering opening, the kind I'd used many times myself to establish rapport. From here I guessed the agents were hoping I'd paint a revealing picture of myself and explain just what I'd been up to, especially if under pressure I developed a case of diarrhea of the mouth and told them something they didn't know or contradicted facts they'd assumed represented the truth.

I took a swallow of my water and recounted everything I could remember. The golf game with Jeremy. The Whestin's party. My two fateful lunches at LaPlaya. Keeping the lines of communication open with Mrs. Whestin to see what else I might learn (would they buy that?). I confessed that I'd probably told her too much but obviously in the end hadn't agreed to go along with her scheme—which, by the way, almost cost me my life. If the FBI could accept all that, I thought I could, too. By the time I stopped talking, an hour and fifteen minutes had whizzed by, and I'd emptied two water bottles.

Crain leaned back, smiled and nodded his appreciation. "Thank you, Mr. McDermott. This helps a lot. You're a lucky man, you know. Wish I could say the same for Mr. Evans and Mr. Hammonds."

Bell pushed off from the wall and took a seat on the edge of the table, his service pistol clearly visible as his suit coat fell open. Which I assumed had been his intent.

"When Mr. Whestin asked you to help him take his company public," he said, "you didn't suspect right from the start that fraud might be involved?"

I thought I'd covered that in my summary but maybe not. Or maybe they wanted to see if I'd give the same answer. It was a game, but one that could get me arrested if I didn't play it to perfection.

"The possibility existed," I said. "But Jeremy—Mr. Whestin—explained that he had a lot riding on the IPO. He said he'd feel better if someone like me took a look at the company's financial statements. That seemed plausible to me."

"And he was willing to pay you...?"

"Five million dollars in post-IPO stock options."

"And a salary of $80,000 a month. Seems a lot for a few month's work, doesn't it?"

Crain was still smiling, ruefully now, as if telling me that his partner was just getting warmed up, and he was sorry about that. Sure he was.

"Not necessarily," I said, "not given the overall size of the IPO. And we'd discussed me staying on afterwards to conduct an audit of the company's internal operations, precisely to see that they were buttoned up when it came to protecting themselves *against* fraud."

The agent reached for a chair and sat down, clearly unimpressed. "You said Mr. Whestin didn't trust his CFO. According to the statement you gave the Sheriff's Office, you found out the very next day, when you had lunch with Mrs. Whestin, that her husband and Mr. Gerard were conspiring to commit fraud."

"That was her story. It seemed pretty fantastic, but—"

"We'll get to that," Bell said. "Tell me, in your opinion, based on what you now know—in large part from the guidance you got from Ms. Laine—would Whestin Group have been able to successfully launch an IPO without cooking its books?"

"Probably not."

He shook his head, leaving the distinct impression he didn't like me. *Back at you, Special Agent Bell.*

Crain's turn again. "So, do you therefore believe now that Mr. Whestin was fully aware that his books were being doctored by Mr. Gerard?"

"Yes. He was the one directing it. But I didn't know that for certain until my meeting with Ms. Laine."

"I understand. 'For certain,' you say?"

"That's right. I had my suspicions. Digging into the documents was the only way to find out for sure. But given my time constraints, I figured I needed to talk with some people in the know. And that led me to Ms. Laine."

"Okay, we're getting somewhere," Crain said. "I'm understanding this a lot better now. So...what did Mr. Whestin expect you to do with any evidence of fraud you found?"

The room was warm and stuffy, and I felt like pizza dough about to be shoved into the oven. I wondered if cranking up the heat was part of the FBI's interviewing technique. *Sweat 'em,* literally.

"He never used the word fraud in connection with my engagement. He just said if I found anything that didn't look right, I was to bring it to his attention. Remember, I told you he didn't trust his CFO. Still, I wasn't positive I'd find anything, but I thought that if I did, and if I had any doubt that any...anomalies wouldn't be handled appropriately, I would go to you guys."

Crain glanced at Bell, who rolled his eyes. "Mr. Hammonds called Special Agent Crain here a few days before his death. Said he thought Mr. Whestin might be blackmailing you, something to do with the sale of Grayson Tool & Die. Was he right?"

Good old Billy Ray. How I missed him, and how I hoped he'd forgive me for what I was about to say.

"Billy Ray and I never discussed a blackmail threat. He mentioned I was a person of interest regarding Grayson, but as far as Whestin Group was concerned, I told him I was investigating a suspicious source for some prepaid cell phones they sold in their communications division."

"And was that true?" Bell asked.

Close. "Apparently an informant told them the phones had been priced substantially below market—and there was a strong possibility the manufacturer had pirated the software that makes the phones work. They wanted me to look into it." Not true at first, but it turned out that way. Lucky me.

"So was Mr. Hammonds right?" Bell asked. "Were you being blackmailed?"

I explained, patiently, Jeremy's claim that he could make it look as if I'd purposely doctored those Grayson statements, and that if I tried to refute that in a court of law, he had the resources to clear himself and convict me.

"So you went along with him," Bell said, deadpanning disbelief. "For five million dollars and a vow of silence from Mr. Whestin."

I adjusted my sling and winced. "If I was going to see what he was up to, I had to play along. And as for the money, I never expected to see any."

Bell gave me one of those *Don't fuck with me* looks, and his right hand brushed across the top of his gun. I wondered if these guys granted potty breaks.

Crain again, playing The Good Cop. It was an act but I appreciated it. Bell was getting on my nerves. "We've read your statement to the Sheriff's Office," he said. "They're in charge of the investigation into the deaths of Mrs. Whestin, Mr. Evans and former Special Agent Hammonds. What they decide to do about that is up to them. From the standpoint of the possibility that you—and perhaps Ms. Laine—were involved in a conspiracy to commit securities fraud, we're reserving the right to keep the investigation open for now. Do you understand?"

I nodded but kept my mouth shut.

"By the way," he said, "we had a dialogue with the local P.D. and the coroner when we found out about Mr. Hammond's death. We didn't know what we were looking for, so we got nowhere. But as for you...you didn't find his death suspicious, knowing Mrs. Whestin had been with him?"

"It crossed my mind, but like you, I had no proof, no idea what else might have killed him. I was in shock then, and I'm not over it yet."

Bell put a hand to his forehead, leaving the middle finger in obvious salute position. I pretended not to notice. He couldn't make me feel any worse than I already did.

One last point," Crain said, "pertaining to Wallace Gerard."

Ahhh, yes, my old friend, who'd disappeared the day after I'd got shot and his lover devoured by an alligator.

"Did you find him?" I asked.

Half of me hoped they had, but the other half could envision the gaudy marquee: *Don't miss this classic he said/he said confrontation, coming soon to a federal courthouse near you!* Clearly I needed a drink with a kick to it.

Crain replied, somewhat evasively, that they thought Wallace was still in the country, "but we aren't able to confirm that."

How comforting. I tried to swallow, my tongue scraping the roof of my mouth like coarse grade sandpaper on rough-cut timber.

"Give me your take on the relationship between Mrs. Whestin and Mr. Gerard," Crain said, scanning the top page in his folder.

I wet my lips and told them what I knew—or thought I knew. Alina, after all, had meant to kill me and nearly succeeded. I could only guess at what her relationship with Wallace might have become with me gone. For all I knew, it hadn't changed even with me in the picture. What a fool I'd been.

When I finished telling my story, the two agents were staring at me, not as a suspect but as something else that didn't have a pleasant aroma about it.

"In other words," Bell said, "Mr. Gerard had a lot to gain if this IPO went through."

"So did a lot of people," I said.

"Yes, but in the end, you were the one responsible for its demise."

"That's the way I'm hoping you see it. But what's this got to do with Mr. Gerard's disappearance? You guys got some inside information?"

This time, both agents gave me the stone cold stare. "Look, I didn't just break up the IPO," I said, hot under the collar now of my own accord. "I broke up what Mr. Gerard thought was his destiny, a top-of-Space Mountain position with Whestin Group and a life with a very attractive, powerful, exceedingly rich woman. Somewhere out there, this man with ties to Algerian terrorists and maybe al Qaeda—I looked it up—has got to be pretty pissed. And you've got nothing to tell me?"

I glared at both agents, but all I could see was the figure of old Tom Jenks manning the Palms Away security gates, studying the surveillance cameras through his inch-thick glasses as Waleed al-Ghamdi slipped past the palmettos, sea grapes and sable palms to blow up my home and everything in it. Including me.

Crain closed his folder. He wasn't smiling. "If it's any comfort, I can tell you that it's not standard operating procedure for these people to conduct a vendetta against an individual. They generally spend their money and sacrifice their bodies on bigger targets."

"Generally?"

He shrugged. "Anything's possible, Mr. McDermott. These people are constantly evolving their tactics as circumstances demand. And besides, there's always that one exception to the rule."

As the agents gathered up their files and our silence reverberated around the room, I could have sworn the bullet in my chest had just moved an inch closer to my left ventricle.

65.

Fourteen weeks later,
4:15 P.M., Tuesday, January 20, 2009

"**R**ainey's season."

That's what Victoria called my one fateful month in the employ of Whestin Group LLC. Just how much my season of trial and tribulation had changed me, I couldn't be sure.

Even so, this had been an encouraging day, beginning with the inauguration of the nation's first minority President, followed by lunch with Frank. And now we were planting geraniums in the lanai with Colleen's help. As the late, great Billy Ray Hammonds might have said, "What are the odds?"

I turned at a sound behind me. "Where you want these?" Frank asked, emerging from the garage with his arms full of potted plants.

"Back by the spa, Pa," Colleen said, laughing gently. She swiped at a spot of perspiration on her forehead, leaving a black streak of potting soil in its place. It looked like a beauty mark to me. Clearly, I still had a ways to go to get this woman out of my system.

Frank ambled to the back of the house. He'd been recovering nicely from his seizure with the help of blood thinners and Dolly's chicken gumbo he said was spiced with a secret herb she grew in her spare bedroom. Just what I needed to hear. Anyway, if he stayed healthy, he said he expected to be driving again by spring, God help us all.

We'd been making progress as father and son. I could see that Frank had always loved me, and that all the rest of it would probably take years to resolve, years I hoped we still had together.

Colleen stood and stretched both arms above her head. "When do you get started?" she asked.

"Next week. If I can find him."

In the holiday spirit last month, I'd agreed to make my first, and so far only, client my father's friend, Pete "Pintail" Patterson. I had no idea if he'd indeed been involved in a Ponzi scheme, but I was fairly certain it wouldn't be Bernie Madoff in scope. Still, it was a start.

I'd met Frank's buddies earlier today for lunch at the marina diner next to the Cape Coral Yacht Club. "Table 4," the group called themselves, a carefree, beer-guzzling, woman-ogling group of men in their 60s and 70s who'd made eighty-five year old Frank their unofficial president. I'd expected to meet "Pintail," but he hadn't shown and hadn't yet returned Frank's calls.

Colleen rested a hand on my shoulder. "You haven't said much lately about your buddies at the Federal Bureau of Investigation. You aren't protecting me, are you?"

Sore subject.

I'd told the friendly folks from the Chicago FBI that if taking on the Grayson assignment today, clean and sober, I'd be appropriately diligent. Beyond that admission, I couldn't prove or disprove criminal intent to commit fraud by anyone at Whestin Group or at Grayson. And certainly not by me.

It was a stretch, but for now I could find a way to live with it if the FBI could. There was a good chance they'd have no choice. Hank Garrett was dead, and his assistant had disappeared. Jeremy had passed away last month after two months in a coma, and neither Wallace nor his commandeered millions had been located. Thus, the FBI no longer seemed interested in pursuing the case, though Grayson's present owners were deciding if they had enough evidence to file a civil suit against Whestin Group.

"Not much to tell," I said. "I don't deserve the FBI's appreciation, and they're not offering it, but with Jeremy and Alina dead and Wallace in hiding, there's not much they can do."

As for my sins in Chicago and Naples, Colleen knew enough to want to call it quits for good. In fact, now that I was medically out of the woods and things were looking better with the authorities, she planned to file for divorce next week. Whether her new life would include Steve Wannamaker, I hadn't bothered to ask, and she hadn't bothered to clarify. Still, I couldn't help but wonder what we'd all be doing on Valentine's Day.

Not that I blamed her for feeling the way she did. If anything, I was grateful she'd forgiven me as much as she had, though she'd soon be walking away with half of our much-depleted assets. A rude awakening for both of us.

"So it's all over?" she asked.

"You mean between you and me?"

"I mean between the FBI and you, silly."

I clipped off a low hanging frond from a pygmy date palm and nodded, though I didn't believe it for a moment. Something told me I'd cross paths again with my special agent pals Crain and Bell. I remembered their warning that they reserved the right to keep the case open, though they didn't say for how long.

"Dolly should be here any minute," Frank said, returning. An embarrassed smile creased his face, which I grudgingly acknowledged with one of my own. I was just happy to see *him* happy. To be seeing him at all.

My phone rang. I gave Colleen a self-conscious glance and could feel myself blushing. According to Victoria's email last week, she was flying in today, staying at a friend's vacant condo for a week of badly needed R&R, which she'd translated as "Rainey & Rainey."

"So, *Mr. McDermott*, I've just landed and would like to know what the job prospects are down here."

"Well, *Victoria*, I hear there's a new forensic accountant in town."

"Put in a good word for me? I brew a mean cup of coffee."

Anything but green tea, sister, and you've got the job.

"Consider it done," I said. "What are your plans?"

"Mostly to get some color on this pale flesh of mine. But I'm hoping we can get together before I go back."

Neither of us spoke for a moment until she asked, "You know what was supposed to happen three weeks from today, don't you?"

The public offering, a thought that gave me the chills.

"Jack Armbruster told me I could stay on as long as I'd like," she said. "He's trying to restructure the debt. Wants to sell off the marginal businesses, tighten the company's strategic focus. How he's going to do all that in this lousy market, I don't know, but Jeremy's son is willing to let him try. He seems to be a nice guy."

I turned my back and brought up, in discrete tones, a question that had been nagging at me since that last night with Alina. "You came to my house with a vial of that...?"

"Succinylcholine—and a syringe I coerced from an old friend at a veterinary hospital, if you're curious. She wasn't too thrilled about that. As for Alina—and this is just a guess—she was a big fundraiser for at least two area hospitals. Getting onto a floor where the nurses knew her would have been no big thing. After that, she just had to wait for the right moment to pluck a syringe or two from an unlocked cabinet."

"Interesting, but I'm just wondering if—"

"What?"

I'd been plagued with the memory of Victoria plunging that needle into Alina's neck as I'd staggered up the lawn to confront them. She'd had no choice, of course. It was self-defense at that point. Yet...why have that syringe with her if she hadn't intended to kill Alina all along? And yet surely Victoria wasn't like her sister, wouldn't have—

"Nothing...forget it," I said, "What are you doing for dinner tomorrow? We can talk more then."

"I happen to be free, though not inexpensive."

"No surprise there. Pick you up at seven?"

"Perfect. Oh, and I might have a client for you. Some heavy hitters in St. Louis have been inquiring as to your whereabouts—if you're interested."

"Might be." I glanced at Frank, who'd been staring at me but quickly

looked away.
"Good. And Rainey?"
"Yes?"
"Call me Vicky."

I climbed into bed that night with my shoulder aching but my mind on how long it would take to sell my house. The line between fat cat and foreclosure victim was becoming thinner by the day. For the thousandth time I kicked myself for not having taken Diego's advice the day he gave it to me.

Which reminded me: I hadn't touched the bongos in weeks, something I intended to rectify in the morning, bum shoulder and all, after scanning the pond again for Sneaky Pete. I hadn't seen the beast since our fateful encounter and wondered how deeply he'd hidden himself. Or if he'd been hauled out of some distant part of the preserve and turned into a handsome ensemble of belt, handbag and boots.

My last thoughts were on Wallace Gerard. I hadn't said my good-byes to him, either. Was he lurking in his own murky preserve of safe houses, waiting to use his millions to do us harm? And was I, personally, on his radar?

Listen to your girlfriend, I heard a familiar voice calling from far away. *The gators want you back.*

My eyes opened, and I tried to force from memory the dream that now left me awake and shivering. I checked the bedside alarm. Somehow I'd slept eight hours, the longest since the night that would haunt me forever. I moved to the edge of the bed and thought about my date tonight, which brought to mind Billy Ray and the morning he saw the Whestin's invitation and tried to warn me away. Another piece of sound advice I ignored.

Funny how the mind works before it's fully awake.

I found myself wondering if our new President was sipping an espresso in the White House right about now and hoped he had a trusted friend to tell him that in the morning, he really should be having a cappuccino.

Author's Note

As one who gravitated to advertising and marketing years ago because he was lousy at math, I still can't fully explain how I ended up creating a financial fraud investigator as the hero of my first novel. But I'm glad I did.

After much research into the world of financial fraud investigation and prevention, I've developed immense respect for these often unsung heroes in the battle against the devastating effects of business fraud. Look into the heart of the major financial scandals of our time—from Enron/Arthur Andersen, WorldCom and Tyco to Global Crossing, Adelphia, HealthSouth and Bernie Madoff. There you'll find highly qualified forensic accountants diligently unearthing evidence to help prove the case for their client, be they the prosecution or the defense. And faithfully doing it "by the books."

More importantly, the vast majority of their time and energy is expended in behalf of small businesses whose internal controls are often much weaker than their large corporation counterparts. It is estimated, by the way, that one-third of all small businesses fail as a result of internal fraud.

In the interest of spinning a good yarn, I've created a deeply flawed hero whose demons compromise his pursuit of the truth. My own experience, however, shows that Rainey McDermott's profile is by far the exception compared to the thousands of men and women who toil worldwide in this vital industry while adhering to the highest standards of ethical behavior. I sleep better knowing they're on the job.

Acknowledgements

I figured writing fiction would be a lonely, solitary endeavor—until I started writing. It would take another book to thank all those who patiently read my innumerable manuscript versions, offered insightful suggestions for improvement and introduced me to valuable technical resources without whose generosity of time and expertise this book could not have been written. Thank you one and all, but especially to my talented writing mentors: Sandra Haven, Lorin Oberweger and Roberta Moore. I think of you as friends. Special thanks, too, to Jeff Schlesinger at Barringer Publishing for the opportunity to make this dream come true, but also for his constant encouragement and support.

A writer, of course, does indeed spend much time preoccupied and in isolation, and thus I would be remiss were I not to single out for special recognition my oh-so-patient wife, Lynn. Thanks, hon, for putting up with it all.